D0575891

Blood
HEAT

HBJ

HARCOURT BRACE JOVANOVICH, PUBLISHERS

San Diego New York London

Copyright © 1988 by Steve Pieczenik

All rights reserved.
No part of this publication may be reproduced
or transmitted in any form or by any means,
electronic or mechanical, including photocopy, recording,
or any information storage and retrieval system,
without permission in writing from the publisher.

Requests for permission to make copies of
any part of the work should be mailed to:
Permissions, Harcourt Brace Jovanovich, Publishers,
Orlando, Florida 32887.

Library of Congress Cataloging-in-Publication Data

Pieczenik, Steve R.
Blood heat / Steve R. Pieczenik.
p. cm.
ISBN 0-15-113216-X
I. Title.
PS3566.I3813B5 1988
813′.54—dc19 87-31020

Designed by Michael Farmer
Printed in the United States of America
First edition
A B C D E

For George, my brother, the last of the just.

For Sharon and Stephanie, my special angels.

And most of all, for Birdie, with special love and gratitude for her tireless support.

Acknowledgments

My deepest gratitude to Steven Waters, Harry Freeman of American Express/Shearson-Lehman Brothers, Jeff Reider, Hannah Baum, Richard Berenzen, Dr. George Pieczenik, Richard Solomon, and Judy Barry Smith.

To Marie Arana-Ward, my inspiring, demanding, yet always gracious editor. And to her assistant editor, Jonathan Ezekiel, for his friendly support. And many thanks to Giles Townsend, my copyeditor, for an exemplary job.

To Robert Gottlieb of the William Morris Agency, a faithful friend, supporter, and agent extraordinaire.

And to Birdie, whose critical reading and comments were, as always, indispensable.

Blood HEAT

1

"*Gaijin! Gaijin!*" Major Futaki Ran, a heavyset man with bright, darting eyes, cursed as he threw the American prisoner to the floor. He kicked the American several times in the face and watched unblinking as blood flowed from the man's broken nose. Sometimes, the major could find a connection with an emaciated prisoner, a look, a gesture, a smile. *Haragei*, or belly language, as the Japanese called it, meant something familiar that could be readily recognized and shared. Unfortunately, nothing presented itself this time.

Ran reached for a corrugated metal cage. A frenzied squealing came from within. Glancing at his assistants, one standing on either side of the groveling POW, he could understand their reactions. Takenaka, the older and more delicate of the two, had screwed his face into an expression of intense concentration. Seeing the *gaijin* crawl about on his hands and knees, trying desperately to stand up, he was trying to muster the courage to carry out the experiment without any trace of fear. Such discomfort was understandable, thought Ran; this was only Takenaka's third human experiment. Kajita, the shorter assistant, was nodding his head eagerly. He handed Ran a pair of thick leather gloves. The prisoner tried to crawl toward the open door of his cell, but Takenaka and Kajita dragged him back and threw him into a corner.

Ran's jaw was clenched into a silent vise as he opened the rusted door of the cage. Even after the glorious victories at Chuhsien, Ningpo, Changteh, and Nanyung, he could not accustom himself to all the rituals practiced in the course of military research. His gaze drifted through the open cell door, beyond the compound, to the rocky, barren landscape ending sharply at the verdant Khingan mountain ranges, forty miles to the north of Harbin, Manchuria. A wave of nostalgia for the fragrant pine trees of Nara, his home town, overtook him. It had been over six years since he had celebrated the *Setsubun* at the Kofuku-ji Temple. The demon-exorcising ritual marked the end of winter. Coming soon was the *Kasuga Matsuri*, held on March 13, when he and his friends would dress in the spectacular costumes of the Heian period and thread their way through the narrow cobblestone streets of the city. Afterward, they would perform the *Okagura* in the garden of the Kasuga Shrine. He missed those days of comforting rituals and old friendships, when warm *sake* and a night of revelry would assure him of a morning's hangover.

Now, the Pingfan Institute was his home. And with his new home had come a self-sacrificing dedication to the fundamental precept of the famous military strategist Sun-tzu: Subdue the enemy without fighting.

Eight years before, the Japanese High Command had turned down the request of General Kiyoshi Ito, Ran's mentor, to create a research center. Yet, despite this opposition, General Ito, starting with only a handful of scientists and technicians, had made the Pingfan Institute into an impressive complex of three hundred scientists, technicians, and soldiers. This laboratory was capable of producing every natural disease known to man—typhoid, typhus, anthrax, cholera, plague, salmonella, tetanus, botulism, brucellosis, gas gangrene, smallpox, and tularemia.

"*Eta!*" shouted Ran.

Takenaka snapped to attention. Who was full of filth, the prisoner or himself? His pinched face at once flushed with embarrassment. The prisoner had grabbed his ankles with feces-streaked hands and pressed his face in terror against the immaculately polished boots. Takenaka looked down with disgust. Memories of his grandfather, who had been an outcast gravedigger in Kyoto, filled his head. He became aware that Ran was sneering at him. What should he do? Kick the prisoner away and risk the humiliation of splattering his starched white laboratory coat, or simply stand awkwardly? Blood already covered his boots.

"Please—help—you have a kind face—" The prisoner tried to pull himself up to a standing position by grabbing the sides of Takenaka's lab coat.

"*Wareware Nihonjin!*" Ran barked and slapped Takenaka's face. Takenaka had hesitated too long. By being indecisive he had disgraced everyone present.

Ran grabbed the dark-haired *gaijin* by his tattered khaki collar and glared into his panic-stricken eyes. What were one man's pleas among the numbing scores of anonymous POW faces and febrile screams? Did it really matter whether this *gaijin* was Chinese, Mongolian, Korean, British, or American? For Ran's purposes, they were all the same: foreigners, outsiders, intruders. They were evil interlopers who wanted to transform his country into a land of eunuchs.

Throwing his prisoner back onto the floor, Ran carefully put on the pair of gloves. For a moment he listened to the sporadic artillery fire that had been growing closer for the past twelve hours. He need have no fear, he told himself, those mountain ranges in the distance, the Great Khingan and its sister, the Lesser Khingan, would offer natural protection. No invaders, except for the magnificent Japanese Kwantung Army, had ever been able to penetrate that barrier. The only vulnerable access routes into Manchuria were the Nun River to Qiqihar and the Lungani to Harbin. Both cut gaps into the Great and Lesser Khingan mountain ranges. But the *gaijin* could never cross those rivers; certainly not, since the Kwantung Army had blocked them off several weeks before.

Ran had risen quickly within the ranks of General Ito's Detachment 731, but his heart and soul were still attached to the Army Intelligence School, where he had been assigned to the *tokumu kikan*. Working under the guise of a researcher for the special duty agencies, he had organized nationalist insurgency groups fighting against the British and Dutch colonial powers. By the age of twenty-five he had helped organize the Indian National Army and the Burma Independent Army. His current assignment under General Ito was to direct medical research at the Pingfan Institute, using the South Manchurian Railway Company as a cover.

"I beg you—no more—experiments—"

A huge gray rat scurried out of the cage onto Ran's right hand. As if waiting for a cue, it paused in his gloved palm. Deftly, Ran grasped it around the neck with his left hand. He reached into a metal bucket and withdrew a few white-yellow flakes, then spat into the flakes and watched as they swelled quickly into granules four times their normal size. As he forced the rat to eat the granules, he thought of the ease with which he had always been able to work with such natural poisons as ricin, Korean bindweed, and bactal. Even infectious diseases, such as dengue fever virus and the *Bacillus anthracis*, lethal as they were, boasted a certain ease of implementation. Simply extract the lethal agent from an infected animal, inject it into a prisoner, and then examine the different organs from the dissected human body. That was standard operating procedure. But this was different. He watched the rat regurgitate the granules containing the *Pasteurella pestis*—bubonic plague. This one was a nightmare.

For a brief moment, Ran couldn't tell which was screeching louder—the *gaijin* or the rat. Would the American prisoner think him awkward? Intemperate? Ran restrained himself from cursing the wretched rat. He squeezed more tightly around the creature's neck, forcing it to ingest its own vomitus, avoiding the frightened, pleading eyes of the *gaijin*.

The sequence of events had become routine. China and Korea had been his testing ground, and he had learned to conduct this same experiment without any hesitation. Only once, at K'uan-Tien, while working on anthrax, did he actually spill a vial before spraying the bacillus into the prisoner's face. Humiliating. He had apologized to the prisoner for his clumsiness and had made a formal apology to each of his eighteen laboratory assistants. Most humbling was having to explain to General Ito how an experienced research technician could disgrace the detachment in front of a *gaijin*. Yes, he would use extra precaution this time.

Loosening his grip around the rat's neck, Ran guided it toward the prisoner's pustular, excoriated face.

"No! No!" The prisoner jerked his head away from the rat's poised teeth and cowered back against the wall of his cell. "Please God! No—"

Without asking Ran for permission, Takenaka thrust his right knee into the prisoner's groin. As the prisoner sank to the floor, Ran plunged the agitated rat into his face.

The rat ripped through the soft flesh. First the cutaneous tissue. Then the muscles. Eventually, the blood vessels and the nerves, until it began to gnaw on the bone supporting the screaming prisoner's eyeball.

Writhing with terror, the prisoner tried to pull the rat from his face. But the more frantically he clawed at the animal, the deeper it sank its needle-sharp incisors.

"Oh God! Oh! Oh!" The prisoner's cries became a drawn-out howl.

Takenaka turned his head aside and vomited on his laboratory coat. On a nod from Ran, Kajita slapped Takenaka across the face.

"Aaagh!" The prisoner's head snapped backward as the rat ripped into his eye socket.

Responding to a hand signal from Ran, Kajita picked up the Yakiba sword from its ritual position on the floor, raised it high in the air above the prisoner, and brought it swiftly down across his throat.

The prematurely balding Second Lieutenant Joseph Parker, USMC, cautiously dismounted from his jeep. He motioned the fifteen-vehicle convoy to stop. Up until this point, the First Battalion, Eleventh Marines had encountered very little resistance from either the Japanese or the Communist Chinese entrenched along the mountain road from Changchun.

"Up ahead, Captain. Over there, two light Nambu machine guns covering that roadblock."

"Get the corkscrew and blow the shit out of them!" Captain Roy Webb, USMC, had learned only two ways of fighting the Japanese since he had landed at Tangku with "Rockey's Rangers," the Third Amphibious Corps, seven months before: turning them out using a flamethrower—"blowtorch"—or blowing them up using demolitions—"corkscrew." The tall and patrician twenty-six-year-old commissioned officer had no preference; he used whichever method achieved the desired effect with the least amount of danger to his men.

Webb lay flat on the ground, watching his sixty-odd men disperse over the rugged terrain on both sides of the dirt road. There was nothing to worry about. It was Parker's job to enter the village of Pingfan, liberate the Chinese citizens, defeat the Japanese, and explore G-2 intelligence concerning its prison camp—and Parker's ass was on the line if the mission failed.

"Sir," said Parker, an unlit panatela cigar hanging from the side of his mouth, "I've ordered some sixty-millimeter mortar rounds placed into both sides of the road."

He was confident of his strategy and wanted Webb to know it. But as the enemy fire grew louder and more intense, it was impossible to determine whether there were two Nambu machine guns cross-firing or simply one firing in concert with a 106-millimeter artillery piece. Parker decided it didn't matter. He had to get rid of whatever was there.

"Let's break out of here before nightfall, before we have to contend with both the Nips and the Commies."

"*Contend*, Captain?" Parker echoed with amusement. He enjoyed ridiculing Webb. He had recognized at their first meeting several months before, at Sixth Marine Division headquarters at Tsingtao on the Shantung Peninsula, that the war was definitely an intrusion in Webb's life. Webb was on his way along life's fast track. In the middle of a skirmish near Chingwantao, an ice-free port some 150 miles north of Tangku, Webb had told Parker, "Let's get this over quickly so I can go back to making money." These two unlikely bedfellows had made an unsigned, unwitnessed commitment to each other. Parker would get Webb out of the war alive, and Webb would take care of Parker for the rest of his civilian life.

Only twenty-two, Parker prided himself on being a good judge of character. When he came back from the war he would become a professional, maybe even a doctor. And Webb was the man who could make it possible. Confidently clutching the trigger of his Browning automatic rifle (BAR), Parker scurried across the road toward his understrength six-man, sixty-millimeter mortar section. He quickly gave orders to the section leader.

"Place them across the road at twenty-five-yard intervals while the Captain and I take a group to outflank the Nambu on the left."

"Hey, Lieutenant, take good care of Johnny Harvard." Even the young corporal was protective of his captain.

"Just make sure our collective asses aren't clipped off," yelled Parker as he ran back across the road, barely avoiding the machine-gun bullets kicking up dust at his heels.

"Wouldn't you say it's about time to use the blowtorch?" Webb's voice was pained. "The noise is getting to be a bit much."

"Captain, I know the noise is a great inconvenience, especially to you. But we can't use the blowtorch because we didn't bring it with us. Remember, sir, you had to make a choice before we left HQ yesterday—either carry a corkscrew or a blowtorch, Ordnance didn't allow both. You chose the corkscrew on the assumption that we would have to blow a lot of Nips out of a lot of caves. Remember, sir?"

"Right. All right, let's get this over with. We're wasting ammo."

"Sir, you can either wait here behind this boulder or join me in a little expedition to wipe out that Nambu." Parker never questioned Webb's courage. He had seen it in action outside of Sixth Marine Headquarters in Tsingtao when Webb had singlehandedly retrieved a wounded corporal caught in enemy cross fire. Back at HQ he had refused a nomination by his superiors for a Silver Star, dismissing his action as simply one of the responsibilities of a senior officer of a corporation. His noblesse oblige was occasionally exasperating. But from that time onward, Parker and the others affectionately referred to him as "Johnny Harvard."

Parker and Webb led the assault group of fifteen men over the rocky terrain alongside the dirt road. Parker ordered three soldiers to set up a Browning M60 machine gun, catty corner from the Nambu.

"Where's my Devil Dog sharpshooter?"

"Here I am, Lieutenant." A tall, lanky nineteen-year-old holding a modified M1 with a viewfinder walked over.

Parker ordered the sergeant manning the M60 to fire a round to draw out the Nambu, and ordered the sharpshooter to sight the enemy and pick him off at will. Within minutes, the combination of indiscriminate firepower and pinpoint accuracy proved fatal to the outmaneuvered enemy.

Six of Parker's men advanced carefully on the oxcarts blocking the road. The sharpshooter continued to fire at thirty-second intervals, but heard only the echo of his own bullets.

Parker ordered the convoy to proceed, but only after Webb had given the order to use the corkscrew and blow up the oxcarts.

Moving continuously down the winding mountain road, the convoy passed through the empty village of Pingfan and reached the rusted metal gates of Pingfan Institute—identified by faded Japanese characters on a wooden board.

"Do you want to blow these gates open too, Captain?" Parker asked, a note of teasing in his voice.

"No, just cover me with the Browning." Webb jumped off his jeep and rang an ornate bronze bell hanging from the decaying stucco wall that surrounded the three-acre compound. He had no idea what to expect. At one time or another he had been briefed that the facility was a prison camp, an intelligence installation, and a maximum-security prison where the Japanese developed all sorts of unspeakable tortures; and someone, somewhere, had mentioned that the Pingfan Institute did experiments for chemical biological warfare—*CBW* was the way it had been designated.

Parker cocked his BAR and Webb rang the bell again. Parker's finger poised on the trigger as the metal doors to the compound swung slowly open.

A Japanese Army major stepped forward. "Good afternoon, Gentlemen. I am Futaki Ran, acting commander of the Pingfan Garrison."

Now it was Parker who jumped from his jeep, making certain that his Devil Dogs had their sights trained on the lone Japanese officer. Parker stood alongside Webb, ready to fire.

"That won't be necessary." Major Ran nodded at Parker's BAR. "This is a garrison of three hundred people—all under my command. As soon as you came into the village, I gave the order to surrender unconditionally." The major's English was impeccable. There was a deliberate, clipped quality to it as if he had been taking lessons from an Oxford don.

Webb walked past Ran toward the center court of the compound. Around him were rows of unarmed Japanese soldiers in tattered uniforms, their backs turned toward him in the customary sign of defeat, bowing from the waist as he walked by. He had fought these slant-eyed, moon-faced bastards, killing and maiming them—in turn, they had fought back. Never would he have expected a bow from them, not even in shame.

A slow walk around the compound revealed how decrepit the

garrison really was. Surrounding the courtyard were about twenty-five single-story, mud-and-straw thatched buildings, some in disrepair, missing a window, a door, or part of a roof. Yet, even in this collective decay, Webb sensed an uncanny orderliness. He wiped his hand along a windowsill of the main building: He would have sworn it had just been scrubbed with disinfectant. Meticulous, thorough, clean, he thought—even in defeat.

"On behalf of my commander, General Kiyoshi Ito, I apologize that he could not be here to greet you personally."

"That's all right, we'll see him in Tokyo."

Ran did not respond. He simply bowed. "Please excuse my English; I haven't spoken it since childhood, when my father made us speak it at home. May I show you around?"

Webb felt something disturbing about this articulate Japanese. Rarely did the Oriental adversary speak English, and never this well.

Suddenly, a pistol shot reverberated through the compound, then the noise of a scuffle. Quickly, Webb followed the sound to a freshly painted adobe building marked with a large red cross. Inside, Parker was trying to restrain an emaciated, disoriented, American POW from pummeling the body of a dead Japanese soldier.

"Kill the sons of bitches! Kill them all!" In Webb's presence the ragged prisoner seemed to come to his senses. He struggled weakly to his feet and made a faint effort at a salute. "U.S. Army Air Corps. Navigator—First Lieutenant Brad—" Without finishing the sentence, the prisoner collapsed to the ground.

"There are three more Americans like him here," Parker told him. "Forty-five Chinese and fifty-five Russians—all POWs. This poor bastard picked up a Nip rifle and killed his guard."

Webb turned toward Ran, hoping to see some expression of contrition or remorse, but the Japanese officer's face revealed no emotion.

"Take a look at this." Parker opened a door and quickly covered his nose and mouth with his hand. He led Webb and Ran through rows and rows of evenly stacked dead bodies, each covered with pustules, boils, scars, or open, festering cavities. The fetid odor was overwhelming.

Webb suppressed a powerful urge to vomit. "What in God's name have you created here?"

"Unfortunately, there wasn't sufficient time to bury them."

Webb bent over one cadaver. The Chinese victim's eyelids were swollen; his dry, cracked lips were caked with congealed blood; and his limbs were stripped of all body fat. The skin of his arms was punctured every ten centimeters with enlarged needle marks. The gruesome body looked as if it had been starved for months; the abdomen was distended with fluid.

"Peritoneal ascites." Ran was matter-of-fact. "Not uncommon among severely debilitated victims of malnutrition and chronic infectious diseases." He pointed to six bodies piled one on top of the other. "That group represents experiments conducted with the anthrax bacillus."

"Anthrax. Christ! That's the goddamn disease our cattle used to die from back in Minnesota."

"Correct, Lieutenant. It kills cattle—and enemies." He pointed to a squashed Occidental cadaver at the bottom of one pile. "The Russians used it against us here in Manchuria in 1935. This should come as no surprise to you, Captain." Ran paused, uncertain whether to use the name inscribed on Webb's shirt.

"I am Captain Roy Webb, Major Ran."

"Thank you, Captain Webb."

"These guys are nothing but goddamn butchers!" Parker spat. He raised his BAR and pointed it at Ran. "Let's get rid of them now!"

Webb lunged forward and knocked the barrel of Parker's BAR up toward the roof, just as the heavy Browning stuttered and a burst of slugs slammed into the ceiling.

"Goddamn it, G-2 gave specific orders not to kill anyone at Pingfan. They want some *live* bodies to interrogate!"

Ran simply nodded his head at Webb in quiet gratitude.

Parker ran from the building to vomit. The odor had sickened him. That was no medical research, that was calculated barbarism. A moment later he returned, wiping his mouth with his mud-caked sleeve. "Sorry, Captain, but one way or another, those slant-eyed bastards have to pay."

Webb nodded his head in agreement. They will, he said to himself. Believe me, they will.

Apparently unruffled, Ran led them into a dark, stone room with a corrugated metal ceiling. He screwed a bulb into a socket hanging from a metal link chain and pointed to the left side of the room. A triangular stack of bombs was neatly piled as if awaiting inspection.

"This is the *Uji* bomb. It produces clouds of airborne bacteria. Each weighs approximately fifty pounds and is made of fragile porcelain to lessen the amount of explosives required to burst it. It carries eleven liters of toxic agent—usually anthrax or *Pasteurella pestis*—and detonates several feet above the ground, creating a uniform cloud over a distance of five hundred feet or more." He paused to measure the reaction of the two Americans, and was satisfied to see that the captain was more than a casual listener. In fact, Webb was staring with a curious intensity.

Ran indicated a smaller pile of metal casings. "We tested over twenty-five hundred of these bombs," he continued proudly. "This is the *Ha* bomb, yes, *ha*—the word for laughter in English."

Webb's eyes narrowed. To him, Ran's extraordinary command of English could mean only one thing—intelligence training. Was Ran an intelligence agent masquerading as a research scientist? Perhaps the bacteriological warfare experiments at Pingfan were controlled by Army Intelligence? There was already enough evidence at Pingfan to incriminate the whole fucking Japanese government. War may be war—especially if it involved gunpowder, shrapnel, and metal casings—but immobilizing your opponent with diarrhea, fever, or a serious infection was against all the rules of the game. Webb's mind was spinning as he listened to Ran describe the advantages of the *Ro* bomb, a lighter, smaller steel casing that could be delivered from a howitzer. Plainly, Ran was a man with valuable information. What would he want in return?

Webb and Parker followed Ran into an immaculate research laboratory, complete with pipettes, flasks, Bunsen burners, and an assortment of large, thick gallon bottles corked with black rubber stoppers.

"Captain, take a look. I don't believe it! The Nips are growing a goddamn flea circus."

"To be precise, Lieutenant Parker, they are *Pulex irritans*." Ran looked at the notation on one jar. "These particular fleas are infected with *Pasteurella pestis*. A victim bitten by these fleas will develop a severe pneumonia, swollen lymph nodes—called *buboes*—fever, chills, and possible death."

"How do you use these fleas?" Webb asked. His mind was racing. He calculated that there were literally millions of fleas in the bottles stacked about the room. Each bottle carried a different type of lethal disease. Why the hell waste bullets, mortars, and armor when you can decimate whole populations with a flea bite?

Ran stepped between the two men, his back toward Parker. "We use them in two ways. First, we can encapsulate them in the porcelain bombs so that they are discharged on impact. The second method, though less precise, is to release the fleas from large metal spray tanks attached to the fuselage of a plane at a very high altitude."

Webb was beginning to admire Ran's pride in his work. Moreover, he seemed to speak with an absolute conviction that his methods were proper and correct.

"Only one year ago our maximum output of disease-carrying fleas was five hundred kilograms per month, on a scale equal to our capacity to produce vaccines to counteract those very same diseases."

Parker spun Ran around to face him. "How the hell can you sound so calm and collected about spreading death and destruction with these piss-ass bugs?"

"Let him go, Lieutenant!" Webb commanded angrily. Of course, Parker was right. There was no moral justification for any of this. But was there a moral justification for war? If Webb had learned one thing from the Marxist literature at Harvard, it was that the only business of foreign affairs was business—capitalist business. Morality was at best an interesting side issue.

"Lieutenant Parker, I am ordering you to wait outside."

"Thank you, Captain." Contemptuously, the lieutenant released his grip on Ran's arm and left the laboratory.

"It is a pleasure to discuss such complicated and sensitive matters with someone who is both sophisticated and . . ."—Ran carefully observed Webb's cool blue eyes—". . . inquisitive." From an unlocked desk he withdrew a tightly wrapped document and handed it to Webb.

"In translation it reads: 'Defense and Security Intelligence Report No. 8: Chinese Employment of Chemical and Bacteriological Warfare Against the Japanese.' This was prepared by the research section of the Kwantung Defense Army, 3036 Unit, written on October 1, 1941." Ran paused for a moment to consider whether Webb might read Japanese. But that was too much to expect of the *gaijin*.

"The report documents a period between September 1937 and August 1939 when there were ten proven instances of bacteriological warfare perpetrated against the Kwantung Defense Army, seven of cholera and three of anthrax. Five of the cases involved contamination of wells; two, drinking from a creek; one, from a river; and two, eating contaminated rice. In each of these instances of Chinese bacteriological sabotage there were a half dozen casualties—some Chinese inhabitants, but mostly Japanese soldiers of the Kwantung Defense Army. In Pingfan today, among our prisoners are five Russian spies who were apprehended in Kempei carrying ampoules and glass bottles filled with dysentery bacteria. We have proof that these agents infiltrated Manchukuo with instructions to target local Japanese commanders and technicians. And as you well know, we are not even in a state of war with Russia."

Ran's point was not lost on Webb. One side was rarely more innocent or more righteous than the other side. Most wars were simply a product of political expediency and public perception. The Japanese had been raping the resources of the Far East for well over twenty years before they decided to attack Pearl Harbor. Why didn't the United States, Britain, or Holland stop them at least ten years earlier? The answer was apparent to Webb: The United States had not been ready to compromise its financial interest in the Far East. Until December 7, 1941, the U.S. had been shipping scrap steel to Japan from the Third Avenue El Subway in Manhattan.

Webb's thoughts were interrupted by the sound of approaching footsteps. As he spun toward the laboratory door, he knocked a jar of infected fleas to the ground.

Ran immediately grabbed a can of insecticide and began to spray its contents over the fleas that swarmed onto Webb. "Those fleas have been infected with *Francisella tularensis*—rabbit fever."

"Does that mean I'll be eating carrots the rest of my life?" Webb jested.

"The incubation period is two to three days, at which point you will have fever, chills, and severe coughing. Thirty to forty percent of the people infected with this disease die."

"Is there a cure for it?"

"We were just beginning to develop some fungal molds, like your new penicillin, that had an anti-tularemia effect. But unfortunately the vagaries of war . . ."

Ran led Webb to a building used as an infirmary. He strapped a blood-pressure cuff around Webb's upper left arm and began to pump the black bulbous ball. Without warning, he slipped a syringe needle attached to a long rubber tube into a prominent vein in Webb's forearm.

"When I tell you, release the pressure on this cuff by turning the knob."

Webb felt his left arm engorge with blood, swelling his arteries and veins three times their normal size. He watched with a combination of bewilderment and fascination as Ran prepared his own right arm with a blood-pressure cuff and punctured the skin of his right forearm with a second needle attached to the other end of the rubber tube. Webb flinched as the needle in his arm scraped against the sides of his vein. Ran showed no sign of discomfort. Seated on a wooden chair alongside Webb, he slowly released the valve on the black rubber bulb controlling his blood-pressure machine and looked on calmly as the blood flowed from his right arm into the tube.

"You don't have to worry about blood incompatibility. I have type O, the universal donor. Now Captain, release the pressure."

Webb turned the knob and felt Ran's blood rush into his veins. There was a cool sensation. He was surprised at how compliant he had become.

"Five years ago I survived a bout of rabbit fever. Through my blood I am transferring to you the antibodies that I developed over the past five years. In principle, you, too, should be protected from the full fury of the disease. If you do get sick, you should get a milder form. At least, it will not be life-threatening."

"Why are you doing this?"

Ran didn't answer. How could he explain the long-cherished Japanese tradition of *on*—incurring a debt of honor. With his blood, Ran had placed Webb in an eternal cycle of obligation. Ran pulled the needle from his arm and unfastened the blood-pressure cuff. He did the same for Webb, who was beginning to shiver.

As blood trickled over their respective forearms, Webb studied Ran thoughtfully. Then he said quietly, "Let's talk."

Ran nodded his head slowly: The *gaijin* understood.

Later that evening the convoy climbed the mountain road overlooking Pingfan Institute. A bright orange-and-yellow fireball illuminated the night sky. Ran turned his head away as he heard the explosion scatter his life's work into the cold Manchurian night.

"One corkscrew did the trick. Just as you ordered, Captain."

"And the POWs, Lieutenant?"

"We took the only American we thought could survive the trip back," Parker answered.

"How's he doing?"

"Not too good."

"I'm sorry to hear that."

Webb patted his double-locked duffle bag and thought of all the written records inside. He contemplated his own future prospects and smiled.

"*Tenno heika banzai!*" The cry rose from scores of youths in white headbands as they circled the Yoyogi Parade Ground and Atago Hill near the American Embassy. A call for continued armed resistance and honorable death, it fell on deaf ears. Passers-by, dressed in simple cotton kimonos, or *yukata,* walked quickly by the teenagers, impressed that the armed American soldiers surrounding the embassy simply smiled with bemusement. On direct orders from General Douglas MacArthur, supreme commander of the Allied Powers (SCAP), all military personnel were to treat the vanquished Japanese with respect and compassion. Under no circumstances was there to be any use of force.

"Those kids belong to the *Sonno Joi Gigun,* a rightist group dedicated to upholding imperial rule and driving out foreigners." The lieutenant volunteered the information as his jeep parted the milling crowd. He stopped briefly for the armed guards at the entrance, and entered the embassy compound. The U.S. army of occupation, in Japan only four weeks since VJ Day, was having more difficulty than anticipated.

"Have they caused any major problems?" Webb asked absently. His thoughts were on the upcoming meeting. He dismounted and ushered Ran through the front doors of one of several badly bombed office buildings on what was formerly three acres of formal gardens.

"*Zangyaku-sei,*" Ran responded, as he glanced through the windows of the small conference room overlooking a phantom city.

Eighty percent of Tokyo had been destroyed by incendiary bombs dropped from the B-29s. Gone was the mosaic of textile factories, office buildings, and wooden houses that had once made the city the pearl of the Orient. As far as Ran could see, it was a wasteland of glazed rubble, surrounded by mile after mile of makeshift shacks and huts built from the scraps of war. American military vehicles and personnel clogged the city; they outnumbered the Japanese civilians in the street. His countrymen were still too ashamed of their defeat to show themselves in public.

Webb led Ran to one of twelve chairs surrounding a rectangular conference table in the bare, high-ceilinged room.

"Please have a seat. I'll tell them you are here." The lieutenant closed the door behind him.

"As I was saying, those youths reveal *Zangyaku-sei*, a brutal and savage spirit," Ran continued.

Webb didn't reply. After what he had seen of the Pingfan Institute, Ran could hardly accuse any of his countrymen of brutality or savagery.

"Please do not judge us too harshly. I know that most Japanese feel *shikata-ga-nai*—resignation—at this time. *Ensei*, I am ashamed to say—a weariness of living."

Ran took his seat, both apprehensive and ebullient about the meeting. Over the past few weeks he had learned several important things about his captor. Above all else, Captain Roy Webb was an extremely ambitious and practical man, with considerable American ingenuity. Having been told initially it would take two months for SCAP to meet with him in Tokyo, Webb had arranged, through the exchange of gifts and favors, to have himself and Ran transported by train from Harbin to Mukden and from there flown by C-47 via Chung King and Manila to Tokyo. He had ordered Parker to stay behind, ostensibly to take command.

When the door opened, an army colonel in his late twenties with sharp, aristocratic features strode into the room. He was followed by a well-dressed gentleman in his fifties. Both took seats opposite Ran and Webb while a cocky Japanese youth, no more than seventeen years old, stood guard at the door. Ran noticed his zoot suit and the amputated pinky on the boy's right hand.

"I'm Captain—"

"We know who both of you are, Captain Webb. It is now more important that you know who we are and why we want to speak with you. I am Colonel Lawrence Swann, chief of G-2 Intelligence. And this gentleman to my left will be called, for the purposes of this meeting, Mr. Smith. I can only assure you that Mr. Smith is a friend of the U.S. government. Tommy here"—Swann pointed to the youth at the door—"is Mr. Smith's personal bodyguard."

"Pleased to meet you." Mr. Smith nodded respectfully.

From the slight accent, Webb surmised that Mr. Smith was not an American. But why the false name?

"Without wasting any of our time, let us agree that the war wreaked havoc on both sides. Japan, however, has suffered a devastating blow. One point three million Japanese soldiers have been killed, and seven hundred thousand civilians have died in U.S. bombing raids. It is SCAP's opinion that the Japanese armed forces have been completely crushed. The prospect of their becoming militant again within the next several decades is nil. Therefore, in concert with SCAP's new program of economic development and political liberalization—*Demokurashi*—we in G-2 are particularly fascinated by the strategic and economic significance of the findings at Pingfan Institute."

"Yes, sir." Swann's emphasis on the word *economic* brought a smile to Webb's face. As always, the business of American foreign policy was business.

"Tell me, Major Ran, why has the Japanese army general staff been so interested in bacteriological warfare? The U.S. certainly has had no interest in developing it."

"Our commitment to developing bacteriological weapons was due primarily to the foresight of General Kiyoshi Ito, who created the Pingfan Institute. Our major strategy was to use such weapons against China and Russia, however—countries that already had deployed them against us in Manchuria."

"The Chinese?"

"Yes, Captain Webb. Between 1937 and 1939 the Chinese contaminated the reservoirs and rivers in Manchuria with cholera and anthrax and caused six hundred fifty deaths."

"What about the Russians?" Swann glanced at his colleague, who was making notes on a small piece of paper.

"In Manchuria we apprehended a group of Russians transporting vials of anthrax, cholera, and dysentery. In the city of Shenho, the Russians had thrown cans containing anthrax bacilli into factories, schools, and trains."

"So that justified developing and exploding over four thousand *Uji*-type bombs?"

"I must remind you that two thousand of those bombs were used in field trials at Pingfan."

"Major Ran, how would you evaluate the success of your efforts at Pingfan?" As he spoke, Mr. Smith made his own evaluation—moderately successful.

"In my own opinion, a great deal more could and should have been done."

"Please elaborate, Major." Mr. Smith's French accent had become more noticeable.

"As in most large organizations, we were unable to achieve harmonious cooperation among different divisions of the military. Quite frankly, we were unable to attract the best civilian scientists, some of whom had already been assigned to other projects."

"If you had to do it all over again, what would you do differently?" Mr. Smith put down his paper and gazed intently at Ran.

The Japanese major did not hesitate: "If I had another chance, I would not do it again." He hoped he sounded appropriately contrite.

"Please, Major, neither Mr. Smith nor I am interested in your moral repentance. This line of questioning is intended simply to uncover the facts at Pingfan."

Webb liked Swann. He had a bottom-line attitude.

"If General Ito had asked me that question, I would have told him that I would never again develop a bacteriological warfare program under government auspices. It was too inefficient. Too unpredictable. Too costly. There were too many bureaucrats in the military who were uncomfortable with the idea of chemical or bacteriological warfare. They made my job particularly difficult, and at times, unpleasant."

"So what would you do?" asked Colonel Swann.

"I would do research through a private corporation."

"Can you tell me, Major Ran, why I should not recommend that you be tried as a war criminal and sentenced to death?"

"Colonel Swann!" Webb jumped out of his seat.

"Sit down, Captain!"

Ran's face became pale. The *gaijin* had fooled him, leading him down the path of self-incrimination. He was at a loss for words.

2

Janet Rydell bolted up in her hospital bed and screamed.

"My baby! You've killed my baby!"

She glanced anxiously around the room with its light-green walls. The last room she could remember had had an October 1989 calendar with little kittens playing. Where were they? They had taken the kittens and killed her baby! All she saw were shadows playing on the curtains that separated her from the other patients in the room. They must be dead, she thought. There was a pungent odor—embalming fluid! That was it! These womens' babies had also been mutilated and slaughtered. God! She didn't even know if it had been a boy or a girl. It must have been a boy. That's what she and Jimboy had wanted. Where was Jimboy? Why wasn't he there, helping her find their baby boy?

She looked out the window and scanned the hospital grounds for help. This was unlike any military compound she had ever seen. She inhaled the acrid scent of what she now identified as cleaning fluid and shook her head in disbelief. This couldn't be Fort Detrick. A fort didn't smell this way. The five-story red brick building in the distance looked like an oversized Japanese tea house. What in God's name was she doing here?

Before her stood two men, one in a green Army uniform and one in civvies.

"Where's my baby? I want to see him!" She spoke to the taller of the two, the one with the short, cropped hair. "Who are you? And what are you doing with Balthazar standing next to you?"

"Janet, my name is Major Ezra Kimball. I was called in to examine you because you are developing a high fever. This gentleman is Dr. Orestes Bradley, an expert in infectious diseases who often consults with us here at Walter Reed Hospital."

"He's the Devil. Don't let him near me. He's taken my baby and cut her up!"

Bradley, a man of medium build in his early forties with dark features and black curly hair, approached the patient slowly. He was a self-assured bachelor with an instinct for bureaucratic survival and an uncanny clinical acumen. Despite a warm, disarming manner, Bradley had a reputation for perseverance, even ruthlessness in obtaining whatever he wanted. He kept Janet's attention focused on him while two female nurses in green scrub suits took position at the sides of the bed.

"Don't come any closer! I know what you want to do to me. I've seen your evil doings."

"I'm not trying to hurt you, Mrs. Rydell."

Bradley noted her pallid, anxious appearance. Even without conducting a thorough examination, he could see she was suffering from toxic psychosis. Some type of infection or chemical reaction was causing her agitation and disorientation. For the director of the National Institute for Infectious Diseases and Allergies at the National Institutes of Health in Bethesda, it was not a difficult diagnosis to make.

"Give Mrs. Rydell seventy-five milligrams of IM Thorazine,

stat." Major Kimball turned toward the nurses who, unlike their civilian counterparts, waited patiently until their superiors barked out medical orders.

Bradley was always surprised to see how deferential the military nurses were compared to his NIH personnel. Military medicine's hierarchical system seemed to attract submissive people.

"Ezra, hold it! Remember, phenothiazines lower body temperatures. And introducing a drug at this point may confuse the underlying picture."

"Nurse, give her fifty milligrams, stat," Kimball ordered.

The head nurse, a gray-haired woman in her early fifties, thrust the five-centimeter needle into the patient's left arm as the other nurse held Janet down.

"Aaaah!" Janet struggled to free herself from their grasp. With a sudden motion she wrenched away. She grabbed the syringe from the nurse's hand and slipped off the bed.

"You've killed my baby."

Bradley motioned everyone to back away.

"Janet, put down that needle. You're going to hurt someone."

He crouched down to make himself a smaller target and started to circle slowly around her, forcing her to concentrate her complete attention on him. Even Kimball, a fifteen-year combat veteran of Vietnam and sundry other unofficial, highly classified conflagrations, stepped back from the action.

However, Kimball, as well as the ward staff, realized that a jab from the tainted syringe was tantamount to Russian roulette with an infectious disease of unknown origin. Who knew what lethal infection she might be carrying? Kimball watched Bradley weaving back and forth, dodging Janet's lunges.

"Janet, I know you're upset. Can we talk about it?" Bradley felt awkward hearing his own stilted words. His eyes were fixed on the infected syringe jabbing at the air around him. Janet Rydell did not need him to listen patiently and interpret her concerns. This sick woman was trying to hurt him in retribution for injuries sustained during the delivery of her baby. But what were they? And how had they occurred? Ezra had only told him there was a postpartum psychotic woman on the Ob-Gyn unit, nothing else—no signs, symptoms, or differential diagnosis. Was Kimball withholding information? Or was this another of Kimball's "tests"?

"Janet, hurting me is not going to solve the problem."

"He had no head. Do you know what a headless child looks like? No, I bet you don't!"

Her question sent a chill through Bradley. The woman was mad. He glanced around quickly and realized he was soon going to be pressed against a wall with nowhere to go.

"Rockabye baby in the treetop."

Kimball caught Bradley's eye and threw a pillow to him. Bradley grabbed it with both hands and thrust it against the syringe.

"No!"

The nurses rushed Janet and pulled her away from the pillow, but not before the needle had penetrated the thin hospital pillow and imbedded itself in Bradley's shoulder.

"Oh Jesus!" Bradley yanked the pillow away from his bleeding right shoulder. Her infection had suddenly become his. A stupid quirk of fate, and Bradley's destiny had become intertwined with that of a toxically psychotic woman.

Bradley's face turned white as he realized what had happened in that one motion, but he calmed the other three patients with a wave of his hand and turned to examine Janet, now restrained by the staff. She was clearly febrile. He placed his fingers on her pulse. It was racing at 134. He was convinced that any more agitation or increase in fever could throw her into an arrhythmia. A few more heartbeats per second and she could sustain a major heart attack. Beads of sweat poured down her forehead. Her eyes appeared slightly jaundiced, but he couldn't be certain under the white fluorescent lights in the room.

"Blood pressure?"

"Ninety over sixty."

In a few more seconds, Bradley thought, she could be in a state of toxic shock.

"Bilirubin?"

"Direct, point three milligrams per hundred milliliters; indirect, point five milligrams per hundred milliliters."

Both serum bilirubin levels were within the normal range. Despite the slightly yellow sclera, there was no evidence from the blood sample drawn earlier that morning of acute or chronic hepatitis or any other bacterial or chemically induced disease that might affect the liver. So what the hell was causing a jaundiced appearance in her eyes?

Bradley had worked long enough with Kimball to know he wouldn't volunteer any information. On the other hand, if properly requested, no information would be denied Bradley. This was part of the accepted rules of the game called medical consultation. Although his presence had been specifically requested by Kimball, Bradley realized that Kimball had major misgivings about having him as consultant at Walter Reed Army Medical Center (WRAMC), the foremost medical hospital and infectious disease research facility in the U.S. armed forces. WRAMC had the latest information on all the newest infectious diseases, whether caused by gram-positive bacteria, gram-negative bacteria, anaerobic bacteria, mycobacteria, fungi, mycoplasma, chlamydia, viruses, protozoa, or parasites. Furthermore, WRAMC had a large body of physicians who knew more about infectious diseases, and treated more of them, than any other medical institution, including the National Institutes of Health. So why did Major Ezra Kimball, M.D., continuously call on Dr. Orestes Bradley's expertise? He was seldom wrong.

The truth was that everyone understood the single overriding principle of military medicine—CYA. Cover Your Ass. Despite the fact that Kimball had an extremely understanding working wife, and the Mormon Church stood ready to support him in any financial mishap, Bradley knew Kimball wanted to make certain he would fulfill his remaining eight years of service without a blemish on his service record. He was a fast-tracker whose ultimate goal was to settle into retirement and collect his annuity of $35,000 per year. Bradley, recognized as the best infectious disease man and epidemiologist in the government, was his CYA insurance policy.

"Let go! Devil! You're hurting me!"

"What hurts you, Janet?" Bradley waved aside the male nurses, but they wouldn't let her go.

"Dammit, let her go! Something's hurting her! Let's find out what it is."

The attendants looked at Kimball who nodded his head.

"Who's the monkey in charge here, anyway? The general or this civvy?"

"Janet, would you mind if this civilian examined your arms for one moment?"

She glanced at Kimball, who again nodded his head.

"He acts like a puppet, doesn't he? Just nodding his head up and down. Can't do better than that, General Kimby?"

"Janet, I'm a major. And my last name is Kimball. I must remind you you're still in a military hospital and must act according to rules and regulations."

"But I'm crazy, General. You can't make me do anything I don't want to. Right, civvy?"

Grabbing her arms, Bradley felt the tiny lymph nodes hidden amidst the bony protuberances of the elbows. They were enlarged.

"Hey, that hurts! What are you doing?"

"Ezra, they're swollen."

"They were negative a few days ago."

"Dammit! That hurts! You son of a bitch! General, get this butcher off me. He's killing me."

"Bilaterally swollen up here as well."

"They weren't there before."

Bradley pushed gently on the swollen lymph nodes beneath both her armpits. They were tender, soft, malleable—and at least a few days old. These nodes should have been detected earlier.

"Urine?"

"Cloudy. A few white cells. Between three and five RBCs. pH, six point five."

"Any proteinuria?"

"Mild."

"And the CBC?"

"Shift to the left, with a moderate leukocytosis."

"How elevated are the white cells?"

"Seven point five."

"Blood cultures?"

"Negative."

"Blood smear?"

"Again, nothing."

"What do you mean 'nothing'?" Janet interrupted suddenly. She became visibly anxious. "I got something. Something very real. Something inside of me. Just like my little baby." Hanging her head down on her chest, she caressed her abdomen. "Do I have another one there, doctor?"

"Would you like another one, Janet?"

"I . . ." She started to cry. "We tried for so long, Jimboy and me. Does Jimboy know?" She grabbed Bradley's hand. "He doesn't blame me, does he? Is Jimboy here? I want to talk to Jimboy."

"He knows that, Janet."

"Are you sure? It was so horrible, doctor! He had no head. No eyes. No ears. How could he eat? He had no mouth. He had nothing. Only an ugly stub on his neck. A child? That was no child! That was Satan himself!"

Bradley noted that her psychotic delusions seemed to wax and wane. Right now, he concluded, she was mentally alert and far more oriented than she had been minutes before.

"Have you been taking any prescribed medications? Any drugs at all?"

"I don't even drink, doctor. I'm a born-again Pentecostal Christian. I don't smoke, drink, or—" She started to laugh. "Oh yes, I do, don't I?"

Bradley glanced toward Kimball, who simply shrugged his shoulders.

"Have you or your husband been out of the country recently?"

"Yes!"

"Where?"

"Maryland!"

The staff snickered and Bradley realized that Janet was normally bright and witty.

"Janet," he repeated, "have you or your husband been out of the country recently?"

Without waiting for her to answer, Kimball shook his head negative. He scanned her chart and reaffirmed his response.

"That's not true, General. Jimboy and I been to the Orient."

"There's nothing in the chart here about an overseas assignment." Kimball signaled the nurses to take her from the room. His obvious discomfort puzzled Bradley.

"Where in the Orient?"

"Everywhere those slanty-eyed bastards live."

Kimball shrugged again, intimating that the line of questioning would prove futile.

"I have little ivory elephants carved in Bangkok." Janet pulled away from the firm grasp of her nurses.

"Bangkok?" Bradley's mind raced through the infections indigenous to that area: cholera, hepatitis A and B, malaria, and a host of parasitic diseases.

"Take her away." Kimball now was clearly disturbed by the discussion.

"Bangkok! One night in Bangkok! That's all I've ever wanted to spend. One night in Bangkok." She paraphrased the words of a popular song.

The staff laughed.

"Get her into isolation!" Kimball exploded.

"Don't ever eat Chinese food without soy sauce!" As she was wheeled into the solitary seclusion room at the other end of the corridor, her screeching voice faded against the padded walls.

What the hell did she mean about soy sauce on Chinese food? Bradley mused.

"Hey, that's your field, Russ. Psychosis secondary to an infectious disease process. Help me find the underlying infection, and I'll tell you what she meant."

"Then send me those blood samples you took from her."

"No sweat. We'll express them over by tomorrow morning. Sorry this wasn't more productive."

"By the way, what's her husband's job?"

"Classified, Russ. Sorry."

"*Merde!*" Helene de Perignod's auburn mane snapped as she spat out the word.

"Offer one hundred thirty-nine. Bid one hundred thirty-three. Down from one hundred thirty-nine as of this morning. Helene, it looks like it's starting to tumble."

The ominous news was almost lost in the cacophony bursting from the smoke-filled trading pit of Cox and Company, broker and cover for Molecular Technology Industries. The stentorian calls for "Buy!" "Sell!" "Go short!" "Go long!" bellowed from traders sitting in front of row upon row of silent, glowing green computer terminals.

"John . . . switch me to the Chicago Board of Options Exchange. Let's play a few spreads." Helene studied the screen carefully. "At one hundred thirty-two sell. Buy at one hundred twenty-nine."

Roy Webb, chairman of the board and chief executive officer

of MTI, the forty-five-billion-dollar chemical and pharmaceutical conglomerate, smiled as he watched his beautiful executive vice-president for finances and acquisitions hover over John Crosby's shoulder. He had never seen MTI stock so volatile, even in a shaky market. Rarely would he or Helene appear in Crosby's corner of the trading pit, the haunt of "quants" and "rocket scientists"—the new breed of traders skilled in one of the hard sciences, who applied their esoteric skills and formulas to the manipulation of stock-index futures, interest-rate swaps, options on index futures, and a variety of mortgage-backed securities.

Webb watched attentively as Crosby deftly executed Helene's orders, punching a series of numbers and commands into the high-speed Cray computer, especially designed for MTI.

"All right, John. Stay long until we see a significant downturn. Then start to sell short. *Comme un fou!*"

"I gather that means crazy?"

"Like the devil, John. Like a crazy man!" Helene turned toward Webb and smiled with the uneasy tension of a perfectionist concentrating on final details. She ran her tapered fingers nervously through her wavy auburn hair. She had done business with all the legendary merchant bankers of the world: The Russian middleman collecting information on the rice trade in Java or gold shipments from Siberia; the Dutch banker bartering Chinese tea for Dutch waterworks in return for Siamese sugar. As the youngest of four daughters of a prominent and noble Toulousean merchant banker, Helene de Perignod felt at one with the Hambros, the King-makers; the Warburgs, the Heretics; the Barings, the Sixth Great Power; Mattioli, the Master of Paradox; and the Rothschilds, the Frankfurt money leaders. And now she was at the top of MTI, which exceeded the combined wealth of all previous merchant bankers and was equal in gross revenue to the gross national product of the oil-rich state of Kuwait.

"MTI: Bid one hundred forty-three. Offer one hundred thirty-eight. Spread five." John Crosby, a thirty-three-year-old former physicist who had taught quantum mechanics at Harvard University, stared into his terminal. He announced the luminescent Quotran numbers scurrying across the screen with the controlled enthusiasm of a seasoned stock trader as he watched the yet-unspecific movement on MTI stock.

"Mets les premiers chiffres a côté. Je voudrais voir si ça va monter ou tomber."

"Helene," John protested, "I've got enough problems tracking these numbers without having to tax my French 101."

Webb waited tensely for a technical trend that would tell him the eventual market direction. Yet paradoxically the peril of the moment excited his passion for Helene. He watched her closely, hardly believing that their five years of personal and professional intimacy was waning. Not yet thirty-six, Helene was just over half his sixty-nine years. Still they managed to hold onto one another, through guile in measured amounts, warmth in large portions, and a heavy dose of mutual respect. He respected her for her vast knowledge and experience of the international markets of New York, London, Tokyo, and Hong Kong. And she, he presumed, admired him for his entrepreneurial guts and financial talents. How incongruous it was, he mused, to see this svelte, attractive artistocrat from the southwest Languedoc region of France, dressed in her latest Emanuel Ungaro suit, supervise a hundred disheveled, monochromatic Brooks Brothers rocket scientists. Still, Webb loved to watch her carefully teased eyebrows arch sharply over her brilliant almond-shaped hazel eyes as she scrutinized the situation. Her thin lips tightened in a strained line, beneath her straight, Gallic nose. Unconsciously, Webb nodded in approval. When Helene frowned at him in mild disgust, Webb knew he had committed another faux pas. How many times had she complained that she didn't want *le grand patron?*

"Bid one hundred thirty-seven. Offer one hundred thirty-one. Spread, six." John continued to read from the screen.

"*Merde! Merde!*" Helene turned toward Webb with the first obvious sign of distress. Not only was there an unusual amount of unexpected activity, someone was trying to force the price of MTI stock downward. She punched out some numbers and graphs on the screen. Webb focused on two semiparabolic curves intersecting at midpoint, a graphic representation of the downward trend of the MTI stock. If the convexity ratio, the distance between the two curves, increased with a few more transactions, there was a better than fifty percent chance that an irreversible Wall Street panic might occur once the stock fell below 125 dollars per share. The momentum of selling might force the price of the stock down to less than half its present value. Possibly as low as sixty dollars per share. At that point, he might as well declare corporate and personal bankruptcy. MTI would have to repay nonsecured demand notes amounting to over twenty billion dollars.

"Bid one hundred twenty-eight, down four."

"What's the hedge ratio?"

"Off the charts, Helene."

"Is there any way we can widen the spread between bid and ask?"

"Not at this point. It's beginning to look like a ski slope."

Who was forcing down the price of MTI? Helene wondered. An arbitrageur who was trying to buy large chunks of the company to be sold at a higher price? A greenmailer who wanted to buy large shares of the company with the sole purpose of making a considerable profit on a buy-back by the company? Or was the run simply the beginning of a bear hug, the initial squeeze before a company takeover?

"One hundred twenty-seven, down one."

"Sell short."

"Helene, we'll lose fifty million."

"Sell short, John."

"But, Helene—"

"Get the orders off!" Webb couldn't stop himself.

Helene turned toward Webb with an expression of both gratitude and disappointment. Eventually, John would have executed her order. She turned impatiently back to the screen. There was a possibility this run might turn into an emergency. However, at 127 they were still some measure away—or were they? Was the

1.5 maintenance ratio of equity over debt out of line? Why the hell didn't Webb tell her?"

"One hundred twenty-six, down one."

"One hundred twenty-five—and falling."

Webb stared at Helene. His thoughts drifted back to his final year at the Harvard Business School when MTI was no more than a petri dish in his kitchen refrigerator. The winter snows of 1947 had been particularly severe, even for Cambridge, Massachusetts. Yet for the most part, it had been a mild year: the fall had been sufficiently golden to be considered an Indian summer; and the summer, like all weather along the Charles River, had been invigorating . . .

Making his way along Harvard Street, a snow-wrapped estuary for sliding cars and slipping students, Roy Webb buried his frostchilled nose into the matted fleece of his collar. As he passed his favorite bookstore, he saw they were closing for the day. He skirted a group of giggling Cliffies huddling together for warmth inside the Harvard Coop arcade, and pushed open the heavy glass door painted with an amorphous logo of intertwining red and black vines.

"Mocha almond with jimmies on a cone, please." Webb glanced around the half-empty store, past the tiny booths surrounding the room. His gaze stopped at a familiar face.

"Captain! It's you!"

"Parker! What in God's name are you doing here?"

"I'm inhaling the culture so that one day I can be as smart as you." Parker grabbed Webb by the shoulder, ignoring the latter's dislike of close bodily contact, and gave him a strong hug. "Sit down, Captain. I see you haven't changed your contrary habits—ice cream in the winter!"

"This is some hell of a coincidence. Are you working around here? Last I heard from you was a postcard from—was it New Jersey or Rhode Island?"

"It was New Jersey. I had gotten a scholarship to Rutgers University."

"That's great!"

"Listen, I don't want to keep you if you're busy. You're probably some kind of a hotshot businessman by now, right?"

"No, I haven't had a chance. Just another Harvard MBA student."

"My condolences, Captain. I figured by now you would be a big bucks man."

"What do you mean, Joe?" Webb bit into the hand-scooped ice cream with an uncomfortable sense of urgency. Parker wasn't here by accident; there was a calculated quality to his conversation. The man looked haggard. His plump, cherubic features had disappeared with what was easily a fifteen-pound weight loss. His thinning hair and day-old stubble made him appear almost sinister. Only his trademark of an unsmoked dangling panatela was the same. He looked desperate, on the prowl, waiting to strike. Yes, Parker's physical presence was a marked contrast to his own patrician jaw and flaxen hair.

Quickly examining his options, Webb decided there was little he could do but sit there and listen to what Parker had to say.

"Another ice-cream cone, Captain?"

"No thanks, Joe. For a freezing winter night, one's enough."

"Married yet, Captain?"

"No, I'm not married. One or two real possibilities, but I have enough problems just getting myself through this MBA program."

"I'm sure, Captain. But a smart guy like you shouldn't have too much trouble. Didn't you go here before?"

"Yes, I went to Harvard College."

"Well, there you are!" Parker slapped the table with his thick, stubby fingers and roared with laughter.

"What's so funny, Joe?"

"You, Captain. You. For someone who acted so savvy at Pingfan, you seem nervous, edgy—know what I mean?"

"No, I don't know what you mean." Webb was becoming annoyed.

Parker leaned over the table and whispered conspiratorially,

"Pingfan. Remember that fuckin' place we blew up so that there would be no evidence left to incriminate your slanty-eyed friend?" He winked, insuring that Webb would not lose the meaning of his poorly disguised innuendo.

"What about it?"

"Come on, Captain. You must have fonder memories than simply 'What about it?' "

"Joe, cut the crap! What do you want?"

"Oh, come on now, Captain, you hurt my feelings. Do you think I came all the way from New Brunswick simply to ask you for something?" Parker shook his head. "No, I don't want something from you. You've got nothing to give me." He pulled out a folded sheet of notebook paper. "Tuition, seven hundred fifty dollars a year. Rent for an incredibly tiny efficiency located on the top floor of a three-story wooden row house on Jackson Street, seven hundred twenty dollars a year. Meals and other accessories, I figure another six hundred a year. That makes a total of two thousand dollars a year."

"Two thousand and seventy, as long as you're keeping track."

"Thanks, Captain. I was always lousy in math. Anyway, I figure your outlay is two grand a year and your intake as a teaching assistant is one grand a year. So that makes a shortfall of one grand a year. Now that's got to come from somewhere in order for you to go to this very fancy school."

"I'm not even going to ask you where you got your information—"

"Good, Captain, because it doesn't really matter. But I can assure you, it ain't too hard in an open society like ours—I mean, people talk."

"It's been good to see you again."

Webb stood and Parker grabbed him by the arm. "Captain, remember Pingfan?"

"What about it?"

"What happened to that little Nip you saved?"

"I don't know what you're talking about."

"Oh, come on, Roy! The Bureau of Taxation and Incorporation in Wilmington, Delaware shows that you're incorporated." Parker pulled out a rumpled piece of paper. "December seventh, 1946—nice touch, Captain. Was that in honor of Pearl Harbor day?—a company which you and some anonymous party are the sole owners of called M–o–l–e–c–u–lar Technology Industries. Pretty fancy, Captain."

"What does that have to do with Ran?"

"Precisely my point. You tell me! Remember, Captain, there were only two ways to attack a problem—blow it up or burn it. Well, I've got a problem . . . I've got some plans for my future, and I want to go out and achieve them. You know, the Great American Dream." One look at the tightness in Webb's face and Parker realized his approach was becoming counterproductive. His voice softened. "You always told me while we were fighting together that if I got you out of the war alive, you'd take care of me, ain't that right?"

Webb walked up to the counter and ordered two mocha almond ice-cream cones. He handed one to Parker.

"Thanks, Captain. That's the Roy I knew in Harbin."

"What can I do for you?"

"Nothing now. But in the next couple of years I'm going to need something against which I can borrow—in order to finance my medical school education."

"So MTI stock would fit the bill?"

"Something like that."

"Look, let me thank you profusely for your valiant efforts in making certain that I came out of the war alive. I'll even write to the War Department on your behalf, recommending you for a Distinguished Service Medal. What more do I really owe you?"

"Gratitude does not count for very much, does it, Captain?"

"They make pretty good mocha almond, don't they? You should see this place in the summer. It's jam-packed. Lines around the block."

Parker reached into his jacket pocket and pulled out several mimeographed sheets of paper and handed them to Webb to read.

Several minutes later Webb stopped eating his ice-cream cone. He rose from the table and beckoned Parker to follow. The two young men walked in silence along Fresh Pond Drive and up the rickety wooden stairs of the three-story firetrap to Webb's cramped efficiency. Webb walked straight to the kitchen, opened the antiquated refrigerator, and pointed to a round plastic covered petri dish filled with a blood-like substance.

"There's MTI! You own twenty percent of that!"

"Five down and still falling!" Crosby's voice pierced Webb's thoughts. He placed his hand around Helene's waist and felt her tense up and pull away. He had never seen her this nervous.

"Sell one hundred put orders," Webb commanded. He was willing to pay the price of offending Helene and usurping her professional role.

"But, sir—"

"John!"

"One hundred twenty . . . one hundred nineteen . . . one hundred eighteen . . . one hundred seventeen . . ."

"Sell short the CBOE options."

"Down one hundred ten . . . one hundred . . ."

Webb watched the printed quotations race across the screen. The quants in the rest of the room ceased their conversations and number crunching. Everyone's attention was focused on Webb.

"Ninety-eight . . . ninety-six . . ."

"Helene, what's our cash position?"

"Two hundred mil, as of close of business."

"Any possibility of borrowing more?"

"Only if we collateralize our remaining equity. And then the bankers want a one point five debt coverage over our net cash flow."

"So that means another—what, three hundred to five hundred mil?"

"Possibly . . ."

"Get it!"

"And then what?"

"Place the entire seven hundred mil into the market. And short it!"

"Roy—you can't. The directors of the New York Stock Exchange will stop trading the stock and slap you with a lawsuit for acting irresponsibly. We'll be driving the company into bankruptcy."

"That's what I want, Helene. A major psychological jolt."

Helene's mood switched from worry to exhilaration as she watched Webb analyze the data on the screen. Webb was responding to numbers and market conditions that were apparent only to him. The strategy might on the surface appear totally irregular and irrational. But she knew, in the long run, it would be brilliant. Her father had described Webb's type of man as possessing *gründlichkeit*, a thoroughness and lucidity of style and expression. *Der Liebe Gott wohnt im Detail*—"the good Lord lives in detail."

"Ninety-three . . . ninety-two . . ."

"Keep selling short."

"But sir, you're driving the price down farther!" Crosby paused to collect his thoughts before presenting an argument to dissuade Webb from committing corporate suicide. He glanced at the faces of his fellow quants, now gathered around his terminal, and continued to read the screen. "Eighty-eight . . . eighty-six . . ."

"Roy, what about our debt-maintenance ratio?" Helene cut in anxiously. "Pretty soon the banks will call in the loans."

"Eighty-two . . . seventy-eight . . ."

"Keep selling!"

"Sir . . . we are. But it's simply accelerating the rate at which the price is falling."

"Good, good."

"Roy—please! This is no time to play a Mexican standoff."

Webb flashed displeasure at Helene's comment.

She once again glanced at the screen. "*Merde alors! Quel acteur!*"

"It's starting to turn around . . . seventy-nine . . . eighty-one . . . eighty-three . . ."

Everyone sighed with relief. The room exploded with an uproar of applause, laughter, cheers, and whistles as Webb walked out.

"Keep the momentum—buy long," Helene ordered. Now she understood Webb's game. "At one hundred ten sell off twenty percent of the preferred in order to pay back our borrowing. But don't let them charge us more than fifty basis points for service."

Helene left the room quietly. She wanted to see Webb privately and bask in the glow of his success. She walked briskly past his phalanx of personal secretaries into the suite she had helped decorate. The series of living-room-sized chambers, decorated with eighteenth-century furniture and set in the elegant sixteenth arrondissement of Paris, made her feel familiar and protected. The walls, covered with *toile de Jouy*, provided a contrasting backdrop for the valuable modern canvases that hung upon them. But the centerpiece was the overbearingly dark French queen painted by Jean Jacques Lagrenée.

As she passed through the chambers, Helene could hear the familiar arpeggios of the Schubert A-flat Major Impromptu coming from Webb's private study. Helene found him sitting at the baby grand Steinway, running his fingers up and down the keyboard in an exercise of self-discipline and aesthetic grace. How like him to counterpoint this moment of financial victory with the exquisite rendition of a romantic melody, she thought. A scholar of Greek and Latin, Webb knew enough not to offend the gods. No victory, whatever its nature, could be proclaimed publicly, and no defeat unduly mourned. Only with the touch of madness, in a moment of sublime creativity, could one proclaim victory without disturbing the gods.

"I'm so proud of you." Helene ran her fingers tenderly through his hair.

"Find the name of the son of a bitch who tried to destroy me today."

Webb's hands came crashing down on the keyboard, ending the piece *fortissimo*.

4

"Uncle Russ!" The small brown-eyed eleven-year-old with a long dark ponytail rushed up to Orestes Bradley and hugged him. "Oh, I am so glad you could come to talk to our science class."

Before he could respond, a pixieish blue-eyed, eight-year-old blonde sneaked up behind him and shimmied up to hang from his neck.

Bradley twisted around to catch Sharon and carefully set her down on the ground. Until he learned whether or not he was infectious, he would have to be cautious.

"Stephanie, are you sure your classmates won't be bored silly with my talk on viruses and infections?"

"Are you kidding? They've all seen you on television. They think you're neat."

He knew his nieces well. Whenever his sister, Judy, took a business trip to promote her famous Kalorama Guest House, a bed-and-breakfast chain she had developed and operated for the past five years, Bradley always moved into her Victorian house in Ritchfield to take care of her kids. He watched them now as they ran through the playground of Ritchfield Elementary School. Its spacious grounds and imposing gnarled oak trees were well suited to this exclusive professional community in the suburbs of Washington, D.C.

Bradley swirled Sharon around until she screamed with a mixture of fear and delight. A thin pale girl about Stephanie's age leaned against a large oak tree and stared.

"Sweetheart, what's that little girl's name?"

"Come on, Uncle Russ, don't stop now! I'm slipping off your neck."

"Sharon, leave Uncle Russ alone, brat! Can't you see he doesn't want you on his neck?"

"Uncle Russ, she called me a brat. I am *not* a brat." Sharon paused, then asked plaintively, "I'm not a pain in the neck, am I?"

Bradley grabbed her by her tiny waist and lifted her up. "No sweetheart. You're not a pain in the neck. But sometimes you and I know that you can be a pain in the a–s–s ."

"Oh, you said a dirty word! I know what a–s–s means, too."

As if she had just remembered her uncle's question, Stephanie beckoned to the frail child. "Come meet my Uncle Russ. He's famous. You'll like him."

As Bradley started toward her, Lydia Cromwell scurried from behind the tree. She darted across the school yard and into the classroom.

Before Bradley could decide whether or not to follow, the school bell rang and Stephanie was dragging him toward the two-story L-shaped building.

Walking through the spotless hallway, Bradley recalled the many times he had come to the school—the ballet recital, the talent show, parents' visting day. And, then, there had been the frightening times at Ritchfield Elementary School. Only three years ago, one little boy in Sharon's kindergarten class, and two girls in Stephanie's second-grade class, had developed an unusual constellation of symptoms: fever, chills, and muscle weakness. After having conducted extensive neurological and chemical blood tests at the National Institutes of Health, Bradley had concluded that they all had poliomyelitis. The last outbreak of polio had occurred at a camp in the Berkshires when he was their age. Both the Salk and Sabin vaccines had not yet been perfected, and, instead, he had received intramuscular shots of gamma globulin.

Bradley grabbed both girls' tiny hands.

The pleasant greeting by the principal, Mrs. O'Reilly, a handsome woman in her early fifties, belied the history of threats and mutual distrust between the two of them. Attempting to close down a public school, Bradley had learned, took more political savvy than medical smarts.

"Come on, Uncle Russ, come inside." Stephanie pulled him into her classroom. "They're all waiting for you."

"Hello, Dr. Bradley. I'm Mrs. Rogers." Stephanie's thin, sprightly teacher stepped up and proceeded to introduce him to her twenty-six eager students.

Bradley divided the class into two groups. He pointed to a pink-cheeked girl and motioned her forward to the center of the classroom. "What's your name?"

"Annie Rodinski."

"Annie Rodinski, you are hereby appointed leader of the Blue group, called the Viruses. Better yet, the Retroviruses. Can you say that?"

"Retro—virus."

"Good, Annie." He winked at a disgruntled Stephanie, who was piqued that he hadn't choosen her as team leader.

"All the members of the Blue team, come over here where Annie is, form a circle around her, and hold hands." He smiled as he watched the thirteen children scramble around Annie.

"Now I need a Red team leader." Twelve hands shot immediately into the air with accompanying screeches of "Please!" "Let me!" "I want to!"

"The red-headed boy over there!"

"Tommie Willoughby, step forward," Mrs. Rogers interjected, making certain Bradley did not forget this was still very much her class.

"Come forward, Tommie, and do what Dr. Bradley asks you to do."

"Tommie, you are the leader of the Red team, the Antibodies."

"Anti . . ." He turned toward Stephanie, his face flushed red, silently pleading for help with the word.

"Wait a minute, Tommie is short one team member." Bradley counted only twelve students.

"Where's Lydia?" Mrs. Rogers did two separate head counts. "Who saw Lydia?"

"She left the classroom when Dr. Bradley came in," Annie replied.

"All right, I'll try to find her." Mrs. Rogers paused briefly before she left the room and added, "Now, children, don't forget, Dr. Bradley is our guest and you must pay full attention to him."

"Would the Blue team come over here. Hold hands and protect Annie. That Antibody over there is trying to destroy you all and capture her." He handed Annie several sticker tabs filled with inscriptions. "Annie, you are the information center for your Blue team. Imagine, boys and girls, that the Blue team is the shape of a real virus. And Annie, located in the center of the virus, is the brains of the virus, containing all kinds of information called genetic material, or strings of RNA. These strings will allow the Blue team to create all kinds of diseases on Tommie over there, who is being protected by his Red team, the Antibodies. Now, Annie, if you can break through the Red team's circle and place these stickers on Tommie's body, you can make him very sick. How many of you have had a bad sore throat?"

Half the children raised their hands.

"All right, how many of you have been sick with a fever, or a rash, or a stomachache, or—" he paused, knowing full well what type of a reaction the next question would elicit, "or a throwing up that won't stop?"

As expected, the children began to laugh. Stephanie exchanged glances with several of her friends, reaffirming that her uncle was, in fact, a really "neat" guy.

Bradley began to hum the only tune he knew: his Columbia University alma mater.

"When I stop, Annie and her Blue Virus team will try to break into the Red Antibody circle so that she can place her stickers on Tommie's forehead. That's what happens in the human body when you and I become ill. First there's a virus that infects the body. Sometimes it remains in our body a long time before we know it's there. At its center can be all types of information that can produce any number of diseases, like German measles or sore throats. As a scientist, I can use special chemicals to change the information in the center of that virus and make it produce a different disease."

Bradley started humming again. He watched the two teams pushing forcefully against each other, shouting, screaming, accusing each other of cheating or playing dirty.

"May I see you, Dr. Bradley, *please?*" Mrs. Rogers had entered the room, obviously flustered by something she had seen.

"All right, Antibodies and Viruses, cool it!"

"Oh no! I've almost got her!" Tommie yelled, reaching over the arms of his teammates.

"Next time, Tommie, I'll make you a vaccine, which will increase the number of antibodies, so you can destroy the virus."

"Dr. Bradley! Please come with me!" Mrs. Rogers led him out of the classroom into the ammonia-scrubbed linoleum hallway.

Her abrupt demeanor caused Bradley to think wearily of the countless years he had spent in public school arguing with teachers who jealously guarded their own authority. He sometimes wondered whether his own rebellious attitude was not due in some small part due to his having grown up without a father in the house.

Mrs. Rogers led him to the girls' bathroom. She called inside,

"Lydia, I'm coming in with a doctor. Everyone else—please leave."

Bradley followed her to a bathroom stall. As the door swung open he recognized the pale, frightened girl who had run from him earlier.

"Lydia, this is Dr. Bradley, Stephanie's uncle. Tell him what you told me."

Lydia turned away from them, and tried to edge farther into the space between the toilet bowl and the ceramic tiled wall.

"Lydia, don't be frightened."

Bradley placed the back of his hand on her forehead. Just as he expected—extremely warm. He would guess about 103 or 104 degrees. He drew her toward him and palpated her neck and underarms. "Does this hurt, sweetheart?" Large, swollen lymph nodes were obviously causing some of her problems.

Bradley lifted her blouse and inserted his fingers beneath the edge of her rib cage.

"Let's see what we have here."

Just as he had feared, her liver was enlarged. On her left side he felt a similarly enlarged spleen. Lifting her blouse to palpate for tenderness around her ribs, he noticed her breasts, larger than normal for a child of her age.

"Call the Bethesda Rescue Squad and ask for an ambulance to take her to Georgetown Medical Center."

"No—no—I don't want to go!" Lydia slid away like a frightened animal.

"Don't you think, Doctor, we should try to call her mother first?"

"Of course, we'll call your mother." Bradley lifted the legs of her pants and noticed her calves were streaked with fresh blood.

"Sweetheart, do you feel dizzy . . . lightheaded?"

"No."

"Are you sure?"

The child did not respond.

"Please, Mrs. Rogers, locate her mother and call an ambulance."

As the teacher left the room, Bradley felt Lydia's pulse; it was racing at 120. In a child of ten or eleven years with high fever, any number of factors could be causing a rapid pulse rate. He grabbed a few paper towels, soaked them in cold water, and placed them on the child's burning forehead. He ran through the possible diagnoses in his mind, but the symptoms taken together did not make sense.

"Lydia, how long have you been feeling sick?"

"A few days."

"Do you remember how and when it began?"

"First, my stomach hurt. And then my throat hurt, and I couldn't swallow."

"Did you notice any of the lumps on your neck or under your arms?"

"Yes. Yesterday."

"Did you tell your parents?"

"My father isn't here. He left home a long time ago." Her eyes filled with tears.

There were a few encouraging signs, Bradley thought. She had been ill only a few days. But with an enlarged spleen and liver, and tender lymph nodes, there was a serious possibility of an acute type of childhood leukemia. But the rapid onset of symptoms suggested an infectious disease. He immediately eliminated the routine childhood diseases: chicken pox, German measles, measles, and roseola. Lydia had no evidence of any skin lesions. Possibly it was infectious mononucleosis? Yet the causative virus occurred most often in late adolescence and early adulthood. He wondered whether, with the early sexual changes, Lydia had a disease of puberty.

"Lydia, your mother is here." Mrs. Rogers had reappeared. "Mrs. Cromwell, this is Dr. Bradley."

A slender, disheveled women in her early thirties glanced quickly at Dr. Bradley, yanked Lydia up by her hand, and without saying a word, hurried her out of the bathroom and down the hall. Bradley followed, begging Mrs. Cromwell to wait for the ambulance, but the agitated woman pushed Lydia into a gray Volvo station wagon and sped away.

Bradley ran to his "arrest-me" red Porsche 928S. The child needed medical attention and she needed it fast. As he reached the car door he was reminded suddenly of Janet Rydell, the hallucinating patient at Walter Reed. Most doctors, he thought, would dismiss a postpartum woman and a prepubertal girl with similar symptoms as pure coincidence or, at best, significant. But as an epidemiologist, he was inclined to see correlations and causalities between disparate entities—no matter how different they might appear to the untrained eye.

As was often his habit, Bradley had left the door of the Porsche unlocked.

"Cops and robbers so early in the morning?"

Seated in the front passenger seat was Dr. Henry Kempe, chief of pathology at NIH. A well-dressed man in his mid-fifties, Kempe was Bradley's closest friend. Warmhearted, cynical, he had cultivated an expensive taste for good food, wine, and the undemanding companionship of light-hearted, sensuous women—or as he chauvinistically called them—"my little beavers."

"What the hell are you doing here?"

"Well, I thought it would be mighty neighborly of me if I could just drop by in between some of your more important federally subsidized household chores—like taking care of your nieces, or chasing old ladies with sickly children down the streets of Ritchfield. By the way, is it safe for me to leave my 911 in the school parking lot? Or are the elementary school kids into stripping down Porsches?"

"Dammit, that woman's got a really sick kid." Bradley was having a hard time getting the key into the ignition.

"May I remind you, lest you forget in your pursuit of old ladies and the Holy Grail, that in less than forty-five minutes you and I are supposed to attend a meeting of the Health Affairs Council at the Executive Office Building to discuss something as trival as an imminent epidemic?"

Bradley pushed his foot down on the accelerator and swung around the parking lot to pursue the Volvo. Kempe could see that the White House meeting would have to wait. Bradley drove down

Wisconsin Avenue, gathering speed as he passed a block of exclusive boutiques selling high-priced fur coats, Gucci handbags, and loafers.

"Russ, I can't tell you how impressed I am with the way this beautiful piece of machinery—a two-hundred-and-eighty-eight-horsepower, V-eight aluminum alloy, water-cooled OHC engine—is being used in congested Washington traffic to chase a woman and her sickly daughter. We should be preparing for the One American Lap which, I hasten to inform you, is only three weeks away. How do you expect to win a seven-day race of eight thousand miles, if we don't practice?" Kempe checked his watch. "You know, I got this new Rolex just for that One American Lap. I'll feel very bad if I've spent several thousand dollars for nothing."

"That girl has got a fever of over one hundred three. Just this morning I examined a woman with a high fever, bilateral adenopathy, and delirium."

"So what? My grandmother has bilateral inguinal hernias and spikes a fever every time she pisses. Would you like to visit her in Milwaukee? You might find some interesting correlation there between the postpartum lady and the schoolgirl. If you want, I can think of one right off the bat."

"Forget it."

Ignoring his friend's ribbing, Bradley floored the Porsche, determined to catch up to the Volvo and ask Mrs. Cromwell some pertinent questions. When did she first notice her daughter's illness? What were the original symptoms? With whom was the daughter in contact? And the one question that was beginning to bother him—was she or anyone else in her family in the military? He cut across Reno Road and Connecticut Avenue and followed the Volvo down the oak-lined torn-up single lane of Sixteenth Street, past the Gold Coast—large, slightly dilapidated three-story mansions, inhabited primarily by the nouveau-riche black upper-middle class of Washington, D.C. He turned right onto Columbia Road and entered the Hispanic neighborhood of Adams-Morgan.

"Since you're into one of your serious, intense moods, I was wondering whether you can explain to yourself how a public health officer with a salary of seventy-two thousand dollars a year can afford to pay fifty thousand dollars for four rubber tires, a sleek metal body, and a Blaupunkt radio with ten speakers?"

"You know that it's my one big fucking indulgence—unlike your Rolex watches, Givenchy suits, and condominiums on Embassy Row and Saint Thomas. Talking about affordability, where the hell do you get the money to buy all that crap?"

"Touchy, touchy! All I wanted to know was whether your self-esteem could tolerate possessing the most expensive Porsche made."

"Stick it!"

"At last, I have your complete attention."

"You know, if I didn't know you any better—as a serious pathologist and dedicated friend who once, only a few short years ago, had only three hubcaps to piss in before acquiring his unexplained 'grand inheritance'—I would think that either you've become an intolerable horse's ass or you've developed a serious case of Alzheimer's." Bradley knew Kempe was right, in his indiscreet way. Like Kimball and all the other federally employed medical personnel, Bradley had acceded to a basic need for financial security at the expense of the opportunity to make big money. Unlike his sister, Judy, only one and a half years younger, already twice married, twice divorced, Bradley had no real entrepreneurial desires or skills. Nearing Columbia Road, a few blocks from his sister's guest houses, he wondered how the same mother and father could have sired two children with completely different ambitions and skills. With the proceeds of her divorce settlements, Judy had gambled first on renovating one, then two, then eventually four Victorian town houses on Mintwood Place, on the simple intuition that travelers were getting tired of staying in oversized, aseptic, impersonal hotels. When she had started four years ago, he had thought she was crazy. Now, her houses were among the most popular bed-and-breakfast inns in the East.

Perhaps, Bradley thought, his Palermo-born mother had been

too protective and indulgent of her first child and only son. He recalled how she continuously assured him he was exceptionally talented and bright, and that *la forza del destino* had meant him to apply his unusual talents to the wellbeing of mankind. In contrast, Judy was *la bella ragazza* who should marry well and be content. As a result, whatever money his mother earned as a receptionist in a doctor's office had gone exclusively to his education. Of the boy playing stickball on 188th Street, in the shadow of the prestigious Columbia Physician and Surgeon's Medical Center, it was assumed that one day he would study at P and S and fulfill his mother's prophecy.

At the corner of Columbia Road and Mintwood Place, the Volvo made a right turn onto Mintwood, a quaint, tree-lined residential street of Victorian row houses. Bradley followed, and watched as the car entered a side alley and parked behind 1854 Mintwood. Lydia and her mother left the Volvo and disappeared into his sister's guesthouse.

"Is Judy Bradley in?"

"Who should I say is calling?" The resident manager, a tall thin man of indeterminate age, with thick red hair and an effete manner, held the front door gingerly.

"Let's make this a quick visit." Kempe nervously scanned the sidewalk.

"Tell her it's her brother, Dr. Orestes Bradley."

"Please come in!" the manager's initial wariness melted perceptibly into a warm, gracious hospitality. "Would you like a cup of freshly brewed coffee? Make yourself comfortable while I see if she's available."

It had been almost three years since Bradley had been here. A great many changes had been made. Bradley looked around the parlor and was impressed. The living room had a warm, inviting quality to it. It was filled with authentic Victorian and Edwardian furniture, oil paintings, and Persian rugs. The only thing missing was a fire in the fireplace beneath the oak mantel.

As soon as the manager walked out of the living room, Bradley walked over to a hall table and opened up the guest register.

"What are you doing?" Kempe hissed.

"Cromwell—here it is, Room Nine. I think it's on the second floor. Come on!"

Bradley hurried up the red-carpeted wooden stairs surrounded by original 1890s covers from the *Ladies Home Journal* and *Harper's* magazine. Kempe followed.

"Russ, this may be your sister's place, but you've got no right to barge in on someone, particularly when you don't have legal grounds."

"A contagious illness and suspicious behavior are grounds enough for me." Bradley knocked loudly on the door marked 9. There was no answer.

"Russ, what's going on here?" Judy Bradley, a slightly overweight, dark-haired woman, looked indignantly at her brother. The manager stood sheepishly behind her.

"What are you doing? I don't force my way into your hospital rooms and disrupt your physical exams." Her firm manner revealed an iron will Bradley knew all too well.

At best, their relationship was civil. But for the most part, Bradley found his sister aggressive and petulant, particularly when she was not able to avail herself of his babysitting services for Stephanie and Sharon. She, in turn, disliked his peremptory manner, his attitude that he owed no debts of gratitude to anyone, save their mother. While Orestes had been designated by their mother as the child who would achieve major accomplishments, Judy had been relegated to the sandbox of neglect. Unfortunately, both children were well aware of these familial expectations. If Bradley hadn't been such a wonderful uncle to her two daughters, Judy would long ago have severed the tenuous family ties.

"Listen, please tell your friend that he and you are welcome here as long as you both behave. Otherwise, I would appreciate it if you and he would hightail your asses out of here." For a split second, Bradley thought Judy had recognized Kempe—and vice versa.

"This is my friend, Dr. Henry Kempe." Judy did not offer her hand.

"Please, Judy, let me in! I've got to talk to Mrs. Cromwell and examine her daughter. The girl is in Stephanie's class. And she may have something quite contagious."

"She's in Stephanie's class? But—" Judy seemed surprised. Staring first at her brother and then at Kempe, who nodded his head in agreement, she took a key-ring off her wrist and flipped keys to find the right one. From inside the room came the sound of movement.

"Is there a second exit from this room?"

"There's an old fire escape that leads to the alley."

As Judy opened the door to the darkened room, they heard the fire escape clang. The occupants had fled.

Bradley started to climb over the windowsill to the fire escape, but Kempe grabbed his shoulder.

"Take a look here!" Kempe covered his mouth with his hands, gagging at the odor of decay that permeated the room as if a cadaver had been rotting for several days.

On a rumpled bed Bradley could make out the contour of a body. He turned on the overhead chandelier light, bumping into a chair in the process.

There was a hoarse cry: "Shut that fuckin' light!"

Kempe switched the light off.

A voice began to mumble: "Who's there? Lydia? I can't see you. Are you there, Lydia? Come here, sweetheart. Tell your mother to bring me some water, I'm thirsty. Lydia!"

Judy answered, "She's not here, Mr. Raymond. Mrs. Cromwell and her daughter left when they heard these men coming into the room."

"Who the hell are you?" the voice demanded.

"It's me, Judy Bradley."

"Leave me alone! I've paid your bloody money."

"I'm not here to collect your money. Your sister already paid for you. . . ."

"And Lydia? Where's my baby niece, Lydia? She wasn't feeling well. Did my sister take her back to one of her fancy doctors in Chevy Chase?"

"I don't know. They just ran out when these gentlemen came."

"Did she tell them anything?"

"No, Mr. Raymond," Bradley answered. "That's why I followed her here from her school. She's quite sick. I'm a doctor. Maybe I can help." He adjusted the closed venetian blind so the afternoon light could filter into the room. Before him was the deathly pale body of a man. He was covered with black spots that looked as if they had been hemorrhaging. Bradley pointed out the ecchymotic lesions to Kempe, who let out a gasp. The only diagnosis that flashed through Bradley's mind was too incredible to believe.

"How long has he been here, Judy?"

"A few days."

"A few days? Come on, he's been here longer than that."

"Take a look at how blue his lips are. He's not getting enough oxygen." Kempe pointed to Raymond's face.

"I got all the oxygen I need. What kind of horseshit are you guys flinging here? Get them out!" Raymond tossed back and forth in the bed, obviously in pain.

"One of my managers admitted him two weeks ago without my knowledge. I think he may have had some kind of relationship with him. By the time I found out he refused to leave."

"Cut the crap, Judy . . . I may be dyin', but I'm not some kind of fag who screwed your resident manager. Why don't you tell your brother the truth?"

Bradley's eyes darted to Judy. How did Raymond know he was her brother?

"What is the truth, Mr. Raymond? *You* tell me!" Bradley opened the venetian blinds gradually, so that more light shone on Raymond. Judy and Kempe stepped back into the hallway.

"Shut the friggin' light. It's killing my eyes. My head feels like I've got a band of street niggers playin' metal drums in there."

"I've got to examine you."

"You got to do nothing except get the hell out of here! And take that lyin' bitch with you."

"Judy, call the police and tell them to send a squad car and an ambulance over here!"

"You don't scare me, Doc! She ain't gonna do nothing. Right, sweetheart?"

Bradley looked at his sister. Was Judy afraid of this man?

"I'll go make the call," Kempe offered.

"No, I'm going to need you here."

"Don't go, Judy!" Raymond pleaded.

Judy took in Raymond's glare and her brother's questioning eyes. She seemed completely paralyzed.

"I have the power to close this place down, Sis," Bradley warned. "You could be running a distinct health hazard here."

Still Judy did not move. Kempe hurried down the stairs and instructed the manager to make the necessary phone call. When he returned, Bradley was already examining Raymond, talking out loud as if he hadn't noticed Kempe's absence.The patient seemed to be more compliant.

"Hyperpyrexia. I'd say close to one hundred five degrees Fahrenheit." Bradley held Raymond's emaciated arm. "I see you lost part of the pinky on your right hand."

"You're a real wizard, Doc."

"May I ask how that happened?"

"Yeah, sure! I got my fingers caught between this fat woman's thick thighs and she wouldn't let me go. So they had to cut it off."

Kempe laughed.

"You like that, shadow man? Remind me to invite you some day to my Comedy Store debut."

"And what about this, Mr. Raymond? This tattoo. It looks like some kind of insect with . . . is it six or eight legs?"

"It's a beetle. See those oriental characters underneath?"

"Yes, I was noticing them."

"You know what that says? No tickee, no laundree." Raymond was enjoying himself. It had been some time since he was able publicly to humiliate anyone in authority. As far as he was concerned, this medical clown and his friend weren't going to learn anything from him other than what they could glean from their physical exam. Who cared anyway? He was dying!

"Do you go to the Orient often?" Bradley asked him.

"Every time I have to get my white shirts hand-washed and starched."

Judy tittered. She seemed to be enjoying the fact that her omniscient brother was being given such a hard time.

Bradley pulled out a packet of matches, lit one, and passed it in front of Raymond's eyes. "His pupils are constricted. What do you think, Henry?"

"A hemorrhagic lesion somewhere in the midbrain . . ."

"Hey, you guys talkin' about me? Talk in English, know what I mean? None of this bullshit medical mumbo jumbo."

Bradley asked Judy to bring him a glass of water. He gently poured it into Raymond's blistered, caked mouth.

"Doc, leave me alone! I'm dyin'! There's nothing you can do!"

"Let's first find out what you have. Then we'll worry about your dying."

Despite her lifelong anger toward her brother, Judy was impressed with his compassion for the man.

"Mr. Raymond, I want to do something now that may bother you."

"So don't do it! I got enough pain." Raymond coughed and wheezed, desperately trying to lift his head to spit up the phlegm in his trachea.

Bradley motioned Kempe over to the bedside. Together, they reached beneath Raymond's armpits and propped him up against the brass bedpost. Raymond coughed up a clot of blood. Carefully, Bradley wrapped it in a handkerchief and placed it in his pocket.

"Doc, my head, it's killin' me."

Bradley gently twisted Raymond's head from side to side and felt the rigidity of his spine. "Meningitis."

Kempe covered his mouth reflexively, as if he might catch whatever microbe Raymond had. "Could be Cryptococcus or some other fungus. His immune system is shot."

"Whatever he's got, he's drowning in it." Bradley tapped Raymond's chest with the third finger of his right hand.

"The chest sounds are flat. You're right—he's completely congested."

Raymond slumped forward, his body became limp and his eyelids started to close. "Look at this—"

Together, they examined a matted group of lymph nodes three to six centimeters in diameter, surrounded by swollen bleeding tissue. Picking up a spoon on the nightstand, Bradley scooped up a small amount of yellow pus oozing from the swollen lymph nodes.

"Buboes!" Kempe exclaimed.

"You're the pathologist, Henry. If this isn't what we think it is . . . then I'll be damned."

"*Pasteurella pestis*—the bubonic plague."

"What are you talking about, Russ?" Judy cut in. "Are you saying that this man has the Black Death? The scourge that killed millions in the Middle Ages?"

"Afraid so, Judy. I'm going to find Mrs. Cromwell and Lydia and put them in isolation. And I'm going to quarantine your guest house."

"What? You can't!" Judy was outraged. It was so typical of her brother to act high-handedly without confirming whether he was right or wrong.

"Tell her, Henry." Bradley placed the specimens of pus in the handkerchief with the sputum, then went over to the sink and washed his hands.

"Russ," came Kempe's response, "we're late for our White House Meeting. We've got to go!"

"Jesus Christ, Henry! Are you going to leave this man to die?"

At times Bradley felt Kempe was more than a bit unfeeling.

"Can we be sure it's the plague?" the pathologist asked.

"No . . . not one hundred percent. Judy," he said, spinning around to his sister, "I know this is asking you to take on a financial loss for a while. But you've got to close the house. I'm reasonably certain he has the plague."

"Do me a favor," she shot back. "Don't close it down until you have definitive laboratory evidence it's not some other disease."

"I never knew you were such a purist in medicine. But, if it makes you feel better, I agree to that. What do you say, Henry?"

"She may have a point. So far all we have is a clinical impression, not a firm laboratory finding. Anyway, the plague has been eradicated from the United States."

"But there's still one or two small pockets of wooded areas where the plague transmission cycle has not been completely eliminated yet," replied Bradley, adding reflectively, "It's a vicious cycle—an infected flea bites a wild rat, which in turn bites man. At some point the cycle has to be broken in order to prevent the spread of the plague." He could see Kempe fidgeting impatiently. The White House meeting was obviously on his mind.

"Are there any cures?" Judy asked.

"Streptomycin antibiotic, two to four grams, for three consecutive days. But first you have to culture the bacteria out from a sample of sputum, blood, or buboes. That's the only way you can make a definitive diagnosis."

Suddenly, Bradley felt Raymond tugging weakly on his arm.

"Moro . . ." Raymond's voice was weak.

"*Moro?* What's *moro,* Mr. Raymond?"

"I think I hear the paramedics coming up the stairs," Judy said. She was suddenly nervous, apprehensive. She shifted her gaze rapidly from Raymond to Kempe to Bradley.

Without warning, Kempe rushed to the bed and slammed his fist down onto Raymond's chest.

"Ugggh!" Raymond's body arched upward off the bed as if he had received a huge jolt of electricity.

"What the hell are you doing?" Bradley shouted.

"He's going into cardiac-respiratory failure! I'm doing CPR, what do you think I'm doing?" Kempe kept pushing down on Raymond's chest.

"Henry! He was just talking to me. How could he be in heart failure? Get off of him."

"Russ, dammit! If we wait till his vital signs drop, it may be too late."

"Right this way, gentlemen." The manager led two paramedics, dressed in blue with red-and-yellow arm patches inscribed D.C. Fire Department, to the bed.

Bradley turned to them immediately. "I'm Dr. Bradley, and I've just examined this man. He has poor vital signs and must be rushed to the emergency room." He pulled out his identification card and showed it to the more senior of the paramedics, a white-haired lieutenant with a ruddy complexion.

"So?" The paramedic replied.

"I'd like you to call ahead to thc George Washington ER and ask them to have an isolation room ready."

"Why?"

"This man has a highly contagious disease."

"Such as?"

"I'm not sure yet. But they should be prepared."

"Gotcha. We'll telephone from the ambulance." The paramedics grimaced at the odor as they lifted Raymond onto an adjustable metal stretcher. He was breathing with difficulty. They moved him down the stairs and into the street carefully.

Kempe, who had left to call the White House as the paramedics had come in, reappeared. "You're a lucky man, Russ. They're running late and will wait until you arrive."

"Good. Drive my car to GW and join us in the ER." Bradley gave Kempe the keys to his Porsche and turned his attention back to the ambulance.

"This guy ain't doin' well at all, Doc. I'll ride in the back here with you and the lady, and we'll head straight towards GW."

Examining Raymond, the lieutenant added, "Doc, I think we got a little problem here. His BP is down to eighty over fifty, and he's very cyanotic."

Bradley could see that the lieutenant was right. Raymond was almost purple and his breathing was rapid and shallow. Through the stethoscope Bradley heard the distinct sounds of cardiopulmonary failure: Fluid mixed with pus was rapidly filling Raymond's chest. In order to get even a small amount of air, Raymond had to breathe twice as fast as normal, placing incredible pressure on his already debilitated heart and lungs.

"Will he make it?" Judy asked, rubbing her hands nervously.

"I don't know."

Bradley placed an oxygen mask over Raymond's face, grabbed a green cylinder of oxygen, and turned the valve. Raymond's breathing became more labored. His face turned a macabre dusky blue. The oxygen was making the situation worse.

"Quick! A cut-down tray!" Bradley snapped.

The paramedic quickly set up the instruments to thread a catheter into one of Raymond's already collapsed veins. Bradley intended to get some cardiac stimulants into him. Maybe Kempe was right to have started the CPR.

"Russ, what are you doing?" Judy cried. "You can't cut him up here—we're just a few minutes away from the hospital ER!"

Bradley ignored her, slipped a pair of sterilized, powdered gloves on his hands, and grabbed the surgical knife. Without bothering to anesthetize or sterilize Raymond's right forearm, he made a sharp incision along the most superficial vein, cutting through the beetle tattoo.

Judy turned her head aside as blood oozed from the cut flesh.

Dabbing the blood away with a series of sterile gauze pads, Bradley slid a two-inch metal needle into the vein. He quickly attached a three-way heparin lock, from which he drew some blood samples, before attaching it to a tube hanging from a plastic bag filled with five percent D5W, one percent calcium chloride, and one percent epinephrine solutions. Bradley wasn't about to let this man die. There were too many urgent questions to which only Raymond could have the answer: Where had he been two weeks ago? With whom? Did he use drugs? Had he recently been bitten by an animal? Where was Lydia Cromwell? How had she gotten sick? Why was he at the Kalorama Guest House? Was it an accident that Lydia was in Stephanie's class?

"Agggh!" Raymond was in terminal respiratory failure.

Bradley grabbed a five-inch syringe needle, carefully measured one centimeter below Raymond's Adam's apple, and forcibly jabbed the needle into his trachea. The oxygen hissed audibly through the newly created hole in his throat. Dark-red, almost black, blood gushed out.

"Dammit! I've hit a bleeder!"

"What about CPR, Doc?"

Without looking at the paramedic, Bradley knew he didn't have to answer that question. Neither of them would elect to give this man mouth-to-mouth resuscitation. Bradley picked up the stained surgical knife and cut through Raymond's throat, creating an even wider hole.

Judy started to gag as a steady flow of blood pooled around the red beefy cavity of Raymond's throat.

"Doc, we're losing him!"

"Push a bolus of epinephrine!"

"Doc, it's too late."

"Give me that!"

Grabbing a ten-inch syringe filled with epinephrine, Bradley counted two centimeters below Raymond's left nipple and plunged the needle filled with the cardiac stimulant straight through the chest cavity, right into Raymond's heart. But he could feel no cardiac activity. Withdrawing the needle in frustration, Bradley slammed his fist onto Raymond's chest and started to push down with both hands.

"Nothing, Doc. We gotta stop—we're at the ER."

The ambulance door was wrenched open. "God, what the hell happened in here? It looks as if someone walked into a meat cleaver!" Kempe helped the orderlies pull Raymond out of the ambulance. The lieutenant placed a green tarpaulin over the motionless body.

Followed by his sister and Kempe, Bradley hurried into the George Washington University Medical Center Emergency Room, showed the security guard his visiting attendant's identification card, and proceeded to the pathology laboratory. He pulled the contaminated handkerchief from his jacket pocket and smeared a sample of Raymond's blood and sputum onto a slide.

"Why don't you try staining the slide first. It might help."

"Smart-ass pathologist!" Bradley took the slide off the microscope tray, and with an eye dropper filled with two different staining fluids, carbolfuchsin and carbolthion, he placed a few drops on both ends of the slide, just to be certain that he would not miss the microorganism because of some error in staining technique. First, he scanned the entire slide under twenty-five-power magnification for any evidence of a bacillary, ovoid, or coccal organism. Then he switched to fifty-, one-hundred-, and two-hundred-power magnification.

"What do you see?" Judy whispered.

Though he searched the slide's surface thoroughly, Bradley could find no trace of the characteristic bipolar "safety pin" structure of *Pasteurella pestis.* It was impossible. How could Raymond have all the classical symptoms of bubonic plague without possessing a clearly identifiable *Pasteurella pestis* bacterium?

"Nothing, huh?" Kempe looked at Judy; both were clearly relieved.

"But Christ! What could it be?" As he massaged the gnawing pain in his right shoulder, Bradley began to turn over the possibility that Janet Rydell's assault with an infected syringe needle had consigned him to the same fate as Raymond. Both the postpartum woman and his sister's guest had seemed to have the same plague-like symptoms. And one had just died—cause unknown.

"For the record, there are potentially three ongoing epidemics. Twenty-four new cases of cholera have just broken out in Hong Kong. The HK public health authorities, however, claim there is no need yet for massive inoculations, WHO international health certificates, or airport quarantine."

Bradley sat down alongside his boss, Susan Engel, M.D., Ph.D., and listened to Richard Kuzmack's rapid-fire delivery. Kuzmack was chairman of the Health Affairs Council as well as the President's science advisor.

"Richard, you know damn well that on the surface twenty-four new cases of a disease do not comprise more than twenty-four new cases. But you never know." Dr. Engel was living up to her reputation for speaking bluntly, a habit of some concern to her superiors. Yet the spry sixty-five year old was an internationally recognized expert in epidemiology, and the first female surgeon general of the United States. She rarely suffered fools—or bureaucrats—gladly. And Kuzmack was playing a little bureaucratic game with her, trying to shift the international monitoring of Hong Kong cholera away from the already overburdened White House Office of Science and Technology. Bradley had to admire his skills. He had clever ways of dispensing his monthly assignments. An ex-Jesuit, he had resigned from Woodstock Seminary because of what was officially described as "personal moral conflicts over doctrine." Kuzmack wielded unusual influence over the science community by his ability to control contracts and grants from several government agencies. Although Kuzmack had only a Ph.D. in ethics and science, both Bradley and Engel had respect for the depth of his knowledge in the three broad areas of science for which he was responsible: the development of new policy guidelines for the emerging commercial areas of recombinant DNA, child development, and an alternative spacecraft to the faulty *Challenger*. A short, wiry forty-three-year-old man, Kuzmack still radiated a religious intensity that was both inspiring and repulsive.

"Susan's correct, you know," a gruff voice cut in.

Kuzmack turned to the new speaker. "But what about you, Joe? Don't you have twenty thousand men stationed around there? Won't they be at risk?"

"No, I've got some light infantry with the Republic of Korea. Nothing around Hong Kong." Major General Joseph Parker, M.D., surgeon general of the Army, twirled his unlit panatela cigar.

"They may well come down with cholera if you guys at Walter Reed don't monitor the situation," Engel snapped.

"Susan, there's very little I can do if my boys decide not to wash their hands. But I sure as hell can get on their case if they've picked up a strain of clap that you people tell us can't be treated with our current antibiotics."

"Joe," Engel persisted, "all we said was that you can't keep treating gonorrhea with the same old combination of tetracycline and penicillin."

"What do you recommend?"

Kuzmack could see that his approach had missed the mark. It was time to go into neutral. "Perhaps you are both correct. But it also may be too early to know much. As chairman of HAC, I authorize Dr. Engel to supervise the monitoring of the Hong Kong situation by the Office of International Activities and the Communicable Disease Center." He paused, but heard no opposition.

"What about the AIDS epidemic?" Parker asked, glaring at Engel.

"Don't worry about it," replied Engel. "We have it under control. The incidence of new cases has gone from one in one thousand to one in ten thousand. Our national education program for safe sex is working. As long as your military boys don't bring it back from overseas, we're all right. Also, our laboratory scientists at NIH are working on a blood screening program and vaccine that look extremely promising."

Eager to avoid another confrontation, Kuzmack interjected, "For the next, far more important, problem, Bob will summarize the situation."

Bob was Army Colonel Robert Squire, a forty-two-year-old fast-tracker who, after having spent the major part of his professional life in counterinsurgency and special operations, now headed up a three-quarters-of-a-billion-dollar operation entitled the Defense Advanced Research Projects Agency. DARPA funded a multitude of different weapon systems, including the M-1 Abrams battle tank and other highly classified projects. His presence at the HAC meetings made Bradley and Engel wary. Kuzmack's response to Engel's queries had been, "I assure you he has a proprietary interest in all health matters pertaining to the U.S. government. Furthermore, you'll find him extremely knowledgeable."

Squire began his summary: "We're beginning to notice in both our military population and their civilian dependents all over the United States, a random distribution of the following symptoms: a prodromal period of malaise, lethargy, some muscle pain, and a low-grade fever of about one hundred to one hundred one, spiking rapidly to one hundred five."

"Bilateral enlarged inguinal nodes?" Bradley interjected.

"That's right, Russ. How did you know? We thought we were the only ones seeing these symptoms. They seem to be mainly in our people coming in from stations overseas."

"How long has this been going on?"

"Three to four weeks." Parker interrupted, turning toward Squire to make certain his facts were right.

"Russ, how come you didn't tell me about this?" Engel asked.

"I just saw my first three cases today." Bradley shot a glance at Kempe, who said nothing. Kempe enjoyed accompanying Bradley to the HAC meetings for the single purpose of informing his friends and colleagues that he had been to the White House that day. Bradley continued, "One was at Walter Reed, and another was at—"

"Joe, what's DARPA doing monitoring military health?" Dr. Engel interrupted in a shrill voice.

Despite the obvious provocation, Squire sat unperturbed, his ramrod back pressed against his chair.

"Come now, Susan," Parker snapped. "There's no need for bureaucratic testiness. The Army is very broad-minded about its interdisciplinary participation."

"Horsefeathers, Joe! Interdisciplinary participation? The only thing that's interdisciplinary over at the Pentagon is that you all eat out of the same public trough."

Engel's comment was followed by an awkward silence, the type Kuzmack disliked for its inefficiency. Valuable energy and time were being siphoned away from the task at hand.

"Please go on, Joe," he said calmly.

"We have counted well over two hundred cases of this unknown disease," Parker began.

"Unknown? What is unknown about bilateral auxiliary involvement, bubo, and high fever?" Engel's voice rose. "In my day we called that *Pasteurella pestis.* Do you know what that is, Bob?"

"Yes ma'am. Bubonic plague."

"Very good, Colonel. But if you're right, we have the makings of a new fourteenth-century scourge."

Kuzmack made a conscious effort to conceal his mounting enthusiasm. For the first time in a long while, he thought, they might have a national disaster worthy of his skills.

Squire took a deep breath, choosing his words with care. "The disease *looks* like bubonic plague. It follows the same five- to twelve-day course. And it terminates in death."

"Death in every case?" Bradley broke into a cold sweat. The throb in his right shoulder seemed to intensify. "Have we been able to culture any pathogens?"

"No, not yet," Squire replied hesitantly.

"What about treatment with streptomycin?" Engel had diagnosed and treated several cases of *Pasteurella pestis* while stationed as a World Health Organization medical officer in Islamabad, Pakistan.

"Negative," Parker responded, in his customary clipped military fashion.

"Chloramphenicol?" Engel persisted.

"Negative."

"Tetracycline?"

"Again negative, Susan." Parker looked uneasily at Engel. "I don't like saying this, but we have no known cause, no known cure, and a definite body count."

"How many dead so far?" Engel demanded.

"One hundred and ten dead out of approximately two hundred cases," Squire replied evenly.

Bradley wondered how this could have been kept so quiet. Admittedly, it was of recent origin. But within the continental United States the incidence of plague was close to zero. Now he was hearing that there had been about two hundred cases within four weeks. It had to be an epidemic!

By federal law all practicing physicians were required to report the occurrence of three quarantinable diseases: cholera, yellow fever, and plague. Bradley dreaded to think of the number of cases that had gone unreported. How many doctors were seeing an isolated case and misdiagnosing it? Or seeing two or more cases, but not believing what they were seeing? And how many were treating patients with a broad-spectrum antibiotic or simply considering them victims of that all-inclusive medical category, Fevers of Unknown Origin? There was a reflexive medical response: If you have an FUO, there is simply nothing you can do about it, except wait out its natural course—death.

Bradley barely heard the desultory argument between Engel and Squire as to what constituted an epidemic. Kempe nodded his head in quiet sympathy. He knew what Bradley was thinking. Bradley recalled Susan's stentorian pronouncements when she had appointed him director of the National Institute for Infectious Diseases and Allergies: "There are only three basic techniques of epidemiologic practice that you will undertake here at the Institute: descriptive, analytic, and experimental." She hadn't said anything more than what was accepted as standard procedure. But that was exactly the point—she didn't want any deviation whatsoever from the three painstaking, rigorously demanding classical approaches. No guesstimates, hunches, or intuitions. But within the five-day incubation period, could he, Bradley, use any of those techniques to save his own life? Or the lives of millions of other potential victims? Or was such speculation futile, premature?

"Since we really don't know anything about this disease—the total number of actual cases, the number of people infected, the cause, the treatment—"

Squire's pronouncement was interrupted by Engel's stern voice. "We've been over that point, Bob."

"But, Susan, I think we need to take some bold initiatives *because* we know so very little."

"What would you suggest, Russ?" Engel turned to Bradley, annoyed that he had dropped out of the discussion.

"A massive program of blood tests on suspected carriers of the disease," Bradley said reflexively.

"We have screened the few individuals who have been willing to come to our infirmaries voluntarily, but so far the number has been minimal." Squire looked expectantly, first at Parker and then at Kuzmack.

"Well, then, don't make it voluntary."

"What in God's name are you suggesting, Russ?" Parker burst out.

"Declare the present condition a public health hazard!" Bradley replied angrily. "Invoke the necessary federal statutes already on the books and require both civilian and military populations to be quarantined until we have a better idea of what is going on. In the meantime, we will make it mandatory for all civilian and military physicians to report any suspected cases." Bradley felt the gnawing pain again in his right shoulder. Was he proposing a drastic approach because of his own personal situation? Was he becoming irrational as a result of his anxiety? If anyone at that table, particularly Susan, suspected that he might be infected, they would hospitalize him immediately—and proceed to attack the disease on their own time schedule.

"I suppose, Russ, that you would like to volunteer the military for this ignominious job?" Parker tapped his thick fingers on the table, clearly annoyed.

"You guys did a brilliant job in Wilkes-Barre, Pennsylvania, in the late seventies, when everything was washed away in the flood and there was a cholera epidemic."

"Thank you, Russ, but as you well know, the governor of Pennsylvania, with the consent of the President of the United States, declared Wilkes-Barre a national disaster."

"Who took care of the massive evacuation and relocation of the Vietnamese refugees after Saigon fell?"

"We did! But again, that was a national emergency," Parker insisted.

"You remember, General, I was in there with your medical corps, treating everything from massive outbreaks of amoebic dysentery to malaria, cholera, and severe malnutrition. Again, you did an exemplary job."

"Your flattery is appreciated, Russ. But the military is also mindful of its constitutional restrictions. Involving ourselves in this not-yet-diagnosed epidemic would be a violation."

"Cut the baloney, Joe. You guys will do what you're told to do when it comes out of the Executive Office Building."

Engel looked at Kuzmack, who was surprisingly quiet. "Well, Richard! What do you have to say that will dissuade me from officially reprimanding my obstreperous, rambunctious Russ, here?"

"Susan, I wouldn't be too harsh on our colleague," Kuzmack responded. "Russ, I personally think that there is some merit to the idea that, of all the government agencies capable of dealing with an outbreak of infectious disease, only the Army is really equipped to handle the logistics for the massive numbers of people potentially involved."

"Richard!" Engel scolded Kuzmack. "You know the Public Health Service has an equally honorable, longstanding tradition of eradicating epidemics."

"Yes, I know, Susan, and I don't mean to slight you or your agency. If, after a rigorous epidemiologic investigation, you can demonstrate the need for an official public health quarantine, then I will recommend it. It will be executed by the military and supervised by the PHS."

"Thank you. You will have the necessary data within a week's time," Bradley blurted. Then he rose, nodded to everyone at the table, and exited quickly with Kempe.

Engel's face showed her exasperation with Bradley's rash promise. Kuzmack, Parker, and Squire looked at one another. Bradley had taken the bait.

7

"Beautiful, *n'est-ce pas?*" Helene de Perignod and Roy Webb stood before the living-room window of her spacious penthouse apartment in the exclusive Ritchfield Towers of Chevy Chase, Maryland, the very first apartment she had owned outright. One million dollars to acquire and another quarter million to furnish. The Paris apartment on Avenue Foch had been paid for by her employers, Credit Lyonnais and then Paribas. The suite on the top floor of the Regent Hotel in Kowloon, with the nightly festival of lights embracing the Hong Kong harbor, had been paid for by her employer Dai-ichi Kangyo, the largest bank in the world. Even her apartment in the fashionable Roppongi area of Tokyo, where most foreigners lived, was owned by another employer, Mitsubishi Bank. Now she stood savoring the quiet beauty of the first piece of the world she had owned. Webb had affectionately termed her tasteful combination of French provincial and Japanese furnishings "Nippon Bouillabaisse."

"Look, *mon cher!* The Capitol building is lit up, just waiting for your political ascendancy," she purred.

Webb smiled wryly, enjoying her teasing. She was always trying to encourage him to run for office. Congressman, senator, maybe even President. He usually replied that holding office entailed too much ass-kissing and too little real accomplishment or responsibility—except that of self-aggrandizement. In a strictly political town, he was one of a select few who wanted nothing more than to lead a commercial life. In some ways this made him an outcast living and working in a city with only two basic commodities—real power and perceived power. Except for its beautiful skyline, Webb found the town parochial and inefficient. Locating MTI headquarters and laboratories fifty miles north of the city had nothing to do with a desire to read his name in the "Style" section of the *Washington Post*, where a recent bon-mot or attendance at some worthy gala was considered by some to confer importance. It simply made good business sense to be located near the Federal Drug Administration in Rockville, Maryland.

"RAI—Research Associates International. Instead, it should read IRA. At least we'd earn some tax-free dollars in a retirement account. Research Associates International is nothing more than a couple of rocket scientists massaging numbers they push through the Federal Drug Administration." Helene pressed up against the muscular body she knew so well.

"They're not rocket scientists, sweetheart. They happen to be eminently qualified epidemiologists and biostatisticians. As you know all too well, they run the clinical studies required for FDA approval before I can put any new drugs on the market."

"*Wagamama-na!*" Helene lapsed into Japanese to emphasize her annoyance with him, but tightened her arms around him.

"No, my dear, I'm not being an egotist."

Webb kissed Helene on the cheek, unwrapped her arms from around him, and walked over to the nineteenth-century hand-carved bureau. He set down his brandy glass and gazed for a moment at a silk painting by Utamaro, the famous seventeenth-century Japanese painter of erotic art.

"Does it excite you?" Helene inquired softly, indicating the scene of two lovers fondling each other. She ran her fingers through his thick white hair, impatient now with his preoccupation with business. Perhaps their love had run its natural course and would not be rekindled.

"I need RAI," Webb said suddenly, as if he had not heard her. "I have a group of new biotech products for which I have to get approval."

"I understand."

Helene picked up a Mexican green-skinned cherimoya, peeled it with a knife, and cut slices of the creamy apple for Webb and herself—a peace offering. He looked tired. She should have known. She had noticed Webb becoming increasingly concerned about MTI's future in months past. Despite healthy third-quarter earnings, MTI was already feeling the vagaries of a consumer population taking fewer and fewer drugs and concentrating, instead, on preventive medicine. Now, even in their limited spare time, he was insisting that they discuss business. As she gazed at his profile, silhouetted against the living-room window, she thought how good the past five years had been to him. And to them. She remembered how they had first met; it seemed so long ago. . . .

It had begun with the clear yellow sun of Cézanne, Matisse, and Van Gogh burning sensuously into Helene's tanned, seminude body as she lazed on a chaise-lounge facing the Mediterranean Sea. Alone at last, free from the social and professional encumbrances of her daily routine as a Eurodollar bond trader at Paribas, she could finally appreciate the long-awaited getaway she had arranged for the beginning of July. Refusing the invitations of her concerned male companions and lovers, she had decided to fly Air Inter to Nîmes and then drive the remaining two hundred kilometers to St. Jean-Cap-Ferrat. This would give her a chance to see again the medieval village of Les Baux and attend one of the jazz festivals in Aix-en-Provence. All, she proudly reminded herself, had been done *sans homme*.

Pressed between Nice and Monaco, St. Jean-Cap-Ferrat is a tiny peninsula bracketed on the north by the Baie des Anges and on the south by the Golfe de St. Hospice. Its estates lie hidden from the Basse Corniche by a maze of narrow cobblestone roads that wind their way through luscious vegetation, palms, and blooming bougainvillea. It had been here, to the exclusive Grand Hotel, some twenty years earlier, that Helene's father, le Comte de Perignod, would take his four beautiful daughters, one shrewish wife, and one moody nanny who, on her off hours, doubled as his mistress. Now Helene had returned to the very same hotel, hidden from the Boulevard Général de Gaulle by a high white stucco wall crowned by terra-cotta tiles.

The incredible vista she remembered from the terrace had not disappointed her: the daily miracle of the blood-red setting sun fusing into the shimmering Mediterranean. Helene had long ago found the place a haven. She smiled as she reminded herself that this time she had very purposefully chosen to vacation here in order to avoid finding love.

At the ripe age of thirty-one, she had had many lovers—some, serious liaisons; others, minor affairs. But for her, love was as much a practical concern as making money. These few days would simply be a present to herself: she would arise when she wanted, walk where she wanted, sunbathe as she wanted. She was beginning to tire of lovers. Running her fingers over her firm body, she was glad to be distanced from her usual reality.

"*Je m'excuse, Madame. Mais, est-ce que je peux m'allonger à côté de vous?*" A man's voice.

"*Comme vous voulez, Monsieur!*" She wanted to be alone, dammit, and nothing in the world would force her to open her eyes. She wanted to preserve the rich and colorful images of the past few days in her mind as a reminder that somewhere in this world of advancing technology and crass mercantilism was a sanctuary where natural beauty was the sole arbiter of reality.

"*Pardon, mais vous savez si cette chaise est cassée?*"

She wanted to be rude. But even in a moment of sensual self-abandon, there were still rules of etiquette.

"Je vous en prie! Je suis occupée. Demandez au garçon! Il va vous aider."

"If I were to ask the pool boy for some help, I'd never get a chance to meet you," the man's voice said in exasperation.

"Ah . . . an American. That explains everything."

"What arrogance! Look, I'll leave you alone, but only if you open your eyes."

"I see only what I want to see." It was now a simple matter of Gallic pride that under no condition would she open her eyes or succumb to his persistence.

"*C'est dommage*, I may not be handsome, but I'm a terrific boxer."

"Why should you presume that I would be the slightest bit interested in what you look like?"

"No reason. But we seem to be having quite a charming conversation despite our temperamental differences."

"Temperamental differences! My God, you are presumptuous. I'm lying here minding my own business and you, in your typical American fashion, come sauntering up and annoy the . . ." She was tempted to finish the sentence, but decided that she would not give him the satisfaction of knowing how much of an impact he had made on her in so short a time.

"I bother the hell out of you. It's okay, I can take it. Believe me, I'm a big boy."

"Are all you Americans alike? You want something, and therefore it must follow that you should have it."

"I can't answer on behalf of all my countrymen. But, as for me, I will give you an unbiased answer if you open your beautiful eyelids. It really won't hurt you. And you have already acknowledged my obnoxious presence by talking to me for, I'd say, the better part of a quarter of an hour."

"Are you always so persistent?"

"Are you always so blindly obdurate?

"Obdurate?"

"Yes . . . stubborn!"

"Dammit! I know what *obdurate* means." Helene sat up on

her chaise and was completely surprised. By the high timbre of his voice and his ingenuous enthusiasm, she had imagined him to be in his middle forties. But his rugged, weathered face made him older.

"Please, let me buy you a drink." He motioned to the waiter. "*Dom Pérignon millésime.*" He turned to Helene. "How do you like your view of the Mediterranean?"

"Are you the owner of this hotel? Are you conducting a survey?"

The man was pleased that her pluck and vitality more than equaled her exquisite body.

"No. I'm in Room two hundred fifteen—just below you."

Laughing, she wondered how he had learned her room number. "You're a clever man . . . and insistent."

"And audacious. . . ."

"Yes, I'm sure you're successful . . . in whatever it is you do."

"There are those who consider me just that. However, I'm not so certain."

Helene was surprised by his answer. This was not the type of man who should have the slightest hesitation about what he said or did.

Bringing a chilled ice bucket, the waiter placed it on the small wrought-iron table between their chairs and pried the cork loose.

"No loud bang!" Helene cupped her hands over her ears.

"At my age, most good things begin with a whimper—a persistent, obnoxious whimper. The loud bang comes later—if you're lucky."

"Ahh, I see, I will now be entertained by the aphorisms of a wizened old man."

"To Youth!" He offered her a glass of champagne and raised his glass in a toast. "May it always remain both wiser and more foolish."

"And to my American Gary Cooper, may he always rescue a damsel in distress. Even if she may not be in distress." Sipping her champagne, Helene watched his cool blue eyes. They were intelligent, determined, and sensuous. A trim, tanned body in a brief swimsuit. Except for the loose, wrinkled skin of his neck, she would say he might be in his early fifties. The full sinewy lines of his arms told her that he was a tennis player or an athlete of some sort.

"You speak English extremely well," Webb said.

"School. Private tutors. And several years in the States."

"Where?"

"Stanford."

"I hear it's beautiful. You deserve each other." He raised his glass in the sign of a toast.

She reciprocated. "And you? Your French?"

"Prep school. Yale. And business here in France."

"And what do you do?"

"I have built a conglomerate in chemicals, pharmaceuticals, and a series of other products." He knew he sounded immodest, but age gave him that prerogative.

"What's the name of your conglomerate?" She liked a forthright man. She waited to be impressed.

"MTI."

"Ah, that would be Molecular Technology Industries. Gross revenues, thirty billion dollars; third-quarter earnings for '84, seven hundred fifty million. A diversified holding company with what is considered to be one of the finest, if not *the* finest, corporate management teams—under your able leadership, Mr. Roy Webb."

"Madame, I am very much impressed." He poured another glass of champagne and toasted her once again. She was as smart as she was beautiful.

She continued, "MTI is the preeminent company developing the latest techniques of recombinant DNA technology and effectively applying them—unlike your closest two dozen competitors—to the manufacture of commercial products, such as your new swine flu vaccine for animals."

"Is there anything you don't know?"

"Yes. What are the next five years in your company going to be like?"

"That depends."

"On what?"

"Whether you join us or not."

"I toast you, Mr. Roy Webb. But, I'm afraid that I never mix pleasure with business. And since I'm not quite certain exactly what type of proposition you are making, I will endeavor to enjoy our present conversation before it ends on a nasty note."

"*Endeavor, nasty*—I see! I think you misunderstand me. I didn't make a pass—at least, not yet. I simply want to make you a job offer for whatever position and salary you see fit."

"Mr. Webb, nowhere in your annual report does it mention that you are either generous, trusting, or ingenuous—or, if you would excuse my directness, foolish."

Webb smiled almost imperceptibly and then launched in: "Helene de Perignod, thirty-one years old, single, attractive, born in Toulouse, France, to a prosperous, aristocratic merchant-banking family with strong ties to the Orient. Parochial school to age thirteen, then private tutors. Graduated number one *École Normale Supérieure Économique et Politique* and received an MBA from Stanford. Then a few years in Tokyo at Dai-ichi Kangyo, Mitsubishi Bank, and an assortment of small private trading houses operating out of Hong Kong and Macao. At thirty-one you're considered to be rambunctious, willful, extremely ambitious, shrewd, and at times, a bit too impatient with recalcitrant clients and slow-witted bosses. You're fluent in French, Spanish, English, and Japanese, and you know a smattering of Mandarin Chinese. And you're one hell of a risk arbitrageur and currency trader. You're registered at the hotel, making certain through a sizable but discreet *pourboire* that no one, including your present employer, Paribas, knows where you are. My job offer is simple: any terms you want, for as long as you want, if you join MTI as a corporate officer. Working, of course, exclusively for me."

"Is this the way you normally recruit your personnel? Ambushing them when they least expect it . . . half-naked and—?"

"And expecting an amorous overture, instead?"

"Well, I must admit . . . a job offer with MTI was not exactly what I had expected at St. Jean-Cap-Ferrat."

"As you said, we Americans will go to any lengths to acquire something we want badly enough. Well?"

"My God! Do I have at least a few minutes to think about it?"

"You have as much time as it takes to consume lunch—truffles, canard à l'orange . . ."

"Enough!"

"And a fantastic chocolate mousse."

"After which you will expect an answer."

"If it's not too presumptuous. . . ."

Helene felt a rush of excitement. Rarely did she meet a man who seemed her match in every way. Webb did not miss the thrill her eyes betrayed. Reaching toward her, he took her hand and, without saying a word, led her over to a white, canopied beach tent nearby. She followed docilely. He closed the tent flap and gently placed his lips upon hers, inhaling the warmth of her breath and the sensuous fragrance of sun and sea.

Helene didn't resist. She was surprised by her body's response to his self-assured passion. She leaned into him and ran her fingers over the nape of his neck, down the sinewy muscles of his back.

He pulled down the bottom of her bikini and lowered her to the white wooden bench. Arching his body over hers, he entered her without hesitation. They moved with graceful restraint.

Tenderly caressing the firm muscles of his thrusting flanks, she looked into his eyes and whispered the only word she could recall, "Now!"

When she awoke that night in the king-size bed of Chambre 215, she was looking into Webb's smile. Alongside her on a table were trays of food.

"As promised—lunch."

Later, they walked down the carpeted marble stairs to the 1979 convertible Rolls Royce Silver Cloud Corniche. Her hair blowing in the warm midnight breeze, Helene watched the shimmering lights of the marina at Beaulieu-sur-Mer, where the bouillabaisse at The African Queen was as good as any found along the Côte d'Azur, even the one she used to eat with her family in Villefranche. They raced along the winding, narrow road of the Basse Corniche, and passing through the tiny fishing villages of Cap Roux and Eze-sur Mer, she recalled the beautifully decorated interior of the chapel of White Penitents, surrounded by the medieval stone buildings used as painters' and sculptors' studios. They passed Pointe de Cabuel, Pointe Mala, and Cap d'Ail and entered Monaco. On Boulevard Rainier III, Helene was astonished by what she saw. Surrounding the Place du Casino, the formerly elegant capital of Monte Carlo, once accessible only to the very discreet and very wealthy, was a gaudy carnival of people and high-rise condominiums. In contrast, Miami Beach, even more crowded and commercial, still retained some semblance of dignity in its faded art deco facades on pink stucco buildings lining Collins Avenue. Monte Carlo had been ruined by crass commercialism. Helene had no objection to anyone making money in healthy commerce, but to amass wealth at the expense of the aesthetic beauty of a country was an unpardonable sin.

"Please, let's go away from here!"

"One stop, that's all." Webb drove along Quai Albert Premier, around the Port de Monaco, and stopped in front of Harry's Discothèque, only to be refused entry because he had forgotten to bring along a sport jacket. He shrugged his shoulders as he returned to the car. Helene stepped out and, in defiance, began to sway sensuously to the persistent drumbeats wafting from the interior of the club.

"It's free out here, and you don't need a *jaquette*."

They both laughed.

Webb awkwardly tried to mirror what appeared to him her formidable footwork.

"Just relax!" Helene danced behind him, took his hips in her hands and pressed her body against him, purposefully arousing him with her circular movements.

"Remember, dancing to rock is just like making love . . . which, by the way, you do beautifully . . . except this time . . . to music."

"Does that mean you want me to hum in bed?"

Her arms encircled his neck while she continued to undulate her pelvis. "I dare you."

Webb turned and steered her lithe body to a secluded doorway. Lifting her thin cotton dress, he lowered his head onto her nakedness. . . .

Helene's thoughts drifted back to the present as she cut open a purple-striped New Zealand pepino and savored its silky texture. It seemed to her their love once had tasted like this fruit—mellow as a pear and sweet as honey.

"What about it, Helene?"

"What about what, Roy?"

"Haven't you been listening to me?"

"Oh yes, I have." She offered Webb a slice of the pepino. When he refused that, she made him another offer of the cherimoya. This time, he took a piece.

"Well, what did I say?"

"You said that I was the most sensuous, exciting creature you had ever met. And certainly one of the best currency traders."

"Of course." He took her in his arms, knowing all too well that this sudden show of affection could not make up for his recent behavior.

"Do you remember St. Jean-Cap-Ferrat?"

"Of course. That's where I recruited you. Half-naked, at that."

She smacked him playfully. "How do you know that I wasn't setting you up so that you would eventually hire me?"

"Well, you certainly went to great lengths to hide your whereabouts."

"That would be precisely the right way to entice a man like you. Don't you always say, make the obvious look complicated and the complicated look obvious?"

"Yes, but why would you want to set me up?"

"Love! Financial advancement!" Coyly breaking away from him, Helene sensed she was finally exacting some slight revenge for his emotional inattentiveness.

"One never knows, does one?"

"Okay, Svengali, now that I know you've set me up, tell me what you think about mezzanine financing for RAI?"

Helene took another piece of pepino and pondered his question. Dammit, if that's the way he wanted it, she'd give him an answer.

Sitting down at a desktop computer in her booklined study, she accessed the menu for a mergers-and-acquisitions model, then placed a cash-flow analysis for years one and two of operations on the screen.

"After year two, it looks to me like your R and D expenses will be about three point six million. Your marketing, if you want to do a halfway decent job, about nine point seven million. General and administrative expenses, eleven point two million." She recited the litany of debits and credits in a playful voice and concluded, "You should receive a total gross revenue of twenty-three point twenty-five million. Take this sum and offset it by the forty-one point six million expenses, and lo and behold, what do you find? That you're in the hole for eighteen point thirty-five million dollars before your obligatory equipment depreciation of ten million dollars, making it a grand total of twenty-eight point thirty five million dollars of red ink. And then there is debt service. Chief—if you don't mind my calling you that—I wouldn't worry about mezzanine financing or any financing. RAI should *pay* you to take them over. But I know you have your heart set on this deal. So . . ."

"I'll first buy it through mezzanine financing, have Swann and Company take the senior position with eighty percent debt-to-loan value at one and a half points over prime. I'll pay them the sum necessary to keep the debt current. Then I'll take a junior position with a subordinated convertible debenture that will give me an accrued annual thirty percent compounded return due in two years."

"That's not mezzanine financing—where's the upfront equity? There is none! It's all debt financing. You've just created a rich man's leveraged buyout without having to force the company to pay fifteen to eighteen percent interest rates up front. But you're still going to sink that company with the weight of all that debt. There's not enough cash in that company to service even the senior debt."

"That's right. And when they start to get into trouble—which should be pretty soon—I buy them out by swapping my defaulted mezzanine financing for common stock and then merge RAI into MTI and give them Class B nonpreferred, worthless MTI stock."

"Well, why don't you just do that right now, instead of going through this entire charade?"

"I want those scientists to feel properly motivated. And not simply raped."

"You really want them, don't you?"

"Let's say they're becoming indispensable. I'm developing more and more new medical products using recombinant DNA, and I could use their expertise."

"What if I find you a corporate officer who is both a good epidemiologist and a good clinician? Would you stop this acquisition?"

"Why are you so opposed to it?"

"Because it's not like you simply to buy a service company without any tangible assets when all you have to do is hire them away or retain them as consultants."

"I *need* that company! It has a unique relationship with the Federal Drug Administration."

"Then hire their expertise."

"No! I want to own it. And freeze out any potential rivals from passing new drugs through the FDA."

"They're not the only company in the business."

"No, but they're the best." Webb couldn't understand why

she was fighting him so much. Perhaps it had nothing to do with the acquisition, perhaps he had been hard on her lately.

"Listen, I'm sorry."

She ignored the apology. "RAI is nothing more than a John Doe operation with a holding company registered in the Cayman Islands."

"So what?" Webb argued. "We've bought other anonymous corporations. *Société anonyme.* You've done it for us in France."

"We're not in France. And never with a company of prima donna scientists. They usually insist on having their names plastered all over the letterhead of the company, as well as any billboard they can stick them to."

"You don't trust me?" He looked at her squarely.

Helene put down the pepino and walked back toward the living room.

"Answer me!"

Her silence was answer enough. Checking her Patek Philippe watch, she noticed that they were already late for Senator William Hall's Georgetown dinner party.

"We're out of time, Roy."

8

"Bill, I apologize for my colleague's tardiness." White House science advisor Kuzmack looked around the table at Senator William Hall's invitees. Only Bradley's place at the table remained unoccupied. Hall was the junior senator from Oregon. A middle-aged, successful businessman, he chaired the powerful Senate Health Subcommittee, a position obtained after a risky, highly acclaimed grab for power. But Kuzmack, the shrewd ex-seminarian, had only to look down the table at the beautiful woman seated next to Roy Webb to realize it was Helene de Perignod who had invited the evening's guests. Only she would have the audacity, in conservative Washington, D.C., to wear a semitransparent, loose white blouse beneath a white handknitted Riviera jacket over black satin pants. Her hair was pulled into a tight chignon, crowning the sharp, elegant features of her face. Her high Bourbon forehead and nose were highlighted by gently arched eyebrows and lush eyelashes.

Large black pearl earrings and necklace adorned her patrician neck. Christ, Kuzmack thought, how incredibly beautiful! A woman worthy of the Medici fortune and equal in shrewdness to Borgia herself. A corporate finance officer who ran her own agenda under the guise of working for her longtime mentor and patron, Roy Webb. In the past, when MTI needed bold action to absolve the pharmaceutical industry of medical liability, it was she, not Roy, who had come to see him. When he had indirectly asked how he, Kuzmack, could benefit from helping MTI, she had replied simply that "good deeds were a reward unto themselves."

Kuzmack picked up one of the five wineglasses in front of him to savor the taste of the unidentified white wine. As the evening wore on, he stopped wondering why Helene, not Senator Hall, had invited them to this charming Georgetown townhouse.

"Bill," he addressed the senator, "in this glass I am drinking—let me see how I can describe it—a well-integrated superior Chablis . . . with just the proper hint of peach. I would say this is a Chablis *Premier Cru*, 1983, Vaillons."

"My compliments, Dr. Kuzmack. You are correct. You really did learn something useful at the Woodstock Seminary." Hall enjoyed presiding over his winetasting parties, always catered by Hobart's, the most expensive, if not the most elegant, caterers in town. Forty-seven and already twice divorced, Hall knew well that in Washington the only relationship that mattered was the one that served as an adjunct to political influence. The basic tenets of the pecking order were clear even to a Washington novice: first, a senator is more important than a congressman; second, a congressman heading up a powerful subcommittee is more important than a senator; third, a senator in charge of an important subcommittee is more powerful than a cabinet secretary; four, all of the above are significantly less influential than the President's appointments secretary. Having understood these fundamentals early in the game, Hall proceeded to build an assortment of political coalitions around a variety of health issues. As he looked down the long mahogany table of his sparsely furnished dining room, his real constituents sat before him.

"I'd like to propose a toast to all my guests—"

"All your guests are not here. And anyway, I can't get straight which of these glasses belongs to me and which to Joseph." Dr. Susan Engel, wearing a simple black dress, without makeup or jewelry, felt out of place at this Georgetown dinner party with its menu of wild mushroom and leek ravioli tossed with sweet young peas.

"Susan, you're always bitching and moaning about turf. That glass on your right is mine and that quarter-filled pinott blank is mine." Parker moved his wineglasses closer to his plate, then began carefully dissecting his food.

"It's *Pinot Blanc*, Joseph. You don't pronounce the *t* or the *c*."

"Thank you, Helene, I always wanted to have my French corrected in front of a group of dinner guests."

"Now, now, Joc. No need to be touchy. We're all friends here, aren't we?" Hall interjected smoothly.

"What's the matter, Roy," teased Parker, the surgeon general of the Army, noticing Webb's stern expression. "Afraid someone is trying to poison you?" He was out to bait Webb deliberately.

Webb ignored Parker's provocation. Bradley had finally arrived, and Bill Hall was relieved to see him.

"Profound apologies to you, Bill, and to your guests." Bradley nodded his head as he entered, embarrassed by the smiles of his colleagues, all of whom were acquainted with his well-founded reputation for tardiness.

"No problem. I hope you don't mind, but we began without you. I think you know everyone here."

"Not everyone," Helene said, raising her eyebrow quizzically. "I'm Helene de Perignod. And you are the director of the National Institute for Infectious Diseases and Allergies, the famous Dr. Orestes Bradley."

"Famous? In God's name, what trouble has he gotten himself into now?" Susan Engel crowed.

"Oh, Susan, Russ here is a big boy. Let him meet this pretty, charming lady. Only fair—right, Roy?" Parker needled Webb in the practiced way he had used to maintain the decades-old tension in their relationship.

"Bill, you promised me a handsome young man on my left," Helene complained. "And there you are, seating Dr. Bradley next to Susan, who has the opportunity to see him as frequently as she wants."

Hall quickly moved the empty chair next to Helene's. Bradley was impressed by her easy forthrightness, but wary of this now publicly acknowledged interest in him.

"The gentleman to my right is Roy Webb, chairman and president of Molecular Technology Industries." Helene pointed nonchalantly toward Webb.

"Nice to meet you. Bill has told me a lot of good things about you." Webb rose and shook Bradley's hand.

"Well, you know politicians—always exaggerating," Bradley replied half-jokingly. Webb liked Bradley's self-assured manner and his obvious wariness of Helene's attempts to manipulate him.

"I understand you're in charge of some very important clinical data and monitoring equipment." Helene ran her finger around the lip of the Wedgwood crystal glass.

"You make me sound quite notorious," Bradley laughed. He had to force himself not to stare at her. She was more than beautiful—she was exotic, unobtainable. Trite, he thought, but true. Beneath her polished veneer he detected a childish mischievousness, a sensuous playfulness.

"Anyone who can track down mysterious diseases and cure them would be quite notorious, I think," Helene replied flirtatiously. She found Bradley attractive in a rugged, casual sort of way. Unlike Webb, Bradley did not appear vain. Thick black curls bracketed a high, intelligent forehead. A forehead like her father's.

"Watch out for Helene—she's crazy about epidemiologists," Webb said, laughing for the first time that evening. He knew the cryptic reference to RAI would not be lost on Helene. Webb was also irked by Helene's obviously seductive behavior. Was she trying to make him jealous? Or was she recruiting Bradley for a senior position at MTI?

"Dr. Bradley," she said, turning in her seat to face him, "I'm a great believer that human minds and talents cannot be bought and sold like corporations. What do you think?"

Bradley realized very quickly that he was being used to resolve some unspoken dispute between Helene and Webb. He resented it.

"I'll tell you what I think, Helene," responded Susan before Bradley could reply. "Most number crunchers in the health field *want* to be treated as if they were high-powered computers with sophisticated software."

"Susan, that's no way to talk about your best and brightest," Parker interjected facetiously.

"On the contrary. The brighter they are, the more independent they feel obliged to become."

Bradley turned toward Helene and jabbed a pointed finger at his own head, pantomiming that Susan was talking about him.

"Susan, don't go around demoralizing our federal officials," Senator Hall piped up. "Our subcommittee will have to allocate more funds for mental health benefits for federal employees." He pointed to Bradley's three full wineglasses. "As it is now, we provide more benefits for our employees than any organization other than the Politburo."

Kuzmack was amazed by Helene's blatant attempt to seduce Bradley. Could it be that she and Webb were no longer living together? The industry rumor had it that there was a chill in their relationship. But that wouldn't account for Helene's behavior. Above all else, she could always be trusted to be discreet. No, it must be something else. Could it be that she wanted something from Bradley—something she didn't have and needed? What was it?

"I see our friend Kuzmack is giving us the once-over, wondering with his convoluted Jesuit's mind what is it that I am up to," Helene teasingly reprimanded.

Kuzmack raised his glass of wine in appreciation of Helene's observation, as well as her audacity in confronting him publicly with such charm. The raison d'être of the party was quickly revealing itself to be nothing more than a shameless ruse for Helene to meet Bradley.

"Since Dr. Bradley was the last guest to arrive, it is only fair we subject him to the wine test, *n'est-ce pas?*" Helene raised Bradley's wineglass to his lips. He took a small sip.

"Of course, there are other tests we can subject him to . . ." Kuzmack couldn't resist trying to smoke Helene out.

"Richard, could you for one moment try to stop being such a pain-in-the-ass Jesuit?" Helene was becoming annoyed with the former seminarian.

"Try this one." Webb handed Bradley a large, half-filled glass.

Taking a few sips, Bradley looked at Helene, who anxiously awaited his response.

"Well, on the one hand . . . it could be . . . but on the other hand . . . I'd say this is a white Chablis." He held the glass with both hands, hoping that no one would notice the nervous tremor. His shoulder was killing him.

"From our chief of infectious diseases we expect a lot more than that." Parker raised his glass to Webb in silent mockery.

"You too, Joseph. I wish you the best of health," Webb replied calmly.

Watching Webb and Parker, Bradley was surprised by the palpable tension between them.

"Come on, now. No copping out. *Essayez!*"

"Sweet . . . flowery . . . a Riesling."

"Very good. And?"

"And . . . let me see. And . . ." Bradley watched Webb as he pointed to his right ear.

"A . . . Riesling of the right ear!"

"Dr. Engel, is this the finest detective you have?"

"Helene, I'm only responsible for him from nine A.M. to five P.M. After that he's strictly at the mercy of his deficient upbringing."

"Where were you raised, Dr. Bradley?" Webb asked.

"The Washington Heights section of New York City."

"I know it well," Webb volunteered. "Before you were even born, I used to date some girls from that neighborhood. There used to be a teachers' college there."

"You make it sound ancient," Susan teased.

"I am, my dear Dr. Engel. I am."

"Well, is the chairman of the board of MTI hinting at possible retirement?" Kuzmack smiled as he asked a question to which he already knew the answer.

"Nothing of the sort. On the contrary, Dr. Kuzmack, I think I will ask the board to invest me for perpetuity." Webb laughed. When Parker guffawed, Webb stopped laughing.

"Now, Dr. Bradley, we still haven't finished our friendly inquisition. What type of Riesling is that?"

Helene tried to help him by mouthing the name *Mittelwihr*.

"Middle Ear." Bradley and Webb laughed loudly together.

"Château de Mittelwihr, 1983, Riesling. A praiseworthy Alsatian wine of ample body and oily texture . . . flowery but not at all sweet, with outspoken, citrusy fruitiness . . . aeration twenty-eight to thirty minutes."

"And this one?" Bradley picked up another glass and sipped it.

"Chablis *Premier Cru*, 1983, Montmains," Webb and Helene answered in unison.

"Wait a minute! May I remind the folks at the other end of the table that Dr. Bradley is also one of my guests. I don't want him running out of here thinking what an inhospitable host I was, and what a bunch of bullies I invited."

"Please, Bill," Bradley said, raising his hand. "Just because I've been deprecated, insulted, and generally degraded by innuendo and direct insult, I hold no hard feelings, especially when a gracious, elegant woman has made me feel totally inadequate." Bradley turned his head away from the startled guests. Only after Helene broke into merry laughter did everyone join in.

"To a man whose sense of humor is equal to his charm and sense of perspective. I ask you to join my toast to Dr. Bradley."

Hall motioned to the wine steward. "Please fill everyone's glass with the Sylvaner d'Alsace 1983."

"Don't you find this all so pretentious?" Helene whispered to Bradley in a conspiratorial *sotto voce.*

"It's only pretentious if you don't really enjoy drinking wine. From time to time I drink a Beaujolais. But I have a very low tolerance for red wines."

"Ah, so you are quite mortal."

"Definitely so. The young god Bacchus made certain that if I had more than two glasses of red wine, I would develop an incredibly painful headache."

"I'm sorry to hear that."

"No, simply a way of teaching me to beware of hubris. I'm not as much in control as I might think I am."

"It would be interesting to test that hypothesis, wouldn't it, Dr. Bradley?" Helene asked mischievously.

"Only the blandishments of a beautiful woman could force me to reveal the answer." Bradley was more shrewd than she had expected, thought Helene.

"Hey, what's going on down there?" Hall boomed.

"Don't be so jealous, Senator. You get to see him before your committee. This is the very first time he's testified before me." Helene reached over and took Bradley's arm.

The feel of her fingers tightening around his forearm sent a shudder through Bradley. He recalled Raymond's final grasp, and the word *moro.* What the hell had he been trying to say? And that tattoo?

Bradley's mind momentarily wandered from the conversation. He had spent the afternoon trying to track Lydia Cromwell down through the Ritchfield Elementary School directory. For the sake of privacy, the school file did not reveal either the name or the address of the sponsor who had agreed to allow his or her residence to be used for the purpose of enrolling Lydia. Not an uncommon practice in the Chevy Chase public schools, according to Mrs. O'Reilly, who suggested he might want to call back the next day. She had laughed when Bradley recommended she close the school until tests could be run to see whether Lydia had the bubonic plague. With no definite proof, and no formal federal order from the surgeon general, there would be no school closing. And when Bradley had argued with Judy to keep Stephanie and Sharon at home for a while, Judy's response, too, had been to laugh.

"Penny for your thoughts?" Without waiting for a response, Helene continued, "I'm afraid we've lost you with our idle chatter."

"No, not at all. I'm simply not a very entertaining companion tonight."

"Don't mind him, Helene, he does that all the time. He's always tuning out." Engel winked at her.

"Well, I see there is nothing left to do except to make certain that the good Dr. Orestes Bradley won't be bored."

"Don't mind her, Russ," said Parker. "Helene is an expert in placing people on the hot seat. Don't be intimidated, just strike back."

Bradley liked Parker. He could always be counted on to be frank and appropriately rude. But behind the casual manner, Bradley knew, was a secretive and ruthless man. You didn't become surgeon general of the Army by being a nice guy. Yet the foot soldier in Parker, the love of combat and camaraderie, appealed to Bradley.

"Joe," Helene said, "I'll make a deal with you. You take care of yourself and I'll take care of *le médecin*."

"To hear you talk that sweet French to me, I'll agree to anything," Parker cooed.

"Oh, I'm sorry!" Helene stood up, wiping at the table linen with her napkin. She had overturned her glass, and wine was running down Bradley's pants leg. "Look what a mess I've made! I am so sorry. I've ruined your trousers."

"I'll get some seltzer from the bar." Hall rose from his seat.

"Don't bother yourself, Bill, I'll take the hapless victim and administer to him myself." Helene took Bradley by the hand and rushed him through the swinging doors of the small, cluttered kitchen to the foyer.

"Let me apologize," she said as soon as she led him into the other room, "I've used the oldest and corniest trick in the book, spilling that wine on you. But if we stayed any longer, I would have been fighting with Kuzmack; Parker would still be trying to annoy Webb; and you would have tuned everything and everyone out. And I don't want that to happen again. At least, not tonight."

"Don't I have anything to say about it?"

"No. Please hand me that coat in the closet and let's get out of here."

Bradley helped her on with her beautiful sable coat and they stepped into the cool night air of Georgetown.

Helene placed her arm through his, her face alive with excitement. "You don't find me too bold, do you?"

"Of course not! It's a daily occurrence for me. Wine purposely spilled on my pants by a seductive abductress. I'm used to it! That's one of the perks of a senior government official."

"Oh, I'm so glad!" She wrapped her arm more tightly around his and felt, for the first time in a long time, young and frivolous.

"God, smell that air." Bradley held her as she started to slide over the slippery cobblestone sidewalk. "Chicory wood burning in a fireplace." He stared at her face beneath the yellow shimmering light of a wrought-iron lamppost. He saw a beautiful woman filled with childish glee.

"I feel naughty. I want to do something dangerous."

"Like what?" As the words escaped his lips, Bradley felt ridiculous. The answer was self-evident. Or was it?

"A game! Let's play a game!"

"A game? What type?"

She released Bradley's arm and ran along the leaf-covered sidewalk. "See how far you can slide." She coasted for a few feet, then she fell to the ground and laughed.

Bradley ran to her. "Are you all right?"

"Only if you promise to leave me here, lying in this field of crisp, golden leaves."

She looked exquisite.

"*Allez-y! Aidez-moi!*" Helping her to her feet, he felt her body against his.

They turned left on Wisconsin Avenue and saw the usual assortment of high-school seniors and college undergraduates milling about the stores. It looked like Oktoberfest—colorful, noisy, and carefree. Strolling leisurely, they glanced through store windows at everything from Chinese kites to punk-rock albums. Standing in front of a small gourmet food store, Helene squeezed Bradley's hand and led him inside.

"I'm thirsty and I want a simple Perrier to cleanse my palate of all those ancient wines."

"A cold soda on a cold October night?"

"Of course." She jabbed him playfully in the stomach, then pressed her cold fingers against his face, "*Froides mains; chaudes amours.*"

"Cold hands, warm heart." Bradley opened the bottle and handed it to her.

"Very good." She took a drink and then offered him some. "Just imagine you're on a hot, sandy beach on the French Riviera. The sun beats down on you. Your body is covered with that wonderful mixture of sand, coconut oil, and sweat. And if you're lucky—or as you Americans would say—if you play your cards right, you might even have a beautiful woman alongside of you."

"Anyone in particular?" He enjoyed her overtures, understanding them to be exactly as they were intended, amusing, humorous, playful, and purposefully seductive.

"*Quien sabe?* We've just met, and in the course of a few short hours I have managed to insult you, spill wine on you, abduct you from a dreary dinner party, and—worst of all—entice you to drink a freezing soda when it's forty-five degrees."

"Not bad. I think we may be getting somewhere."

"Where are we going, *mon ami?*"

"To play something fast and dangerous." They left the shop and turned left on M Street. It was a long but invigorating walk to Dupont Circle, a Greenwich-Villagelike area in downtown Washington.

They entered a nondescript five-story apartment building dating back to the 1950s, when most of northwest Washington was being built. Bradley greeted the Pakistani concierge at the front desk and led Helene down a recently carpeted hallway. He opened the blue metal door and turned the light on.

It was what Helene might have expected—a two-bedroom, two-bathroom, bachelor apartment decorated in inexpensive, Scandinavian teakwood furniture. On one wall was the popular black-and-white print of Don Quixote and Sancho Panza. The other walls contained rows of diplomas, citations, and signed photographs. The living-room shelves were stuffed with professional journals, reprints, and books. Every flat surface was piled high with papers.

"Is this what you consider fast and dangerous?"

Bradley helped take off her coat. "Not exactly. Let's warm up before we go downstairs to the garage and take my car out for a drive around town."

"A Porsche 928S."

"How did you know?" Bradley walked over to the liquor cabinet. "Rémy Martin V.S.O.P.?"

Helene nodded her head in agreement and picked up a toy version of his car, which served as a paperweight. They both started to laugh. Drink in hand, she planted herself before a brightly polished silver frame containing the picture of two young girls.

"Your daughters?"

"No, I wish. They are my nieces. The dark one with the hazel eyes is Stephanie. She's eleven years old, with the poise and charm of a teenager. The other one, Sharon, is eight. She has beautiful blue eyes and blonde hair, and a mind like a steel trap."

"Well, it sounds as if both girls take after their uncle."

"Thank you. Such flattery is always welcome." Bradley raised his glass, inhaled the aroma, and drank.

"You never married?" Helene sat comfortably back in the sofa, her arms stretched over the dark-brown pillows.

"Too busy. Too ambitious. Never enough time. Pick any one of those answers and it'll fit."

"You mean there was never a woman?"

"Once. A nurse, when I was a resident. Warm. Kind. Caring. She wanted to marry me."

"And?"

"I wasn't ready. I had milestones to pass. We lived together near Greenwich Village for about five years. Eventually, we parted. There was no place for the relationship to go, so we turned against one another and destroyed every remnant of warmth. Since then I have lived with a series of women for brief periods, always leaving before the issue of commitment could become a serious topic of conversation."

"Trust." She stood up, walked over to him, and placed her arms around his neck.

"Is this the kind of game you like—fast and dangerous?"

"No, as a matter of fact, in this case, I like it slow . . . very slow . . . and easy." Bradley paused; his mind was racing through the facts about the plague. The contagious stage was technically called the pneumonic phase, and certainly he was not there yet. He had no cough, no fever, nor swollen lymph nodes. But if he were infected, even droplets of his saliva could be fatal to her.

She was kissing him gently on his neck. "Unbutton me!" she said softly.

As Bradley opened the last button of her loose white blouse, Helene unfastened a heavy gold bracelet with a bold inscription on the back.

"What's that say?" he asked, hoping to buy time, wondering whether or not he dared go any further.

"*Sauve qui peut.*" Half-naked, she took Bradley's hands and placed them on her breasts. Her full brown nipples were erect. She began to undo his belt and smiled when she saw that he was warm and ready.

"And what does that mean?"

"Survive at all cost!"

The irony of the words jarred him to quick decision.

"No, Helene." He reached down, picked her blouse up off

the floor, and draped it around her shoulders. "Not now," he said gently. "Not just now."

She stepped back to look at him, and brought her hands up to her breasts reflexively.

Major Ezra Kimball's Chemical Bacteriological Warfare Threat Assessment Group was for real. It was the first of its kind—a unit of the Army Medical Research Institute of Infectious Diseases (AMRIID) within the Department of Defense, trained specifically to fight a chemical or biological war. The unit was an interdisciplinary one composed entirely of minority group members. Kimball well recalled the response of Colonel Bryant Stockwell, his superior, when he had argued the case for developing the unit. The Director of AMRIID had said, "The only minority in this friggin' pack is you and me—two WASPS lost in a dungheap of upwardly mobile frito banditos, kikes, chicks, and niggers. They're your dirty quartet, so don't pawn them off on me as some noble experiment in human enrichment."

Now Kimball was on the field drilling his motley foursome. "The enemy, designation Bkhv—Soviet chemical troops—is one battalion strong, fully deployed. What's his configuration, Private Ramirez?" Kimball shouted the question through a thick haze of gas: twenty-three percent cyanide, thirty-eight percent chloropicrin, and thirty-nine percent chloroform—toxic at five minutes or more exposure. In truth, he felt no better off than his four trainees blindly scrambling around gasping for air, who were cursing him for having forced them to take off their gas masks.

"No pain, no gain!" Kimball snapped. "You people need a lasting memory of what this shit can do to you."

Corporal Jorge Ramirez sputtered. He was a first-year community college dropout who had joined the Regular Army to become a lab tech. A tough kid, he refused to allow Highpockets Kimball to intimidate him.

"Well, Ramirez?"

"Soviet configuration, sir! Facepiece: an ShM-one rubber helmet, plus a modified Soviet GP-forty civilian respirator." Ramirez gasped for air and tried to relax his diaphragm muscles in order to control his rate of respiration. He felt as if someone had just poured caustic lime down his throat.

"Also an OP-one hooded coat, sir!"

"And?"

"Leggings and gloves made of lightweight rubber."

The six-foot, barrel-chested Kimball liked the short, swarthy Latino. Ramirez had the necessary drive and ambition to succeed at the Fort. Also, it didn't hurt Kimball's personnel OER if a member of a minority group was number one in the regiment.

"And?"

Leaning against the Quonset hut wall, arms across his forehead, Ramirez tried to answer Kimball in between coughs. Corporal Louis Rappaport, another member of the team, groped through the mist and pulled Ramirez to the ground.

"Smart move, Rap." Kimball picked up the smoking canister of gas and flung it toward them, forcing Ramirez and Rappaport to scuttle to the other side of the tiny hut. The two other trainees continued circling the periphery, gagging and choking, but hardly taking their eyes off the World War II carbon-filtered gas masks lying idle on the wooden shelves around the room. Ramirez regained his strength, ran across the room, picked up the canister, opened the door, and flung it outside.

"Smart little motherfucker, aren't you?" Kimball pulled down his gas mask and turned on the switch to the portable air-compressor, the M-106 Mity Mite.

"*Puta!*"

"What did you say, Ramirez?"

"I said that you can never outsmart a smart major."

"Ramirez, you haven't finished."

"Sir, I can hardly breathe!"

"On a battlefield, they are not going to be as understanding or forgiving as I am. We're not going out of here until you can complete the full description of the Bkhv. If you don't know your enemy, you sure as shit can't fight him! And he'll get you first!"

"ZFO-fifty-eight clothing with an L-I light protective suit made of heavy-duty rubber cloth."

"Why do those SOBs wear rubber?"

"So they can fuck you on the battlefield without getting venereal disease," Rappaport whispered under his breath.

"I didn't hear that, Rap."

"The L-I suit can be worn for as long as twenty minutes at temperatures above thirty-eight centigrade, or for four hours at temperatures below fifteen centigrade."

"*Muy bien*, Ramirez."

"Thank you, Major. *Puta!*"

"I heard that, Ramirez. A *puta* is a whore who fucks around, and you just fucked your buddies by making them stay here for another two minutes." Kimball checked his watch to reassure himself of the two-minute safety margin. "Your lungs aren't going to be worth shit if you don't get out of here in the next minute and a half."

All four raced for the door.

"Wait, Ramirez! No one leaves until you can tell me the basic ingredients of a Soviet Army decontamination kit."

"Soviet decontamination kit, sir! The IPP-S-one kit contains a dichloramine concentrate, while the I-DP weapon-decontamination kit contains an ampoule of each of the standard degassing solutions, one of DT-six and one comprising two percent caustic soda, five percent monoethanalomine, and twenty percent ammonia." Despite the excruciating pain in his chest, Ramirez loved to answer this question because he loved to hear the major's predictable retort.

"You're one smart Puerto Rican."

"*Muchas gracias*, Major. I owe this all to the Army, sir!"

"The Army has one more question for you, Ramirez."

"Yes, sir."

"Who is the biggest user of guinea pigs?"

Ramirez didn't answer. Instead, he sank slowly to the ground.

Kimball rushed to him and placed his index finger on Ramirez's carotid artery: tachycardia. He ripped open the young soldier's protective overalls and placed his ear against his chest. Fluid was rushing into his lung. Pulmonary edema! Kimball realized he had miscalculated the time of exposure to the cyanide gas. How could this have happened? He had run this simulation many times before. Never once had any of his chemical bacteriological warfare trainees succumbed to the gas mixture. True, it could be lethal—but at three times the dose and twice the time of exposure. Something was definitely wrong. Kimball dragged Ramirez from the gas-filled hut and took a medical kit from his backpack.

"Rappaport, call an ambulance!" he barked. "Williams, get over here, help me set up an IV." Corporal Thaddeus Williams, a wiry black man in his early twenties, temples prematurely speckled with gray, opened the green metal suitcase carried by every CBW platoon. Corporal Anne Drake, an Army registered nurse on detail from Walter Reed Medical Center, rushed alongside Williams.

"D5W, Doctor?"

"D5W, butterfly on the dorsum of the hand, and a Lasix push."

"How much Lasix, sir?"

Without answering her, Kimball had shoved the syringe of forty milligrams of Lasix into the IV socket along the plastic tubing leading from the bottle of D5W, and was pulling back the syringe, making certain no air bubbles were trapped. A pulmonary embolus was the last thing he needed.

"Ambulance on its way," Rappaport said. He handed Kimball a cylinder of oxygen while Drake and Williams inserted a six-inch rubber catheter into Ramirez's penis.

Listening to the screeching siren, Kimball shook his head. No doubt about it, he had fucked up. How could it have happened? Cyanide had a safety margin of five minutes open exposure without paraphernalia, without deleterious side effects. Ramirez had had a good two to three minutes left.

Kimball examined Ramirez's pupils, making certain they had not yet dilated.

"Major, would you please sign here, on Form 125-K, approving our removal of the victim Jorge Ramirez from the premises?" The paramedic placed Ramirez on a stretcher.

Kimball scribbled on the bottom of the page. With Ramirez out of action for some time, he would have a hard time qualifying the entire unit for CBW recognition by both the Army Chemical Corps and the Army Medical Corps, which he needed in order to satisfy the procurement, testing, and operations requirement for both the Army Munitions Command and the Test/Evaluation Command.

With a salute he dismissed the paramedic and returned his attention to the problem at hand: how to make these ambitious misfits into the foremost experts in chemical and bacteriological warfare in the world. He had only ten days.

"Can I help, Major Kimball?" Corporal Anne Drake was unusually attractive, despite her baggy Army fatigues. Her Slavic features showed intelligence and warmth.

Standing at attention, pencil-straight in their dark protective clothing, Drake, Rappaport, and Williams looked like the smorgasbord of ethnicity and technology he had intended them to be. In only three months he had made the four strangers into a cohesive group. But without Ramirez, the self-appointed leader, the bonding among the four could disintegrate.

"Can we black folks speak up, sir?"

Kimball nodded at Williams.

"I know we've all been subjected to an unusual trauma . . . why with the—"

"You don't need the *why* in the sentence, Corporal."

"Thank you for the correction, sir." That was his first clue to relax. "Although Jorge may have just blown a gasket, I speak on behalf of the three of us. We'd like to continue, sir."

Drake and Rappaport raised their right fists in a parody of black solidarity. "All the way, sir!" The three responded with the gusto they knew Highpockets—the nickname derived from the fact that Kimball took long marches with both hands in his pants pockets—would enjoy. They were proud of the fact that they had been selected for their intellectual capabilities and for their racial and ethnic differences. Kimball's quartet had qualified for the first selection of a minority CBW team in the history of Fort Detrick.

As Kimball had explained to them, on different occasions, their racial differences offered a unique laboratory for experimentation in ethnic warfare. Only Kimball was old enough to remember when, during the Vietnam War, the Defense Advanced Research Projects Agency at the Pentagon had funded a group of scientists at Fort Detrick to develop weapons to exploit the emotional and physiological differences that normally occur among specific population groups. He recalled a group of Cherokee and Blackfeet Indians being transported from their reservations in large yellow school buses. They had been unceremoniously deposited at the far end of the Fort and quartered in two sparkling white barracks with brown tepees attached to their sloping metal roofs. Each morning, the scientists drew the Indians' blood and separated them according to blood groups. Ninety-six percent of the Cherokee Indians had Type O blood; ninety percent of the Blackfeet had Type A blood. Kimball remembered how a page seven news item in the *Washington Post* had almost blown the entire project when the acting commander of Fort Detrick was accused of having "rounded up" problem Indians for military training. Of course, the story was soon squelched by the higher-ups, and no one ever printed, if in fact they discovered, the real reason for studying the two Indian tribes.

"Corporal Drake, what's your blood type?"

"O negative, sir."

"Is that characteristic of you Polacks?"

"Only those in the western regions of Silesia."

"And you, Williams?"

"Sickle-cell anemia, sir."

"Who the hell passed you on the Army physical? Don't you know it's against Army regulations to have this blood disorder?"

"Yes, sir!" Williams snapped briskly to attention and smiled broadly. "You informed me very specifically of this regulation. Article Eight forbids anyone with sickle-cell anemia to be drafted into the Armed Services."

"So why the hell did you join?"

"Because I wanted to serve my country. And you offered me bonus pay if I would serve as your guinea pig."

"Are you crazy?"

"Yes, sir. I believed everything you promised me: thirteen fifty a month; a chance to learn a practical skill, like chemical bacteriological warfare; and a chance to do experiments as well as the opportunity to learn how to become a scientist."

"And a chance to die an ugly death at an early age."

"Yes, sir."

"Do you want to die, Rappaport?" Kimball spat out the question, then listened intently. Rappaport was the only one of the four who couldn't or wouldn't join in his rituals of self-mocking banter.

"Not if I can help it."

"Not if I can help it, *sir!*"

"Not if I can help it, sir!"

"How do you intend to prevent this great inevitability of life?"

"By making certain that I don't act like one of these dumb fucks."

"You mean Drake and Williams?" Kimball took Rappaport

by the shoulder and turned him ninety degrees around to face Drake. "Tell her she's a dumb fuck."

"You're a dumb fuck."

"May I, sir?" Without waiting for a response, she drew back her fist and slammed it into Rappaport's face.

Rappaport reeled back, stunned. "What the hell?" He pulled back his fist ready to retaliate when Kimball stepped forward and blocked his punch.

"Strike her and you strike me. That's a court-martial."

"I have no intention of hitting you, sir."

"You're having a hard time adjusting to this unit, aren't you, Rappaport?"

"I'm not sure I understand what we're supposed to be doing, sir. We're supposed to be training . . . preparing ourselves for chemical and bacteriological warfare, but that's where I get confused. What the hell are we doing playing around with bacteria? That stuff has been outlawed by an Executive Order since 1972."

"Your attitude sucks, but your hostility makes up for it." Kimball waved his hand indicating to the three of them that it was all right to relax.

"Let me repeat. We are not in any way, shape, or form violating the Valentine's Day Declaration banning biological weapons. We are only making certain that we have a biological preparedness . . ." He paused as he quickly dismissed any thoughts of Project Blood Heat from his mind, then continued, "Just in case the Soviets decide to violate the 1972 Biological Warfare Convention and employ the Bkhv's bag of microbiological tricks." He started to laugh.

"You're full of shit, Major. You know it, I know it, and these two know it." Rappaport became more agitated, waving his arms as he spoke. "You act as if we're playing some fucking game. You're supposed to be the tough, mean-assed CO who has our best interests at heart. Well, I just don't buy it."

Kimball pulled Rappaport toward him by the collar. "Your friggin' lightweight overalls are made of boron nitrite fibers, a material that can stop a thirty-caliber bullet fired at a range of thirty meters. They cannot—I repeat, cannot—stop Lassa fever, which will hemorrhage ninety percent of all those exposed." Picking up Rappaport's gas mask, he waved it dramatically in the air. "This cannot protect you against Ebola fever." Grabbing a little metal kit hanging from Rappaport's belt, he took out a metal syringe. "Nor can this atropine defend you against Marburg Fever."

Kimball restrained his anger. "Listen and listen well! The United States Army *must* be prepared to counter a biological war launched by the Soviets. Just remember the Soviets had over three hundred civilians die in an outbreak of anthrax in Sverdlovsk only a few years ago. What the hell were they doing manufacturing anthrax bacillus? You tell me, Rappaport!"

"We just want to be able to defeat the enemy without too much loss of lives or destruction of property, ain't that right, Major?" Williams replied cynically.

"I see we have a conspiracy here." Kimball broke the stern lines of his weatherbeaten face with a smile and a raucous laugh that seemed to heighten a wicked gleam in his darting brown eyes. "Relax. Rappaport is right. You have to think of CBW as a kind of make-believe game in which we are not really supposed to be preparing for a type of warfare that is no longer supposed to exist. So I have to do whatever is necessary to make certain that the nonexistent players like yourselves are ready to fight this war that no one is preparing for in the first place."

Kimball paused to consider the effect of his words, but his thoughts kept returning to Project Blood Heat. He still couldn't mention it to them. They weren't ready yet. Soon, perhaps.

He strapped the combat chemical-survey meter, a Soviet-issued VPkhr, to his back, handed two multi-dialed green boxes of already obsolete, photoelectrically triggered, colorimetric nerve gas alarms, models USE-41 and M6A1, to Williams and Drake, and led the group down a wooded hillside toward the metal chain-link fence surrounding Fort Detrick. From these hills Kimball focused on the distinctive wooden geodomes half-buried in the ground beneath endless miles of aluminum and cast-iron pipes running above ground. It reminded him of his hometown brewery. At this point in his career, he was just about on his life schedule, give or take a few years. Not yet thirty-six, he had two more years before he could be considered for a light colonel.

From residency onward, Kimball's professional life had been a series of short way-stations toward his current permanent assignment at Fort Detrick. His first post in CBW was at the U.S. Army Chemical Center and School at Fort McClellan in Anniston, Alabama. A staff of seven hundred had taught four thousand students the rudiments of CBW. It was there he had learned about the different categories of chemical weapons. The poison and nerve gases like tabun, sarin, and soman, codenamed "G agents," were organophosphate chemicals that inhibited neuromuscular transmission, paralyzing or killing the exposed soldier. Equally lethal was the VX nerve gas developed by American-captured World War II German scientists. Officially, the United States, France, and the Soviet Union had stopped manufacturing these gases in the late 60s. Unofficially, there were still large stockpiles of these nerve gases stored in Toulouse, France. The West Germans, as far as Kimball could recall, had the largest stockpile of the poisonous gases used and developed during World War I, including phosgene, mustard, and hydrogen cyanide.

Later, in Vietnam, he had learned about the more popularly known CS gas. Less toxic than CN, which caused severe irritation of the respiratory passages, CS had received great notoriety in the Vietnam War for its use both in controlling crowds and in flushing out Vietcong from their underground tunnels so that they could eventually be killed by more conventional weapons. The U.S. had sprayed eighteen million gallons of Agents Orange, White, Blue, or 2-, 4-, 5-picloram and cacodylate over much of Vietnam's jungles.

But what Kimball found especially fascinating was the whole group of incapacitating chemical weapons called psychochemicals. He was intrigued by the notion that one could incapacitate an enemy by using pot or LSD. He had been much amused by a publicity campaign initiated by the U.S. Army Chemical Corps while he was at Fort McClellan. It had been called "Operation Blue Skies," and in it the Army had tried to justify its work in chemical weapons on humanitarian grounds, because instead of killing the opponent, one simply disabled him temporarily. Although Kimball agreed with that rationale, he had prided himself in correctly predicting a serious public and congressional backlash to the program. Sure enough, one year into Operation Blue Skies, Congress cut back funds for CBW by fifty percent.

After a year and a half at Fort McClellan, Kimball was transferred with high honors to the U.S. Army arsenal in Pine Bluff, Arkansas, where he received his first introduction to the field of biological weapons and their psychological effects on personnel. He learned how to appreciate the advantages of these weapons, their ability to kill or incapacitate a whole army with minute quantities of toxin. At Pine Bluff Arsenal he learned that biological agents could be spread by guided missiles or dispersed from storage tanks in airplanes as an aerosol, slurry, or powder. He recalled that sunny day when an F-111 screamed over a simulated cardboard city. It had dropped a five-hundred-pound Bigeye—a spray bomb of tiny spores of anthrax, an animal bacteria causing high fevers, rashes, massive blood infections, and death. It was estimated that most of the inhabitants of such a city would have been seriously ill or dead within two weeks.

The M6A1 alarm went off as they reached the bottom of the hill. Kimball watched his squad don their face masks and disperse along the chain-link fence to assume the position for a CBW counteroffensive. He smiled to himself. They were damned good. When Ramirez returned in a few days, they would be ready to commence final preparations for the most controversial maneuver of his career—Project Blood Heat.

10

At the corner light opposite the Bethesda Naval Hospital complex, Bradley made a left-hand turn from Wisconsin Avenue into the National Institutes of Health. The campus consisted of three hundred manicured acres of rolling hills covered by winding roads and red brick buildings housing scores of laboratories. At NIH, research was conducted in everything, from the genetic determinants of affective disorders to the effect of radiation on cancer growth. The southern boundary of the campus was a modern church-like building, the prestigious National Library of Medicine, with its advanced MEDLAR computer information-retrieval system. On the northern part of the campus, a fourteen-story building of black glass housed the clinical research center in which Bradley had his offices and laboratories on the top three floors.

Usually the campus looked aseptic and sterile. Today, thought Bradley, it seemed alive and beckoning. Was it the memory of

Helene's eagerness that made his senses so vibrant? So much feeling had passed between them that he had insisted they meet again tonight, to sort things out. Despite the constant pain in his shoulder, it seemed to him his condition had not degenerated. He parked his car in the space reserved for him, walked briskly through the lobby of the "black box," and bounded up the stairs two by two.

"Russ, if you've got a minute, would you come in?" It was Kempe.

Bradley would normally have stopped by to chat, but he felt particularly pressured to start examining the epidemiological data he needed to present his case before HAC. If, in fact, he needed to declare a public health emergency and spend the next few years of his life working on a cure for this twentieth-century bubonic plague, he might as well begin now. It was really Dr. Allan Wilson, chief of Genetics Research, with whom Bradley had to talk. Wilson was the only one who could tell him what had caused Raymond's and Janet Rydell's illness—an illness that was possibly his own.

"Hey, since when do you walk past one of my morning invitations?"

It was true. Bradley seldom passed up Kempe's company. Whether they conversed about Kempe's hedonistic pursuits of wine, women, and song, or his slides of fetuses, they both enjoyed their morning chats. Bradley shrugged and followed Kempe into his office.

On the dark grey stone worktable sat an endless array of five gallon jugs filled with yellow liquid and withered fetuses. There was an eerie, almost ghoulish feeling to the room with its antique Bunsen burners, frayed rubber tubing, and assortment of jars, bottles, and flasks. It gave one the impression of a cross between a neighborhood funeral parlor and a nineteenth-century apothecary shop.

"Take a look at these slides," Kempe said. "Fetal lung tissue—really quite extraordinary."

Bradley was astonished that the mystery of stillbirth still fascinated Kempe after twenty years of work in the area. At major scientific conferences he would present a finding he termed the "Kempe phenomenon"—pink hyaline bodies scattered over an embryo's lung resulting from an infection in the mother's womb. His colleagues, envious that Kempe, unlike most non-NIH scientists, didn't have perennial funding problems, considered those pink hyaline bodies to be nothing more than an artifact from red stain.

Kempe sat Bradley in front of a microscope and adjusted the slide.

"Right there, near the fetal windpipe. Move it over to the left."

"Well! What do you see?"

Bradley had rarely seen Kempe so excited. The last time was when they had promised each other that one day they would each drive their respective Porsches in the One Lap of America race. They had often talked excitedly about that event. A competing driver merely had to circumnavigate the 8,400-mile periphery of the entire United States in seven driving days, using only public highways and interstates. Kempe's face was as full of boyish enthusiasm now as it had ever been in discussions about the One Lap.

"Come on, you must have seen it!" Kempe increased the amplification of the Zeiss lens and stepped back.

Bradley felt he was wasting his precious time, but he tried to be responsive. He looked directly under the mouth, ventral to the inchoate spinal cord. Suddenly he saw it: a series of overlapping small circles of cartilage, with a membrane covering the openings of the trachea.

"It can't be!"

"Russ, that's exactly what I thought. You know how sensitive I am about my hyaline bodies. I examined this slide thirty times—and did a tissue biopsy. Using Loeffler's, and human and rabbit blood agar, I grew *Corynebacterium diphtheriae.*"

"Diphtheria! Impossible! We eradicated that fifty years ago. The DPT vaccine made sure we haven't seen a case in God knows how long."

"Believe me, I know. The mother must have had some antibody titer to the diphtheria toxin."

"What if, for some reason, she hadn't received the DPT vaccine? Could she have passed on the infection to the fetus through the placental barrier?"

"I thought of that. But the diphtheria toxin is twenty angstrom units in diameter, and the placental barrier blood vessels won't allow any molecule larger than ten angstrom units to pass through."

"Henry, what are you trying to tell me?"

For a fleeting moment Bradley recalled Janet Rydell's bizarre description of her aborted fetus: *He had no head . . . only an ugly stub on his neck.* Could these two cases be related? Bradley placed the two phenomena into a mental category he termed "bizarre occurrences."

"Do you have the mother's medical chart?"

"Of course. Nothing unusual." As Kempe handed him the chart, Bradley was surprised to notice that his friend's hand was shaking.

"The mother is a twenty-five-year-old divorced white radiology technician in nuclear medicine who works at Frederick General Hospital, Frederick, Maryland. Negative family history; perfect physical health, except for tonsils and adenoids at age fourteen. This is an extremely healthy lady."

"Well, what do you think?"

"Not much. The diphtheria membrane is probably a freak accident, a result of chromosomal damage secondary to all those rads she's been shooting into her cancer patients."

"That's a possibility, but you don't often get a recurrence of an eradicated disease in a completely new setting."

As Kempe withdrew the slide from the microscope, his tremor became unmistakable. "Oh shit!" he swore as the slide slipped from his fingers.

Bradley helped him pick up the pieces. He looked quizzically at Kempe and placed one of the pieces in his pocket.

"Henry, what's wrong? Is there something you didn't tell me that I should know about this case?"

"No . . . of course not . . . what else could there be?"

Bradley noticed Kempe was perspiring; his face was deathly pale.

"Listen, Henry, sit down. You're not well. Why don't you go down to the infirmary and let them check you out?" He felt Kempe's forehead. It was cold and clammy. As Kempe pulled away from him to stand up, Bradley felt a few matted, slightly enlarged lymph nodes just below his earlobe. Had Kempe caught something from Raymond? The incubation period was certainly too short. But something was wrong.

Kempe walked over to the sink, took a cup of water, and swallowed a small brown pill. "Thanks for coming by! I'll be sure to get a check-up."

"Are you sure you're okay, Henry?" Bradley was reluctant to leave him.

"Sure, Russ. I'm all right." Kempe led him to the door. "Thanks, buddy. Hey, listen, don't forget—only a few more weeks till the One Lap."

"I'll be there waiting for you at the finish line."

"Don't count on that!"

"All right. Just take care."

Bradley was concerned. He sensed that Kempe was trying to tell him something; he had acted too frightened. What was it about the diphtheria membrane that had excited Kempe so much, he wondered. He left the lab rubbing his right shoulder.

The corridor outside Kempe's office was crowded with dented metal desks, three-legged chairs, an old medium-speed refrigerated Sorvall centrifuge, and a stack of cardboard boxes containing rows of dusty triangular Ehrlenmeyer flasks. Waste! What incredible bureaucratic, governmental waste, thought Bradley. There was nothing wrong with that Sorvall centrifuge that a little maintenance couldn't fix.

Pure research was no longer being measured by the quality of the output, but by the size of the research budget and the number of scientific papers published each year and presented at international conferences. Gone were the days of the intellectual asceticism that had produced such scientific giants as Watson, Crick, and Sanger—all Nobel prizewinners, each of whom had relied on his individual abilities to conceptualize, analyze, and solve complex problems of the genetic code rather than waste his time formulating Requests for Proposals as a year-end device to force the government to spend its appropriated funds.

Fortunately, the professionals working around the clock in the fourteen-floor mausoleum were a group of extremely competent and creative scientists who, like himself, had their own sense of how things should be run. And, for the most part, they produced good work.

Bradley hurried toward Dr. Allan Wilson's laboratory. As chief of Genetics Research at NIH, Wilson had a lab three times larger than anyone else's, and it aptly reflected his personality. Unlike the other researchers, most of whom were medical doctors, the chainsmoking Wilson, a Ph.D. geneticist and molecular biologist, maintained all of his old laboratory equipment in pristine condition. For that reason alone, his research, no matter how theoretical, was always funded—it cost approximately one half the amount of any other research in the country. But the institution had to pay a definite price for Wilson's presence. The rate at which Wilson attracted postdoctoral candidates to his laboratory was equaled only by the attrition rate of his technical staff.

Matters of administration rarely bothered Wilson. As a matter of fact, Bradley had concluded that very little seemed to perturb Wilson, an unusually thin, stoop-shouldered protégé of the Molecular Research Council at Cambridge University, England. After graduating valedictorian from the all-male Hotchkiss prep school near Lakeville, Connecticut, Wilson had gone on to Harvard University, where he had managed to obtain the second lowest graduating average in Harvard's three-hundred-year history. It was a position accepted with pride.

The neatly organized laboratory, with its P4 protective encasement (a completely secured, separate room with an independent ventilation system), held rows of shiny aluminum hoods with powerful air vents for sucking air away from the young Ph.D. postdocs working feverishly on their respective DNA research. In the far corner of the room was a bathysphere-shaped, medium-speed, refrigerated Sorvall centrifuge. A hanging, heavy steel incubator was filled with agar plates of bacteria and bacteriaphage, growing their full complement of colonies. As Bradley entered, he passed Wilson's only recent indulgence, an ultra-high-speed centrifuge with four T150 titanium rotors, each costing four thousand dollars. Along the walls were shelves of glass beakers, flasks, and triangular bottles with screw tops.

"Russ, welcome! What brings you to these ignoble quarters?" Wilson set down the flask he was holding. His self-effacing humor had an irritating, patronizing quality to it that put Bradley off. Yet there was a basic scientific integrity and decency about the man.

"You've just come from your friend Kempe, and now you're looking for some intellectual stimulation." Wilson never made an attempt to hide his contempt for Henry Kempe, whom he considered a second-rate scientist and a first-rate spendthrift. "Has he found any new hyaline spots?"

"All right, Allan, take it easy. You've made your point. How's your work going?"

"If that's more than a rhetorical question, then come with me. I've got something very interesting to show you." Wilson knew Bradley was keenly interested in the progress of his research. He led him to a small hospital room across the hall. "Meet John!" he said grandly. "John, this is Dr. Bradley."

John was ten, but had the appearance of a six-year-old. He was strapped down to a bed with leather manacles attached to metal guards. Twisting and turning his wracked, frail body, he was clearly trying to free his hands, which had unevenly amputated fingers. Bradley gagged at the smell of urea emanating from the writhing child. The small body and head, as well as the Mongoloid face, clearly marked John as both physically and mentally retarded. He had massive contusions over his forehead, and masses of scarred tissue from old, crusted lesions. Bradley was staring at the stumps that remained of John's fingers when the boy spat into his face.

Wilson handed Bradley a tissue. "Amazing, isn't it, how self-destructive the human body can become just because there is a slight defect in one single gene out of the one hundred thousand in its chromosomes?"

As Bradley wiped the spit from his face, he calculated that John had about ten more years left of this primitive behavior before he died. In the meantime, either NIH or John's parents would keep him alive. Morally, Bradley found this unconscionable. Although he was committed to saving lives, he felt that there should be a clear code of ethics concerning euthanasia, whether it would be for a terminal cancer patient or a severely retarded, self-mutilating child like John, who had Lesch-Nyhan syndrome, a rare, inherited genetic disorder. He lacked an enzyme, hypoxanthine-guanine phosphoribosyltransferase (HGPRT). Without that enzyme, uric acid crystals collected in John's kidneys, joints, and brain, accounting for his self-mutilation and mental retardation.

Wilson steered Bradley out of the fetid room into a laboratory filled with cages of scurrying mice. "These little buggers sense that something is wrong, especially when I come into the room. Maybe I smell like catnip."

Bradley did not laugh. He was still thinking about the child.

"This rodent sanctuary is the place I expect to create John's salvation. Amidst these little beasts is the answer I have been waiting for." He pointed to a series of charts located above the cages, and spoke with the clarity and condescension of a lecturing professor who takes pride in condensing a complex process into five easy steps.

"First, I take a normal copy of the affected gene, containing, of course, coding for the missing HGPRT enzyme; then I insert it into a gene of a normal retrovirus. I splice the gene open with restriction enzyme and close with ligase, then I mix the defective bone-marrow cell with the newly engineered virus. Not bad, huh?"

"Have you tried this procedure on a human?"

"We're just getting to federal guidelines for this type of gene therapy. John will be the first patient to receive it."

"There seem to be quite a few risks along the way."

"I'm well aware of them. The most serious one is the retrovirus we're using as a vector for insertion of the normal gene into the defective bone-marrow cell."

"Why a retrovirus?"

"Because it's an RNA virus that can multiply extremely fast in the human body and at the same time remain dormant as a DNA copy in the chromosome for quite a long period before it's reactivated."

"What about using the retrovirus as a . . ." Bradley paused. He wasn't supposed to know about Wilson's other research experiment, the one he conducted by himself after hours—the one no one had wanted to fund because it was too dangerous.

"Allan, I want you to do me a personal favor."

"You've got it as long as you don't ask me to work with Herr Doktor Kempe."

"Here's a handkerchief with a sample of a patient's blood and sputum. I think you're the only one who can tell me what type of vector is in this blood sample. It's extremely important that you find out—any way you want. I want to know the different types of sequences of DNA or RNA that you find."

"Including hemoglobin or methemoglobin?" Wilson was challenged by Bradley's proposition to examine these traces of unmarked blood. "Is there some illegal or classified shit here?"

"No, not as far as I know."

"What do you mean, as far as you know? That doesn't sound like the omniscient Dr. Orestes Bradley."

"Please, no head games! Not this time. Mark the sample—Mr. Raymond."

"No problem. Anything else?"

"Yes." Bradley rolled up his sleeve and picked up a piece of black rubber tubing lying on the Formica tabletop. "I want you to take my blood and perform on it the same type of analysis you do on the other one." By having his own blood examined, Bradley could then compare any organism present with that in Janet's and Raymond's blood.

Wilson opened a desk drawer and withdrew a five-cc plastic syringe and needle. He tied the tubing tightly around Bradley's right arm and gently inserted the needle, drawing out enough blood to fill the tube.

"Is this another part of the clue to figure out 'Who done it'?"

"Obviously, whatever you find is to be kept strictly between you and me. Is that clear?"

"You're not, by any chance, implying some sort of threat, are you?" Wilson had an uncomfortable feeling Bradley might know about his moonlighting experiment.

"Allan."

"All right! All right! I'll mark this sample *Mr. Smith.*"

Wilson untied the rubber tube and held the two different specimens of blood high in the air. "You don't have to answer the question if you don't want, but am I supposed to suspect that these two different blood samples have similar infectious vectors?"

"Now that you've guessed forty-nine and nine-tenths percent of the answer, you have only fifty and one-tenth percent left."

Bradley started to leave. Then he remembered the piece of Kempe's glass slide in his pocket. Handing it to Wilson, he added with a smile, "Make it a triple header, and your wish is my command."

"You know you've just sold your soul to the Devil, don't you?" Wilson had visions of requesting increased funding—especially for that special experiment.

"It may well be worth it if you find the correct answer."

"How will I know?"

"I'll worry about that when you've got the results. I need them as soon as possible."

"Hell, this sounds like fun. Real hush-hush—and a deadline. Anyone going to get murdered?"

"Maybe, Allan." Bradley said. Then, as he closed the door of

Wilson's lab behind him, he added to himself, "Perhaps millions."

Bradley had a strong affection for Wilson. Because of scientists like him—erractic, blunt, and innovatively brilliant—he could justify the interminable hours of "shit work" he had to tolerate in order to carry on the business of his division. Wilson was easily worth all the bureaucratic nonsense he had to put up with from Engel, Kuzmack, Parker, Squire, and even Kempe. Directives of the policy-planning staff were usually nothing more than a paper assault on Bradley's turf, attempting to tie him down with busywork while the others went about cutting up the massive one-hundred-billion-dollar government health program in a manner that suited their personal needs for power and influence. But if, in the process of staving off this bureaucratic onslaught, he could preserve the integrity of a program like Wilson's . . . it was well worth the time and battles.

As Bradley walked into his cluttered, unpretentious office he was accosted by an unexpected visitor.

"Dr. Orestes Bradley? I'm Special Agent Brian McDonald with the Federal Bureau of Investigation. I'd like to ask you a couple of questions, if I may." Dressed in a dark-blue suit, the youthful McDonald had a pleasant, alert face despite his serious demeanor. He withdrew a black leather wallet from inside his jacket and flashed his identification.

"Russ, I'm sorry I couldn't get him to come back later. I told him you were extremely busy, but he said it was very important." Dr. Andrea Novak, Bradley's attractive assistant, obviously felt bad she had not been more successful in blocking the intruder.

Bradley waved McDonald's identification away and sat down at his gray metal desk strewn with journal papers, memos, and pink telephone messages. McDonald stood patiently in front of the desk like a pupil awaiting the teacher's attention.

"Andrea, did Dr. Kimball send any specimens over from Walter Reed?"

"No, Russ. None arrived."

"Would you get him on the phone and find out what the lab-test results were on Janet Rydell, the female patient I saw on the Ob-Gyn ward. Also, find out from the Ritchfield Elementary School the whereabouts of an eleven-year-old fourth-grader named Lydia Cromwell. I need the usual things—home address, telephone, and the name of her pediatrician. If possible, I'd like to talk to her mother." He already had tried unsuccessfully to obtain this information, but perhaps Andrea would be more persuasive with her woman's touch. "As soon as you finish, prepare an epidemiological grid for me on the computer. I think we've got a new riproaring epidemic."

Bradley looked up at McDonald: no response. Bradley was impressed by someone he could not intimidate. "Now, Mr. McDonald, please sit down. How may I help you?"

"Thank you for affording me some of your valuable time, sir."

It was obvious McDonald didn't like Bradley. He seemed irritated at the scientist's self-assurance, plainly regarding it as flippancy, in view of the seriousness of the occasion.

"Did you ever meet a Mr. Albert Raymond?"

"Well, yes."

"You seem uncertain, Dr. Bradley."

"May I ask you what this questioning is all about?"

"You may, in due time. But at this particular moment, if you don't mind, I would like to direct a few questions at you. And then, if we have the time, I will be more than happy to answer any questions you may have."

"Excuse me . . ." Andrea burst into the room. "The woman you examined yesterday at Walter Reed has been discharged. I thought you might like to know right away."

"Discharged? Impossible! What about her blood samples?"

"There's no record that any CBC or blood culture was sent out from the lab. And no orders were given."

"Get me Dr. Kimball."

"He's not available."

"What the hell does that mean?"

"He's on a detail somewhere. His office will be happy to have you talk to the physician covering his service."

"Forget it! What about Lydia Cromwell?"

"I'm working on that." Andrea rushed out as quickly as she had come in.

"May we continue, Dr. Bradley?"

"Raymond? Yes, I met him briefly yesterday morning. But I can't tell you very much about him, other than the fact that he was quite sick."

"Why did you see him? Was he a patient of yours?"

"No, he wasn't. My sister—" Bradley stopped. He stared at the intent face across from him.

"I'd like to know why you went to see Mr. Raymond at the Kalorama Guest House at approximately ten-thirty A.M.," the FBI agent repeated.

"You already seem to know quite a bit."

"Did your sister call you to see Mr. Raymond?" This was plainly one of the questions McDonald needed answered before he would leave. "Did she tell you how she knew Mr. Raymond?"

"No."

"Were they lovers?"

"What!" Bradley could hardly restrain himself from standing up and throwing McDonald out of the room. "Lovers! You must be crazy! That guy was nothing but—"

"Scum. Alfred Raymond, alias Roger Peters, alias Joop Van der Haag, alias thirteen other names under ten different passports—American, Canadian, Australian, South African, so on and so forth. Twice arrested in the United States for unlicensed export of weapons to the following countries: Iran, North Korea, Cuba. Twice indicted and convicted for smuggling narcotics, but he escaped just before sentencing years ago. Prior to his most recent arrival in the States he spent a considerable amount of time in Japan. Doing what, we don't know. In short, an unsavory man the FBI was particularly interested in apprehending. He has always managed to elude us—thanks to people like your sister."

"What does my sister have to do with him?"

"That's what I'd like to find out. We know that he stayed at her guest house, ill, for almost two weeks, during which time she tried to nurse him back to health. During that period she never consulted a doctor or even brought him to a hospital. As a result, we can only assume she was in some sort of collaboration with him. For what purpose, we're just not certain. He was pretty sick when you saw him, wasn't he?"

Bradley nodded in agreement. It was impossible for him even to consider the possibility that Judy was tied up with hard drugs, gun smuggling, or any other illicit activity. Certainly, she was stubborn and independent-minded, and their relationship was frequently filled with sibling rivalry and jealousy. But what McDonald was intimating was ludicrous.

"Do you know what Raymond died from?" The FBI man pressed.

"Not exactly. I have a hunch."

"Would one of those hunches be murder?"

"Murder?" By the bubonic plague? Bradley was not amused.

"The autopsy report reveals a substantial level of pyridium."

"Pyridium! That's impossible! The urinary tract analgesic?"

"That's right. The generic name . . ." McDonald consulted his notes. ". . . is phenazopyridine hydrochloride. A patient exceeding three thousand mg., or with more than three days' worth of therapy, can develop severe methemoglobinemia resulting, as in Mr. Raymond's case, in severe fatigue, weakness, and shortness of breath."

"Why do you think this was murder?"

"Autopsy revealed several old needle tracks where the pyridium could have been injected. But most importantly, Raymond had a blood level of seven grams of methemoglobin, with an equivalent amount of oxygen deprivation. No pyridium pills were found in his stomach, so the only way it could have gotten into the blood was with a needle. Your sister is the primary suspect, and we'd like to know where she is."

"This is crazy. She's not a murderer. Why in God's name would she want to kill him?"

"Precisely what we need to know." McDonald stood up to conclude the interview. "In case you may not know, Dr. Bradley, anyone who willingly withholds any information on a murder is legally an accomplice." He turned and closed the door behind him.

Bradley picked up the telephone and dialed Judy's house. He had to find her before the FBI did.

11

"Hey, Bradley, beam me up!"

"Sorry, Andrea." Bradley sprinkled some sunflower seeds into his hand and cracked them gingerly with his teeth.

"I have some bad news for you. That sweet little girl's mother is a real bitch. What the hell did you do to her?"

"What do you mean?"

"She let me know in no uncertain terms through Mrs. Rogers that you were nothing more than a meddlesome physician who had no business sticking his nose where it didn't belong. Furthermore, she is seriously considering filing charges against you for child molesting if you don't leave her and her daughter alone."

"Not bad for one day's work—an accomplice to murder and a child molester."

He turned to his desk. "Put a matrix on the Wang. I want to start tracking some symptoms. See who's got them and where they're located."

"Trying to prove a point again?"

"This time I may have gotten some egg on my face."

"There is one thing I forgot to tell you."

"What's that?"

"The girl's mother wanted me to warn you that when her husband comes back from his overseas assignment he'll take his M16 to you if you ever bother them again."

He wondered if the woman had found out that Raymond had died—and that Lydia might be next.

"So what's strange about my being threatened with a military execution?"

"Well, Mrs. Rogers let me see the school's records, and the woman is not married. She's a civilian stationed at Fort Detrick—classified job. But guess whose address is on the school enrollment form? Ms. Judy Bradley."

"That's impossible!"

Bradley angrily dialed his sister's phone. Again, no answer.

Andrea made her way around the littered office to the Wang. "What do you want punched up on the screen?"

"Let me see our menu for data collection."

"What's the profile of the disease?"

Andrea typed out the necessary instructions on the keyboard. A display sprang into view: COLLECTION OF DATA. 10 BASIC SOURCES OF SURVEILLANCE INFORMATION.

Bradley glanced down the menu. There were ten basic ways to collect, describe, and track epidemiological data. Morbidity, the most commonly analyzed variable, was usually provided by practicing physicians who treated a disease and reported its occurrence to the local or state health department.

Andrea punched the symptom "high fever" under the morbidity category. The total number of cases was two hundred and fifty percent larger—5,000, compared to 2,000 cases the year before.

"What do you think, Russ?" She could almost predict Bradley's response.

"Could be influenza. Let's take a look at the regions."

The data confirmed that certain regions of the country had close to a two-hundred-percent increase in the number of cases of fever over 102 degrees Fahrenheit reported to the state health officials. In the mid-Atlantic region, Maryland and Virginia ranked highest on the list. Andrea punched out the morbidity rate for fevers in the southeastern region.

Bradley was bewildered; he couldn't identify any consistent pattern in which this disease spread. "What in God's name is in Arkansas? Swine flu? Break it down some more."

"Coryza—five hundred. Influenza, Russian type—two hundred. FUO—two thousand."

Ah, there it was, the catchall term, Fevers of Unknown Origin. "Let's swing across the country."

"Illinois, Utah, Texas, California, New Mexico, all have about the same number of FUOs as last year."

"Switch to the sentinel-physician reporting records." Bradley wanted to crosscheck his morbidity data with a random selection of physicians who were most likely to see infectious diseases: pediatricians, internists, family practitioners, and infectious disease specialists.

"Look at this. In five states, New York, Maryland, Arkansas, Utah, and California, there seems to be an inordinately high rate of coryza, with fevers above one hundred and two degrees Fahrenheit, rashes, and lymph node swellings. Over three hundred physicians in each of these states have provided this information."

"Survey the mortality data. What do you get?"

"Arkansas, Utah, and Maryland again all have about the same mortality. In this past month almost three hundred patients in each of these states died with hundred-and-two degree fevers, swollen lymph nodes, and rashes."

They soon realized the data were more frightening than either one of them had suspected. In the past six months, over 1,500 patients had died from this disease consisting of fever, rashes, and swollen lymph nodes—bubonic plague symptoms. What's more, the number of victims was doubling every two months. Bradley now had the necessary evidence to convene another HAC meeting. And, more importantly, he had the evidence to request a mandatory quarantine for any patient presenting the triad of symptoms: high fever, swollen lymph nodes, and rashes. A public health emergency had to be declared! They had to isolate the fast-spreading organism. But why was there an unusually high concentration of cases in Maryland, Utah, and Arkansas? Bradley wondered. What did these areas have in common?

"Can we get some better definition on the demographics of those three states?"

Andrea pressed several keys. "Over eighty-five percent of the reported deaths in Maryland this week were around the town of Frederick. Wait a minute! Look at this! In Arkansas, seventy-five percent of the deaths were located near Pine Bluff."

"What's Pine Bluff?

"Beats me."

"And Utah?"

"A general distribution similar to Maryland's, with a heavy concentration around a city called Dugway."

"What about Washington, D.C.?"

"A little more than a hundred cases."

"Any reported cases from Walter Reed?"

"None."

"That's not possible. I just examined a woman on Kimball's ward. There's no question she had the . . . plague, or whatever it is. Check all the military hospitals. Bradley recalled that Squire had admitted that the military had seen two hundred cases.

"None."

"That's impossible."

"Take a look."

Andrea was right. None of the military hospitals, from Colorado Springs to the Presidio in San Francisco, had reported any cases.

"Wait a minute. Match up the geographical areas served by

the civilian hospitals located near these military hospitals and look what we see."

"A two-hundred-percent increased incidence of the symptomatic triad in this past month alone. And guess which ones they are?"

"Frederick General Hospital in Frederick, Maryland; Dugway Mormon Hospital in Dugway, Utah!"

"And Pine Bluff Memorial Hospital in Pine Bluff, Arkansas. Right?"

"Right." Bradley strained his memory. What single factor connected these facilities? The three hospitals were more notable for their dissimilarities than anything else. The plague was affecting a cross section of the population, without any preference for race, age, or socioeconomic status. Checking the list of hospitals approved by the Joint Committee for Accreditation of Hospitals, Bradley discovered that all these hospitals were private, nongovernment-supported institutions that were in good standing.

"Do you think it is significant that Lydia's mother works at Fort Detrick?" Andrea asked.

The question started Bradley's mind racing. Mrs. Cromwell could have transmitted the disease from Fort Detrick, or Raymond might have brought home some serious contagion from abroad. In either case they would have infected each other. On the other hand, he knew that military bases often acted as a reservoir for different types of microbes. Still, the bubonic plague was rarely found in a population of young military recruits; it was commonly associated with rats wandering in the wooded areas of Montana, New Mexico, or Texas. And the hospitals in question were in the very midst of major urban areas. Suddenly, another thought came to Bradley: the mother of the fetus with the diphtheria membrane had worked at Frederick General Hospital. And Fort Detrick was in Frederick.

"Look what happens when I punch in the category 'Military Base' after each one of the three locations."

"Dugway Proving Ground, Dugway, Utah. Pine Bluff Military Base, Pine Bluff, Arkansas. And Fort Detrick—Frederick, Maryland."

"Each one of those private hospitals is located in the vicinity of a military base. In each one of those hospitals we have state and local health reports of an incredible number of bubonic-like cases. And no cases reported from the military hospitals!" Andrea anticipated Bradley's next question and punched up the category "Classification of Base." Her eyes widened when she saw what was on the screen before her. "Look at that, will you?"

"Incredible!"

"All three of them, research and development centers."

"Can we get a breakdown on the nature of the R and D?" Bradley asked.

"Every time I try to access it the computer spits out 'No information available.' "

"Is there any other way to access that information? Through military channels?"

"Legally or illegally?" Andrea knew Bradley was not the type to break the law to get what he wanted. But he wasn't against pushing the system as hard as he could. "There is one way," she said.

"How?"

"I can access the DARPA net, but it could cost me my job. DOD places an automatic trace on every electronic signal that enters their computer bank. At their discretion, they decide whether I have committed a criminal act."

"What's the DARPA net?"

"Squire and his predecessors at the Defense Advanced Research Projects Agency at DOD set up a specifically secured network of computer links around the country, connected to military bases, universities, and private industries. All are related to DOD R and D, and are funded primarily by DARPA. If I can get into the net and get out within thirty seconds, I might be able to avoid the tracer."

"Let's go!" Bradley leaned over the computer terminal in anticipation.

"O.K. Keep an eye on the second hand for me."

"Here goes the countdown: thirty . . . twenty-nine . . . twenty-eight . . ." Bradley watched Andrea rapidly punch the keyboard. Apparently, this had not been the first time she had tried to enter the DARPA net.

"Russ, I think I'm getting inside . . . look at this: 'Dugway Proving Ground. R and D type: classified Top Secret. No distribution. No contractors. DARPA restrictions.' "

"twenty . . . ninteen . . . eighteen . . ."

" 'Pine Bluff Military Base. R and D type: classified Top Secret. No distribution. No contractors. DARPA restrictions.' "

"Twelve . . . eleven . . . ten . . ."

" 'Fort Detrick. R and D type: classified Top Secret. No distribution. No contractors. DARPA restrictions.' "

". . . two . . . one . . ."

"Out!"

Lawrence Swann II sat a bit too imperiously in the leather wingback chair, Helene decided. Sitting back comfortably on the sofa, her arms stretched across its overstuffed cushions, she watched the distinguished chairman and CEO of the four-hundred-million-dollar investment-banking house, Swann and Company, nurse his Johnnie Walker. She knew he was on edge, even in this austere, male-dominated club at 15th and G streets. But, so far, her plan was working. She had insisted they meet at the most inconvenient time possible for Swann, just when he had to review the daily orders and meet with his division managers. She had him where she wanted him.

Swann, a thin, dapper man in his late sixties, had inherited the firm Swann and Company directly from his grandfather immediately after his father had committed suicide. Investment banking had turned into more of a service business than young Swann had bargained for. His major clients were demanding of his time, and they called the shots. MTI was a major client. Helene knew well that he would meet her wherever she insisted they meet.

"Larry, what happened yesterday? Did the traders at your Cox subsidiary get nervous?"

"What do you mean?" Swann bridled at Helene's provocative tone.

"You know exactly what I mean."

"There were several large orders to sell the stock short. That's all, Helene. You know that happens all the time."

Leaning over the inlaid coffee table, Helene made sure her voice conveyed her annoyance. "You're telling me that I should take losing seventy-five million dollars as just an everyday occurrence? Larry, you can do better than that. A stock doesn't fall almost twenty points in one day without someone forcing it down. Now, who was it?"

Swann turned to the white-jacketed waiter, "Another one, please."

"Well?"

"Helene, there's really very little to say. Some big traders sold short, and that's it."

"That's all there was to it?"

"Pretty much."

"Larry, we've known each other for too long. Give it to me straight. Who was selling MTI short and why?"

"Why are you asking me? Swann and Company isn't the only banking house in the country."

"No, but you're our biggest market maker, Larry. You're supposed to be our buffer on the trading floor precisely so that there won't be too great a volatility in our stock. Instead, we found ourselves on a wild rollercoaster ride yesterday. Up and down, up and down. You didn't buffer us very well."

"Are you threatening me, Helene?"

"I won't even bother to answer that question." She sensed that not acknowledging the threat made him feel even more vulnerable. Watching him fidget with his second glass of scotch, she knew she had him on the run. "Larry, you know perfectly well that Roy doesn't like to waste seventy-five million dollars of good corporate treasury money simply to stabilize MTI stock. He likes to know that he got something for it."

Swann looked at her intently, shook his head, then placed his drink on the table and stood up, ready to walk out of the room.

"Sit down, Larry, don't make a fool of yourself. Everyone's watching." She knew he would be mortified. "Larry, I'm not asking you to break professional confidence with a client. I simply want to know what type of organization would be interested in driving down the price of our stock."

A quick mental calculation of his recent profits from MTI's stock movement convinced him to respond. "A Cayman Island subsidiary of an anonymous society."

"Where is it registered?"

"I didn't ask. I'm in the business of making money, not interviewing for pedigree."

She smiled at the intended slight, but moved in even harder. "Every Cayman Island *société anonyme* must have a place of incorporation."

"I told you, the Cayman Islands." He had adopted a slightly apologetic tone, to convince her there was nothing more to pursue.

"Very well, Larry, I concede the point. I shall find out on my own." Her next question required more delicacy. "I imagine you know nothing about Roy's tender offer for RAI?"

"He's mentioned it to me."

"Are they a legitimate company?"

"As far as I know. They have a handful of some of the best-trained epidemiologists and toxicologists, a lot of them from Harvard and Yale. They also have a strong earning curve; and with the right hands-on management, like Roy's, they could do a hell of a lot better."

"I understand they would take some equity and debt."

"Quite frankly, I'm not sure what they'll take." He knew that Helene was trying to negotiate the terms of an agreement before they had agreed on a price. She was fishing for information to determine how low his clients would go if offered a premium price all in cash.

"I assume RAI are your clients?"

"The assumption is correct."

"Have you met the owners?"

"No. I met a representative of a representative who has a certified letter of agreement giving me the authority to sell the company to any qualified buyer."

"For the usual fee, I presume?"

"The Lehman formula for brokering a business deal is an accepted price structure. Why the interrogation?"

"Because I had the mistaken impression that you were considered MTI's principal investment banker."

"Well, I'd like to think we are."

"If this RAI deal goes through, you've made an effortless four hundred thousand dollars for nothing more than picking up a phone."

"Helene, I've never questioned your price structure."

"You're right, Larry." She stood up and extended her hand. "I assume these clients are also registered anonymously in the Cayman Islands?"

Before he could respond, she was walking toward the large oak doors of the club sitting room, smiling. She had just discovered the answer to the question that had been gnawing at her since yesterday: *why* someone was trying to drive the price of MTI stock downward so quickly. Now it was only a matter of finding out who.

Unfastening the holster strap of his Sig-Sauer P226 pistol, Major Ezra Kimball, commander of the Threat Assessment Group, felt an extra measure of comfort. It was one of the finest pistols in the world. Within thirty seconds, CBW Exercise Wurzburg, the precursor to Project Blood Heat, was to begin here at Edgewood Arsenal in Aberdeen Proving Ground, Aberdeen, Maryland. Signaling to his TAG team to spread out over the rolling green hillside, he felt his heart race with excitement. The five H-34 helicopters began swooping in only a few feet over their heads, spraying an aerosol-borne form of anthrax from their HIDAL spray tanks over a population of white sheep grazing lazily at the bottom of the hill. Within the hour, all the sheep would be dead! And Kimball's TAG unit would meet a similar fate if they weren't careful. They would have to cross a quarter of a mile of hilly terrain, all the while exposed to real battlefield conditions: 105-millimeter howitzer shells; anthrax bacilli sprayed from the H-34 helicopters; and toxic picloram powder dropped from the C-123 cargo planes. The unit's battle task was simple: to neutralize chemical and bacteriological toxins for the accompanying Army and Marine units and assist in the capture of a hypothetical army unit, "Red John," located on the other side of the mountain. One mistake and it would be all over for TAG and Project Blood Heat.

"Look over there, Major." Ramirez pointed to a group of C-123 cargo aircraft flying at five thousand feet equipped with renovated MC-1 spray systems, dropping white, pink, and green powders.

"Put your fuckin' hood on and keep your ass out of the way of those live artillery shells."

Watching his TAG team adjust their protective gear, Kimball ignored the cacophony of mortar and artillery shells whooshing in all around him, but he could not ignore the sheep's bleats of agony as the white, pink, and green powders of picloram 2,4D enshrouded them in inevitable death. He stepped over the bloated carcasses, hemorrhaging at the mouth, and was reminded of how sick Ramirez had been only a few hours before. Kimball had treated him as he would have dealt with any sick soldier on the battlefield. After a massive push of IV fluid and chloramphenicol antibiotic, Ramirez had seemed to recover completely, and was ordered to join the others in this exercise. But now, Kimball, ever the clinician, had his doubts. Ramirez seemed to have a problem breathing. Kimball couldn't ignore the tinge of blue around his face. And the swollen lymph nodes. Something wasn't right.

"Ramirez, what are you doing?" Kimball yelled into the ICPCS head mike attached to his helmet. He could see Ramirez was having trouble walking a straight path, stumbling over the carcasses of discolored, bloated sheep.

"Rappaport, what's with Ramirez?"

"I don't know, sir. I think he may have been discharged too early," Rappaport replied over his mike.

Ramirez continued to stumble forward, apparently deaf to Kimball's orders.

"Sir!" Williams's voice suddenly filled Kimball's helmet.

"Yes, Williams."

"We're coming in for some heavy shit!"

"Keep your head down, keep your eye on the objective, and don't panic."

No sooner did Kimball finish his words than the five H-34 helicopters swooshed in low again and released Weteye cannisters, which exploded several hundred feet above the ground and sprayed sarin nerve gas over every visible square foot.

"Get your fucking asses down on the ground and keep your hoods on tight. Use your decontamination kits! Be careful! That stuff can kill you." Kimball listened as the handful of sheep that had survived the defoliant powder bleated in their death agony. They thrashed in a pool of their own blood before being trampled by the hooded Marine and Army troops that marched behind the sleek M-1 Abrams tanks. Blood Heat should be a cleaner operation, thought Kimball, as he ran down the hill toward Ramirez.

Kimball threw himself to the ground as a 105-millimeter shell came whizzing in directly above him. He started to crawl on his belly toward Ramirez, who was desperately trying to break away from the grip of both Rappaport and Williams. Kimball hoped they could restrain him, but Ramirez seemed highly agitated. If he managed to escape and remove his helmet he would surely die either from asphyxiation or from poisoning by one of the chemical or bacteriological agents.

Hearing the deafening roar of the 105-millimeter howitzers firing at random, Kimball knew a barrage of deadly VX shells would soon be followed by a screen of chemical barrier five hundred feet deep. The TAG unit would have exactly five minutes in which to scale the side of the hill—some six hundred feet—and capture Red John.

Drake rushed to help Rappaport and Williams keep Ramirez pinned to the ground. Over the ICPCS speaker in his helmet, Kimball could hear Ramirez screaming for his mother in Puerto Rico while Rappaport was trying to convince him that he was in the middle of a battlefield exercise.

"Let me go . . . you gringo motherfucker! My mother wants to see me!"

"Take it easy! We're right here," Rappaport consoled him.

Deja me tranquilo! Puta!

"No, man! We can't leave you alone!" Williams was using all his strength to hold him down.

"Major, we can't keep him down much longer. He's flipped out!" Drake said. She had taken the red rubber cover off an atropine syringe, ready to inject Ramirez, when the young Puerto Rican bolted and ran down the hill toward the tanks and combat soldiers.

Kimball watched grimly. The chance of Ramirez surviving the battlefield was shrinking fast as the incoming CBW artillery became more varied and lethal.

Against the livid, smoke-filled air, stained by the cloud of deadly poisons, the onslaught of combat soldiers clad in their space-aged protective covering and respirators, hurrying alongside the massive M-1 tanks, gave Kimball the eerie feeling that he had entered a time warp far into the future.

Kimball started to run toward Ramirez; then he stopped: Ramirez was taking off his hooded PASGT helmet.

"*Mamacita, vengo!*"

Kimball drew his pistol and took aim. Almost reflexively, he reviewed the wisdom he had sought to impart to his unit: Biological agents should consistently produce either death, disability, or plant damage; should be able to be manufactured on a large scale;

should be stable under production and storage conditions, in munitions, and during transportation. Squeezing the trigger gently, Kimball recited the list of desirable characteristics: difficult for a potential enemy to detect or protect against; short and predictable persistency if the contaminated area is to be promptly occupied by friendly troops; capable of infecting more than one target through more than one portal of entry. And most importantly, he recalled as he heard the crack of his pistol, it produced the desired psychological effect. Tears welled up in his eyes as he watched Ramirez fall to the ground.

It was the only humane thing to do.

12

Bradley pressed his foot on the accelerator of the 928S and felt his muscles ache. As he made his usual left-hand turn from Barrington Street, the principal thoroughfare of Ritchfield, onto Hartford Avenue, he felt lightheaded. At the corner of Hartford and Litchfield, he pulled over, parked his car, and leaned his head back against the black leather seat. Feeling the universe spin around him, he wondered how much time he had left before he would be helplessly debilitated by Mrs. Rydell's disease. If only he could get to Judy before the FBI found her. There were so many questions: Raymond, Mrs. Cromwell, Lydia, and now the murder charge.

Past the unkempt front yard filled with ivy, weeds, and half-dead azaleas, Bradley walked up the concrete steps of Judy's crazily mismatched home, a bizarre fusion of nineteenth-century Victorian and twentieth-century modern. He hoped he could control his dizziness long enough to deal with Judy and move on.

Kempe had called from his home just before Bradley had left NIH. He hadn't sounded well. "I need to see you right away, Russ," he had said, but he wouldn't say why.

Bradley leaned against the doorbell. No one answered. He peered through the half-opened thin-slatted blinds; the house appeared abandoned. Unsuccessfully, he tried to pry open some of the large wooden porch windows before he remembered that Judy always left an extra key for the kids hidden beneath the wooden stairs in back of the house. As he walked around the side, he thought he saw someone inside the house pass quickly by the kitchen window, though it could easily have been a shadow.

The quarter-acre backyard contained a wooden swing set and Stephanie's secondhand bicycle, which he had bought in a small shop in Bethesda next to his favorite Chinese restaurant. Stepping over a plastic baseball bat and sponge ball, he remembered promising Sharon to teach her how to pitch "the way the older boys do"—overhand. He reached beneath the steps of the floating wooden deck and felt around for the black metal box in which Judy normally hid the key. It wasn't there.

He walked over to the sliding glass doors and saw that the living room looked as neatly ordered as always. Judy had long ago banned the girls from play in what he once labeled her "mausoleum of opulence," the only room in the house filled with antiques and folk art collected from her trips around the world. Counting on his sister's negligence, Bradley easily pried open the faulty lock on the glass slider with a combination of body blocks and the adept use of a carpenter's nail.

Entering the Persian-carpeted living room, he made his way carefully past the antique Russian samovar and the baby grand Steinway. He swore as his head struck a bronzed parrot hanging from the ceiling above the overgrown planter. As he stood there rubbing his forehead, he noticed the red light glowing on the telephone answering machine. He turned the dial to rewind and played back the messages.

"Hello . . . anyone there? Mommy? Are you there?" The voice sounded like Sharon's. "I'm at Lucy's house. I've just eaten dinner. Can I have a sleepover tonight? I already did my homework for tomorrow. Please? Pretty please? Call me soon."

Was that yesterday or today? And who was Lucy? He would have to check her name in the school directory, which was usually floating around somewhere in the kitchen.

An angry voice followed.

"Ms. Bradley, this is FBI Special Agent Brian McDonald. This is the fourth message I have left on your machine. Please call me at . . ."

Every FBI agent sounded alike, thought Bradley. They all had that proper, rigid, recriminating tone of voice.

"Judy?" This voice was rough, and the words sounded garbled, almost as if the speaker were drunk.

"Kob . . . esh . . . i," pause ". . . dea . . ."

The static made it difficult for Bradley to understand what was being said. A few beeps, like electrical circuitry, interrupted the message. Bradley was about to turn the answering machine dial back to replay, when the same voice returned, sounding even less intelligible.

". . . to . . . na . . . no . . . na . . . do . . ."

Bradley turned off the machine. Was there someone in the house? For a moment he thought he heard footsteps cross the upstairs hallway, but all was quiet. He turned the machine back on. The voice now became increasingly unclear. But there was a nervousness, a slight quavering quality in the timbre of the voice that bothered him.

"Mor . . . o . . . mi . . ."

More of me? Is that what the man was saying? No, not quite. It sounded more like *moromi*—foreign. Italian? French? Oriental? Maybe Japanese.

"Nad . . . o."

As Bradley heard the last syllable, a powerfully built man wearing a woman's nylon stocking over his face turned him around and threw him into the wall of bookshelves. He grabbed Bradley's head and started to bang it against the edge of the shelves. The room became a whirl of blurred images.

When he awoke, Bradley felt as if his head had been hit by a truck. Examining himself in the living-room mirror, he could see the black and blue marks around his throat where his assailant had grabbed him, as well as some contusions on his forehead. He turned on the telephone answering machine, but he heard only high-pitched whirring noises. The tape had been erased.

He found an ice pack in the freezer and placed it on his forehead. He tried to recall the last message. First, there was something about *Kobe*. A name? A place? He strained to recall the words preceding and following it. But the sensation of ice interfered with his concentration. The words *more of me* flooded his thoughts. Were these words related to the last syllables Raymond had uttered? And what about the word that ended in *do?* The thing made no sense at all.

He slammed his fist angrily on the kitchen table. Where the hell was Judy? Clearly, someone else was looking for Judy and didn't want him to know about that message. And what was her relationship to that unsavory character with the beetle tattoo and the amputated finger? Was he a hard-core drug addict or dealer, and why was he staying at Judy's guest house? Was Judy on drugs? Were they working together? Was she really willing to sacrifice her life and those of her children for this social misfit? Why had the Cromwell woman used Judy's address to register Lydia? His sister had a lot of questions to answer.

Bradley leafed through the worn pages of Judy's telephone book, looking up the words *Kobe*, *more of me*, and *moromi*. He flipped through the pages hoping to find names that ended in *do*. Then he looked up Cromwell and Raymond. Nothing. He went through the book again, found an entry for Yolanda, Judy's Jamaican housekeeper, and dialed the phone.

"Hello, Ellis resi—i—house." The familiar sound of a giggling eight-year-old made Bradley forget his pain and bruises momentarily.

"How are you, honey?"

"Hi, Uncle Russ. Where are you?"

"Here at your house."

"I bet you don't know who's speaking." Sharon always wanted to be certain that she was never mistaken for her older sister.

"Oh yes, I do. Your name is Heather O'Shaughnassey, you're seventy-five years old, and you live on top of a mountain with a bald eagle."

"Oh, Uncle Russ . . . you're funny! But you still don't know who I am."

"Is Stephanie there too?"

"We're making brownies."

"Is your mommy there?"

"No. Yolanda said she had to go away on a trip and that we'd be living with her until Mommy comes back."

"May I speak with Yolanda?"

Bradley heard Sharon scream for her.

"Hello, Dr. Bradley. Don't worry none. The kids are fine with me."

"When did you see my sister?"

"About noontime. She came runnin' into the house. She looked kind of upset and very hurried."

"What do you mean?"

"She ran upstairs to her room, took out a small bag, and packed in a big hurry. Gave me close to three thousand dollars in cash so I could pay my own wages and have some money left over to take care of the kids."

"Did she say where she was going, or for how long?"

"No, Dr. Bradley. I asked, but she didn't tell me. It's not like her."

"Are you all right with the kids there?"

"Oh, we're perfectly fine. I'll drive them to school each morning, do my shopping and chores, and then drive them back here to sleep, until she comes back."

Her last words sent a shiver through Bradley. She might never come back.

"If you need anything, Yolanda, you know where to reach me. Don't hesitate to call."

"I won't, Dr. Bradley. Believe me, I won't. Stephanie just told me to tell you she'll call you later because she's making these brownies."

"No problem. Tell them . . . I love them both very much. Are they feeling all right?"

"Doctor, if you could see how many brownies they just ate, you wouldn't ask me that question."

"Take good care of them."

"I will."

As he hung up the telephone, Bradley noticed a black Ford Torino with Washington, D.C., license plates parked diagonally across the street. He couldn't see the face of the man sitting behind the driver's seat, but a plain, two-door American-made car with District plates, parked for no apparent reason across the street, was definitely an outsider—maybe his assailant. What was he waiting for? What did he want?

Bradley checked Judy's bedroom. The place was in chaos. The mattress was overturned. All the drawers had been emptied. The wall-to-wall carpet was strewn with broken ceramic.

Rummaging through the books, papers, and clothing, Bradley clearly understood two things: Someone else wanted to find Judy—and that someone wanted him gone. He ran toward the bedroom window to take another look. The black Ford Torino had disappeared.

Bradley sped through Bethesda's Wisconsin Avenue toward Kempe's three-bedroom rambler. When he arrived, he saw the front door was wide open. He hurried up the steps.

"Russ!" Kempe struggled weakly to his feet as he saw Bradley enter. "Thank God!"

Bradley led his gasping friend over to the living-room sofa and laid him down. A cursory examination revealed the same symptoms he had seen in Raymond, Janet, and Lydia. Kempe's lymph nodes were bilaterally swollen and tender. His temperature was at least 104 degrees Fahrenheit. Blue and black hemorrhagic areas covered his entire body.

"Russ . . . methyl . . . ob . . ." Kempe could barely speak. It seemed as if each utterance cost him a breath. He pointed to a table on which a plastic syringe lay alongside a bottle labeled Methylene Blue and held up blue-stained fingers. He motioned Bradley to inject him with the chemical.

As he filled the syringe, Bradley's mind raced through the symptoms again. Taken together they, too, fit the picture of bubonic plague. But Kempe was also extremely cyanotic. It looked as if he wasn't receiving enough oxygen, or the oxygen he was receiving wasn't sufficiently aerated. Methemoglobinemia. An inborn error of metabolism that reduced the red blood cell's capacity to carry the normal amount of oxygen, thereby making the victim actually look blue. Kempe had exactly the same symptoms that Brian McDonald had described for Raymond. Except the autopsy report had incorrectly concluded that Raymond was killed by an overdose of pyridium. He, too, probably had methemoglobinemia.

"If you want me to inject you with the methylene blue, just nod your head."

Eyes closed, Kempe nodded his head.

"How did you get these symptoms?"

"I–I–" Kempe opened his eyes but could not speak.

"How did you get both the plague and methemoglobinemia? We saw these two illnesses in Raymond, do you remember?" Bradley inserted the needle into Kempe's antecubital vein and saw fear was in his face.

"A–a–agh . . ." Kempe's face broke out into a cold sweat. He became more agitated, moving restlessly on the couch, grabbing first Bradley's arm then the thick black leather pillows.

Was Kempe's severe agitation the result of one of his diseases? Or the IV rush of methylene blue?

"The slide . . ." Kempe said suddenly. He seemed to improve. His breathing became more regular; the cyanotic blue of his lips and fingers faded; his voice became more forceful.

"What slide?"

"Diphtheria . . . over . . . the . . ." Just as quickly as the improvements appeared, they disappeared. Once again his body seemed to withdraw into a shroud of cyanotic death.

Bradley looked on the table for some clue to what Kempe was trying to say. All he saw were used, blue-stained syringes and gauze pads saturated with dark-red blood. The disarray of the usually impeccable living room indicated that Kempe had been searching blindly for something.

"Try again, Henry."

"Ray—"

"Come on, keep talking—don't give up!"

Kempe again raised two fingers, motioning for another IV.

"Does Raymond have something to do with this?"

"M . . . o . . ."

"Mo?"

"Mor . . ."

"Moromi?" Bradley pushed another two-cc bolus of methylene blue.

Kempe began to shake uncontrollably. His head jerked backward, catching his tongue in a vise of teeth as his jaw clamped shut. A *grand mal* seizure. Blood began to froth from Kempe's mouth. His breathing became less regular, more shallow. His face flushed deep crimson, then turned ashen gray.

"Come on, buddy! Don't leave me now!" Bradley grabbed Kempe's mouth and tried to pry it open. Soon, he heard only the bubbles rushing through Kempe's flattened lungs.

"One more lap, buddy? Remember, you promised me one more lap!" Bradley banged on Kempe's chest with his fist.

"I'll let you drive my 928. Listen, you son of a bitch, the Kempe phenomenon is real. I know those hyaline spots aren't artifacts. They're a real scientific discovery. I'll make Wilson publicly retract everything he's said about you." Bradley stopped banging on Kempe's chest. It was too late. Kempe was dead.

Tears welled up in Bradley's eyes. Wiping them away, he looked around the spacious living room. It had been weeks since he had visited Kempe. There were several large multicolored Chinese porcelain vases, Japanese *netsuke*, and original prints of men and women engaged in different sexual positions.

As he examined the collection, he realized that these things were new. Two, perhaps three, months ago, they hadn't been there. But why hadn't Kempe told him about the acquisitions? He could hardly contain himself every time he bought a new chronometer or cellular telephone for their impending One Lap race. Why were these objects bought with such uncharacteristic silence and modesty? Bradley recalled how sickly and nervous Kempe had appeared the day before. The only thing he had wanted to talk about was that slide of the fetus with the diphtheria membrane. But every time Bradley had suggested a plausible explanation for the anomaly, Kempe, in uncharacteristic fashion, would pooh-pooh it.

What did a fetus with diphtheria have in common with the bubonic plague and methemoglobinemia—if anything at all? And how the hell had Kempe acquired the symptoms of both these diseases? What was the connection between Kempe and Raymond? One word dominated Bradley's thoughts: *moromi*. What was it? Why was it on Judy's answering machine? On Raymond's and Kempe's dying lips?

Dr. Allan Wilson, chief of Genetics Research at NIH, opened the door of the incubator, a white porcelain metal box with a prominent temperature dial registering a constant 37 C body temperature, and removed a petri dish containing agar with *E. coli* bacteria. By now he should have some interesting findings, he hoped. Holding the agar plate against the light, he saw the clear little circles he had expected. The altered retroviruses had killed the *E. coli* bacteria. He examined the opaque material around the tiny holes just to make certain he wasn't observing an artifact. With a sterile toothpick he scraped the inside of the clear spots, inserting the residue into a metal-capped test tube containing a broth of milk-proteins, vitamins, sugars, and yeast extract. Goddamn little buggers! They eat better than I do, he thought.

Wilson's hand trembled with excitement as he swayed the

metal-capped test tube back and forth beneath the burning brilliance of a naked light bulb, awaiting an ancestral commandment from his illustrious scientific predecessors—Darwin, Huxley, Rutherford, and Newton. He was about to commence the experiment that could prove that an RNA retrovirus could act as a shuttle vector between microbe and man, man and man, DNA and RNA.

Multiply! he commanded his retroviruses, as he transferred the contents of the metal-capped test tube into a 250-milliliter polypropylene centrifuge bottle, making certain to balance it with yet another water-filled bottle. He placed both bottles into the head of the refrigerated Sorvall centrifuge and set the time for thirty minutes, at a speed of fifteen thousand rpm. To pass the time, he grabbed a handful of playing darts and threw them, one at a time, at a blue necktie decorated with a yellow RNA molecule motif that hung suspended over the blackboard. Each successive dart received greater momentum as Wilson recalled the ludicrous reasons for his having been denied membership to the RNA Tie Club seven years before. The club was an elite group of twenty international scientists working exclusively on deciphering the genetic code. The rejection had been surprisingly painful.

Wilson muttered angrily to himself as he pulled the darts out of the wooden blackboard. The members of the RNA Tie Club had applauded unanimously when he had presented the idea that a DNA copy of a retrovirus and a bacteriophage could be used in designing a shuttle vector. It was true that some members had laughed when he proposed splicing together the two different viruses, using the enzyme ligase. But then he had asserted matter-of-factly that the resulting hybrid virus plasmid vector could shuttle DNA instructions from a bacteria to a human cell and back. At once, several of the scientists had been alarmed that such a vector could devastate human life if improperly utilized. Yes, he reassured himself, turning off the centrifuge, his revolutionary ideas had guaranteed his exclusion from the elite club. But once he could prove that a retrovirus could shuttle different genetic instructions to and from man, then he would be vindicated.

Wilson examined the clear, supernatant liquid in the upper half of the metal-capped test tube. He had an extremely dilute concentration of DNA material. To concentrate the solution Wilson addded polyethylene glycol and sodium chloride in order to absorb most of the water without damaging the DNA or the virus. He centrifuged this solution again, creating a white pellet at the bottom of the tube. Wilson resuspended the pellet with a five-milliliter buffered solution, adding .01-molar magnesium chloride, along with five milliliters of redistilled, equilibrated phenol. He shook it vigorously in a screwtop test tube and again placed it into a centrifuge. But this time he placed the test tube into a desktop, missile-shaped, low-speed centrifuge, setting the dial for thirty minutes at three thousand rpm.

He examined the titanium rotors of his ultra-high-speed centrifuge, reflecting with satisfaction that there was no field other than science that would spend over four thousand dollars for four rotary buckets in order to spin down an experiment worth no more than five dollars. As he readjusted the balance of the buckets, he wondered what it would be like if he simply took two viruses, trapped them in a filter, and spliced them together, without having to go through this elaborate technical process.

Wilson then removed the test tube from the centrifuge and examined it carefully. As he had expected, it held three clearly delineated layers: on the bottom, a bright-yellow liquid composed of all the nonprotein organic material; in the middle, a white cloud of denatured protein; and on top, a clear layer of water.

He smiled: Now for the final step. Using a pipette, he added a few drops of potassium acetate, dropping the pH of the solution down to an acidic level of 5.5. He then added a cold ninety-five-percent solution of ethanol, placed the entire solution in a siliconized corex test tube, and placed it in a freezer.

One hour later he removed the test tube from the freezer and carefully examined it: There it was! A white, cotton-like precipitant in the middle of the tube—DNA from the *E. coli* bacteria. He then spun the precipitant down and poured off the alcohol supernatant.

Selecting a pipette from the wooden rack, Wilson sucked up one hundred microliters of Tris buffer pH 7.4 and dropped it into the test tube. The white precipitant disappeared.

Opening the freezer, Wilson removed an Ehrlenmeyer flask plugged with cotton, marked SV40-DNA. Simian virus 40 was a monkey cancer virus that he had grown in primitive human tissue cells, using the same basic procedure he had been utilizing for extracting the DNA from bacteria.

As he examined the flask, Wilson thought of the serious harm this virus could inflict on an unwitting population. Close in genetic composition to a human virus, the simian virus could transmit to exposed humans those ailments that were specific to monkeys. Severe hepatitis, cancer, as well as dangerously infectious diseases might occur. The members of the RNA Tie Club were already talking about imposing a moratorium on any further research or experimentation with SV40.

Wilson turned on the ultra-high-speed centrifuge and watched as it began to gather speed. This was a marked improvement on the previous day's performance, when loosened rotor buckets had made the machine almost inoperable.

He turned off the machine and quickly prepared a new solution. Then he poured the final ingredient into the test tube—ligase enzyme, the biological glue that could span the evolutionary scale between bacteria and man. As he shook the test tube, the clear aqueous solution became cloudy. Wilson frowned in puzzlement. Something was wrong! The ligase was a clear liquid. So were the DNA extracts from the *E. coli* and the SV40 virus. What had happened? Something in the test tube had precipitated out. Could it be the newly created shuttle virus? There was only one way to find out. He placed the test tube in the rotor bucket of the centrifuge and closed the heavy door. Fastening the snaps around the rim of the door, he turned the dial to 125,000 rpm and listened to the quiet hum of the motor.

All at once, there was a grinding sound, as if the gears in the centrifuge drive were ripping each other apart. There was a sudden explosion. For a split second Wilson was stunned by a blinding light, then all was darkness.

Of the hours that followed, he remembered little. But from time to time the clouds of pain and unconsciousness cleared, and in those moments a single thought formed and re-formed with a demented urgency: He had to tell Bradley what he had discovered!

13

"*Konbanwa.*" Helene bowed her head gracefully as she greeted Bradley at her door. She knew her flowing blue silk Japanese kimono, with its dark-red obi wrapped tightly around her waist, transformed her into the image of a Japanese *geisha*. She saw it on Bradley's surprised face.

"*Dozo oraku ni.*" She beckoned him forward into her private world decorated with Japanese prints, Chinese lacquered screens, and Persian rugs.

Bradley marveled, as he walked over the glistening living-room Isfahan, woven with red, yellow, blue, and caramel-colored silk threads. If he had one of these rugs, he thought, he would hang it on the wall. Certainly, it would never be walked upon. That was obviously one major difference between the monied class and wishful thinkers.

"*Ocha ikage desuka?*" Helene pointed to a black tray with two translucent porcelain teacups and a handpainted teapot. She lifted one of the empty cups, held it up to the light, and handed it to Bradley.

Bradley took it and held it to the chandelier, staring into its thin porcelain.

"There's a woman's face painted on the inside. She's staring right at me."

"*Hai!*" Helene bowed her head in agreement.

"Hi!" Bradley broke into a smile. "That's the first word I've understood this evening."

"No." Helene abandoned her Oriental restraint and started to laugh, or more precisely, to giggle as if she were an embarrassed Japanese woman, sounding and acting purposefully childish in order to disarm her male adversary. There was an underlying tension, a residue from the night before.

"*Yame nasai!*"

"Please, not again!"

"Repeat after me: *Ya-me na-sa-i!*"

"*Ya-me na-sa-i.*"

"Good! You've just informed me in not-too-polite terms to cut it out. Which is what I intend to do . . . immediately."

"Thank you." Bradley sat down on a thick brown leather couch. "How do I thank you in Japanese for the help you've just given me?"

"*Domo arigato.*" Helene bowed, left the living room, and returned with a tray of raw fish slices, each draped over a small clump of rice and wrapped with a band of black seaweed.

"*Sushi.* I've only had it once before."

"Try one. They say that if you eat enough high-protein raw fish you become incredibly . . ."

There was definite mischief in her eyes. Bradley was impressed by the ease with which she carried herself. Obviously aware of her own striking presence, she was neither defensive nor ostentatious in her demeanor. The worst thing that could happen this evening, Bradley decided, was that he might genuinely enjoy himself.

Looking around the opulent living room, Bradley felt out of place. As little as he knew of MTI's scientific achievements, he was certain that their executives were extremely well paid. And Helene, as one of their most senior executives, had to be one of their best paid. Her manner suggested old, tutored wealth. But her surroundings revealed her as an individual comfortable with the present.

"Try that red fish. It's called *maguro*. It's oily tuna." Delicately lifting the *maguro* with chopsticks, she placed it onto a small plate and picked up a small triangular bottle covered with Japanese inscriptions.

"Soy sauce, try some." She poured the soy sauce into a shallow cup. "Dip your *maguro* lightly into the soy sauce. It covers the fishy smell of the raw fish and gives it an extra tangy flavor."

"No, thank you."

"You might like it. No respectable Japanese would eat *sushi* without soy sauce. And besides, you say no to me far too much."

Bradley smiled and waved the soy sauce away. "How did you become so involved with Japan?"

"I spent several years working for major banking firms in Tokyo." Helene watched Bradley carefully place the *maguro* in his mouth, tearing the fish apart with a combination of his hands and teeth.

"If you'd like, I can cut it up into smaller pieces."

"No . . . I'm fine. All I need is a microwave and a few decent metal utensils."

"Listen, you really don't have to eat it. Why don't you try some slightly warm *sake?* It will relax you." She ran her fingers over his furrowed brow. He looked troubled and exhausted. "Are you all right?"

"Is that a rhetorical question?"

"No. It's really quite a selfish question. If you appear distracted, then I have a very hard time enjoying myself. Is there anything I can do?"

Taking her hands in his, he pressed them together and held them against his face.

"Does that feel any better?" she asked.

"Yes. All my worries have suddenly disappeared."

"You want to share them with your favorite *geisha?*"

"A good friend of mine, Henry Kempe, died today."

"Oh, I'm sorry. Had he been sick?"

"Apparently, yes."

"Apparently yes? You don't sound very certain."

"I thought there might be something wrong with him yesterday. But today he died from what I discovered to be a case of bubonic plague and an unusual genetic disorder called methemoglobinemia."

"Bubonic plague? Russ, you must be kidding! That disappeared in the Middle Ages."

"So we thought—until now. I've seen four cases of plague-like symptoms in the past two days."

"Aren't you afraid of catching it?" The implication of that question was very clear: Was she in danger of catching it as well?

"Yes and no! The people who have died from these symptoms showed no evidence of having contracted the bacterial disease. So far, we haven't been able to culture out the bacteria."

"What does that mean?"

"I really don't know. What's even more weird is the fact that Kempe and one of the others who had these plague-like symptoms also showed signs of methemoglobinemia—it's a pretty esoteric disease."

Helene stood up and resumed the role of the gracious *geisha.* Bradley watched as she carefully poured the clear *sake* into a small porcelain cup. Each studied motion was graceful. Her transformation into an attentive Oriental hostess was at once impressive and frightening. The other evening she had acted the role of a self-assured, cocky, almost brash seductress. He wondered which of the two personalities he preferred—the assertive, independent Occidental, or the gracefully accommodating Oriental? He wanted to reach out and hold her again. But instead, he fixed his gaze on a small hand-carved ivory figurine hanging on a ribbon suspended from her red obi. It was a carving of an elderly Oriental man wearing a circular skull cap, seated with folded knees in front of a checkerboard.

"I see you're looking at my *netsuke*. Isn't it wonderful? This case, called an *inro*, is attached to the *netsuke* with a thick string passing underneath my obi." Helene unwound the red obi, removed the *netsuke*, and handed it to Bradley.

"It looks so delicate. You can even see the black and white pieces on the board. Kempe had a few of these *netsukes* in his apartment. Are they common?"

"Actually, they're becoming increasingly rare." Helene took his hand and led him to a black, highly lacquered modern bureau on which sat three rows of *netsukes*.

"In the 1930s, when the *netsukes* were first being sold at auction in England, they were worth only a few dollars, at most. In fact, they were so cheap the dealers bored two holes in them, beaded them together on a string, and sold them by the pound." Helene showed Bradley a *netsuke* of an old hunchbacked woman carrying a load of firewood. "Notice the two holes in the back of the head. I'd say that fifty years ago this may have sold for the modest sum of one dollar."

"And now?"

Helene handed him a strange-looking *netsuke*, a black gorilla carrying a large red piece of wood on his back.

"How much do you think that's worth?" Bradley asked.

Her shrug was studiedly nonchalant. "Let us say that it has to cost more than one dollar."

"Kempe had a *netsuke* very similar to that one." Bradley pointed to a South Sea Island coral diver made from ebony, coral, and gold.

"I'd say this one—and Kempe's, if it's the same—is worth around one hundred thousand dollars."

"You're kidding!"

"Fortunately, I'm not. At a recent Sotheby's auction, a pair of miniature ivory horses made by an eighteenth-century Japanese artist named Okatomo sold for a quarter of a million dollars."

"I'd say Kempe had about a dozen *netsukes*. They could be worth one million dollars."

"Possibly more."

Helene smiled at the look on Bradley's face. The fact that his friend could own such an expensive collection seemed to bother him. She felt a rush of feeling for him that she struggled to restrain. It was an emotion she had not experienced in years. Five years. Since St. Jean-Cap-Ferrat, when she had first met the strong, invincible, aggressive Roy Webb. Yet, as she had learned painfully, these admirable masculine traits too often meant sullen moods during periods of stress. For hours on end Roy could appear distracted, forlorn, as if someone or something important had been taken away from him a long time ago.

"Did you ever hear the name Alfred Raymond?"

"Not that I recall. Should I have heard of him? Is he an investment banker?" Helene tossed her auburn mane.

"Hardly."

"A corporate executive? A scientist?"

"He's—never mind."

Helene watched the nervousness with which Bradley ran his hands through his thick black hair. She wanted to go to him, try to comfort him once again, let her kimono unveil its secrets. But he was too tense, too distracted. And, given their uncertain encounter last night, she wanted everything perfect this time.

"Mor—o—mi. Does that mean anything to you?"

She ignored the question. Her mind focused on the image of her handsome, stately father seated at the dinner table, listening to his daughters' collective impressions and complaints about their trying school day. Her older sister would always dominate the conversation by complaining incessantly about Sister Antoinette, whom she once described inadvertently as "the bitch," an indiscretion for which she received a sound slap.

Approaching Bradley, she realized why distant men appealed to her. They were a challenge, requiring her to employ all her emotional, intellectual, and sexual skills in order to attract their attention—or perhaps more accurately, her father's attention. Bemused, she thought that this was a hell of a time to conjure some Freudian interpretation of her emotions. But she smiled at the thought that whatever emotional entanglement might ensnare her, she had forewarned herself. *Au moins!*

"*Tais-toi!*" She gently took his arms and pulled him down onto the Persian rug. Without saying a word she loosened his tie and shirt and trailed her fingers down his neck and around his shoulder blades.

She could see his eyes begin to glaze over. It was working as it had in the past—*Shiatsu,* the ancient art of acupressure. By using her fingers—or her hands, feet, elbows, or knees—she could release the pressure building up along the fourteen major meridian lines of his body. When she felt the large muscles along both sides of his spinal cord relax, she felt a surge of erotic feeling; she became more excited, more lubricated.

She slid her hands up his body and pressed her fingers into his shoulders. With a violent, jerking motion, Bradley sat up and faced her.

"What's the matter? What did I do?"

"It's my shoulder. I should have told you before. A little accident at the hospital."

"Anything serious?"

"I don't know." He took her in his arms and held her tight against his chest.

Wilson groaned as he slowly became aware of his surroundings. He could recognize familiar cues—an intravenous bottle, a green surgical sheet smelling of phenol draped over his body and much of his head. Out of the corner of his eye, he could see the iodine-tinted corners of adhesive tape running across his forehead.

"Dr. Wilson. I'm Maureen Callahan, your surgical scrub nurse. I know you can't answer me, but if you can hear me, just blink your eyes once. That's fine."

Her voice sounded so angelic and sweet and self-assured,

Wilson felt the sudden impulse to weep. Where was he? What had happened to him? How badly was he injured?

"I know you have a lot of questions on your mind. They will all be answered in time. But let me tell you that you're a very lucky man. Had you not been immediately brought here to the emergency room at Bethesda Naval Hospital, you might not be alive right now."

Bethesda Naval Hospital! What the hell was he doing in a military hospital? He wasn't part of the military. Certainly not the Navy.

"Don't worry. You haven't been drafted. We have an inter-departmental agreement that allows us to treat anyone injured at the NIH campus across the street. So you're in good hands. As a matter of fact, you're really lucky. You have one of our senior attending civilian consultants who happened to be here when you were brought in and volunteered to treat you at no extra expense." She bent down and whispered in Wilson's ear. "He's the best civvy around. He works all over the place—at the university hospitals in the District, as well as those high-powered big-bucks companies."

"Hello, Dr. Wilson. I'm Dr. Ran, the surgeon in charge of putting you back together."

All Wilson could see was a green figure hovering over him with a coal miner's light wrapped around his forehead, blinding him whenever it pointed his way. Ran's voice sounded professionally reassuring, but there was something strange in his pronunciation. A barely perceptible self-consciousness, as if Ran wanted to make certain that he was articulating correctly.

"Unfortunately, you can't see the X rays of your head that I'm holding here," the green figure said. "But you have two distinct injuries that we must treat sequentially and immediately. The first is a nondisplaced alveolar fracture of the lower mandible, and the second one is a serious compression of your first three cervical vertebrae."

Jesus! Wilson thought. Was he going to be in a wheelchair for the rest of his life? How the hell was he going to continue his laboratory research? NIH would have to redesign the lab completely for a cripple. Suddenly, he felt a painful pressure on both sides of his tongue—he couldn't breathe! As the pain from the front of his lower jaw shot through his mouth and up into his eyes, he started to gag on the saliva flowing into the back of his throat.

"Nurse, Gumbco suction."

"Yes, Dr. Ran."

Wilson felt his head awash in pain. A sharp instrument pierced the back of his mouth, sucking parts of his throat into a plastic tube. He could neither speak, move, nor indicate any discomfort.

"What I am doing, Dr. Wilson, is applying increasing pressure to your lower mandible with my index fingers. I'm trying to reduce your temporomandibular joint manually before I fix your fractured mandible. If you understand, blink once."

Despite the excruciating pain, Ran's soothing, experienced voice was becoming an unexpected source of comfort. Wilson blinked his eyes once.

"Good. I see that we can communicate. Communication is very, very important, don't you think?"

Wilson blinked his eyes again.

"Very good. From now on things should go a lot more smoothly. In a second or so, I'm going to push downward on your jaw and try to insert it back into the temporomandibular joint. I will tell you now that it can be quite painful. But only for a very brief moment. Blink once if you want some pain medication and twice if you don't."

Ran lowered his green-masked face into Wilson's field of vision, again blinding Wilson with the bright light. Tears welled up in Wilson's eyes. Ran watched as Wilson blinked once.

"Nurse, please get me seventy-five milligrams of Demerol and 10 milligrams of Valium."

Wilson heard Nurse Callahan move to the other side of the room. He felt increasing pressure from Ran's index fingers, firmly anchored into the slippery tissue of his mouth.

"The light is hurting you. Dr. Wilson, I am truly sorry."

Suddenly, Ran's tone changed from one of measured comfort to a cold, whispering, insidious threat as he leaned close and whispered, "I know that you've been working in secret on the SV40 virus. Don't bother right now about how I know. Let's just say we share a mutual interest in recombinant genes. But my interest in a shuttle retrovirus began long before yours did."

Wilson's face was awash in uncontrollable tears. Ran was right. The bright light was incredibly painful, so mercilessly irritating his optic fibers that if he tried to close his eyes they still opened reflexively.

"Blink your eyes once for yes, twice for no. Then your reconstructive surgery can proceed more quickly. Less painfully."

There was an ominous pause. Wilson could hear Nurse Callahan preparing the Demerol and Valium syringes across the room. He felt Ran's fingers push down farther into his lower jaw. Any moment Wilson expected to hear a crack, and envisioned a permanently loose lower jaw dangling from his face.

Once again, Ran leaned close to his ear: "Did you find before your unfortunate accident that the SV40 virus was an effective shuttle vector between bacteria and man?"

Wilson wanted to shake himself loose, grab Ran by his own jaw and slam his face against the metal table. But all he could feel was his lower jaw being gradually ripped away.

"This procedure has such a simple, ingenuous name: manual reduction of a dislocated temporomandibular joint. It really is quite a simple procedure. Would you like to learn how to do it?"

"I'm ready with the syringes, Dr. Ran. Would you like me to bring them over?"

"No, I'm fine here. Just get the Erich bars ready. I should be finished with this procedure in a few minutes." Ran switched his attention back to Wilson.

"Dr. Wilson, all I have to know is whether you have effectively developed a shuttle retrovirus that can go from microbe to man or man to man. Please, Dr. Wilson, I beseech you . . . one blink means yes, two blinks, no. And try not to lie because I already have a pretty good idea. However, I want to be certain. You can understand that feeling of incomplete scientific certitude. It creates unnecessary anxiety and fear in the scientist. What good is a scientist who is both frightened and uncertain? My God, he's worse than useless."

Wilson tried to keep his eyes clear, simply as a matter of stubborn pride. From time to time he had to close them to clear the welling tears. However, he knew the response Dr. Ran wanted—a clean, undisguised series of eyeblinks, a natural, manmade Morse code between the victim and his torturer. Wilson was determined to blink his eyes when he wanted to, in whatever random, meaningless pattern he determined.

"I know you don't have a medical degree. But I am certain that an intellect of such insatiable curiosity as your own would be fascinated to learn how simple, and I might add, efficacious, this procedure can be. For example, all you need to do is to insert both your index fingers along the buccal sulci of the lower mandible and *push* downward."

Aaagh! His mind screamed with pain. All the paralyzed muscles of his throat and mouth constricted in a moment of useless empathy to release a silent scream of excruciating pain that only the mute Wilson could hear.

"The more you *push downward* . . . the greater the chance of successfully inserting the lower jaw properly into the temporomandibular joint. *Down!*"

Wilson could feel his jawbone ripping away from the joint as if Dr. Ran were skinning a live chicken.

"*Down.*"

As Ran applied pressure, he could feel the taut tendons stretching from Wilson's temporomandibular joint to the condyles of his lower jaw. Any further pushing and he risked the chance of permanently damaging the tendons and muscles—an outcome he preferred to avoid. He needed a live, functioning, articulate Wilson in order to uncover the answers for which he was searching.

"Then, with the thumbs placed on your chin, thus, we push *upward* and *backward* like this."

The pain was unbearable. It felt as if Ran had taken a hammer and chisel and fractured his entire lower jaw. Wilson was sure the searing pain running straight from his chin to the joint was the only thing left connecting his jaw to his face.

Ran leaned close: "Does Dr. Bradley know about your experiment?"

At least if he couldn't protect himself, Wilson thought, he could try to protect Russ, who had spent a good part of his professional life protecting him from the rapacious bureaucracy. He blinked twice.

"Well, how noble! My deep respect and admiration go out to you, Dr. Wilson. You are, as I have been amply informed, a man of impressive moral character. I like a man who protects his friends. But of course, how can I be certain that you are telling me the truth?"

Wilson blinked his eyes quickly: Twice—pause—then twice again. Another pause—then two more times.

"Yes, yes, I understand; but that 'no' is only part of the other answers I need to uncover. You are not making it very easy for me."

Wilson felt like a baby, gurgling and blinking. But it was to no avail. Ran, whoever he was, would not be satisfied until he had uncovered more answers.

"Up . . . *pushing* up . . . that extra bit . . . upward . . ."

"Dr. Ran, are you ready for the Erich bars?" the nurse's voice came from across the room.

Wilson groaned inwardly with frustration. Why couldn't she hear what Ran was saying to him? Jesus Christ, couldn't she see what he was doing? She'd have to be blind or deaf.

"The retrovirus shuttle," Ran whispered. "Was it successful?" He thrust his fingers downward and then upward one last time.

Wilson smiled as he closed his eyes and heard the loud, cracking sound.

14

Bradley glanced nervously at his rear-view mirror and pushed his foot down on the accelerator. His hastily arranged appointment with Kimball was for 10:30 A.M., and as usual he was running late. Heading north on Wisconsin Avenue, Bradley heard the Fuzzbuster chirp. Not far away, something was emitting high-intensity microwaves. Bradley dropped his speed and scanned the streets, searching for the distinctive yellow Maryland state trooper's car or the unmarked Ford Torino. Neither was around. He pressed down on the gas again and sped through Bethesda, past the Armenian and Iranian carpet stores; Japanese, Italian, and French restaurants; and an old second-run movie theater. The NIH campus rolled by on his left, the Bethesda Naval Center on his right. He sped through the entrance of Route 270 north toward Frederick, Maryland.

His frustrated desire to possess Helene had capped two days

of disaster. His sister had disappeared. Kempe was dead. A lowlife named Raymond had died. And this vermin may have been involved in both Judy's disappearance and Kempe's unusual death. Also he, Bradley, had uncovered four cases of a disease whose symptoms mirrored the bubonic plague—of which one had already cultured out negative for pathogens. Moreover, two of the cases were associated with another unusual disease, methemoglobinemia. And, to the best of his knowledge, he had uncovered a nationwide epidemic of bubonic plague centered around three military installations—Pine Bluff, Dugway Proving Ground, and Fort Detrick. Capping it all off was the unbearable irony that he might become one of the plague's victims.

Now there was the disturbing news that Allan Wilson had been seriously injured in a freak explosion. Dr. Andrea Novak had telephoned Bradley at his home but had dissuaded him from visiting at the hospital until later that evening. According to her, Wilson was still in the recovery room and scheduled for a second operation that day. Bradley had never heard of the surgeon, Dr. F. Ran. But Bradley was reassured after several discreet phone calls that Ran was a highly respected general surgeon and researcher whose specialty was antibiotic-resistant bacteria strains. In fact, the military hospitals were lucky to have Ran as a consultant, one professional colleague had informed Bradley. Wilson was getting top civilian care provided at bargain rate prices. A hell of a deal, the colleague had joked.

How had this incredible accident happened? Bradley wondered. He glanced nervously at his holy trinity of high-speed driving—Fuzzbuster, rear-view mirror, and speedometer—and accelerated to one hundred miles per hour, past the gentle hillocks of central Maryland, past farms and the corporate headquarters of high-tech industries.

He forced himself to concentrate on the only positive thing that had happened to him: Helene. An uncertain promise: alluring yet controlling, open yet hidden. She had managed to extract from him his entire life story. He, in turn, however, had learned nothing about her except the basics: birthplace, education, and employment.

Since she had worked closely with Roy Webb over a five-year period, Bradley inferred that she must have had an affair with him. He felt a twinge of jealousy. But he understood that the emotion was premature.

Perhaps it was her feeling of non-belonging that perplexed him the most. She was a spiritual nomad; her ability to "adapt" made him uneasy. Last night she had made him feel as if he were the only man in her life. Yet, on another evening, she had no problem appearing attentive to Webb, fending off Kuzmack's hostile nonverbals, flattering Dr. Engel, pleasing the host, and finally trying to seduce him.

Christ, he thought, she was continuously on the offensive—probing, questioning, doubting. She seemed particularly interested in the potential infection sources for the bubonic plague. Could it be microbial, viral, or some hybrid form, like mycoplasma? Growing up Catholic, he had been taught to expect women to be passive, submissive, not controlling. What did she want from him? Yes, she had conveyed to him the feeling that he was special, but why did he feel as if he were just one more man in her collection? Was he beginning to fall in love with her?

At the brown brick buildings of Fairchild Industries, only a few minutes away from Frederick, the Fuzzbuster began to emit a warning alarm. His speedometer read 105 mph. He quickly pumped his brakes. No yellow car with a red gumball in his rear-view mirror. It wasn't until he made a turn off 270 North onto Route 15 that he saw the state trooper in his standard Smokey the Bear costume aiming a speed gun at him. Damn, thought Bradley. He slowed down on West 7th Street and drove carefully past the Frederick Shopping Center and the endless rows of 1950s red-brick ramblers with their neatly manicured lawns. He drove up to the marked police barrier at the entrance of Fort Detrick.

"Excuse me, sir. May I see some identification, please?"

Bradley handed the young policewoman his green Public

Health Service card, which for all practical purposes looked exactly like a typical military ID.

"Yes sir! Pass on by!" The young woman snapped to attention and waved him on.

Bradley nodded in appreciation. "Major Kimball's office?"

"Building Thirteen—we call it the good-luck building. Down past the water tower on your left, two stop signs, hang another left. You'll see a group of three-story buildings with all sorts of pipes coming out. Thirteen is one of those buildings."

Bradley drove slowly over a yellow speed bump on the two-lane road. A green diamond sign with a medical insignia informed him that he had just entered Fort Detrick. He passed a series of two-story federal buildings surrounded by children's jungle gym sets, leaf-covered plastic swimming pools, and an assortment of deteriorating toys. A chain-link fence separated these living quarters from the one-story red brick colonial buildings that contained, according to the signs, a fire department, the command headquarters, the judge advocate's office, and a community club. A small handpainted notice under the Porter Street sign announced THIS SUNDAY'S PICNIC WILL BE POSTPONED. In the distance, the Catoctin mountain range affirmed Bradley's impression that most forts were little more than suburban recreational areas for the military working class.

At the water tower Bradley made a left turn and passed a series of glass plant houses encircled by a chicken-wire fence bearing a sign inscribed: Agricultural Research Laboratory, U.S. Department of Agriculture. Behind the USDA buildings were wide-open fields traversed by huge electrical power lines. The Fort seemed to have a silent, eerie quality, thought Bradley. Few vehicles were on the road, and there were no people walking on the sidewalks. Where was everyone? Like most military installations Bradley had visited, the grounds were kept immaculately clean. Although most of the 1940s buildings had been torn down and replaced with modern, efficient units, there were a few corrugated metal Quonset huts still left from World War II. These were strewn alongside clay tennis courts, an unmarked gas station with one gas pump, and a small wooden shack marked: Building 901, FBI Resident Agency. Bradley's mind darted back to Brian McDonald.

Bradley turned left onto Daughten Street, past another pair of water towers, and the scenery suddenly became more ominous. Daughten was bordered on both sides by long, rectangular three-story brick buildings surrounded by chain-link fences and large shiny metal pipes rising mysteriously from the ground. The cast-iron pipes entered the three-story brick building from the ground floor and exited from the third floor, traversing twenty feet above the street before entering the building on the other side. The scene reminded him of a miniature oil refinery, except for the fact that all the windows in both buildings were completely bricked up. The only ventilation, Bradley surmised, came from the large metal pipes, compressors, and vents on top of the flat roof.

Bradley stopped the car and leaned forward to read the sign: Frederick Research Facilities, Building 427. A familiar-looking woman, accompanied by a black paramedic dressed in a white lab coat, hurried past the convoluted aluminum pipes. He stared at the woman's face, and realized that she was Janet Rydell. From a distance of one hundred feet, she showed all the physical characteristics of drug-induced Parkinsonism: a slow shuffling gait combined with a pill-rolling motion of the fingers.

When the paramedic caught sight of the red Porsche following him, he grabbed Janet's arm more tightly. Bradley's radar detector started to buzz again as he approached the geodesic dome, at first slowly and softly, then increasingly louder and more quickly. Bradley watched the paramedic punch a code key in a little metal box on the side of the geodesic dome and lead Janet through its brown door. The door closed quickly behind them. The sign on the chain-link fence outside the dome read: Building 111, U.S. Army Medical Bioengineering Research and Development Lab. Restricted Area. Authorized Personnel Only.

Across the road, at the corner of Wood and Miller Streets, a large hydroelectric plant was surrounded by concrete cross stanchions supporting large transformers and thick, heavily wrapped cables. In front, two trailer vans sported signs that read: Flammable Liquid Prohibited.

As Bradley drove past Building 111, the Fuzzbuster suddenly became silent. Building 111—what were they doing there? Why was Janet Rydell taken there? And why hadn't Kimball sent her blood samples?

Building 13 resembled all the other nondescript three-story, red-brick boxes. A green metal sign nailed to the front door simply read: Major Ezra Kimball, M.D., USAMC. Appointments Only. Bradley knocked on the door. No one answered. He knocked again. It was 11 A.M. and he knew he was a half hour late, but he couldn't believe Kimball would have left without leaving a note, even if he hadn't seemed very happy about Bradley's request to meet him. In fact, Kimball had sounded unusually nervous.

"So you finally arrived?" Kimball's irritated voice startled Bradley. He stood hands on hips, dressed in khaki camouflage fatigues.

"Ezra! Where's your legendary Mormon compassion?"

"Andrea calls me, so I stop what I'm doing and haul my ass over here. Then I wait. And wait. And all the while, you're out on the road leisurely burning some rubber—no doubt checking out all the speed traps for your turnabout with your buddy Kempe."

"He's no longer my buddy."

"What's the matter, did he get tired of your fuckin' tardiness?" Kimball inserted the key into the lock and flicked on the fluorescent light.

"He's dead."

"Who's dead?" Kimball rolled up some maps and hurriedly filed some pieces of paper.

The room remained cluttered. Above the metal desk, hanging on the yellow wall, were a series of photographs depicting American soldiers gathered around a sign. Clearly World War II memorabilia. The rest of the wall was covered by an assortment of framed diplomas and awards. At the far end of the room were three relief maps partially draped with a tarpaulin.

"Kempe died with symptoms not too dissimilar from those of Janet Rydell. Remember her?"

Kimball stopped his filing and faced Bradley. He sat down slowly on his desk top, noticeably shaken. "I'm so sorry. Are you sure? Bubonic plague?"

"I didn't say that, Ezra. I said he died from the same thing your patient had. Was that bubonic plague?"

"On the surface it looked like it. But I'm not really certain." Kimball seemed defensive. He shook his head. "It's hard to believe. I just saw him at a conference last week. He seemed as healthy as you and me."

"Whatever happened to Janet Rydell?"

"I really don't know. She may have been transferred to isolation on an infectious disease ward."

"Weren't you worried she might have some variant of the plague, Ezra?"

"Well, there certainly was some concern after you had left. But no, I wasn't worried. I have no doubt we'll figure out what her problem is. What are you getting at, Russ?"

"Nothing. I just want to know what happened to her. I was waiting for her blood samples in order to run a sequence on them and identify the pathogen. You remember, I was stabbed with the needle used to draw blood from her. You could say I have a vested interest in keeping track of her."

"Of course, of course. If the blood samples aren't already on the way over to your lab, I'll make a point of getting them out ASAP"—Kimball made a notation on a pad—"I've got it marked down here: COB phone WRAMC to deliver blood samples to Dr. B. Stat! All right?"

"If they arrive, I will be very happy."

"What do you mean, *if?*" Indignant, Kimball stood up. "You know hospital systems. Patients get lost; records get misplaced."

Bradley shrugged his shoulders. Why was Kimball lying to

him? Janet had been secretly transferred from WRAMC to Fort Detrick and was either being evaluated or treated in Building 111. What kind of game was he playing?

"Russ, I'm sure you didn't come all the way up here to ask about a patient."

"That patient is a pretty important one."

"I read you loud and clear." Kimball ripped the top sheet from his notebook and held it up as evidence.

"You know, Ezra, you're not an easy fellow to reach. Even Andrea has a hard time."

"I've never denied I have other duties in the Army beside being a practicing clinician. By the way, how did Andrea find me?"

"Through Walter Reed. She told the personnel officer there was a medical emergency and you had to be found, stat. You know bureaucrats, Ezra. They're scared of refusing a request on the basis of a medical emergency."

"Very clever, Russ. So what's the medical emergency?"

"What do you people do here?"

"That's classified, Russ. And unless you have a real need to know, there's no way in hell I can tell you."

"Suppose I demonstrate that need to know."

"I'll consider it if I deem it sufficiently serious," Kimball countered. He thought he would enjoy a little gamesmanship. On most occasions it was he who had to implore Bradley to come over to Walter Reed for an evaluation. Now the situation was reversed, and he wanted to savor it.

Bradley was undeterred. "I've been assigned by Kuzmack, with the joint approval of General Joseph Parker, surgeon general of the Army, and U.S. Surgeon General Dr. Susan Engel." He paused, making certain that his reference to Kimball's superiors was not lost. "My job is to monitor this resurgence, for lack of a better term, of the bubonic plague, document its incidence, and develop measures to counteract it."

Kimball nodded, indicating he would not argue about jurisdictional legitimacy.

Bradley continued: "The epidemiological data show a broad national distribution of cases ranging in symptoms from a simple FUO to a full-blown picture, with skin rashes, hemorrhages, pneumonia, and buboes—just like Janet's."

Kimball's face remained serene.

"The data show an inordinate distribution in three states and around three particular areas in those states."

"Is that my cue to ask you which states and which areas?"

"My gut tells me that you know the answer to that question," said Bradley.

Kimball walked slowly around the room, straightening the pictures on the wall.

Bradley had the uncomfortable feeling that this was no typical bureaucratic game. On one hand Kimball was hiding information from him. On the other hand, the major seemed to be goading him on, almost encouraging him to ask for that very information.

"What do Fort Detrick, Dugway Proving Ground, and Pine Bluff, Arkansas have in common?"

Kimball ignored the question. Instead, he motioned Bradley over to one of the pictures. He pointed to a small sign written in English. "I don't know if you can see the lettering on this sign. It reads Pingfan Institute. Have you ever heard of it?"

Bradley stared at the photograph. There were about 120 men grouped around the sign. The soldiers in the back rows wore helmets and held rifles. The first two rows consisted of wounded American soldiers wrapped in an assortment of bandages, looking extremely emaciated. He examined each of the faces, as he had done previously on every WWII photo he had ever seen, hoping to find a soldier's face resembling himself. It was totally possible that his father, who had been killed in the Pacific theater, could have been one of these men.

"Well, Russ?"

"I'm just looking for faces I might recognize."

"Well, there *is* one."

Bradley felt his heart race. His mouth became dry.

"Over here, toward the center. This thin, scrawny guy with a cigar hanging from his mouth. Can you guess?"

Bradley studied the photo. "No. Nobody I know comes to mind."

"Think hard. It's somebody you know quite well."

The face had no meaning.

"Second Lieutenant Joseph Parker."

"You're shitting me!"

"Look carefully. I'll wager you any money he's still smoking that same cigar."

"Anyone else I know here?"

"At one time Pingfan was the largest research and development center for bacteriological warfare in the world. At the peak of World War II, they employed close to three hundred people to study the effects of tularemia, botulism, anthrax, and bubonic plague on mass populations. The head of the institute was a guy named General Ito, who commanded Detachment 711 based at Pingfan, near Harbin, China. He's the one in the center, manacled to his assistant. His job was to send his "researchers" around the countryside to slaughter a few thousand Chinese peasants and Russian POWs so that they could study the effect of those bacterial agents on them. By the way, throw in American POWs. To give you an idea of how efficient that slanty-eyed motherfucker was, they had over 4,500 incubators used solely for breeding fleas infected with the plague. In three months alone, Ito and his assistant were able to produce over forty-five kilograms of fleas, with an estimated one hundred forty-five million parasites."

"How many Americans were there?"

"I don't know. I think maybe a few hundred."

"What happened to them?"

"An advance column led by Parker and some captain liberated Pingfan. But from that point on, I'm not clear about the story myself. There was some kind of explosion, and only a handful of people survived."

"And one of them was Parker?"

"Yes."

"Do you know who the captain was?"

"No. But the scuttlebutt for some time was that it was some big muckamuck."

"Any way to find out which Americans were there—liberators and prisoners?"

"I can take you over to the archives. There may be something there."

"So is that what Fort Detrick, Dugway, and Pine Bluff have in common—bacteriological warfare?"

"Come on, don't make it all sound so ominous."

Bradley looked carefully at each of the other glossy framed photographs. He pointed to some equipment and uniforms that he had never seen before. "What are they?"

"Those funny-looking canisters are an East German model R-2 spray and S-2 atomizer. Their sole function is to spray the enemy—that's us—with lethal and nonlethal chemical agents intended to burn, mutilate, paralyze, or kill."

Kimball walked over to the back of the room, where a group of maps were hanging one on top of the other. He picked up a gas mask and tossed it to Bradley.

"That's a standard Soviet-issued SBM gas mask specifically designed to protect against cyanide blood-poisoning agents and phosgene-type choking agents."

"Wasn't that what the Germans used in Verdun in 1917?"

"Yes. Phosgene gas. Often called the "Red Cross agent" because there is very little you can do about it, once you've inhaled it, except call the Red Cross. Without this SBM gas mask, you can literally choke to death. The Germans were smart; they knew all too well that one enemy soldier incapacitated by phosgene or mustard gas—which, by the way, causes incredibly painful blisters at any point of contact—was more valuable than a dead one, because one disabled American soldier forced two other battlefield soldiers to aid him. So, in effect, they took three soldiers out of battle where they normally would have taken only one."

Bradley then glanced at the maps on the wall bearing the classification Secret/Sensitive—No Distribution. Why would a map of the Patuxent River, running through Montgomery County, near Scaggsville, Maryland into the Triadelphia Reservoir, the Rocky Gorge Reservoir, and passing by the Washington Suburban Sanitary Commission, be classified at all?

"That's a Soviet-made MSP-18 treatment kit." Kimball snapped open a metal case and took out a metal syringe. "In Russian, this is called a *shyrits-tyubik*. When you inhale some phosgene and you begin to feel the eye and skin irritation, you jam this auto-injectable, atropine-filled syringe right into your thigh, and presto, you feel better."

"Why would atropine, an anticholinergic agent, be effective on phosgene?"

"Because phosgene's principal symptoms are gasping, cough, chest pain, pulmonary edema, nausea, vomiting, and eventual death within twenty-four hours from fatigue and cardiac failure—all caused by bronchial constriction."

"You don't have any qualms about your work here?"

"Nope! And the Russians don't about theirs. The Soviet's CBW capability is like the communicable viruses they've developed—it's spreading to other countries, like Iran, Iraq, Libya, Syria. Our intelligence suggests that they taught Vietnamese and Lao troops how to use chemicals against their enemies in Laos and Cambodia. When they invaded Afghanistan in 1979, the Soviet Army had between eighty and a hundred thousand CBW specialists using both lethal and nonlethal chemical agents, sprayed either out of the East German model R-Two or that S-Two atomizer."

"Ezra, what's your role here?"

"To develop TAG—the Threat Assessment Group. A primary defensive unit in charge of preparing U.S. troops for chemical/biological warfare."

Bradley's mind was spinning. What should he ask about first? About the maps? About Janet? About Kimball's assignment? Was the Army manufacturing the plague bacillus at Fort Detrick, Dugway, and Pine Bluff? Was Building 111, into which Janet disappeared, the place where they were developing the *Pasteurella pestis* pathogen?

"Don't look so distraught. In 1979 the Soviets had a major accident at a CBW plant in Sverdlovsk. Anthrax contaminated the surrounding farms and animal feed. Thousands of Soviet citizens died without the world knowing one thing about it. That was accidental. Their basic battlefield strategy, however, is quite purposeful: a high-speed offensive through battlefields contaminated with nuclear, biological, and chemical agents. The United States is not prepared to fight such a well-equipped, well-trained adversary, particularly after Nixon's executive order forbidding the manufacture and storage of CBW weapons."

"How the hell can you justify this, Kimball? In the afternoon you treat and heal people infected with diseases you manufacture that morning." Even Bradley had to admit he was beginning to sound somewhat hysterical.

"Would you agree that war is inevitable?" Kimball took another direction.

"To a certain degree."

"Since World War II, the last war to end all wars, we have had anywhere between forty and sixty major conflagrations. Recently, over one million people died on a battlefield stretching from Teheran to Baghdad—all in the name of religion and power. But the reasons for war are irrelevant. And they become increasingly irrelevant as the technology exceeds man's capacity to understand and manage it. Wouldn't it be better to fight wars which don't kill, but simply incapacitate people?"

"Soon, you'll convince me that it would be inhumane for mankind *not* to fight a CB war."

"You must admit that a CB war does make a basically inevitable horror somewhat more palatable. With chemical weapons we can paralyze and incapacitate soldiers without having to kill them. Of course, there will be deaths. But compared to the apocalyptic destruction inflicted by nuclear war, CB war is far less costly in lives and dollars, and it is far more manageable and containable."

"Does this type of reasoning also apply to the creation of a new type of the bubonic plague?"

"We are prohibited by both the legislative and executive branches from manufacturing or storing any bacteriological agent."

"And what's in those buildings I passed?"

"Basically R and D centers. We are developing vaccines, antitoxins, and antidotes against the CB agents we may encounter in a battlefield situation. We call them defensive weapons, for want of a better term."

"So neither Fort Detrick, Dugway, nor Pine Bluff is engaged in the manufacture or dissemination of chemical or bacterial agents?" Bradley already knew the answer. If Kimball could lie about Janet, he could lie about this. The term *defensive weapon* was disconcertingly suggestive.

"I already told you. Both Nixon's edict and the 1972 Biological and Toxic Weapons Convention prohibit our manufacturing such weapons." Kimball laughed. "But I know you don't believe me." He took out a paper marked Confidential/No Distribution. "Read it! Each one of these companies and universities has an ongoing research relationship with the Pentagon. I can't tell you what they are doing specifically, but you know damn well that it's hard to make a new virus or pathogen. I'll admit that among those grant recipients there are probably a few who believe that with the new recombinant DNA technology it would be possible to develop new and better CBW pathogens. I'm not one of those believers. I told you exactly what I believe in—a strong, intelligent, effective CBW defense."

Bradley found the list incredible. In it were the names of some of the most prestigious companies and universities in the country.

"What's the face for, Russ? Those guys are researchers first. Only second do they happen to be working for the Defense Department. No big thing. You're a clinician/epidemiologist first, and you happen also to have a Navy rank."

"Come on, Kimball! The PHS is known as the Yellow Berets. We have nothing to do with the military except PX privileges."

"You skim off the best parts and sanctimoniously throw back the rest."

"Oh, by the way, could you see if there's anyone working here by the name of Cromwell?"

Kimball leafed through the Fort Detrick directory. "No Cromwells."

"What about Raymond? It's a long shot, but look up Anthony Raymond."

"No Raymonds anywhere."

"Thanks."

As Kimball led him out of the door, Bradley could hear the ominous whirring of helicopters in tight formation. Six Huey gunships were headed toward the open fields beyond an electrified barbed-wire fence that marked the boundary of no-man's-land.

"Dissemination is the critical problem in bacteriological warfare," Kimball volunteered. "You have to be able to keep the bacterial agents viable long enough to be effective. Humidity, oxygen content, irradiation can either enhance or diminish the viability of a pathogen."

Bradley watched the helicopters release a yellow powder over the field.

"After the choppers are gone, my TAG team will go into the field and measure the pattern of dissemination. They'll record the altitude at which it was dropped, the rate and direction of the wind, the barometric conditions."

"And this is part of a sanctioned defensive strategy?" Bradley marveled.

Kimball ignored the implied rebuke. "We're trying to determine the ideal conditions for a large-scale biological attack. And we've discovered some useful information. For instance, we've learned that such conditions include an attack at midnight over an extended line at an altitude of approximately three hundred feet. The wind direction and speed should be a constant twelve miles per hour. The pathogen should be in aerosol form, no less than five microns in diameter. Its toxicity should dissipate only very gradually over a long period of time. The pathogen should be disseminated over an area of thirty miles at a rate of approximately one and six tenths gallons per mile."

Why was Kimball volunteering this classified information? It made no sense. More incredibly, he was leading them both toward Building 111. Bradley knew that if he could find Janet he might be able to evaluate the course of his own disease. For the moment he only felt a slight queasiness. At another time he might have related it to the information Kimball was so willingly imparting.

"How would you create an epidemic of plague?"

Kimball didn't answer. Bradley watched carefully as Kimball played with the sequence of keys in the electronic lock at the entrance to Building 111.

They entered and descended a brightly lit tunnel into a beehive of solemn activity. Men and women in white lab coats went quietly back and forth from one glass cubicle to another. Each seemed to be involved in a different stage of recombinant DNA work. Bradford saw nothing unusual: gel electrophoresis, gas spectrophotometry, paper chromatography, high- and medium-speed centrifuges, with no precautions more sophisticated than standard aluminum ventilation hoods. Not a highly secured P4 lab—used for extremely dangerous experiments—anywhere in sight.

After a few minutes, Kimball led Bradley back up the stairs to the sentry station.

"If there is anything else I can do for you, please give me a call," he said, offering his hand.

"There is one more thing," Bradley said, "the word *moromi*, have you ever heard of it?"

"No. Is that supposed to mean something?"

"I don't know. Thanks again."

Bradley started his car, drove past Building 111 toward Gate 17 on the southwest corner of the base, and headed toward Frederick General Hospital. Strange, he thought, his radar detector was silent.

15

Wilson's eyes dilated with fear as Ran ignited a small welding torch and passed the searing blue flame over two gleaming steel wires.

"Don't worry, Dr. Wilson! No chance of my blowing us up. I had Mrs. Callahan shut off all the anesthesia valves before she left the OR. I hope you don't mind my dismissing her before our operation was over. It was over, as far as she knew. But with the diagnostic review groups and our hospital's concern for cost containment, I felt it would be negligent of me to keep her here on overtime. I'm certain you understand."

Wilson stared at the green-masked sadist who had just dislocated his lower jaw. An upward pressure radiated from his lower jaw, through his frontal sinuses, to his eye sockets. He kept blinking his eyes in an irregular pattern intended both to annoy Ran and distract himself from the exploding pain in his head.

Ran placed both wires on an operating tray and began to palpate Wilson's face, pushing and probing with his thick fingers over Wilson's forehead and nose.

"It's a pity you never had the chance to study medicine. I think you would have appreciated its artistic imprecision."

His hands spanned each side of Wilson's face, pressing downward over both of Wilson's cheekbones. His thumbs thrust deep into Wilson's eye sockets. With a little more pressure, Wilson realized, Ran could pop both eyes.

"In medicine it is important that potential problems be anticipated before an operation. You could have any of three types of facial features. At this point I must assume you have one or more of each type, or none. Medicine is such an inexact science, don't you agree? We have to work with such gross subjective markers: point tenderness, facial asymmetry, localized ecchymosis and hematoma, disturbances in eye movement, malocclusion—my God, listen to me, I'm giving you a crash course in medicine, when all I really want are a few simple answers."

Ran picked up one of the Erich bars with a set of pliers and inserted it just below the gum line of Wilson's upper jaw, wrapping it tightly around his upper molars. He used the other bar for Wilson's lower teeth. This completed, he slipped a twenty-six-inch soft alloy steel wire around the neck of Wilson's top molars and started to weave it up and down, through the arch bars, drawing Wilson's jaw and teeth into tight alignment. With his pliers, he began to tighten the wire.

"Remember, one blink—yes. Two blinks—no."

Wilson's pain was excruciating. His head had become a vise responding to the slightest twist of the wire. He continued to close and open his eyes in a random fashion as Ran tightened the wire threaded throughout his mouth.

"Just think of this as a new set of braces that would cost anywhere from two to four thousand dollars. I'm giving them to you free! After this is over, you'll have a perfect set of teeth. And I will have my answers. Let us begin again: Did you convert the retrovirus II into a shuttle vector?"

The acrid taste of the metal made Wilson want to vomit.

His stomach was churning bilious fluids back up to his esophagus. He knew that if he started to vomit with his mouth sewn shut, he would choke on the liquid and possibly die from asphyxiation. He blinked once.

"Good . . . good . . . Now you're getting into the proper spirit."

Wilson blinked twice, once, then twice again.

Ran twisted the wire tighter and monitored Wilson's eye movements and facial expressions very carefully. Stubborn *gaijin!* he thought. One more turn of the wire and Wilson's eyes stopped blinking.

"I'm glad to see I can impose some order here. The last thing I need right now is chaos. By the way, did you know that my last name, Ran, means "chaos"? I digress. That is not a question I want you to answer. But here is one: Have you ever heard of Moromi?"

Moromi? thought Wilson. That didn't even sound English. For the first time he decided to play along with Ran. He blinked twice.

"No!" Ran waited to see if he would blink again; he didn't.

"Has your boss Bradley discovered yet what Moromi is?"

Wilson blinked once and then twice.

"Yes . . . and no." Ran paused for a moment. "I understand: You don't know."

Wilson blinked once.

"Very good, Dr. Wilson. I see you want to cooperate."

Wilson blinked once.

"Have you been able to develop a retrovirus that can carry a disease totally separate from the one it itself causes?"

Wilson now understood what Ran was looking for. The question explained the mystery slides Bradley had given him, the blood sample with methemoglobinemia and the bubonic plague. But how did Ran know about his SV40 retrovirus experiments? No one was supposed to know about them, not even Bradley. He always conducted those experiments after the normal working day, when his

NIH administrative and research obligations had been completed. And he had always been careful to clean his lab of any evidence of the experiments because they had not been authorized. At best, it would have taken another five years to obtain the clearance—if then. He couldn't afford the delay. There was increasing evidence in the scientific literature that too many other scientists were imitating his type of experiment, possibly undercutting his discovery.

Wilson had made a clear decision to proceed without authorization. And his decision had been vindicated. He had been the first person, or so he thought until now, to create a retrovirus that could convey new genetic material from microbe to man. But who had seen him work? Could it have been Bradley? No. Had Bradley found out, he would immediately have confronted Wilson with his transgression. It had to have been someone capable of spying discreetly, fox in clown's clothing. Only one person fit that description.

Wilson blinked his eyes twice.

"No! I don't believe you!" Twisting the wire several turns, Ran watched Wilson's eyes fill with tears. Wilson cursed Henry Kempe as he felt his face contort into a grotesque grimace.

"Stubborn, aren't you?" Ran hissed. "Well, now, have you ever heard of Project Blood Heat?"

Wilson's pain was becoming intolerable. If he answered yes to that question, clearly Ran would want to find out more. If he answered truthfully, no, Ran might not believe him.

"Ah, I see that my friend is in too much agony to answer even a simple question. Well, we must do something to alleviate the pain." Ran took a metal syringe and injected its contents into the intravenous bottle of D5W.

Within seconds, Wilson felt a warm glow surround his mouth. He knew the pain was there, but suddenly it didn't bother him.

"Wonderful opiate, morphine. And seventy-five milligrams is seventy-five times more wonderful than no opiate." He paused to appreciate Wilson's relaxed facial expression.

"Project Blood Heat! Have you heard about it?"

Wilson closed both eyes. The warm, painless sensation was too precious an experience not to enjoy fully.

"Project Blood Heat! Do you or Bradley know anything about it?"

Wilson blinked his eyes once. Why not? Ran was suddenly nice. Why not play along and make Ran feel good, as if he had uncovered a major security leak in the plan. If he answered yes, it might make Ran think twice about continuing with Project Blood Heat, whatever it was.

"Blink accordingly if the date of onset is one week, two weeks, three weeks, etcetera. I would appreciate an immediate response because I have a syringe filled with apomorphine in my right hand, which, as you know, can eliminate the effects of the morphine."

"One week . . . two weeks . . ."

Before Wilson could blink, he felt his head turn, his stomach churn, and whatever involuntary peristaltic reflex he had left, push his undigested food back up into his throat.

He started to blink rapidly, hoping that he might hit an accceptable number.

"Three weeks . . . four weeks . . ."

The bile was reaching his tightly wired mouth when he felt the pressure on his jaws lessen. It was too late. The wave of nausea swept over him.

The 10K Forms on RAI revealed exactly what Helene had suspected. She sat nervously in the art deco confines of her office suite, going over her calculations once again. RAI was a publicly owned corporation, where the majority of shareholders were listed as John Doe. One SEC form had listed Daruma & Company, 2120 L Street, N.W., Washington, D.C., as having filed the standard SEC request for permission to obtain 6.5 percent of common stock in RAI. That was about a seven-million-dollar investment. In itself, the investment was paltry compared to the thirty- to one-hundred-million-dollar transactions that occurred on a daily basis at MTI. But it was odd that RAI's stock price had fallen just about the same time Webb had tendered an offer to acquire them—for cash.

She continued her calculations on a yellow legal pad. Working from RAI's balance sheet, which listed the total number of John Doe stocks outstanding, and the SEC filing, she discovered that over fifty-one percent of the outstanding common stock was in the possession of people other than direct owners or officers of the company. It was not unusual for major arbitrageurs on Wall Street to buy up the stock of a company they suspected might be acquired or sold for a higher price. But RAI had the financial profile of a company about to enter Chapter Eleven bankruptcy rather than a successful merger.

She pressed the intercom button on her desk and asked her secretary to see if Webb was free. Less than a minute later, when the response came back that Webb was too busy, Helene made her way directly to his anteroom.

A tall, powerfully built, blond man came out of Webb's office and strode past her without any sign of recognition. His face was serene and handsome; his eyes a piercing blue. She had seen him once before, weeks ago, working with security guards at the plant. What in God's name was he doing here, in Webb's office?

The small light on the wall did not switch from red to yellow, indicating that Webb was still unavailable. Unwilling to wait in the anteroom, Helene walked into his office and found him at his immaculately neat mahogany desk.

"Well, how is my Mata Hari this afternoon?" Webb stood up and greeted her warmly as she entered his office.

"Don't be a horse's ass!" Helene had no patience for his sarcasm.

"Well, aren't we touchy? Why don't you sit down over here on the sofa, my sweet financial advisor." He took her arm.

She pulled away from him. "I'll come back later if this isn't a good time."

"No, this is a wonderful time. Anytime I see you is a wonderful time. No matter how late you come in."

"Roy, I had things to do."

"I'm sure." He had to admit he was getting a certain delight in provoking her. What she did with her nights was not for him to question.

"I tried to reach you a number of times, but your secretary informed me you had not come in yet. That was ten thirty."

"I didn't realize I was accountable to you for every waking hour of the day."

"Certainly not for every sleeping hour."

"Well, well, well!" She walked delicately around Webb as he continued to lean against his desk top. "So, finally, the irresistible, seductive chairman of the board of MTI deigns to notice me as something more than his executive vice-president for finances and acquisitions. And what's the first thing out of his mouth? An adolescent barb as to whether I got laid last night."

"I don't like it when you talk that way." Webb was angry, not so much with her as with himself—for allowing himself to appear so vulnerable. The secret to their relationship had always been that he was sufficiently demonstrative to keep her attracted, yet restrained enough to make certain he would never become too dependent on her. He called it a "titrated relationship." Just enough love, tenderness, intimacy, and challenge to keep both parties engaged. Looking at her now, prowling in circles around him, running her fingers through her loose hair, he had to admit he had been ignoring the titration factor.

"Two nights ago, I sought out an eminent physician-epidemiologist who I thought would be an extremely important resource for MTI, especially when it came to evaluating personnel at RAI."

Webb held up his hand. "That's precisely why I was trying to reach you all morning. I've just concluded negotiations for RAI. I wanted you to be the first to know."

Helene held the SEC forms tightly in her hands. Her rage was overwhelming. The message was clear: He no longer trusted her enough as his principal officer for new acquisitions to invite her into the final stages of negotiations. Little by little, he was letting her go. First as a lover and now as a corporate officer. Tears began to fill her eyes, but she focused all her energy, fought them back, and said in a steady voice, "As the principal financial officer of this corporation, might I be so presumptuous as to ask what exactly was the deal? And, if it doesn't sound stupid at this late date, why did you make the deal?"

"I made the deal for the reasons I already told you! I need RAI. That company will help me push some new MTI products through the FDA. If I can get them into the marketplace quickly, I can keep our revenue base high this year. I'm tired of cycling every other year with new health policies from Washington that restrict our growth."

"Cut the speech, Roy. You don't have to sell me free enterprise. My grandfather was trading in the Orient when your family was stoking coal on a freighter from Ireland."

"Germany."

"Who cares?"

"I do! If you're going to get nasty, which it looks like you're doing, then I'd appreciate it if you would be accurately nasty."

Helene continued to pace the room nervously. "What was the deal, Roy?"

"Better than I thought." Webb's face lit up. He rubbed his hands together, a little boy eager to open up a newly received birthday present. "Instead of using MTI cash reserves, they're willing to take an agreed-upon sum of MTI common and preferred stock, warrants, and debentures."

"And if they exercise all their options, what percent of MTI stock would they own?"

"About eleven percent."

"How much do you own?"

"You know how much I own."

"Twenty-three percent. You're the largest single shareholder. And you've just created the third largest shareholder—RAI—thanks to your generous offer."

"You think I made a bad deal, don't you?"

"No. I don't think it's a bad deal. A bad deal would be giving away five percent ownership of MTI. This deal stinks."

"Take it easy, Helene. You might say something you'll regret afterward."

"What could I conceivably say that I haven't already said? If these sweet, innocent epidemiologists at RAI exercise all their options and ally with any one of your board members . . ."

"Like who?"

"Like Swann, whom I mistrust more by the day. Or . . ." She hesitated, thinking of the second largest shareholder whose name was anathema to Webb.

"Then what?"

"Come on, Roy. You're too smart for that kind of game. You're the guy who could devise more shark repellents in one day than Goldman Sachs, Lehman Brothers, and First Boston combined."

"You really think that's likely?"

"Likely? I wouldn't know about likely. But possible, yes. With Swann's backing, RAI would control eighteen percent of the total stock of the company. And if they want—you're out."

"That's the risk I took when I went public."

"Nonsense. That's the risk you've decided to take now for reasons only you know . . . you and maybe that goon who walked out of here a few minutes ago."

"Are you going to resign?" Webb asked.

"Do you want me to resign?"

"No. You know that."

"I don't know anything, other than what I have already seen. You screwed yourself and the company because you were hot for a bunch of microbiology space rangers." She threw the forms on his desk and headed for the door. As the largest single stockholder of MTI, he had, according to the bylaws that he had personally written, the complete right to make an acquisition without the normal procedure of obtaining approval from the board of directors. In the doorway, she turned. "Read those some day when you have time. You should get to know your business partners."

The next steps were clear to her: *Sauve qui peut.*

Frederick General Hospital was a two-story brick affair like most of the hospitals in the less densely populated regions of Maryland, and also like them, its L-shaped brick structure was immaculately clean and well kept. If it were a show horse, concluded Bradley as he drove into the parking lot, the hospital would win a prize as best-groomed.

As usual, the parking lot was filled with Chevy vans, Volvo station wagons, horse trailers, and souped-up Mustangs with thirty-six-inch rear tires. His Porsche stood out like a bleeding sore thumb.

The pungent, almost nauseating aroma of carbolic acid cleaning fluid greeted his nose as he entered the hospital. It reminded him of Kimball and their conversation about chemical and biological warfare. The more Bradley thought about it, the more convinced he was that Kimball and others at Fort Detrick were creating a pathogen that caused an illness resembling the bubonic plague. There was enough circumstantial evidence—Janet's illness, Lydia's illness, the recombinant DNA facility in Building 111—to make him think the U.S. government was covertly involved in the creation of the plague through genetic manipulation. But what was the actual pathogen? How was it genetically engineered? A mutant bacteria? A new virus? And what would he do with the evidence if he came upon it? Go to Dr. Susan Engel—that was a first step. But did she already know about the CBW? She had warned him to be careful in dealing with the military.

He remembered that in the late fifties and early sixties the Army had conducted covert operations under the auspices of its Chemical Corps Special Operations Division to determine whether potential terrorists could poison a city like New York. Army agents had stood on the pavement above the gratings over the New York subway and sprayed in "harmless bacteria." According to one article, the U.S. Chemical Corps found that serious illness could be spread to thirty percent of the population, which would swamp the hospitals and bring the New York City health services to a virtual standstill. The overall conclusion was that the rest of the United States was also highly vulnerable to similar germ warfare attacks.

Bradley walked down the endless corridors of highly buffed linoleum floors until he came to the right office. "Dr. Sandra Rosen, please."

A plump receptionist, seated behind a black desk sign that read Internal Medicine/Pathology, said, "She's waiting for you in her lab."

Bradley walked through a dimly lit corridor in which every other fluorescent light was out. Dr. Sandra Rosen, a frail, high-strung internist-cum-pathologist well into her sixties, was bent over a worn Leitz microscope, a half-smoked cigarette stuck in the corner of her mouth. Without looking up, she beckoned Bradley forward with her right hand.

"Over here, Russ. Take a look."

Bradley bent over the microscope and saw a group of crenated red blood cells.

"Crescent-shaped red blood cells in a three-month-old child. Well, Dr. Hotshot sleuth, what's the diagnosis? I assure you this one is a lot more complicated than your mysterious outbreak of polio." Rosen slapped him on the back, clearly pleased to see him.

"Hemolytic anemia. The infant's red blood cells are being mechanically destroyed by either a lack of oxygen or some mechanical obstruction."

"Let me look at you!" She cupped his face with her arthritic hands. "You're still as smart and handsome as ever. So what's the diagnosis?"

"Hemolytic anemia, primary or secondary."

"What about sickle-cell anemia?"

"I'll buy that."

The microscopic picture was consistent with that of someone with an inherited defective gene for S hemoglobin. The cases were relatively rare in Africa, and most of the victims died in childhood.

But in the United States, one in six hundred blacks had the trait.

"However," Bradley added, "you also have to bear in mind several other potential causes, like rheumatic fever, myocarditis, osteomyelitis, and a few neurological disorders."

Rosen placed an X ray of the infant's skull over a brightly lit box. "Look at this . . . what is it?"

"Radial striations of the skull." Bradley saw dark, opaque lines crossing over the infant's still-unsealed, porous skull.

"And the dark areas around the parietal bones and cervical spine?"

"Osteoporosis."

"Correct. The infant's bones are losing calcium density." She threw up another X ray.

"Splenomegaly and hepatomegaly."

"Enlarged spleen and liver."

"QED sickle-cell anemia."

"Now you're talking *tachlis*."

"Tachlis?"

"Now you've got your feet on the ground. If you hear hoof-beats, don't think of zebras. Hotshot!"

"So what's unusual about sickle-cell anemia in an infant?" He smiled, realizing he was imitating her heavy New York accent.

Rosen reached up and, with Bradley's help, pulled down a large jar containing a small infant's body curled up in a bath of formaldehyde.

"Take a look! What do you see?"

"An infant's body."

"Yes. But what kind of infant?"

"A male infant."

"Oh, you're such a *goyisher kop*. Look!"

"It's hard to tell with all that wrinkled skin, but that infant looks Caucasian."

"Strange, huh?"

"Maybe the parents had some mixed blood several generations ago."

"Believe me, these parents are pure KKK rednecks." Rosen

took another bottle from the far side of the cluttered Formica work table. It was half the size of the other.

Bradley picked it up and looked through it at a small fetal specimen completely covered with discoloration. "Third trimester miscarriage—therapeutic."

"So far, so good. Not quite a *mavin*, yet, however."

"All right, Sandra, let me ask *you* a question! Did you ever see a fetus with a diphtheria membrane?"

"No!" Rosen replied impatiently.

"There's a woman who works here in radiology who had a child with a diphtheria membrane."

"No such person. No such fetus."

"How are you so certain?"

"I see anyone or anything that involves a pathology examination or anything more serious than a hangnail. Anyway, let's get back to some serious work." She handed him another jar. "So, smarty, what's this?"

"The profuse discolorations indicate a systemic hemorrhage in almost every part of the body."

"Good . . . good. So what would cause a systemic hemorrhaging in a fetus that would eventually lead to a miscarriage?"

"Hints . . . hints . . . hints."

"Believe me, on this one you're going to need it."

"It's either a vascular problem or a hematological one. I don't know of any vascular problem that occurs this early in life. So I would say it's a clotting factor disturbance or deficiency."

"Maybe you are a *mavin* . . . a real *mavin*." She slapped him on the back with resounding approval.

"But that's as far as I can go without speculating too much."

"This fetus is a hemophiliac with a factor eight deficiency."

"Hemophiliac? In the third trimester? The disease doesn't usually manifest itself until early childhood."

"That's right, *boychik!* But if you want to hear the real stinger, guess the sex of that fetus?"

"I don't understand the question." Bradley was clearly bewildered. "It has to be a boy. Only boys get hemophilia."

"Well, that fetus is a girl."

"It's not possible."

Rosen went to a stand of dusty wooden shelves and rifled through a series of slides. She pulled one out, examined it cursorily by holding it in the light, placed it under the microscope, and invited Bradley to look.

She was right! It was a female, covered with extensive areas of hemorrhage. And hemophilia. He was incredulous: two cases of methemoglobinemia; one case of prenatal diphtheria; one case of nonblack sickle-cell anemia; and now, one case of female hemophilia. All inversions of the normal biological process. And each one a complete genetic abnormality.

"Was each of these fetal abortions associated with a mother who had a history of fever, rashes, or buboes?"

"Yes. The mothers or the fathers had at one point or another symptoms resembling the bubonic plague."

Now Bradley was excited. Suddenly, it all started to make sense. "Did you culture out *Pasteurella pestis* bacteria from either the fetal specimen or the parents?"

"We did get blood samples from both the fetuses and their parents."

"And?" He already suspected the answer. All he needed was confirmation.

"No bacteria grew out. But we did pick out a high antibody titer in both the parents' blood samples and the fetuses: retrovirus II, a slow-acting RNA virus."

The picture was becoming clear: Through genetic manipulation a retrovirus II had been created that not only carried the necessary genetic information to produce the bubonic plague, but also to create genetic abnormalities like methemoglobinemia, sickle-cell anemia in whites, and hemophilia in girls. But why? Why would someone want to create a disease as ravaging as the bubonic plague? Or a completely new disease entity in the next generation of children? Bradley was at a loss for credible answers. He was reluctant to ask the next question, but he had to.

"I presume most, if not all, the patients with the plague-like symptoms . . . ," he hesitated, "worked at . . ."

"At where?"

"At Fort Detrick?"

"No, not one of them."

It just couldn't be! Bradley thought. The military connection *had* to be right. His hand went automatically to the tender area over the left lymph node in his neck.

16

"That's not possible."

"Of course it's possible." Rosen took Bradley's arm and rushed him down the shiny corridors to a pair of wooden doors marked in bold letters: Isolation. Following procedure, each donned a green scrub suit and mask from a billowy canvas bag before proceeding into a brightly lit ward. Two concentric circles of patient rooms, surrounded a nurse's station filled with signs. Rosen stopped at the bedside of an attractive black woman, who looked up apprehensively at the two doctors.

"Mrs. Stevens, this is Dr. Bradley. He's an expert on the kind of disease you have. I've asked him to examine you. Do you mind?"

Mrs. Thelma Stevens threw aside the bed covers.

Bradley quickly examined her. Jaundiced sclera. A white-plaqued tongue. Dry mouth. Temperature 105 degrees F. Rapid, shallow respiration. Bilateral swollen and tender lymph nodes. Small areas of ecchymoses. But no evidence of cyanosis or methemoglobinemia.

"Have you been overseas recently?"

"No."

"Have you been bitten by a flea, rat, or any wild animal?"

"No."

"Do you work at Fort Detrick?"

"No."

"Do you or your husband work in a laboratory or a place where they are experimenting with new bacteria or viruses?"

Mrs. Stevens didn't answer. She turned her head away from Bradley. Tears were in her eyes.

Rosen drew Bradley aside and handed him the chart hanging over the foot of the bed railing. Next to the question requesting information about employment, the patient had written "self-employed." Under the name of the insurance carrier, which might have been a lead to her employer, was written "self-insured."

"Husband just deserted her and two kids. He left her without any means of support. Rather than write 'welfare' she wrote 'self-employed.' "

"Do you know anything about the husband?"

"He's a jerk. *Boychik*, not every patient can give you the answer you're looking for. A little patience . . . a little uncertainty never hurt anyone." She patted his hand.

The next patient, a forty-two-year-old heavy-joweled white man whose loose, wrinkling skin made him look as if he had recently lost weight, was waiting impatiently for his turn with the doctors.

"Nice to see you, Dr. Rosen. You've come by to give me my daily hug?"

Rosen gently tapped the patient on his hand and introduced Dr. Bradley.

"Sure, he can examine me anytime he wants. A friend of yours is a friend of mine."

Bradley's examination produced the same diagnosis as Raymond's and Kempe's—bubonic plague plus methemoglobinemia.

"Where do you work?"

"Hey, Dr. Rosen, you didn't tell him where I worked?"

"No. He didn't ask me."

"Oh I get it! It's one of those games. Sure, I'll play."

"It's not a game. It's very important for you to tell me where you worked."

"But Dr. Rosen, you told me that I didn't have to tell anyone."

Bradley looked quizzically at Rosen. His pager beeped and registered a number he didn't recognize. It would wait.

"Don't worry. I'll keep my promise." Rosen walked Bradley to the foot of the next bed and handed him the chart of the woman who had aborted the female fetus with hemophilia.

"Thanks for not pushing the point, Russ. I see you're a quick learner. I had promised the gentleman you just examined that I wouldn't reveal where he got infected."

"Where was it?"

"He was with a hooker in one of those redneck joints in downtown Frederick. By profession he's the superintendent in a garden complex. He's got a wife, three kids, and his mother-in-law lives with him. He's pretty certain he picked up his crud from the hooker."

"Do you know where I can find her?"

"I'll try to find out. Stay here and read that chart. I'll be back in a minute."

The patient's chart corroborated what Rosen had just told him.

Bradley walked up to a white, middle-aged female patient who grew increasingly agitated as he approached.

"Leave me alone! I didn't do anything! Leave me alone! I didn't tell anyone, I swear I didn't tell anyone."

"What are you afraid of?"

"Nothing. I don't know you. I'm not afraid." She began to thrash about. "Dr. Rosen, please! Please!"

Two orderlies appeared at the sides of her bed to restrain her. Rosen pulled Bradley toward the doors.

"What do you think you're doing, Dr. Hotshot?"

"I almost had something from her. I need to know where the hell this plague is coming from, and she knows! And Mrs. Stevens knows! And goddamn it, you may even know. . . ."

"Sometimes you can be a real self-centered *putz*. You have no more right to the truth than these poor suffering people. It's going to take two days and one thousand milligrams of Thorazine to quiet that patient down now. You've scared her. And she was plenty afraid already!"

"Of what?"

"Of anything and anyone who tries to get more information out of her than she wants to give. She's an unmarried secretary in a dentist's office and could have gotten the disease in a hundred and one different ways. What are you going to do, badger her until she's psychotic?"

Bradley looked at Rosen in disbelief. How was it possible that she didn't grasp the absurdity of protecting a patient's privacy when they were facing a disaster of this magnitude? "I've got a phone call to make."

"We've all got phone calls to make. Listen, hotshot, the hooker's name is Crystal. She works at Jack's Bar and Grill on Sutherland and Deheny, downtown."

Bradley blew Rosen a kiss as he walked to a pay telephone.

"Don't forget! Be a *mensch!* It doesn't cost extra. And you'll get what you want." Rosen returned to the isolation ward.

Bradley dialed a number and listened to the line ring. "Hello . . ." He clutched the receiver. It was Judy.

The timetable had been accelerated. Instead of three weeks, Kimball would now have less than one week to run through a simulation exercise before he implemented Project Blood Heat. He had Squire to thank for the rushed schedule. Squire had become unduly nervous after Bradley's visit, even though Kimball had assured Squire he had given Bradley only unclassified information as a way of confirming that he knew nothing about Blood Heat.

Kimball watched as the Chinook helicopter strained to lower the flocculation basin, a rectangular steel casing with giant revolving paddles in between a sharp-edged rapid mixer on one side and a cylindrical glass-encased venturi meter on the other. As soon as Drake and Williams had connected all three parts, Rappaport would attach water pipes to both ends. The purification system for the reservoir would then be in place. The TAG unit could rehearse its assignment in the dark.

"Come on, petunias, let's not drag our asses."

A powerful whirlwind, the downdraft from the Chinook rotors, drowned out Kimball's words.

"Make sure your sweet asses aren't blown away. Otherwise, we can't play TAG anymore."

"Yes sir! But there ain't nothin' here, sir, to blow our asses away."

"What's the matter, Williams, not enough shit for you?"

"Well, sir, we thought we'd be seeing some action. Not dumpin' some crud into the river!"

"Just keep working, Williams. This is as important a mission as you'll ever have. And we're gonna do it right. Make sure you keep your fucking fingers out of those goddamn mixer blades."

"Yes, sir!"

Williams was by far the brightest and most adept of the team. And the one at the present moment most in need of humility. He was far too arrogant. Just as Ramirez once had been.

Kimball enjoyed watching Drake run through her assignment. Ramirez's bizarre and meaningless death on the simulation exercise had somehow inspired Drake to work harder, to become more committed to the principles of CB warfare, and to assume a more defiant posture in general.

"If you SOBs finish this on time, drinks on me."

"Thank you, sir." Williams winked at Drake. Rappaport gave her the high sign.

Watching the behemoth Chinook helicopter pull away from

the group, Kimball had visions of the Vietnamese village in which he had been dropped from the Jolly Green Giant with canisters of *Pasteurella pestis*. First, there had been the larvae beds to set up—covertly, of course—in the Cham Thanh district of In Tan province. Then, bypassing platoon upon platoon of supposedly nonexistent Vietcong, he had placed the larvae beds on the route from Duong Zian Hoi to Vinh Cong.

A few months later he was sent to do the same thing in the villages of Huong My, Minh Duc, and Cam Sun in the district of Ny Cay in the Mekong Delta. In response to the North Vietnamese News Agency accusations that "killer insects" had been let loose, the U.S. government denied any responsibility. But the American public was smart: A public outcry ensued. A committee of socially conscious doctors accused a New England firm of manufacturing, on contract to DOD, large quantities of bubonic plague and tularemia bacilli.

Physicians from all over the country had pressured their respective congressmen to stop the crash program, but the secretary of defense had denied the existence of such a contract. Denial. Distortion. All part of the business of CBW, in the name of national security.

In 1951, General Matthew Ridgway had sent three Japanese bacteriological warfare experts named in the celebrated Khabarovsk war crimes trial to help the U.S. allies in Korea. Subsequent to their arrival in Korea, a rash of bubonic plague symptoms had occurred in the town of Kan-nan in northeast China, and in Kuan Tien Village in Liaotung province, near the Yalu River.

Then there was the infamous outbreak of cholera in Dai Dong, when a simple country girl came across a straw package containing clams and cooked them for her family, friends, and neighbors. Within a few days, several hundred Chinese were dead from vibrio cholera. The clams had been found on a hill alongside a water pumping station and reservoir that the prior day had been completely destroyed by U.S. F-86 fighters.

Kimball's eyes roamed over the expansive fifteen-hundred-acre military facilities so close to Washington, D.C. He was quietly proud to be part of the center for bacteriological warfare research at Fort Detrick. Described in the employee-recruitment brochure as "one of the world's largest animal farms," the Fort employed at its zenith six hundred scientists, all participating in one of three categories of research—defensive; neutral; and, at one time, offensive. The projects included everything from process development to weapons design and small-scale production. The Fort, unlike both Dugway and Pine Bluff, directed its efforts toward breeding into pathogenic organisms precisely those features, such as antibiotic resistance, that other medical researchers would like to eradicate. And unlike the other research centers, it only published fifteen percent of all its data.

In past years, a great deal of attention had been focused on such bacteriological warfare agents as brucellosis, dysentery, anthrax, glanders, and tularemia. Watching his TAG unit work feverishly, Kimball realized how high the cost in human life had been to achieve the recent advances: twenty-five cases of anthrax, twenty-six cases of brucellosis, seven cases of human glanders, sixteen cases of tularemia, five cases of psittacosis. Then he thought of Ramirez and wondered how many other cases of bubonic plague were on the base. In the past, the normal procedure would have been to report Ramirez's case to the Frederick County health officer and then to the Public Health Service, which would coordinate its reporting procedure with DOD. But all that had changed with Project Blood Heat. Even Fort Detrick's professional relationship with the National Academy of Sciences and the American Society for Microbiology had been suspended for a while.

Unlike Dugway Proving Ground, Fort Detrick did not specialize in performing tests on human volunteers. Sometimes the projects seemed a little farfetched—like Project Pacific Bird, run by the Smithsonian Institution, with an initial funding of 2.5 million dollars from Fort Detrick. Ostensibly, the project was designed to study the migratory habits of birds; but, in reality, the project was designed to evaluate the effectiveness of using migratory birds to carry and disseminate bacteriological agents.

Watching Rappaport help Drake with the rotary mixer blades, Kimball concluded that Blood Heat was no more farfetched in concept than Pacific Bird. But it was a hell of a lot more important. If properly executed it could save millions of lives. If something went wrong, well . . .

As far as Kimball was concerned, bacteriological weapons were the most important part of strategic deterrence. They were cheap, effective in small amounts, and primarily strategic. They could be used both overtly and covertly. In many ways biological weapons were far more efficient than nuclear weapons. They could be manufactured quickly, defense was extremely difficult, and unlike nuclear weapons, manufacturing plants could be easily disguised. Pathogens could be easily produced in any brewery or other industry where fermentation was part of the manufacturing process.

The disadvantages of BW were minor compared to the advantages. Sure, it was dependent on meteorological conditions for spreading by aerosol, the preferred means, and there was always the possibility that a BW weapon might spread backward onto its users. But the truth was that no matter with what prejudice one approached the issue of bacteriological weapons, one invariably came to the same conclusion: that bacteriological warfare was an impressive, inexpensive weapon system.

The roaring sound of the turbine motors broke Kimball's moment of reflection. Dammit, they had finally got it started.

"Fantastic! I owe you guys that drink."

"*All right!*" Drake cried, and she turned to slap Rappaport on the back.

Without warning, Rappaport's sleeve was caught in the blades of the rapid mixer. His arm followed. At the first piercing scream, Kimball turned his head aside. There was nothing he or anyone else could do to save Rappaport. With the powerful turbine at maximum rpm, the helpless soldier's body was seized like a rag doll and disintegrated in an instant.

For a moment the team stared, horror-struck; then Drake let

out a sob. White-faced, Kimball moved to shut off the motor as Williams went to comfort the weeping corporal. They had lost a man, but one thing they had to save—Project Blood Heat.

Daruma and Company was exactly as Helene had imagined it: a small suite sparsely decorated with wooden Oriental furniture. It was located in one of the new hi-tech office buildings on the 1400 block of New York Avenue. An Occidental secretary led Helene into a room where two Oriental men were already seated on a pair of facing sofas below a set of seventeenth-century Japanese water prints from the Kyoto school. The coffee table between them held two unfinished drinks.

"Welcome, Mademoiselle de Perignod. I am Mr. Masajo Daruma. Please call me Tommy. I believe you know this gentleman." Daruma stood up and bowed, keeping both hands slightly behind his back, as was the custom. Although he had offered her an opportunity to be informal, he knew all too well that she would decline it. After all, she was a de Perignod, a family name he had learned to respect.

Helene held out her hand to Dr. Futaki Ran and wondered what he was doing there. Her Languedoc instincts told her the less said, the better.

"Hello, Helene. I'm glad to see you under such pleasant circumstances." Unlike Daruma, he stood up and shook her hand.

Ran was the most important research consultant at MTI. Yet, despite his warm eyes and soft features, Helene had never trusted him. After five years at MTI, she still didn't know whether he was a part- or full-time consultant, or even whether he lived full-time in the United States. She knew nothing about his personal life, and only guessed that he had a strong working relationship with Webb. In the truest sense of the word, he was a mystery to her.

Daruma looked more avuncular than malevolent. He had a broad face with narrow, intense eyes. Although he appeared deferential to Ran, Helene had no doubt Daruma was very much in charge of the meeting. If stripped of his Oriental politeness, Daruma would prove shrewd and ruthless.

"Sit down, Mademoiselle de Perignod. You are French, I understand." Daruma motioned with his left hand.

"Yes, by birth and heritage."

"And the *de*, if I recall French protocol correctly, denotes nobility."

Ran silently nodded his head in agreement.

Helene sat quietly, her hands folded neatly in her lap. She was glad she had worn her gray tweed suit. It evoked the image of a well-mannered, properly educated mademoiselle. She knew very well that her modest, unassuming demeanor would fool no one. But like the kabuki parts the three of them were about to play, this part, for the moment, suited her need.

"I am honored that you took the time to call and visit me."

Saru. Daruma reminded her of a monkey, quietly swinging from one bar to the next in his cage until he achieved a vantage point from which to spit or throw something at the visitor.

"Needless to say, I, too, am equally honored to be able to spend some quiet, uninterrupted time with you."

Nezumi. A rat! Ran reminded her of a creature moving stealthily through the darkness, ready to inflict a lethal bite.

"Please excuse my rudeness—"

"*Nanika nomi masho*," Ran interrupted Daruma.

"*Nanika onominina rimasuka*."

Daruma was evidently the more polite of the two, thought Helene. He had asked her whether she would like a drink. Ran had insisted that they all have a drink. Clearly, both men had done their homework. They knew she spoke Japanese fluently, for no Japanese man would ever think of insulting his female guest by demanding she understand what he was saying and requiring her to reply in Japanese, otherwise. It was all part of the charade. But it was also clear that she would be treated as a *gaijin*. They were to be considered her superiors, in control of the meeting. To her slight advantage, she surmised, without any major effort on her part, she was creating a minor rivalry between them.

"*Dozo okamainaku!*" Helene watched Ran flinch ever so slightly.

She could have simply replied, No, thank you! But instead, she responded by telling them both not to trouble themselves, simultaneously revealing that she was not accepting their posture of politeness.

"*Ocha ikaga desuka?*" Ran did not give up. He wanted her to understand that according to protocol, she was to accept whatever was offered her.

"*Domo arigato gozaimasu.*" A simple *domo* would normally have sufficed. But the full formal expression of thanks was, in effect, mocking them—Helene was thanking them profusely for something she had not yet received and would not receive. The message was not lost on either man.

"What can we do for you, Mademoiselle de Perignod?"

"Well, Mr. Daruma, the real question, as you and I and Dr. Ran know, is what can *I* do for *you?*"

"I'm sorry, I don't understand. You telephoned me only this morning, and on very short notice I agreed to see you."

"Why did you agree to see me?"

"Because it was polite to do so."

"Was it polite for you to call Dr. Ran immediately afterward?" Helene watched Ran. He exhibited no visible reaction. For a moment she had some doubts about her provocative tactic: It might backfire. Furthermore, with Ran present she could assume Webb would soon discover whatever transpired—so in fact there were four people in the room.

"Dr. Ran and I have been friends for a very long time. I trust his business judgment," Daruma told her.

"Is he part owner of Daruma and Company?"

Ran exploded. "Mademoiselle de Perignod! I wasn't aware you were so blunt or so—"

"Rude? Dr. Ran, I'm sorry you find me so. But I fear that our time is short and without some plain speaking we will accomplish very little other than a most pleasant acquaintanceship."

"From a pleasant acquaintanceship, one can develop many other pleasant things." Ran's voice sounded conciliatory.

"Why is Daruma and Company interested in acquiring RAI?"

"Because we are interested in acquiring those parts of companies in the high-technology area, sound investments that we feel have a chance for growth."

"RAI is highly overvalued. You're paying thirty times earnings. That can hardly be considered a sound investment. Moreover, there are no hard assets, only the expertise of a few epidemiologists."

"Then why is Roy Webb interested in RAI?" Ran was growing impatient with her.

"Don't you know, Dr. Ran?" Helene returned his stare, making certain he understood she would not be intimidated by him.

"As you and I know, Roy Webb is a very secretive man."

"Even by Japanese standards."

"Yes, even by Japanese standards." Ran laughed. She had a sense of humor. A biting tongue.

"As I have said, we feel RAI is a sound investment."

"And therefore, do you feel that the MTI acquisition of RAI is a wise investment, too?"

"I will not be presumptuous enough to decide what is or is not a shrewd investment for Mr. Webb. I will simply add that Mr. Webb's reputation in the Orient is very strong. He is widely regarded as a man with great vision and foresight."

Daruma quietly nodded in agreement.

Helene was surprised by what she heard. The greater the praise, the less merit there was in the person being praised. Each of them understood that much. If they shared her opinion of Webb's misjudgment, why did they buy into RAI and, by marriage, MTI? Now was the time to change her tactics.

"The name Daruma is an affectionate name of the father of Zen Buddhism and the name of a well-known *netsuke* of Daruma crossing the Yangtze. The Daruma name grows in value either way—spiritually or aesthetically."

"Or financially. . . ." Ran smiled.

She was indeed someone with whom they could deal.

"*Kansha shimasu.*" Daruma bowed his head in gratitude, then he stood up. Raising his right hand, he began to talk.

Helene was eager to hear their proposition. But her attention was drawn to Daruma's right hand. She had seen it only once before. The pinky of his right hand had been deliberately amputated at the mid-point. That could mean only one thing: *Yakuza*—the dreaded Japanese Mafia!

17

Jack's Bar and Grill was small. Under garish neon lights, the Formica-topped bar provided undersized, over-greased hamburgers and french fries all day long. Bradley was surprised to see so many people there in the early afternoon. About two dozen patrons were dressed, unexpectedly, in office attire. Beneath the blaring rock and roll music were ordinary workers quietly socializing on a Friday afternoon, hustling the next drinker for a potential date.

As he pushed through the crowded bodies, Bradley thought of Judy waiting for him in downtown Baltimore. On the telephone she had sounded confused, frightened, and lost. All she would say was "Come quickly. They're coming for me." Who? Why? She couldn't or wouldn't answer the questions. Their rendezvous was at the aquarium at the Inner Harbor, and he had assured her he would be there within the hour. She had asked about Sharon and Stephanie, wanting reassurance that if anything happened to her, he and Yolanda would take care of them. Before he could answer, there was silence on the other end. And then the click. He felt guilty taking a few minutes to track down a lead.

Bradley felt as alone in this crowded bar as he could ever feel. He had lost a large part of his youth in the diligent pursuit of a medical career. He glanced at one young woman seated at the bar who seemed by turns both deeply absorbed with and indifferent to her companion. Bradley vaguely remembered that sense of temporary engagement. For a brief moment he envied anyone who could take a few hours out of her work schedule for nothing more serious than an afternoon's liaison.

He suddenly felt the need to see Helene, the mysterious, sensuous woman who had so recently taken control of his life. He had tried unsuccessfully throughout the day to avoid thinking about the other night. There was in Helene the same controlled focus of attention. Her apparently ingenuous intensity carried with it the same hint of opportunism. Well, he would just learn to enjoy the moment! The rest be damned!

On closer examination, the blonde bartender was more attractive than Bradley had originally thought. He leaned forward to catch her attention. "Could you tell me if someone by the name of Crystal works here?"

"No, I don't think she does." The bartender turned to attend to a group of patrons at the opposite end of the bar.

Bradley followed her.

"Listen, it's extremely important that I find her."

"We serve hard liquor, wine, and soft beverages. That's it, mister. Nothing else." She went back to filling several glasses with draft beer.

"All I want to do is ask her a couple of questions that concern the safety and health of a lot of people. A lot."

"Get this, Jack," she shouted to the stocky, bearded owner of the bar. "This guy wants to know information that concerns the safety and health of a lot of people. Do you want to deal with him, or should I call around and see if there are any social workers here who can help him out?"

"May I help you, sir?" Jack took Bradley's arm in a muscular hand and led him to a quiet corner of the room.

"My name is Dr. Orestes Bradley. I am the director of Infectious Diseases and Allergies at NIH, down on Rockville Pike—"

"I know where NIH is; they botched up my wife's breast cancer treatment. So, Doc, what do you want?"

Bradley noticed the other patrons in the room focusing their attention on him.

"I need to find someone by the name of Crystal who supposedly works here."

"Why?"

"She has some very valuable information . . ."

"Very valuable information . . . like what, Doc—who screwed whom?" His sarcasm achieved its desired effect. Nearby, eavesdropping patrons laughed.

"I just want to ask her a few questions. I assure you, she would be saving a lot of people's lives—perhaps yours and the lives of some people in this room." Bradley glanced toward the woman bartender, preoccupied with washing several long-stemmed glasses.

"You're really into this lifesaving kick, aren't you, Doc? Where were you when my Betty was dying and all they could tell me at your great lifesaving NIH was, 'I'm sorry, but there is very little we can do for her now'? Doc, take your life-threatening diseases and get the hell out of here." Jack waved his arm over the room, suddenly angry. "Can't you see you're bothering my customers? They're listening to this argument and they're not drinking. And that's bad for business."

"Please, I'm not interested in ruining your business or provoking any kind of disturbance . . ."

"Provoking any kind of disturbance? Those are fancy words." Jack shoved Bradley.

Bradley could feel the tension in the room. That's all he needed—a brawl in a redneck bar and grill.

"I apologize." Bradley hoped he could get to the door before Jack stopped him. "I'll be leaving."

"Wait a minute, not so fast! You owe me some money." Jack planted himself between Bradley and the door.

"I didn't order anything."

"That's the point, Doc. You didn't order anything and neither did my customers while you were creating this unnecessary disturbance."

Bradley looked around the room. Everyone was waiting for his response. Or for a fight.

"How much do I owe you?"

"Oh, I'd say about . . ." Jack looked around the room, grinning broadly, encouraged by the smiles from his patrons, ". . . about one hundred and fifty dollars."

The room burst into laughter.

"One hundred and fifty dollars? That's a lot of drinks."

"We're big drinkers here."

Bradley sidestepped Jack and started toward the front door again.

Jack grabbed Bradley by the shoulder and screamed, "Where the hell do you think you're going?"

"Out that door. Your drinks are too fucking expensive!"

"You owe me money, buddy!"

"Send the requisition slip to the defense department. They're stupid enough to pay you." Bradley raised his left arm, blocking Jack's right.

"Give it to him, Jack." An attractive blonde had excitement in her eyes.

"Honey, I'm gonna make mincemeat out of this smart-ass doctor." Jack cocked his right arm backward for a second punch, but was stopped in the middle of his swing. Someone grabbed his arm from behind and swung him around.

Two men wearing blue seersucker suits and sporting neat short-cropped haircuts pinned Jack against the bar.

"Who the fuck are you?"

"Agent Brian McDonald of the FBI. This is my partner. If you strike Dr. Bradley again I'll have to arrest you."

Bradley edged backward toward the front door. McDonald deserved a medal, coming to his rescue. But if he remained for the thank-yous, McDonald would turn around and seize him for conspiracy in his sister's disappearance.

"Hey, let go," Jack blustered. "I was only joking."

Just as Bradley slipped out through the front door, McDonald turned and saw him.

"Oh shit, we've lost him again! Hold onto this jerk." The FBI agent ran to the front door, only to collide with the bartender, who was also running for the exit.

Jack broke away from the agent holding him and jumped on McDonald's back. While the three were knocking and pushing one another, the bartender ran to Bradley's car.

"Wait!" She yelled.

"Yes?" Bradley raced his engine in neutral, anxious to take advantage of his lead time.

"I'm Crystal."

"Why didn't you tell me that before?"

"I couldn't. No one knows me by that name except a few private clients."

"Private clients?" Bradley didn't understand.

"I have a husband and two boys. Bartending allows me to keep a few dollars off the books, but I don't make enough money to send two boys to parochial school by puttin' beer in a glass."

"Then just tell me, who is Raymond? Where does he work?"

"If I tell you what you want to know, can my family get free medical help if we come down with whatever disease you were talking about?"

"Sure, sure, just hurry it up!" Bradley saw McDonald and his partner making a run for their Ford Torino.

"I don't know any Raymond. But whatever I have, I'm certain I caught it from my husband. He's got a high fever and isn't feeling too well."

"Where can I reach him?"

She didn't answer.

"Where does he work?"

"At a small private company. On the docks."

"The name?"

"Trans Nippon Shipping."

Bradley pushed his foot all the way down on the accelerator. Zero to sixty miles per hour in six seconds, just as the Porsche manual promised. He smiled as the Torino disappeared somewhere behind him.

"Trans Nippon Shipping," Bradley repeated the name to himself as he raced up I-95.

How could Crystal's husband have become infected with a virus that caused the bubonic plague if he worked as a shipper on the docks? Unless someone was shipping the virus into the United States using a professional carrier. But who? From where? To whom? The answers, Bradley decided, should be at the main headquarters of Trans Nippon Shipping, wherever that might be. If a live virus—or retrovirus—was being shipped into the U.S., did Kimball have a role in it?

Warning sounds came from Bradley's Fuzzbuster.

Bradley wiped the glass over the dashboard with his fingertips. The speedometer looked blurred. But he was unable to make the haze disappear. He rubbed his eyes with the back of his left hand. Something was making him tear. The more he rubbed, the worse his vision became; soon it was difficult to see the road through the streaming tears. As he started to slow down and veer off to the embankment, he saw what he thought was McDonald's Torino in the rear-view mirror. Bradley pressed his foot on the accelerator and felt the thrust of the engine push him back against the black leather seat.

A smear of colors rushed past as if some temperamental artist had thrown a palette at his windshield. Changing lanes, he wove in and out among the cars, trying to clear his vision by dabbing his eyes with his sleeves. The faster he went, the less he saw. As he reached to turn on his high beams as a warning to oncoming cars, he felt a burning sensation in the palms of his hands, as if he had just touched a scalding iron plate. Suddenly, his hands were in agony. He could barely hold onto the steering wheel.

Cars around him were beginning to honk. He had to slow down. But how far behind him was McDonald? Blindly, Bradley groped for the big black lever in the middle of the dashboard to turn on the air conditioner. He slid the black rectangle over about two inches and pushed another knob to lower the temperature in the car. The cool air on his face was soothing. The haze in his eyes began to clear. Carefully, he drove into a shallow ravine along the shoulder of the highway.

He sat for a moment in silence, his eyes closed. When he opened them, he examined his hands. Each had two large blisters, already so swollen and painful they needed to be lanced. How the hell did he get them? Checking his eyes in the rear-view mirror, he saw they were completely bloodshot, as if someone had thrown lye into them. Now he felt a dry burning sensation in his throat, and he began to cough. Could these be some previously unrecognized symptoms of the plague? The backs of his hands were developing large red rashes, typical of contact dermatitis. Something he had recently touched was causing the rash, the blisters, and the impaired vision—but what?

Bradley shut off the air conditioner and put his hands to his nose. They had a garlicky smell. Was it something he had touched at Jack's Bar and Grill? Or one of those damned formaldehyde specimens in Dr. Rosen's laboratory? Or worse, one of Rosen's patients?

He sniffed the steering wheel. It smelled just like his hands. Was something on the steering wheel causing the irritation on his hands and in his eyes? Or had he spread whatever was on his hands onto the steering wheel? He ran his right index finger along the parts of the steering wheel he had not touched before. Within a few seconds he felt a prickly, irritating sensation on his fingertip.

From the storage compartment, he pulled out a little medicine bag containing all the basic tools for a road emergency. First he took the bottle of mercurochrome and painted his palms. Then, in a cloth on the passenger's seat, he placed a five-cc plastic syringe. With his right hand he punctured first one, and then the other, blister on his left hand. He pulled back on the syringe and drew the clear, yellow fluid from the blister. He repeated the same procedure with his left hand, extracting the fluid from the palm of his right hand. He wrapped both hands in gauze and washed his eyes out with the bottle of sterile water kept in the medicine bag. Bradley recalled his graduate seminars in environmental irritants, as well as Kimball's lecture on the signs and symptoms of chemical warfare agents. Dry hacking cough, severe irritation to the exposed mucosal lining of the body, lachrymation, blisters—they added up to one thing. mustard gas! Someone was warning Bradley to stay away from Fort Detrick and the whole issue of bacteriological weapons.

18

Coming off the ramp past dilapidated freight yards, Bradley turned left onto Charles Street. The principal street of downtown Baltimore was an amalgam of sooty red sandstone buildings supported by decorative buttresses and archways, and modern glass skyscrapers. A string of major hotels surrounded the latest tourist attraction, the Inner Harbor, with its three-story fast-food emporium offering everything from handmade chocolate-chip cookies to stir-fried Chinese food. Baltimore was a city clearly no longer just a way station between the federal government and the more prominent cities of the eastern seaboard.

Bradley parked a few blocks from the aquarium, a building designed in the shape of a twisted conch, with large glass portholes cut in its concrete walls. He looked around to see if he was being followed. The Torino had evidently continued past as he sat in his car lancing the blisters on his hands. For a split second he thought a blue Cadillac Seville was also following him, but he dismissed the idea as a product of his edginess. He paid the six-dollar entrance fee to the aquarium and walked in, wondering if Judy would keep the appointment.

The ground floor was laid out as a concrete walkway ascending to dimly lit upper floors as it wrapped itself around a cylindrical glass tank that served as the core of the aquarium. A kaleidoscope of exotic colors and shapes swam before him. The darker, more prosaic-looking fish, swimming lackadaisically, were in fact the deadly electrics: electric rays, electric stargazers, electric catfish from Africa, and, the most powerful of all, the South American electric eel. A cowardly scuba diver, Bradley had once spent time familiarizing himself with the different species of fish living in the deep corals off Eleuthera, an island of the Bahamas.

Through his own negligence he had once been stung by a South American knifefish, a low-voltage electrical fish. He had survived without serious trauma, but had come away from the experience with a healthy respect for the power of electricity—and fish. Now, as he looked through the luminescent shimmer of the cylindrical tank, Bradley felt as if he were slipping into the depths of the sea.

A side tank contained puffers, a deceptively phlegmatic porcupine fish, playful and amusing until their sharp spines emitted one of the deadliest natural toxins known to man, tetraodontoxin, an alkaloid quite similar to the deadly poison muscarine found in some toadstools. As he glanced toward the entrance looking for Judy, Bradley caught the gaze of a tall man with blonde hair who at once looked away and disappeared in the crowd of people gathered around the bottom of the tank. A meaningless occurrence, it served to heighten his uneasiness.

Bradley wove in and out among the tourists, watching the yellow guppies and silver-bodied three spat gourami. Thank God, he thought, a breath of the ordinary. Checking his watch, he saw that he was only a few minutes late. On the telephone, Judy had beseeched him to be cautious.

When he reached the top floor, Bradley looked down into the tank. Other than a red metal guard rail and a metal grill across the top of the aquarium, nothing separated him from the predatory fish below. Staring into the shimmering water, he felt feverish and faint. The lymph nodes beneath his armpits seemed significantly larger; his bandaged hands still burned from the remnants of the mustard gas. If he didn't find some answers quickly, he might run out of time.

"Russ!" Judy's voice came from behind him. "Don't turn around, just keep walking. You're being followed."

"How do you know?"

"I know. Listen, I don't have much time to talk."

He defied her instruction and turned to look at her. Although she wore a large black kerchief around her head and over half her face, he could see her once-attractive brown eyes and tweezed arched eyebrows covered by clusters of excoriated pustules. She must have just begun carrying the disease prior to his visit to the Kalorama Guest House. And once she started to develop some visible signs of the disease, she fled.

"Ugly, isn't it? My whole body is that way."

"Just like Raymond's!" Bradley whispered.

"Yes."

"Was he your lover?"

"What difference does it make now? There are going to be millions more like us. Ironic, isn't it, that I should be involved in the transport of a lethal virus when my brother is such a famous clinical epidemiologist?" She shook her head in disgust.

Bradley reached out to her, but she pushed him away.

"Russ, we were never close before. Let's not start pretending now."

The shimmering luminescence of the aquarium cast an eerie green glow over her face. A harbinger of death. She smelled putrid, as if her body had already decayed. Wearing the same dress, coat, and penny loafers he had seen her in two days ago, she looked like a derelict.

"The kids, are they all right?" she asked.

"Yes, they're fine. They're with Yolanda."

"Tell them their mother's gone on a very long business trip . . . and . . . I . . ."

He reached for her hands; but she pulled them back.

"You must stop this epidemic, Russ. It's killing too many people. It's gotten out of hand."

"What do you mean, it's gotten out of hand? You make it sound as if it were an experiment run amuck."

"Raymond . . . remember Raymond? An unusual man with unusual skills."

"Yes."

"Wait, Russ. My brain isn't moving as fast as I want it to. It's burning inside."

"Let me take you to the hospital. Then you can do all the talking you want to."

"No, we don't have time. He's here. I know he's here. They sent him here to find me. And to get you. They know all about you and that woman."

"What woman?"

She went on, ignoring the question. "Raymond was a courier. Kempe, Raymond, and I transported the virus – "

Before she could finish, a tall man with blonde hair was upon her, pushing her over the railing.

"Leave her alone!" Bradley grabbed the man's thick, muscular arms. But the more he tried to pull the stranger's arms away from Judy's throat, the tighter her assailant's grasp became and the more forcefully he pushed. Frightened tourists scurried down the four flights of ramps to locate the guards. Judy's screams barely left her frail body as her assailant lifted her into the air and hurled her down onto the aquarium. She struck the protective grill with a sickening crash and lay motionless, face down, sprawled across the tank. Both of her arms had fallen through the grill, and hung lifeless in the water.

Bradley was paralyzed. As he tried to turn away he felt two

powerful hands grab him by the collar and shove him backwards onto the railing. The track lights from the ceiling shone directly into his eyes. The pressure around his neck was intolerable. In a few more seconds, he knew he would black out and be thrown over the side. As his assailant's grip tightened, Bradley's field of vision started to narrow and darken. Jesus! he thought, I'm passing out! He could hear the water bubbling beneath him, ten feet down. The sound began to fade. Vaguely, he could hear screams all around him. The room went black.

"I am very sorry to have left you all alone for so long, but I had some personal business to take care of. Now my mind is totally clear and I can concentrate entirely on healing you."

Wilson heard the familiar voice and opened his eyes. Ran was dressed in the same green surgical scrub suit with a green gauze mask covering his face. If only I could catch a glimpse of that son of a bitch! thought Wilson.

"I gave you a sedative, so you should have had a good sleep."

Sleep? Had he been asleep? Was this all an incredible nightmare from which he would awake? Wilson tried to look around. He knew he wasn't in an operating room. There was too much natural light flooding the area. Over his head in a convex mirror, he could see the end of his bed and the upper part of Ran's body. Beyond that he saw nothing.

"Aren't you pleased, Dr. Wilson? Your condition has improved markedly. You are no longer on the critical list, so we can dispense with unnecessary nursing care. You'll be pleased to know that your jaw has been successfully set back in place. Most important, you will be able to leave this abysmal hospital in a few short weeks. Do you understand me?"

Wilson recalled the signal. He blinked once.

"Good . . . good. A little halothane anesthesia did nothing to impair your excellent memory. You know, things have turned out a lot better than I would have imagined."

Wilson was becoming nervous. Ran's conciliatory, almost apologetic tone of voice frightened him.

"Now, now, there's nothing to be nervous about."

Wilson watched Ran take a folded gauze pad from a surgical tray and with a large pair of forceps gently wipe away the sweat beading rapidly on Wilson's forehead.

"Something must be making you anxious. Trust me, there really is very little else we want to know from you. So far, you've been extremely informative. I know you have developed an SV40 shuttle vector. I know that Bradley must be aware of it, which unfortunately makes him potentially dangerous because it would not be very difficult for him to figure out what it is that we are doing. Hopefully, at this moment, someone will be ridding us of the Bradley problem."

Wilson's mind was teeming. We? Who was the "we" to whom he referred? The military? The government? The Russians? The Japanese? The Arabs? Who was it that was trying to kill Bradley? And what the hell was Project Blood Heat? Did that have any reference to the scientific definition of blood heat – the incubator temperature of DNA?

"Well, Dr. Wilson, I am sorry to say we have one more procedure to perform." Ran held up an X ray of Wilson's spine. "As you can see, I still have to fix the fracture on the dorsal part of your cervical vertebrae. In order to treat that properly I have to place your head in traction. Skeletal traction. A highly regarded and approved procedure. Then we will put you in a Stryker frame for several weeks."

A Stryker frame! Images of a boyhood friend lying unconscious on a bed after a terrible motorcycle accident that made him a paraplegic passed feverishly through Wilson's mind. A prong had protruded from his friend's head, attached to a thick rope that had been stretched over a pulley and tied to weights.

"To begin, I am going to perform a minor surgical procedure on the temporal bones on both sides of your head."

Wilson could feel a wet cloth on the right side of his head.

"First, I'm going to shave all this beautiful hair just above your sideburns, all the way to the area right about here."

Wilson watched Ran spread shaving foam over the right side

of his head. He picked up a sharp, shiny straight razor and used both hands to guide it across Wilson's scalp.

"It is extremely important that the razor be moved smoothly and effortlessly, without any sudden jerky motions. Otherwise, you can well imagine the bloody mess one would create. And we really don't want that, do we?"

Wilson blinked twice. The ceiling mirror revealed it all. The right side of his head was completely shaved. But his next vision made him break once more into a cold sweat.

"What's the matter, Dr. Wilson? I assure you there is nothing to be afraid of."

Ran had picked up a drill. A goddam drill to bore a hole into my head! thought Wilson. He closed his eyes as he heard the harsh scream of the tool come closer. The noise increased in intensity as the serrated edges of the drill bit pierced the epidermal layer of the scalp on its unimpeded passage straight down to the epidural membrane of the brain.

Bradley refused to let his mind go unconscious. He felt the blood rush back to his head as his attacker released one hand from his throat, trying to fend off the tugs from a courageous bystander. Bradley pushed his palms into the assailant's face, squeezing some of the mustard gas through his saturated gauze bandages.

The man released his grip on Bradley as his hands went to his eyes. "Aagh . . ." Bradley dropped onto the concrete floor.

He picked himself up and ran down the ramp, pushing aside the gaping onlookers. A moment later he heard a gunshot, and he turned in time to see the tank containing the brightly colored marine angelfish shatter. Shoals of orange-yellow rock beauties and black-and-yellow-striped french angelfish flipped about in the rapidly draining water.

Flattened against a tank of eels, Bradley looked up the ramp. For the first time he studied his assailant. He was huge and dressed in a conservative pin-striped business suit, his flaxen hair still neatly combed. He was rubbing his eyes with a handkerchief. Bradley looked over at the tourists crouching against the railings, petrified with fear.

A second shot ricocheted against the concrete near his feet. If Bradley didn't manage to run the remaining hundred yards down the ramp toward the exit, he knew his chances of leaving the aquarium alive would be slim. There was only one more tank before the exit – the shark tank. After that, there were no more to hide behind.

As he started toward the exit, his legs went limp beneath him. There, suspended in the tank in front of him was the remnant of a human arm. Deep-red blood still spurted from a severed artery in the shoulder socket. Bits of half-eaten, gnarled fingers floated around like confetti. Three thoughts went through Bradley's mind like rapid fire: shark attack . . . woman's arm . . . Judy.

He felt the nausea rising from the pit of his stomach. But the sound of shoes slapping the pavement behind him quickly reminded him he had no time to lose. In that split second he realized that he had one last chance to stall his pursuer. Taking off his suit jacket, he wrapped it as tightly as he could around his right hand. The killer was less than thirty feet from him by the time Bradley ran back to the puffer tank. He crouched below the little glass tank, his body pressed closely against the concrete wall behind him. For the first time, Bradley could see his assailant's face as he approached. It was a surprisingly handsome and benevolent face, with pale blue eyes.

Twenty-five . . . twenty . . . Bradley counted the remaining feet between him and the approaching killer. With his left hand, Bradley fingered the pen in his coat pocket.

Fifteen . . . ten . . .

He watched as the killer took aim coolly and edged closer.

Eight . . .

The gun was pointed straight at him through the glass. Two shots. That's all it would take, calculated Bradley. One to shatter the glass tank, and the second bullet to pierce him.

Bradley cast the pen out to the side and against the wall. It hit with a sharp snap and skittered across the floor, momentarily distracting the killer. In one quick motion Bradley jumped up, reached into the tank with his wrapped hand, scooped out a startled sandy-colored porcupine fish and flung it straight at the killer's face. The man reeled backwards, clawing the deadly fish from his eyes. He fired, but the shots went wild, grazing Bradley's scalp as he sprinted for the exit.

In the safety of the parking lot, Bradley's mind began to review the horror of the past few minutes: the image of Judy's mangled body; the eyes of the killer; the eerie light of the marine tanks.

By the time Bradley reached his car, warm blood was trickling down the right side of his face.

19

"How's that feel, Captain?" The twenty-one-year-old Navy corpsman was proud of the three sutures he had placed over Bradley's right eyebrow. It was a privilege to have been allowed to work on Bradley, known among the corpsmen and interns as someone who went out of his way to see that even the lowest-ranking staff members got the experience they had been promised upon recruitment. Usually, a senior NIH medical officer was treated only by a physician of equal rank.

"Well, Mr. Jones, what's my prognosis?" Bradley liked the young man. He was enthusiastic, attentive, and, except for one minor slipup that Bradley attributed to nervousness, had done an excellent job of suturing. The bullet had only grazed Bradley's scalp. As he fled the aquarium, Baltimore City police cars had converged on the scene. The security guards at the aquarium had been mysteriously unavailable. Had they been paid off?

"The bandage gives character to your face." The corpsman grinned with self-satisfaction.

Bradley nodded in approval as he checked the stitches in a handheld mirror. His mind kept returning to the puzzling relationship linking Kimball, Fort Detrick, and the epidemic. Did Parker, Squire, and Kuzmack fit in somewhere? A conspiracy involving White House personnel was too fantastic to believe. What was it that Kimball had really been trying to tell him? What was Trans Nippon Shipping? Was that firm related to the epidemic? The questions swarmed like angry bees. He didn't have the energy to fend them off. More than anything, he wanted some time out. He wanted to see Helene.

"So this is where my chief of epidemiology hides out." Susan Engel stood next to the chief of the emergency room, who was a tall, thin, emotionless man.

"What are you doing here?" Bradley stood up to embrace her, but she pushed him away.

"Sit down! What the hell has been happening to you and your people?"

"What do you mean?"

"Kempe is dead; Wilson is upstairs in traction, his neck and jaw busted after some freak accident with his centrifuge; and you're in here with a gunshot wound in your head."

"Flesh wound on the scalp. How is Wilson? I want to see him."

"He's as good as you can expect from a man whose lower jaw and cervical vertebrae were broken. He can't say a word." She turned to the naval officer next to her. "Captain Brooks, this is Captain Dr. Bradley, erstwhile gunslinger, sleuth, and fugitive."

"How do you do? I hope you found your treatment quite satisfactory?"

"Everything was fine." He wanted to add that he had received as competent care from the noncommissioned officer as he would have received from a line officer, but that would have been an unnecessary provocation. "Susan, how did you find out I was here?"

"Well, my dear, that's an interesting story. Do you have another decade to listen to me? Not that you ever listened before." She pulled out a copy of the *Washington Post* from the monogrammed leather attaché case Bradley had given her on her last birthday.

"Panic mounting nationwide as the number of bubonic plague cases climbs tenfold in two weeks. Tens of millions of people are expected to die in the next several months if the federal government does not quickly develop an effective campaign to contain the disease. . . ."

"Who the hell said that?"

"Your good friend Senator Hall."

"What? Why would Hall make inflammatory remarks? He is usually calm and supportive in a national emergency. Remember him during the polio epidemic?"

"Listen to this. You've got some lovely friends. Hall has personally requested a Senate investigation of NIH and its ongoing efforts to curtail the disease . . ."

"What the hell is that about?"

" . . . and he has made you personally responsible for the cure and prevention of the disease. And guess who else?"

"You!"

"Good guess! After I read this stuff about you and me, I immediately called Dr. Novak. You remember her?"

"Of course, she's my deputy."

"Well, it would be nice if you treated her as if she really *were* your deputy." Engel was shouting now. "Because she had no idea where you were until a few minutes after I spoke to her. An FBI agent, Brian McDonald, called to inform her that you had been seriously injured at the aquarium in Baltimore. What's the matter, your Porsche not enough of a toy for you? In the middle of an epidemic you have to go visit some guppies?"

Bradley had never seen her this angry. It was clear she had no idea what he was up to. Usually he kept her completely apprised of his investigations and movements, but the onslaught of events had overtaken his good intentions.

"Do they know where I am?" he asked.

"Who is they?"

"McDonald and company."

"He's waiting outside for you. And I should inform you that they have a padded wagon waiting for you as well."

"You're shitting me!"

"I wish I were. I'm only standing here in front of you because I asserted my rights as your physician and invoked the sacrosanct Hippocratic oath which states that first comes the doctor, then the minions like the FBI."

Bradley was smiling until he walked over to the window. An unmarked van with a chicken-wire grating covering two blacked-out windows was parked at the ambulance entrance.

"You weren't kidding!"

"Sweetheart! I got here before they did so you could have a chance to explain to me what is happening. And if for some reason a foolish old lady should turn her back on a criminal like you, I can honestly say that I didn't know how you got away. Not all of my protégés are on the FBI's Most Wanted list. Dr. Brooks, here, is willing to help."

"That's right, ma'am. As one Navy man to another." He clicked his heels and stood at attention.

"There are two major problems," Engel stated.

"What are they?"

"You've got exactly four days to formulate the government policy expected of you. Where can you stay and be out of trouble while you're working?"

"I'm not sure."

"Didn't you want to isolate and quarantine all the infected victims? What if – "

"Yes, but . . . I'm not so certain anymore."

"What made you change your mind?"

"Well, I have a feeling that if I can get to the source of the infection – the people who are manufacturing a retrovirus II that is carrying the bubonic plague, as well as an assortment of genetic abnormalities – then I can stop the spread of the disease."

"Russ, what are you talking about—retrovirus, genetic abnormalities?"

"Susan, do you trust me?" He grabbed her by the shoulders and looked straight into her eyes.

"You're trying to seduce me, Russ. That's taking unfair advantage of a sixty-five-year-old lady."

"I promise you— "

"What can you promise me? That you'll have a federal policy in three days?"

"You said four days!"

"You just lost one day by trying to be seductive . . . I need that day for some leeway with Kuzmack and the White House. I'm serious! Three days!—that's it! If you haven't developed federal guidelines for containing this epidemic through isolation, quarantine, or whatever you choose—don't bother to come back to your job. I won't be able to protect you against the press or the Hill, or the White House. Or your friend Hall. Furthermore, those gumshoes out there will be more than happy to lock you up for questioning. And your military status in the Public Health Service can't protect you then. Whatever charges they have against you will be adjudicated in a civilian court, not military, where you might have a chance."

"You know, I always loved your optimism." Bradley walked over to a hamper in the corner of the room and put on a green surgical scrub suit with matching hat, mask, gloves, and foot coverings. He headed for the door as if he were off to perform a major operation.

"Where are you going?"

"Upstairs, to see Wilson!"

"Sir, I'm afraid you can't!"

"What do you mean, Captain?"

"On routine CBC and physical exam we discovered that you . . . might have . . . the plague, sir."

"I know."

"You're really something," Engel scolded. "Here you are,

supposed to stop this disease, and instead, you're walking around spreading the goddamn thing."

"Susan, I have no other choice. I have to find out who's creating this epidemic, and why."

"NIH regulations require that you be confined to an isolation ward for no fewer than fifteen days."

"I don't have fifteen days. None of us do. Not unless I can find out what's going on. And I can't do that here. We'll just have to make believe that I am an ambulatory quarantine unit."

Only two things could happen now, he realized: Either he would develop the classical symptoms of the disease and die within the next three to seven days, or if he had received just the right amount of plague toxin, he would develop an immune response instead. At this moment, he didn't feel he was contagious. But if he were to develop a bubonic pneumonia, then he would become extremely dangerous.

Captain Brooks looked quizzically at Engel. Through the porthole window of the OR door, Bradley saw McDonald pacing back and forth in the waiting room accompanied by three other agents in dark-blue suits.

"Captain Brooks, do as he says." Engel walked toward the door, turned back, and waved her index finger at him. "Three days! That's all! If you're maimed, mauled, mutilated, or slaughtered in the interim, make certain that I don't read about it in the *Post.* By the way, try not to be too hard on your friend Hall. He was only trying to cover his political ass."

"At my expense!"

"Why not? You're becoming quite a media personality." Waving the newspaper high in the air, she walked out of the room.

"Follow me, sir." Brooks led Bradley through a side door into a glass-enclosed walkway.

Glancing sideways over his green surgical mask, Bradley saw Engel begin to engage McDonald and his agents in animated conversation. Bradley quickened his steps and crossed in front of Brooks, making it difficult for McDonald's eyes to spot him. They walked quickly down the remainder of the walkway, up three flights of stairs, and past the nurses' station on the postsurgery critical care unit.

"He's in there." Brooks pointed.

The room was completely dark except for a tensor light that shone directly on Wilson. He lay there, stretched out on a Stryker frame, his jaw wired completely shut, his head wrapped in tape. Only his eyes responded to Bradley's arrival.

"Wilson, it's me . . ."

Wilson looked up, his eyes dilated with fear. Beads of cold sweat broke out on his forehead.

"What's the matter? It's me, Russ."

Wilson glanced sideways toward Brooks.

"He's Captain Brooks, chief of the ER, downstairs." Bradley removed his surgical mask.

Wilson blinked. Tears ran down his cheeks.

"He was frightened, sir. It seems he's more relaxed now that you're here."

"Al, are you afraid?" Wilson blinked his eyes once.

"Does one blink of your eyes mean yes?"

Again, Wilson blinked his eyes once. He paused for a few seconds and blinked his eyes twice.

"Two blinks means no?"

Wilson blinked his eyes once.

"Are you frightened about your condition?"

Wilson blinked his eyes once.

"Yes. All right. Would you like me to read to you what's written on the chart?"

Wilson blinked his eyes once.

Bradley walked to the end of the bed and picked up the medical chart and X rays. He held the X rays in front of the light shining from the tensor lamp.

"A linear fracture of the lower mandible. Bilateral subluxation of the temporomandibular joints. Linear fractures of cervical vertebrae C3 and C4. Al, you've hit the triple crown. What do you think, Captain?"

"Well . . . I'm not sure." Brooks opened the chart and read through the medical history and the surgeon's notes.

"Something bothering you?" Bradley pressed.

"Yes. The surgeon performed three different procedures and wrote that a scrub nurse assisted in all of them."

"So?"

"There are nurse's notes in the back of the chart for only one procedure – a manual reduction of the dislocated temporomandibular joint. But the two more complicated procedures – the bilateral insertion of the Erich bar around his teeth and the skeletal traction using Gardner-Wells tongs – were performed without a scrub nurse."

"Is that right, Al?"

Wilson blinked his eyes once.

"Who was the surgeon working on him?"

"Dr. Futaki Ran, one of our finest, if not the best, attending civilian surgeons."

"Is that unusual for him?"

"Well, no . . . not really. He's both a brilliant clinician and a researcher who does a lot of work in postsurgical infections. But he's kind of a loner, a quiet, highly respected, Japanese-trained surgeon. Why would he write that a nurse helped assist him when in fact there was no one there?"

"He was performing an operation that he didn't want anyone else to see."

Wilson blinked his eyes once.

"Well, then, Dr. Ran must have been extremely cautious with your friend, performing a backup procedure that he didn't want to have to justify to an OR nurse or anyone else."

"What do you mean?"

"Here, in the chart, it says that he did a manual reduction of the temporomandibular joint."

"And?"

"He also placed Wilson in a Stryker frame, which realigns

the cervical vertebrae and decompresses whatever pressure there may be on the spinal cord."

"Captain, I'm missing the point."

"Dr. Ran wrote in his own notes that he performed a successful reduction of the lower mandible with his fingers. Why, then, did he specify the use of a Stryker frame to reduce dislocation of the temporomandibular joint? For the cervical injury he could have used a less intrusive procedure than burring some holes in the patient's skull in order to place those tongs."

"Like what?"

"A Georgeade frame, which simply would have been placed around his head. Furthermore, come over here." Brooks pointed to the weights hanging from the edge of the bed just above Wilson's head. "The necessary weight required to realign a cervical fracture is calculated according to the following formula: weight equals three times the C number, times one pound. So a bone injury at C-five level determined by X, say, would be treated with fifteen pounds of traction. Dr. Wilson's fracture is at the C-two and C-four level, which means the maximum weight on the Stryker frame should be twelve pounds. Dr. Ran ordered close to twenty pounds."

"Why?" Bradley lifted two of the four-pound weights.

"Don't!" Brooks placed his hands over Bradley's. "Put them back gently. A sudden decompression of weight could cause the spinal column to shrink back suddenly and snap the vertebrae."

Bradley slowly put down one four-pound weight.

"Are you all right, Dr. Wilson?"

Wilson blinked once.

"All right, Dr. Bradley. Put the second one down slowly."

Wilson's pupils started to dilate.

"Dr. Wilson, are you in pain?"

Wilson blinked once, waited, and then blinked again. Brooks took out a pocket flashlight and shone it in Wilson's eyes. The pupils did not constrict. He read the blood pressure from the electronic monitor on the wall.

"Dr. Bradley, I think we have a problem." Brooks walked

over to Bradley and spoke in whispers. "I think he's in neurogenic shock."

Bradley was alarmed. He touched the skin on Wilson's arm. It was warm and dry. He gently lifted Wilson's legs. They were completely flaccid. The electronic monitor's reading confirmed the diagnosis. Pulse was elevated and the blood pressure was dropping. Blood pressure was fifty-five over forty. Temperature was 95.6 Fahrenheit. Brooks was right: When Bradley had suddenly removed the weights from the frame, Wilson's spinal cord had gone into shock and lost control of the nervous system.

"Twenty-nine milligrams of IV dexamethasone push!"

"Yes, sir!"

Brooks took a bottle of steroids, stuck in the syringe, drew out twenty-five cc of fluid, and injected it into the plastic Y-tube feeding into Wilson's arm. Both men watched as Wilson's pupils constricted. The steroid was working. The monitor indicated that his vital signs were returning to normal.

"Al, was that an accident in your lab?"

Wilson blinked twice: no.

"Were the blood samples and specimens I gave you all destroyed?"

Wilson blinked once: yes.

"Do you know who did it?"

Wilson blinked once: yes.

"Do you know why they did it?"

Again, Wilson blinked once.

"So someone was trying to kill you?"

He blinked once: yes.

"Because of the work you were doing on the shuttle vector?"

Wilson blinked once: yes. But how did Bradley know? He hadn't told him.

"I know what you're thinking. Don't worry! It's okay. Kempe hinted some time ago that you might be working on a shuttle vector – a retrovirus II that would transport certain genetic information from a bacteria to man. And if the bacteria happened to be *Pasteurella pestis*, then the shuttle vector could be used to create the plague without the need for fleas or rats to disseminate the disease. At the time I didn't take his suspicions seriously, so I never confronted you. And, most importantly, I didn't want to lose you, for whatever reason."

Wilson's eyes flooded with tears.

"Did you prove that you could manufacture a virus that could carry the bubonic plague as well as several other diseases and shuttle between bacteria and man?"

Wilson blinked once: yes!

"Goddamn!" Bradley turned to Brooks, staring wildly. "That means he knows who has been manufacturing this bubonic plague, but he can't tell me! Can he move his hands at all?"

"No, sir!"

"Then how the hell can he communicate with me?" The only way was to read off a list of names. "Was it — "

"It's no use, sir!"

All vital signs were flat. Wilson's body had gone into irreversible shock.

It couldn't be! Helene had finished examining both sets of consolidated statements of income for MTI. The one Daruma and Ran had given her showed expenses to be three times the amount officially reported by MTI on October 1. Provisions for losses were over 750 million dollars in Daruma's statement, versus 250 million in MTI's statement. Where had the other 500 million dollars gone?

Webb, with the help of one of the venerable top eight accounting firms in the world, Winthrop, Hoyt, and Hanson, had developed two sets of data: one for himself and one for the public. Helene took another sip of the warm *sake* and continued examining the items listed under Liabilities and Shareholders' Equity. Both short-term and long-term debt were 2.5 times greater than officially reported by Webb. No wonder they were selling MTI stock short. The company was approaching bankruptcy! And Webb had known it all along. He had used her, asking her to find out why and who on Wall Street had been badmouthing the company. Oh, what a fool I've been, she thought as she opened the door of her office and hurried down the empty corridor toward Webb's office.

"I'm sorry, Helene, but Mr. Webb gave the strictest orders that he was not to be disturbed by anyone." Webb's personal secretary rose up from her chair as if she were a physical barrier to Helene's entering. "Orders are orders."

"Tell him I want to see him immediately."

"He's in a very important meeting."

"Tell him he'll be in another very important meeting – the resignation of his vice president for finances – if he doesn't see me now."

"Yes."

Before Webb's secretary could convey the message, Helene had walked through the double set of doors. She halted in surprise.

"I believe you know everyone here." Webb did not seem annoyed by the intrusion. He stretched his arm out to the group seated around the conference table in a symbolic gesture of introduction.

Kuzmack stood to shake Helene's hand. "Good to see you, Helene." His eyes darted back and forth between her and the other conferees. He seemed unduly nervous.

"What a pleasant surprise!" Parker continued puffing on his contraband Havana cigar. "Come and join us. We're almost finished here. I think we could use some wise counsel."

"Thank you, Joe. I'll take that at face value." She knew perfectly well that he was neither pleased to see her nor much interested in her opinion.

The conference room looked unusually cluttered to Helene. On the wall next to Webb, a series of maps displayed the Washington, D.C., reservoir system with a blowup of the Patuxent River and the town of Scaggsville, Maryland, marked off as if it were a designated target of some sort. Next to a wooden mock-up of a water pumping station were the words Project Blood Heat in bold red letters. At the far end of the table sat two neatly scrubbed men dressed in green Army uniforms with shiny silver bars on their dark-green epaulets.

"I'm sorry, dear . . ." Webb began.

The word "dear" sounded strained and cold to Helene. Webb was angry. Good, she thought, I'm angry too.

"The handsome gentleman on my right is Major Ezra Kimball, a physician at Fort Detrick."

"How do you do?" Kimball stood sharply to attention.

"Goodness, Major! I feel as if *I* should salute." The remark hit its mark; the tension was broken by quiet chuckling.

"No, ma'am, just shake hands."

"All right, then. I'll be happy to oblige." Helene walked over and shook Kimball's hand. "Nice to meet you, Major Kimball."

"Thank you, ma'am."

"And you, Colonel, who might you be?"

Squire turned toward Parker, who nodded his head.

"I'm Colonel Robert Squire, Director of DARPA, DOD."

"I know DOD, but what's DARPA – a code word?"

"It stands for Defense Advanced Research Projects Agency."

In any other setting she would have asked him what he did. But under these circumstances she knew better.

"I think we've pretty much covered everything, haven't we, Roy?" Kuzmack was obviously annoyed that Helene had intruded on the final minutes of their meeting.

"We only have one minor point to resolve. Whether within three working days we proceed with Project Blood Heat or not. Is that right, Joe?"

"I really think we've accomplished pretty much everything we've had to. Up to this point."

"I'll leave, Roy," said Helene quickly. "I have no intention of disrupting this meeting. What I want to see you about can wait." She turned toward the door.

"Stay! As part of my senior management and one of my trusted advisors . . ."

Helene smiled to herself: He knows! He knows I'm furious with him. He probably realizes I've discovered the discrepancies in the company's financial statements. He's trying to reestablish my faith in him in the quickest, most dramatic way possible – by allowing my uninvited presence in this restricted, top-secret meeting. It's his way of saying he is sorry.

"What do you say, Robert? Is it a go, or no go?" Webb asked Squire.

"Well, sir. I say we need a few more weeks. What do you think, Ezra?"

"You all know how I feel," Kimball answered. "I've already lost two valuable men. I'm down fifty percent in my TAG capability. I need the extra time."

"How long would it take you to properly train and equip another two TAG members?" Webb was obviously impatient.

"Anywhere from three months to half a year."

"Come on now, Ezra," Parker shot out irritatedly, "you're stretching it, aren't you? Hell, we train baby-assed recruits in eight weeks. Those bug passers are already Army. All they need are a few extra lessons, here and there. Nothin' more."

"General Parker, I beg to differ with you. It's a very sophisticated operation, sir." Kimball felt self-conscious in Helene's presence.

"Okay, gentlemen, I think we have an idea of some of the basic differences. Let us not try to resolve them here, in the midst of hot tempers and haste." Richard Kuzmack, too, plainly disliked having this discussion in front of Helene.

"Cut the crap, Richard. One way or another we will have to decide 'go' or 'no go' before we leave this room, and I intend to stay here until I get an answer. Perhaps we should ask my vice-president, Mademoiselle de Perignod, what she thinks of the matter?"

Webb's threat was implicit. Either they reached a decision soon, or his beautiful intruder would learn the delicate secrets of Project Blood Heat.

20

An ominous premonition clouded Webb's thoughts: Within the next few days, his entire life would change. And for the first time he wasn't certain which direction it would take. He glanced at Helene, sitting somberly at the conference table, and quietly cursed her. One way or another, she had always managed to get her way. This time it would have to be different. He had no other choice.

"Within three days, we proceed with Project Blood Heat," Webb announced. "We can't wait until Major Kimball is up to full complement."

"What about the – er, nuisance factor?" Kuzmack looked significantly at Parker, who was blowing circles of smoke from his cigar.

"Richard, to the best of my knowledge, Bradley has not uncovered anything yet."

At Bradley's name, Helene started. What had Bradley to do with Project Blood Heat?

"If I may interrupt, sir, Dr. Bradley did come to see me. And I am certain he will be back." Kimball was annoyed by Webb's cavalier attitude toward his Threat Assessment Group.

"By that time we will have accomplished our task," Webb said, wary of Kimball's resistance to proceeding with Blood Heat.

"Roy, I wouldn't be so cocky if I were you. He can be a persistent boil on your butt. And after a while, there is nothing you can do with a boil but lance it!"

"Then we'll lance it . . . If, however, events do proceed at a faster pace than expected, we reserve the right to implement Project Blood Heat almost immediately. Right, Joe?"

"Okay, Roy. That means from this point onward we have to be prepared to launch."

"But, sir . . ." Kimball was concerned that both Webb and Parker had completely unrealistic expectations of his TAG capability. He had only a two-member team now, and still couldn't accept more than a five percent margin for error.

"Ezra, you don't look comfortable." White House Advisor Kuzmack had the authority to call off the entire project. But he didn't want to countermand General Parker or Webb. Either man could make his life quite miserable by mustering both congressional and bureaucratic pressure against him. A few selected leaks to the *Washington Post* could destroy his career completely.

Kimball glanced at Webb and Parker. It was clear neither man would stop the project now. The momentum was too great.

"Well, Major Kimball?" Kuzmack waited impatiently as everyone's attention focused on him.

"Two members are better than none," Kimball said resignedly.

"Glad to have you on board, son." Parker inhaled contentedly on his cigar.

Webb stood up, indicating that the meeting was over. He shook hands with the participants as they filtered out of the room.

"I think you're making a serious mistake to discount Bradley," Kuzmack whispered to Webb. "Bye, Helene, always good to see you."

Webb waited until everyone but Helene had left the room. "How good to see you, my dear."

"What the hell is Project Blood Heat? Some American Indian ritual?"

"It's a massive vaccination effort to try to stem the bubonic plague that seems to be out of control."

"Involving DARPA and Fort Detrick? Come on, Roy. I'm not that stupid." She exploded more quickly than she had expected. She had wanted her anger to seethe out slowly, ominously.

"The Army is the only organization capable of handling a massive inoculation program. Who the hell do you think took care of thousands of victims in the Wilkes-Barre, Pennsylvania flood? The U.S. Army. And when the Vietnamese refugees were streaming into the United States after the fall of Saigon, it was the Army that fed, sheltered, and clothed them, and then inoculated them for every conceivable disease under the sun. And when Castro threw out one hundred and twenty thousand Cubans from his prisons and mental institutions, who do you think was prepared to take care of them – your friend Dr. Bradley and his Yellow Berets?"

"I didn't realize you were in charge of the Army recruitment program."

Helene flinched as Webb slammed the table with his fist.

"Where the hell do you come off, barging through doors? I gave explicit instructions that I was not to be disturbed by anyone."

"Why wasn't I invited to this meeting?"

Webb could hear the hurt in her voice. "It didn't involve you. This was a matter of product development for our principal contractor, the U.S. government."

"Why wasn't your VP for either new product development or government contracts here?"

"Dammit! Are you telling me how to run my corporation?"

"This company won't be yours much longer if you keep running it this way – secretively. It is a publicly held company. There are performance standards and codes of conduct that the SEC and your financial backers expect you to abide by."

"What the hell are you talking about?"

"I'm talking about keeping a double set of books. One for you, and one for me and the other suckers."

"Where the hell did you get that idea?"

Helene was taken aback by his righteous indignation. She had expected him to dismiss her charges with offhanded sarcasm.

"I can't tell you."

"You can't tell me! But you make a goddam accusation that I am unethical and downright criminal!" His face flushed. "Dammit, woman, I've compromised my credibility with those men out there to let you come in here, and just because . . ." He jammed the swivel chair against the wooden table. "Because . . ."

It had been such a long time since he had told her how much he loved her. He couldn't release the words.

"You asked me to investigate the rumors that were spreading around Wall Street, so I did. And I discovered that a group of traders, possibly insiders, felt this company was not in very good financial health."

"Is that where you got your idea about a double set of financial statements—from a bunch of slick inside traders?"

"No. It's irrelevant where I got the information. The point is that I feel left out of all the most crucial activities of this company."

"Like?"

"RAI."

"I asked you about it, and we didn't agree. You were opposed to the acquisition; I was for it. You weren't left out. I simply didn't take your advice."

"Why didn't you?" She despised herself for sounding petulant. Webb was making her doubt her own professional judgment both about RAI and about her assessment of the financial condition of the company. She was certain RAI would turn out to be a financial disaster for MTI. It was nothing more than a Trojan horse ploy by a group of RAI investors to drive down the value of MTI stock through rumors and selling short. At the right moment, those same investors would turn around, exercise their warrants and options to purchase MTI stock at a devalued price, and take over the company. Why didn't Webb see this? Why didn't he want to see it?

"I told you before, Helene, it is a company MTI needs now . . . badly." Of course, there was one other company that he wanted even more than RAI, and she would be indispensable for that acquisition – but he had decided to wait until Project Blood Heat was over.

"What could be so bad that it requires you to divert several hundred million dollars of hard cash into a secret research and development program?"

"What the hell are you talking about? You can walk all over this building and you won't find one secret project. All the experiments and expenditures can be accounted for by me or by the accounting firm. I don't know where you get this nonsense about secret funding."

Helene stared incredulously at the anguish on his face. She should tell him about her meeting with Ran and Daruma. As far as she knew, he may already know about it and be testing her loyalty. But what if Webb was right and Ran was lying? What if there really were no shortfall of cash or secret projects being underwritten by a diversion of funds? Was it Ran or Webb she should trust? She had no reason to trust Ran. But she had lost her trust in Webb. And he in her.

What a fool she had been to allow herself the childish indulgence of a protracted love affair. Staring at the maps on the wall of the conference room, she felt her heart pound. She had lost his love, his trust, and his patronage. She must revert to her old ways, to a time when the precept of her life was embarrassingly clear—*sauve qui peut.*

She left the room, not bothering to turn around, fearful that he might try to assuage her pain and wipe away the tears welling in her eyes. She walked quickly down the carpeted hallway to her office.

Her secretary had already left for the day. Her office was dark. She turned on the light, walked over to her Mosler safe, and withdrew from it a small handful of private documents. Everything she owned was in those papers. As the sole executrix of her father's estate she was entrusted to dispose of the considerable family assets in any way she deemed financially appropriate. However, the companies he owned were run by local managers over whom she had very little operational control. That's the way her father had wanted it. She picked up the telephone, reflected on Daruma's and Ran's proposition, and made two telephone calls: one to the president of Dai-ichi Kangyo Bank in Tokyo and the other to a trusted friend at Daiwa Securities. Within twenty-five minutes she had borrowed and spent twenty-five million dollars. She was certain her father would understand. Folding a few thin sheets of her father's papers, she placed them inside the pockets of her skirt.

Startled by an unexpected noise, she looked up.

"I'm sorry. I didn't mean to frighten you." Bradley stood in her doorway.

"How did you get into the building this late?"

"I showed the guard my PHS pass and he let me in. Do you think I could have a simple 'I'm glad to see you'?" Arms outstretched, Bradley walked toward her. Then he stopped, realizing that he wasn't yet sure whether or not he was dangerous to her.

Helene turned away and started sorting papers on her cluttered desk.

"What's the matter? You look upset."

"Nothing that concerns you."

"I called your office and your secretary told me you were in a meeting. I figured you couldn't turn down an impromptu sushi."

Helene locked her attaché case and looked up at him. She forgot her hurt and anger toward Webb when she noticed the Band-Aid over Bradley's eyebrow.

"What happened?" She came up and ran her fingers over his sutures. "Are you all right?"

"I was only wounded. But you look devastated."

"Is it that apparent?" She turned away and began to sort papers again, both glad and resentful that he had come. Here he was, coopting her moment of grief. And yet, throughout the day she had longed to see him.

Sitting on the edge of her desk, she crossed her long legs provocatively. She made a deliberate effort to sound enthusiastic.

"Tell me, Dr. Orestes Bradley, what really brings you here, at this late hour of the day?"

"Truthfully?"

"If possible. However, if you find that you must lie, try to make it credible."

"I wanted to see you . . . very much. Does that sound believable enough?"

Helene ignored the question. "You look like a victim from the Hundred Years War."

"It looks that bad, huh?"

"Worse."

"If you can believe it, I've been beaten up—almost done in, as they say. I can't even believe it myself. Someone almost fed me to the sharks. I think the guy must have died from the way his head struck a concrete floor. But whoever sent him after me is still very much intent on killing me—and several million other people."

"What are you talking about? You're not making sense. Come sit down. . . ." She ran her fingers through his hair.

"I just ducked out of Bethesda Hospital, where one of my admirers, FBI Agent Brian McDonald, was waiting to interrogate and probably arrest me. My sister is dead. I watched one of my best scientists and friends die in a Stryker frame, because his surgeon had constructed his operation and recovery in such a way that his death was inevitable. And I wish I could make sense out of it all."

"Wait a minute . . ." She pulled her hand away and slid off

the desk. Bradley hadn't come to see her. He might be emotionally upset, but he would not foolishly risk danger or arrest simply for another dalliance with her. "Did you ever hear of something called Project Blood Heat?"

"No, why?"

She didn't answer.

"Are you all right?" he asked. Dismissing her moodiness, he continued, "I want you to help me, Helene."

"How?" Her voice became softer, more hesitant.

"I need to find out about a Dr. Futaki Ran, the surgeon who operated on my friend and who, I understand, is a consultant to your company."

Futaki Ran! Helene was taken aback.

"*I'd* be happy to help you in any way I can." Webb strode into the room, effusively warm. "I'm sorry, I wasn't informed that you were coming. But I'm glad you took me up on my invitation to visit MTI." He smiled at Helene, who glared back.

Beyond Webb, Bradley saw a dark-haired, uniformed man blocking the entry door to Helene's suite of rooms.

"Oh, don't mind him! I have a group of security guards who make certain I don't get kidnapped right beneath their noses. If he bothers you, I'll send him away. I don't think you'll kidnap me. What do you think, Helene?"

She was puzzled, distracted by the confusing thoughts that circled her brain.

"Never mind. Helene is frequently lost in her interminable schedule of numbers for corporate financing." Webb took Bradley by the arm and started to walk toward the bank of elevators. "I can't tell you how conscientious she is. She thinks of nothing but the company. Corporate strategy. Corporate financing. Corporate acquisitions. Now, that's her real *forte*, isn't it, Helene?"

Helene shot him a poisonous look.

"Who was it you were particularly interested in?"

"Dr. Futaki Ran."

"May I ask why?"

Webb, Bradley, and Helene entered the elevator together. As the doors closed, the security guard slipped in. The elevator stopped at the ground floor and they walked together through the landscaped four-story atrium.

Looking through the brightly lit, glass-encased walkway of the main administrative building, Bradley realized that the MTI grounds were far larger than would be guessed from a car passing by on Route 270. They reminded him of a newly erected university campus: glass and steel buildings surrounding intimate courtyards. Enclosing the entire campus was a well-disguised electrical wire fence. Guards dressed in dark-blue police uniforms were stationed every few hundred feet.

The group walked through a corridor bracketed by small laboratories. Webb's bodyguard remained behind, chatting with a night guard at the entry of the building.

"We're equipped to handle any type of major research project. At present, we're engaged in developing efficient cloning vectors in *E. coli* used in various prokaryotic and eukaryotic proteins, such as human growth hormones and interferons. We've committed a significant amount of research dollars to the project." Webb looked pointedly at Helene, then turned back to Bradley. "We're studying the problem of cell membrane organization and we're developing DNA probes that will characterize different tumor genes. This work, as you know, Russ, has the potential for diagnosis and treatment of various forms of cancer."

Helene scrutinized Bradley's face, wondering whether he believed what Webb was telling him.

Bradley simply peered through the doors of the various laboratories, saying nothing. So far, there were no restricted areas, no extra-hooded ventilation systems, no extra safety backup systems, any of which would indicate laboratories engaged in developing dangerous microorganisms.

Webb opened the door to a brightly lit laboratory where a man peered intently through the binocular lens of an electron microscope. When he heard the guests enter, the man quickly closed a small metal box of electron microscope grids and locked it in a metal drawer under his work table.

"Dr. Futaki Ran, this is Dr. Orestes Bradley, director of the National Institute for Infectious Diseases and Allergies. Dr. Bradley, this gentleman, working late into the night as usual, is Dr. Futaki Ran, the principal research consultant to MTI."

The two men shook hands. Ran simply nodded his head in Helene's direction.

"How long have you been with us, Dr. Ran?" Webb queried.

"More than forty years, now."

He was taller than most Japanese men, thought Bradley. Was this mild-looking gentleman capable of torturing Wilson?

Bradley was impressed by the spaciousness and neatness of the lab. He noticed one large 100,000-magnification electron microscope with a point resolution under five angstroms; a Sorvall centrifuge, as well as several high-speed centrifuges; and on a marble slab tabletop beneath a series of personal photographs, an automatic synthesizer that created segments of DNA. But Bradley saw no equipment designed for bacteriological warfare and no decontamination units or suites.

"I am very much honored by your presence, particularly at this very late hour." Ran bowed as he spoke.

"A few hours ago I visited my colleague and friend, Dr. Wilson—"

"Oh, I am so very sorry. They just telephoned me from the hospital."

"Yes, he died while I was there, I—"

"A most unfortunate happenstance."

Helene was not amused by Ran's patent manipulation of Bradley. He had not allowed him to finish one thought. And what a flatterer.

"He died of neurogenic shock."

"Please sit down." Ran moved a chair in the group's direction. No one sat down.

Helene looked at Webb, the epitome of confidence and self-assurance.

"According to your own notes, you performed a manual reduction of the lower mandible," Bradley pressed Ran.

"That's correct."

"And then you secured both his jaws with Erich bars."

"Correct again, Dr. Bradley."

"And then you reduced the cervical fracture by placing him in a Stryker frame, using Gardner-Wells tongs to secure his skull."

"You're extremely knowledgeable about surgical procedures."

"I try to be. I'd like to know why you placed him in a Stryker frame to reduce his temporomandibular joint, when you wrote that you had already successfully reduced it by hand."

"Well," Webb interrupted, "I didn't realize that you two doctors might engage in discussion of surgical procedures. I don't know about you, but I have to get up early tomorrow." He was nervous. It was now clear that Bradley was here to accuse Ran of medical negligence. Webb had not anticipated this scenario.

Ran ignored Webb and launched into an answer. "In my surgical experience I have found that a redundancy of a surgical procedure has frequently saved countless hours of worrying about the efficacy of a simple manual procedure, not to mention subjecting the patient to the trauma of yet another operation at a much later time."

"Can you tell me why you placed twenty pounds of weights on the frame when only twelve was required?" All of a sudden, Bradley had a strong desire to see the microscope grids in the metal box he had just seen Ran lock away.

"What are you asking me, Dr. Bradley?"

"I'm asking you why there was eight extra pounds stretching his neck. Eight pounds which, when removed, broke his vertebrae and snapped his spinal cord."

"Are you questioning my judgment?"

Webb interrupted again. "I think it really is time for us to say goodnight. Perhaps you two should continue this conversation in the morning. Everyone must be tired . . ."

"Dr. Bradley, I assure you that in my thirty-plus years as a surgeon, I have found that, for the more complicated cases, the factor of five rather than three is a far more precise and safe guide when selecting weights."

Bradley barely heard Ran's defense. What he saw on the wall of the laboratory was of greater importance—the same picture hung on Kimball's wall. There was Parker with his cigar; and Ran, toward the center; and the captain. Bradley glanced quickly at Webb, then back at the picture. Now he knew who the captain was, the one whom Kimball couldn't remember: Roy Webb. So their relationship went back to World War II, when Webb was the conquering hero and Ran was the vanquished soldier who had indispensable knowledge about bacteriological warfare. Theirs was an association that had endured for over forty years.

Bradley stopped and glanced at another photograph on the wall, one of a group of emaciated American soldiers, dressed in tattered pajamas. He peered more closely at a dark-haired American in the photograph who looked very familiar. The blood drained from his face.

The prisoner in the photograph was his father.

21

"Get the electron microscope grids out of the drawer, Helene!" Bradley yelled as he lunged at Ran.

As both men tumbled to the floor, like boys in a schoolyard scuffle, Helene picked up a long flat utensil lying next to the microscope and jammed it into the drawer.

"You son of a bitch! You killed my sister and my friend—"

Webb grabbed Bradley by the shoulders and tried to pull him off Ran. But Bradley was stronger than Webb had imagined.

Helene shoved the implement into the small space between drawer and tabletop; she suspected the electron microscope grids might provide answers to her own questions about Webb's secret diversion of funds into Project Blood Heat.

Hearing the commotion, Webb's bodyguard rushed into the laboratory.

"Get him off before he kills the professor." Webb pointed at Bradley.

Helen pushed downward and pried up on the drawer.

"What are you doing?" a voice thundered.

She looked up. Webb was staring down at her. The guard had pulled Bradley off Ran and was holding him with his arms pinned tightly behind his back. When Bradley stopped struggling, the guard relaxed his grip.

"Well?"

Helene's eyes darted between Webb and Bradley. "I wanted to see for myself, as executive vice-president for finances, what type of research you were funding."

Webb looked at Ran, who removed a set of keys from his pocket and opened the desk drawer. He handed the metal box of electron microscope grids to Webb.

"Please believe me, Mademoiselle de Perignod," said Ran, "I am by nature and culture a man of peace. I do not like confrontation. If these are what you or Dr. Bradley seek, I have no problem with your seeing them."

"She didn't want those electron microscope grids, I did."

"Why, Dr. Bradley?"

"How many American soldiers did you kill at Pingfan?"

"You're becoming a real pain in the ass, Bradley!" Webb stood holding the metal box, uncertain how far he should allow the conversation to continue.

"Do you remember an American soldier by the name of Bradley, B–R–A–D–L–E–Y? But how could you? There were so many, weren't there?" Bradley's voice was filled with rage; his face, with revenge.

"Please, Dr. Bradley. I understand your sentiments very well. My entire family perished in your B-29 fire bombings of Tokyo."

"Did you use your own family members as guinea pigs at Pingfan?"

"Do you regard your patients hospitalized at NIH as guinea pigs when you experiment with a new protocol of medicine?" Ran replied coolly. "Is every new medicine for which you don't know the side effects a deadly weapon with which to kill patients? Or are those patients and medications avenues to a cure that could otherwise ravish thousands of innocent victims?"

Bradley walked back to the wall covered with photographs.

"You tell me what happened, Roy," he snapped at Webb.

"What do you mean?"

"How many American soldiers were at Pingfan?"

"I don't remember."

Ran spoke up. "At one time or another there were three hundred and forty-two Americans, six hundred and forty-seven Russians, two hundred and thirty-three Chinese, one hundred and fifty Koreans, twenty-nine British, forty-seven Dutch." He provided the figures as if it were 1943.

"What happened to them, Roy? Weren't you the officer in charge of liberating the camp?"

"*Institute*, Dr. Bradley. It was a research institute."

"What happened, Captain Webb? What happened to three hundred and forty-two Americans?"

"Dr. Bradley, you asked to see Dr. Ran. Well, you've seen him. I've showed you our research facilities. Is there any other way I can be helpful to an official of NIH?"

"Did all the Americans die at Pingfan?"

"Yes." Webb was quite emphatic. "Is there anything else we can do for you?"

"May I see those grids?"

Webb looked at Ran.

"Please." Ran took the metal box from Webb and handed it to Bradley. "There is nothing I have to hide. Certainly, not from an esteemed research colleague."

"I don't think we owe Dr. Bradley any further assistance." Webb grabbed the box of grids away from Bradley.

"On the contrary. We owe him all the cooperation that we can provide. Unlike you, Mr. Webb, I am at a slightly greater disadvantage. You see, Dr. Bradley has incorrectly assumed that I have killed his father. You and I know that is certainly not the case. But since we cannot bring back his honorable father to testify to my veracity, I must, by force of circumstance, prove my innocence to him. And to anyone else who may question it. Isn't that right, Mademoiselle de Perignod?"

Helene wondered what Ran was up to now.

"I am afraid we have outvoted you, Mr. Webb." Ran held his hand out for the box.

Webb felt the tension in the room mount. Ran had placed him in a no-win position. If he didn't hand over the grids, Bradley would assume he was guilty of some atrocious transgression—the murder of American POWs. Webb handed the metal container to Ran, who, in turn, handed it to Bradley.

"Please be seated, Dr. Bradley. I suggest you look at the first grid at forty-thousand-power magnification. I assure you, you will find it most interesting." Bradley sat down on the stool in front of the RCA electron microscope and looked at the fluorescent screen. He pushed several buttons on a console located to the left, trying to adjust the proper magnification. At ten thousand magnification, he couldn't see anything.

"Move your magnification up to forty thousand. Each grid will have a different magnification characteristic. And please, listen very carefully to what I say. Don't believe everything you see."

Bradley looked down into the lens. Using a combination of his hand and the electronic viewfinder, he searched the grid.

"Now, in the center of the grid . . . do you see what I am describing?"

"No, not quite . . . I don't see . . ."

"Please, Dr. Bradley, be patient for just a minute. You're having difficulty adjusting my equipment. What type of electron microscope do you use?"

"A Phillips."

"Well, there you are. It will simply take some time for your eyes to adapt to the dark. On this grid, you must use forty thousand amplification. Not more. Not less."

Bradley looked down through the lens at the new setting.

"In the center of the field, you will find a large oval-shaped T cell."

"The nucleus?"

"That's right, the thymus cell, the workhorse of the body's immune system. The one on the left."

"Yes, counterclockwise. At forty thousand magnification."

"Do you see that large T cell surrounded by all those tiny macrophages?" Ran asked him.

"I think I see it."

"Good. I have identified that particular type of T cell, observed at forty thousand amplification, as the first letter—"

"Letter?" Bradley looked up.

"Oh, I am so sorry, did I say *letter?* I meant *cell* . . . Where am I now?"

"The first line of defense for the immune system."

"Yes."

"I see it very well now," Bradley answered him. "The T cell is the first line of defense of the immune system. But I have to turn to the left in order to see it at the forty thousand amplification level."

"That cell is extremely important, as you know, in combating the lethal effects of the retrovirus II when it invades the human body."

Webb relaxed. The conversation was intelligible and innocuous. Half the genetic researchers in the country were working on T cells. It was the most basic and least restricted of all research experiments.

"The next grid must be seen at a fifty thousand amplification. But this time, to the right."

"On the right side of the screen?"

"Yes, there you will see a giant neutrophil," Ran answered.

"I see it. White lymphocytes surrounding it."

"That's right. At MTI, we're extracting the chromatin material and inserting it into a viral vector to produce all sorts of interesting models of disease."

"Ran, I think that's enough," Webb barked.

"Roy, don't worry! I haven't told Dr. Bradley anything he doesn't know already. Isn't that right, Dr. Bradley? T cells and neutrophils are still part of the preclinical medical school curriculum." Webb relaxed and Ran continued. "Using the chromatin material from the neutrophil, and a shuttle vector, we can provide individuals with a specific disease an assortment of immunological protection."

"Derived from the DNA extracts of the T cells and neutrophils."

"Yes. You understand it quite well."

"I think I do understand now. How unfortunate that Dr. Wilson was working on a shuttle vector before his accident with the centrifuge."

Helene was confused. Only twenty minutes before, Bradley had been ready to indict and convict Ran for the premeditated murder of Wilson. Now Bradley's palliative tone sounded as if Wilson had accidentally caught his hand in a desk drawer.

"I am dreadfully sorry about Dr. Wilson's accident. But one must look on the bright side of all misfortunes. If Dr. Wilson had not been the victim of that tragic accident, we might not have met."

"Yes, I see."

Bradley watched as two security guards walked by the lab and waved to Webb. A bodyguard stood silently by.

"Let's finish with this mutual admiration business. It's getting late, and the security guards are waiting for us to leave," Webb insisted.

"Very well, Mr. Webb. As I was saying, Dr. Bradley, the retrovirus shuttle vector, with the new genetically designed immune capability in the DNA, also carries a disease state . . ."

"Like methemoglobinemia?"

"Yes . . . that's one."

"Prenatal diphtheria?"

"That's another."

"Hemophilia?"

"Yes."

"Bubonic plague?"

"Yes. In fact, we are presently working on a vaccine which

will protect against the effects of bubonic plague," Ran offered.

"Using the retrovirus II, genetically altered."

"That's right. Now look at this last grid—sickle-cell anemia. You must review it at thirty thousand magnification."

"I see."

"Move it to the left. Like the first one."

"Yes, I see it now. Crenated red blood cells."

"You wouldn't believe where that blood came from. A glutamic acid in the hemoglobin protein has been replaced by valine."

"I understand."

"What do you mean, Dr. Ran?" Webb was becoming suspicious of the technical conversation.

"You know that it is quite rare to capture a sickle-cell crisis on an electron microscope."

"And you manufacture all your vaccines here?"

"No, Dr. Bradley. As a matter of fact, none of them are produced here. But I am afraid Mr. Webb is correct. You have received more than enough information for now."

As Bradley stood up, Webb pushed him aside and sat down at the microscope.

Ran motioned to Bradley and Helene to leave quickly.

"What the hell is going on here?" Webb searched through the lens. "These grids are empty." He picked up the metal box of grids and threw it against the wall. Knocking Ran to the ground, Webb turned to chase Bradley and Helene down the corridor.

"Stop them!"

The two security guards and Webb's bodyguard joined him.

"Don't let them out of the building!"

"How do we get out of here?" Bradley shouted to Helene as they sprinted down the hallway.

"Down there!"

He followed her to three darkened laboratories at the end of the corridor. Gunshots cracked above their heads and shattered the glass in a door. Bradley reached through the broken pane and unlocked the door. They hid behind a lab table.

Bradley struck a match from his pocket and held it in the air.

The light it cast revealed a desk filled with rows of bottles of eviscerated fetuses floating in formaldehyde. On the side of each bottle was a Japanese inscription.

"Juvenile diabetes. Muscular dystrophy. Sickle-cell anemia. Hemophilia." Helene read aloud in a horrified voice.

"All childhood diseases!"

"What does it all mean? I'm not sure I understand."

"For some time now, Webb, with the help of Dr. Ran, has been in the business of creating unusual infectious diseases, like bubonic plague, on contract to the Army for its biological warfare unit. At the same time, he's programmed the specific DNA that causes the bubonic plague to create other unusual genetic or metabolic defects. That's why everyone I've seen with bubonic plague has also had either methemoglobinemia or some other bizarre disease. Instead of curing diseases, as any normal pharmaceutical company strives to do, Webb and Ran have been manufacturing new illnesses through the use of recombinant DNA technology."

Bradley pulled Helene down to the ground as a beam of light pierced the darkness.

"So *that's* why he wanted RAI!" Helen whispered with a shudder. "MTI profits have been going down as modern-day diseases have either been cured or eradicated with new discoveries and wonder drugs. And what's the best way to raise profits? Create a whole new set of diseases for which MTI will manufacture a whole new group of genetically engineered drugs."

"And to have these new drugs quickly approved by the FDA would require the talents of a company like RAI." Once Bradley had said it out loud, it all seemed too diabolically simple. "Did you know anything about this?"

Helene made a sound of impatience. "I won't answer that question."

"But you are his financial comptroller."

"And you work for the federal government. If I recall correctly, you even have a military rank. Shall I make you responsible for DOD's bubonic plague?"

"*Touché!*"

The sound of hushed footsteps outside the laboratory made it clear the security guards were cordoning off the area.

"In a few seconds they'll find us," Bradley whispered. "Quick, give me your jacket!"

"My jacket? What are you going to do with it?"

Bradley helped her remove it, then rolled it up in a ball. He grabbed a pathology specimen bottle containing a large quantity of formaldehyde, opened the bottle, and completely soaked the jacket with the liquid.

"What are you doing?"

"Saving our lives."

"Webb will never let us out of here alive," Helene commented grimly.

"No doubt. Once he's finished with Ran, we're next."

"What happened between you and Ran?"

The light came on suddenly. Surrounded by a phalanx of armed security guards, Webb stood in the doorway of the laboratory.

"Dr. Bradley! I was trying to accommodate you and this is the kind of gratitude I get. My vice-president for finances is cowering behind a lab bench fearful that I might attack her and her gallant young—"

"Be careful, Roy. Jealousy doesn't suit you," Helene interrupted coldly.

"If I've learned nothing else from you, my dear, it is the importance of panache. Isn't that right, Helene? Do whatever you do, but do it with style."

Bradley looked around the room. Four security men guarded the door, and three more stood behind them. It was clear Webb had instructed them that he wanted Bradley and Helene alive, or they would have used their weapons by now. Bradley glanced at the steel doors on two sides of the room that led to adjoining laboratories. Three windows overlooked the MTI campus.

"I wouldn't try to escape. The entire building is surrounded by my security guards who, I assure you, are impressive marksmen." Webb paused, appearing to savor the situation. "So! You never did answer Helene's question. What were you and Ran talking about, considering all those goddamn grids were empty?"

Helene flinched and looked at Bradley quizzically.

"He asked me to imagine what different cells would look like at different levels of magnification." Bradley realized there was only one way out of the room; he had to keep Webb talking.

"A T cell at forty thousand?"

"Yes."

"But how could you imagine the difference in morphology between a T cell at fifty thousand and the same cell at forty or thirty thousand?"

"I guess I was born with a vivid imagination." Bradley handed Helene her soaked jacket and, still crouching, scurried around the bench.

"Then can you imagine what a thirty-eight-caliber bullet looks like speeding straight toward your eyes?"

"No. I do static imaging. Nothing more exciting than pathology slides moving to the right or the left." He jumped up and grabbed another specimen jar filled with formaldehyde. A bullet barely missed the top of his head.

"That wasn't very smart, Dr. Bradley. One more stunt like that. . . ."

Bradley crawled back to Helene and pulled the cover from the jar. Their eyes started to tear from the pungent fumes.

"Let's go, Roy," Helene said. "This doesn't serve anybody's purpose." Handing Bradley her jacket, she slowly poured the contents of the jar along the left wall of the room. Two guards silently signaled her position to Webb.

"My dear Helene, you and the doctor are free to go. No one will stop you. I only have a few questions for Dr. Bradley that center around his conversation with Dr. Ran."

"How is he supposed to know what Ran was talking about? He never met Ran before. You introduced them." She crawled back to Bradley, who was busy pouring off the remaining formaldehyde. Time was running out.

Webb motioned to his guards to approach Helene and Bradley cautiously.

"Now there's a clever lady. A real clever lady. You're going to have to keep a close eye on her. She's a lot more shrewd than I will ever be."

Bradley said nothing. He grabbed Helene's hands and they edged slowly to a position in the center of the room, alongside a rusted tank of hydrogen that fed Bunsen burners on top of the lab table. He watched as the guards moved slowly about, encircling the room. No one said anything about the obvious formaldehyde smell. Clearly, Webb was aware of the danger, but if he ordered his men to rush them, he risked the chance of creating a living inferno.

Helene spoke: "Roy, you're making an ass of yourself."

Webb's body stiffened. When he spoke, his voice was clipped. "T cell, neutrophil, sickle cell—what do they mean?"

"That MTI is in the dangerous business of manipulating the genetic code in order to meet its quarterly financial projections."

"You can do better than that, Dr. Bradley. Try again. T, N, S—what would those initials mean?"

"I have no idea!" Bradley lit a match; it blew out.

"Oh, come on! Don't you remember that nice lady bartender at Jack's Bar and Grill? Didn't she tell you where her husband worked, where he contracted the plague, which he passed on to his wife, who for a few dollars passed it on to Dr. Rosen's patient?"

"I don't remember." Bradley struck a second match; again no success. Helene took the book of matches.

"Why are you so stubborn?"

"Leave him alone, Roy! He doesn't know what you're talking about." She lit a third match, but it flamed only for a brief second.

"This is all very touching. But if he didn't know what Ran was talking about, why was he so willing to pretend he saw blood cells that weren't there? And collaborate with a man who had ostensibly murdered his father at Pingfan?" Webb was becoming impatient. He motioned to the guards to allow Ran into the room;

the elderly doctor seemed fine, except for a slight bruise on his cheek.

"You son of a bitch!" Helene couldn't resist a smile.

"It's good to see, Helene, that you still appreciate gamesmanship. My God, Bradley, you certainly are naïve. You don't expect evil men to transform into altruists simply because they feel a little guilty?" Webb chortled.

"And if you don't mind my saying so, Dr. Bradley, you certainly weren't above being an opportunist, taking advantage of my Oriental sense of shame to help you in your vainglorious pursuit of destroying MTI," Ran added.

"Why did you two play out that charade with me?" Bradley asked angrily.

"The famous Chinese military strategist Sun-tzu always counseled that in order to neutralize your opponent, you must first find out through good intelligence what he does or doesn't know about you as his adversary. Then confuse him about the real state of your capability."

"And what did you learn about my knowledge of you, Dr. Ran?" Bradley cupped his hands, providing a cover against the draft that was blowing out the matches.

"That you know about Trans Nippon Shipping," Webb interjected.

"Trans Nippon Shipping?" Helene repeated. She struck another match. This time it didn't extinguish itself.

"Yes, Helene, our MTI subsidiary in Baltimore," Webb replied patronizingly.

"But I thought we sold that off a long time ago!" Helene was incredulous.

"We did—to our overseas partners."

"Overseas partners?" Helene exclaimed. What overseas partners did Webb have? Unless, of course, he was referring to . . .

"Whatever." Webb summarily dismissed her question.

"And those electron microscope magnification numbers that Ran was spouting?" Helene moved closer to Webb.

"Come, come. Think about it. Forty thousand left. Fifty thousand right. Thirty thousand left."

"The combination to a safe. The safe at Trans Nippon Shipping where I would find all the incriminating documents."

"Very good, Bradley," Ran interjected.

"And now?" Bradley lit another match in his left hand. He held it poised. Helene's match was almost used up. It was now or never.

"Well, I'm sorry to say that now you know too much about our operations and exactly what we intend to do," Webb replied menacingly.

"No, I still don't know what you intend to do." Bradley gripped Helene's formaldehyde-soaked jacket tightly.

"Don't tell me you don't know about Project Blood Heat. I happen to know Kimball briefed you on it."

"What about it?"

As Bradley applied the flame, the jacket quickly took light.

Ran spoke: "Please, don't take us for fools. Suddenly you want to know how much we know. Very good, Bradley. You are a quick student. Sun-tzu would be proud of you."

Losing patience, Webb motioned the guards to move in. At once Bradley flung the flaming jacket straight at Webb and, in a single sweep, sent the remaining formaldehyde bottles hurtling to the floor. The room burst into flames.

22

"Jump!" Bradley covered his head with his jacket and grabbed Helene's hand.

"I can't!" She held his hand tightly as the flames approached. The wall of fire petrified her.

"Please, Dr. Bradley, I think we can straighten out any differences we might have." Ran's conciliatory tone of voice was strangely appealing.

Bradley watched Webb, Ran, and two security guards slowly advance, dodging the flames lapping at their legs. He wondered how long it would take the fire to ignite the cylinder of hydrogen fastened to the side of the table.

Within seconds, four security guards burst through the door carrying the emergency fire hose from the glass case in the corridor. As they struggled to turn on the water, Bradley knew he had to act quickly. He unfastened the leather strap around the hydrogen tank and held the tank high in the air, his hand on the valve.

If he turned the valve only slightly to the right, he could release enough hydrogen through the Bunsen burners to blow up the room.

"Don't do it, Bradley!" Webb signaled the guards to remain where they stood.

"Dr. Bradley, you are far too smart a man for such foolish, self-destructive behavior," Ran spoke steadily.

"You're right. But how do I know that after Helene and I are apprehended, we won't be tortured and then neatly disposed of?"

The surrounding flames were receding. In a few more seconds Bradley and Helene would be vulnerable again.

"You have our promise."

"Your promise, Webb? How can you expect me to have faith in a mass murderer?"

"Because of our mutual interests, Bradley, which are strictly scientific, not moral. We live in an imperfect world where injustice and hypocrisy are essential ingredients for productivity."

"Is this Webb's course in Ethics 101?"

"No, just a simple statement of fact. Let's get the hell out of here. That tank is going to blow any minute."

"No one is going anywhere until you tell me about Project Blood Heat."

"You disappoint me, Bradley. You have all the bits and pieces but not the wherewithal to put them together. Blood Heat is a pilot project conducted by the U.S. government to inoculate several million residents of the Washington, D.C., metropolitan area against the bubonic plague, employing the artificially created live vaccine created by Dr. Ran and his team. It's that simple. We use a retrovirus II as a shuttle vector between the *Pasteurella pestis* bacteria and man. Through recombinant gene splicing, we altered a retrovirus II so that through water, air, or oral transmission, the virus could produce a mild plague-like reaction in the human, which would allow the body to build up sufficient immunity to protect itself against a more deadly variant. It's similar to inducing a mild form of chicken pox in a child so he can never contract the disease at a later, more dangerous age."

"Where and when is Project Blood Heat to commence?"

Still dousing the fire, the guards approached cautiously.

"Please, Dr. Bradley, we don't have much time."

"Where and when, Dr. Ran?"

"At the Patuxent water reservoir near Scaggsville, Maryland."

"When?"

"Two A.M. Tonight."

"Tonight? *Merde!* You son of a bitch!" Helene shouted.

"Because of Bradley's meddling, Helene, we just decided to move our timetable up. We can't afford to risk being exposed. Normally, we would have waited three days." Webb was glad Parker had had the foresight at the afternoon meeting to place the military on alert. All that had been required to initiate the project was a simple telephone call.

"Did you think you could get away with both creating and curing the bubonic plague?" Bradley asked as his hand began to move slowly over the rusted valve of the hydrogen cylinder.

"Wait just a minute, Bradley. I never said MTI purposely created the epidemic. Let's talk about DOD, DARPA, Kuzmack, Parker, Squire, Kimball, and some of your pals. DARPA gave us a contract to develop the plague as a weapon for the government. There was an accident during shipment and people around the three major receiving stations started to develop symptoms."

"Around Fort Detrick, Dugway Testing Ground, and Pine Bluff?" Bradley was having a hard time opening the valve.

"Correct."

Suddenly, Ran instructed a security guard to increase the water pressure in the hose and to direct the water at the hydrogen tank. Bradley wrapped his arms around the cylinder just as the jet of water streamed over him and slammed Helene against the wall. With a sudden effort, he turned the gas valve to the right, ready to flee with Helene before the room exploded. Nothing happened. The Bunsen burners were too wet to ignite spontaneously. The flames that had encircled Bradley and Helene and held back the guards disappeared. Bradley took the last dry match in his book, lit one Bunsen burner manually, and threw it on the table. The small blue flame erupted into a blazing incandescent yellow torch.

The smell of burning flesh permeated the room. Bradley and Helene ran through the smoke and confusion. Shots rang out and Bradley dropped to his knees, pulling Helene down with him. Together, they crawled toward a red sign on a metal fire door at the end of the hall marked Authorized Personnel Only. The door refused to open. Helene pushed Bradley toward the stairwell next to it.

As he mounted the steps, Bradley realized he was having a hard time breathing. In the laboratory, he had thought it was the effect of the smoke scorching his lungs. But this shortness of breath was something else: dyspnea, one of the most pronounced symptoms of the plague. He felt warm. Extremely warm. He started to cough. His lymph nodes were beginning to hurt again. He held tightly to the railing as the stairwell began to spin around him. The guards had begun to follow them.

"Are you all right?" Helene ran back down several steps, and supported his body with her shoulder.

"I'll be all right."

She held him, fearful he might fall if she let go.

Bradley forced himself to think: He had to stop the guards. His eyes searched the landing a half flight up for the mandatory wet standpipe and folded water hose.

"Help me to the landing." Bradley circled his arm around her shoulder.

"Christ, you're heavier than you look," she said as she struggled up the steps under his weight.

At the third-floor landing Bradley opened the emergency fire case and began to unfold the hose from its rack. A guard one flight below pulled a revolver from his shoulder holster. Helene held the hose as Bradley loosened the water valve.

The guard fired. Several more guards joined the first, revolvers in hand. Bradley pushed Helene down flat. He kept tugging on the valve, stuck from disuse.

"Why don't we stop this cat-and-mouse game?" Webb's voice

thundered. "It's exhausting all of us." Standing several steps below them, he signaled his guards not to fire. "Helene, tell Russ to give up."

One more turn, thought Bradley. Just one more turn. He could hear the squeak of grinding metal. He mustered all the strength his aching body contained.

"Leave that valve alone and come with me. I guarantee you, no harm will befall either you or Helene. I will show you whatever you're looking for."

"What is Moromi?" Bradley shouted. He needed to keep Webb preoccupied.

Webb's face blanched. He looked disgustedly at Helene.

"No, she didn't tell me." Bradley felt a slight give of the valve.

"Who told you about Moromi?" Webb asked.

"Just before you had my sister killed . . ."

"What did she tell you?" Webb started up the remaining steps.

Suddenly, the valve gave way. The water shot out with such force that it knocked Webb down the flight of stairs and forced the guards off the landing and back into the hallway. Bradley and Helene climbed to the fourth-floor landing and into a long corridor flanked by glass doors.

"Corporate suites. We're approaching the *sanctum sanctorum*," Helene rasped.

Helene led them to Webb's office which, except for the eighteenth-century furniture, looked to Bradley like a wing of the Museum of Modern Art. Over the wainscoting on the walls hung millions of dollars worth of paintings. Bradley recognized a Léger, a Miró, a Kandinsky.

"Ridiculous, isn't it?" Helene sneered.

"No, why?"

"Because there's more value on these walls than in this entire company." She led him through a smaller anteroom, where she would normally wait for Webb to greet her. The plush Persian Isfahan carpet, settee, and dark, brooding oil paintings re-created a distant past. They continued into Webb's inner office.

"What the hell are we doing here?" Bradley protested.

"Lock the door! They'll be here in a few minutes," Helene answered, rifling through Webb's massive mahogany desk.

"What are you looking for?"

"The combination for a safe."

"I don't see a safe."

"You will in a moment," she assured him.

"Show me the safe. I think I know the combination."

"How would you know the combination?" She walked over to the far wall and tapped lightly on a dark-brown wooden panel. She grinned as it separated from the others to reveal a safe.

"Voilà!"

"Merci." Bradley knelt beside her and moved the tumbler once to the left and stopped at four. Then he turned clockwise to five. And then he turned counterclockwise again to three. The safe door opened.

"Hah!" Helene erupted. "We make one hell of a team of safecrackers." She kissed him on the cheek.

"So this is T.N.S., Trans Nippon Shipping!"

"So to speak." She took a handful of documents and started to search through them. "This is where Webb keeps his most private papers, lists of clients, records of business transactions, bills of lading . . ."

"But I thought Webb said T.N.S. was located somewhere in Baltimore."

"It is. That's where the loading docks are located. But the basic paperwork is done in this office by none other than Mr. Roy Webb himself. I suspect he doesn't allow anyone other than Dr. Ran to look at these papers." Webb had done an excellent job of hiding T.N.S. from her, but now all the pieces were falling into place.

"Why do you think Webb allowed Ran to tell me about T.N.S.?" Bradley marveled.

"Exactly for the reason he gave you. Webb is a very clever man. In giving you information, he would be able to read your response as an indication of how much you really knew." She withdrew one paper from the pile. "Here it is."

Bradley grabbed it. The same Oriental character of the beetle that he had seen on Raymond's forearm was the logo on the paper. The bill of lading was written in English.

"This is what you've been looking for," she said soberly.

"What do you mean?"

"That eight-legged beetle is the company logo for Moromi."

"Moromi?" Bradley was suddenly aware of the sounds of the guards searching the corridors and offices. He took the bill of lading. "This paper has a list of names under the heading of Courier: my sister, Alfred Raymond, and Henry Kempe. What did they transport? What is Moromi?" Helene knew more than she was saying.

"We have to leave," she pressed him.

The guards were pushing against the locked doors to Webb's office. Helene led Bradley to a side door hidden behind a medieval wall tapestry of ladies-in-waiting.

"Like all good schemers, Webb could have guests come and go without even his secretary's knowing it." Helene opened the narrow door using a key from Webb's desk.

"I won't ask how *you* knew about the door," Bradley said testily.

"Come on. There will be time for jealousy later."

As the paneling on Webb's office door splintered open under a sharp blow from one of the guards, Helene shut the side door tightly and bolted it from the inside. It was dark, but she knew the way by heart. She had frequently entered Webb's office from the narrow metal stairway parallel to the internal fire exit they had just been on.

Bradley became dizzy walking down the small metal steps. He grasped the center pole around which the stairs were tightly wound. "Are we almost there?"

"A few more yards."

Their footsteps reverberated with a thunderous clang.

"How many more doors to break down?" he kidded her.

"I see your sense of humor is back."

"It's not often I'm saved from danger by a beautiful woman."

"Tais-toi!"

The noise as the guards clanged down the metal staircase was intolerable. When Helene finally opened a door into a brightly lit corridor, Bradley was stunned. As far as his eye could see were cubicles filled with technicians working busily in white laboratory coats, completely oblivious of them.

"Occasionally, I come down here to remind myself what the industrial future will look like," Helene whispered.

Bradley looked more closely. "Everyone working here is Oriental."

Helene nodded. "Here in the basement we have over two hundred Japanese technicians working in shifts around the clock."

"I presume they report directly to Ran?"

"Yes."

Each cubicle contained a conventional Zeiss microscope, a small- and medium-sized Beckman centrifuge, a DNA synthesizer, a few metal chairs, and one lab table. Again, Bradley saw no evidence of increased ventilation capacity or the enlarged airflow hoods that might be needed to rid the air of a pathogenic organism. No one, to Bradley's surprise, was wearing a protective suit. There was no evidence that Webb and Ran were manufacturing pathogens as contagious as *Pasteurella pestis.*

"Down this hall there's an entrance to a tunnel that leads outside. But I'm not certain where it comes out because I've never gone beyond this point."

Bradley took out the bill of lading and examined it again. The letterhead was written in Japanese, as were some inscriptions Bradley suspected had to do with the nature of the cargo. He read the three names written on it. "Listen to this: 'Delivery dates September fourth, September twenty-fourth, October fifth'."

Helene took Bradley's arm, pulling him away from his attempts to decipher the bill, but he persisted.

"This is Moromi, isn't it?"

"The bill comes from Moromi Industries, which according to that letterhead is located on the outskirts of Tokyo."

"So that's where they manufacture the diseases."

"Come on. We can figure this out later on."

"No, wait, Helene! The labs down here must receive shipments from Moromi Industries. They must modify them to make them either less lethal or polyvalent, in order to carry other diseases. All the necessary work is done at Moromi and the *Pasteurella* is shipped here from Japan—it has to be! That's how Judy, Raymond, and Kempe became sick. They personally delivered the highly infectious specimens. It's an ingenious way for the military to skirt the law. They simply have a private company develop the pathogen and manufacture it in an overseas laboratory. It's shipped here for altering and then sent to Fort Detrick or Pine Bluff. No one's the wiser unless something goes wrong—like a sample of bacteria escaping or hundreds of people accidentally dying."

Ahead of them was a closed metal door, with a small control box on the wall containing numbered buttons.

"*Merde!* I don't know the combination of this door."

"One of those technicians must know it."

"No time," Helene said weakly.

Across the room, at the other end of the laboratory, stood Webb and one of his guards.

"Three lousy numbers!" she hissed.

23

Bradley pulled Helene through the small entrance as the steel door automatically closed behind them. With his shoe, he smashed the control box on the wall, making certain the door could not be opened from the other side. They were in a dark, empty tunnel.

"Are you all right?" Bradley looked into Helene's weary eyes and they embraced, ignoring the roar of engines above them.

"Darling, how did you know those three numbers?" she asked.

"Helene, if my instincts are correct, Webb has moved up the timetable on Project Blood Heat, just as he said he would. He must have telephoned Kimball and—"

"No. Enough projects. Enough Blood Heat! Just you and me. Here." She slipped her hands under his shirt. "I'm afraid, Russ." Her body was shaking.

"Shhh! It's all right!" He ran his hand through her thick hair and felt an incredible jolt of passion.

"How did you know?" She gazed at him with infatuation.

"It was a lucky guess."

"Be serious!"

"No, it was."

"I don't believe in lucky guesses." She ran her hands through his hair. "You're too smart. You see more than you say, and you say only little. You are not easily fooled by appearances. In many ways you are quite Oriental . . . perceptive, rigorous, and at times . . . deceptive. Tell me, how did you figure out those three numbers?"

"There is only one way MTI can deliver contagious pathogens and work closely with Dr. Kimball at Fort Detrick, and that is to be connected to the Fort through an underground tunnel. When I was at the Fort two days ago, I discovered a geodesic building—Building One Hundred Eleven—which emitted microwave radiation as well as gamma rays. Yet when I finally got inside, probably at the other end of this very corridor, I saw only a few ordinary labs. So I assumed the radiation was coming from an underground source near Building One Hundred Eleven. Until today I didn't know what would emit such active microwave activity. Now I know—Ran's underground laboratories at MTI. And now I know why a woman I had examined at Walter Reed, with plague-like symptoms and a bizarre miscarriage, entered this building and mysteriously disappeared. She went next door, to Dr. Ran's laboratory, to receive her test dose of *Pasteurella pestis* and be evaluated."

"This is all very interesting, my Sherlock Holmes . . ." Helene circled her arms around his waist and drew him closer to her. "But the number—how did you know the number?"

"If you were a technician and you wanted to move quickly between MTI and Building One Hundred Eleven, what number would immediately come to mind?"

"One-one-one."

"That's what I thought."

"It's a pity we weren't playing the lottery."

"Always dissatisfied. Having your life saved isn't good enough, is it?"

"*Laisse-moi tranquille!*" She playfully nuzzled his cheek.

"We still have to get out of here."

They walked, arms linked, through the long, dark tunnel, which led them past empty laboratories.

"Is this the building in which the Army is producing the plague bacteria?" Helene asked.

"As you know, the plague is normally transmitted by bacteria grown within the bodies of infested rodents. But with the new genetic techniques that Webb has developed, they're able to bypass the rodent stage altogether and harbor the bacterial DNA material in a slow-growing virus that is lethal to man. It's called a retrovirus II. That's what Kimball and his TAG team are about to discharge into the Patuxent River."

They walked up a steep flight of stairs and paused before a closed door. The electrical box next to the door indicated the doors were on manual override. Bradley turned the knob along the front panel and found himself outdoors, in a field in Fort Detrick, looking at the gleaming headlights of a moving convoy of unmarked military trucks.

He threw Helene to the ground, clamped his hand over her mouth, and lay motionless, watching the caravan.

After the trucks had passed, Bradley and Helene made their way to the chain-link fence surrounding Building 111.

"Are we going to report this convoy to the authorities?" Helene was shivering from the cold night air.

"And who would you suggest? The White House advisor Kuzmack? Or the Army's Surgeon General Parker? I don't know who's *not* in on this. There's no way this project could have been undertaken without their knowledge. Either we act now or it will be too late. We have to stop Blood Heat ourselves at the source—a reservoir somewhere around Scaggsville."

"But what if this mobilization isn't Project Blood Heat?"

"Then we have a quiet evening on the Patuxent River."

Opening a gate in the chain-link fence, they crouched behind a six-foot-long tank of propane gas and watched a convoy of M-1 Abrams tanks pass by.

"Look over there—the tank with metal tubes sticking straight up into the air. The barrel is sealed. The surface of the tank is greased. Those two snorkeling tubes make me think that this particular tank is going swimming."

About one hundred feet away from the tank, an Army flatbed truck with a folded metal bridge lying in it started moving. The truck wasn't going any faster than five miles an hour. Bradley calculated they had a good chance to jump on the back without being seen. They could hide behind a part of the bridge once they were on board. For a moment, Bradley's mind flashed back to his Porsche, still parked in the MTI lot. Nothing he could do about that now.

He counted the number of seconds the truck was in darkness, as it passed between lampposts.

"Ten . . . nine . . ." Bradley held Helene's cold hands, rubbing them with his. "Eight . . . seven . . . six . . ."

"Why are you counting?"

"When I say jump—jump!"

As the truck passed into the penumbra of the lamppost, Bradley hoisted Helene onto the back edge of the truck. But as he tried to grab the metal edge, his hands slid off. He ran to catch the tail end of the truck, all too well aware that the tank convoy was not far behind, their treads grinding ominously over the asphalt.

"Grab my hands!" Helene extended her arms toward him.

"If I do, I may pull you off the truck."

"Grab them!" Helene could see his exhaustion. At best, he could only run a few seconds longer. She lay down and braced her shoulders against a steel bolt fastening the bridge to the truck. Bradley's hands grasped her outstretched forearms as her body strained desperately to anchor him. As she pulled him toward her, her arms scraped against the edge of the truck and warm blood instantly oozed forth. It dripped down her wrists and into her hands. She set her face in determination—she couldn't let go.

Finally, his elbow caught a firm place on the end of the truck. Her arms became light again. He was up. She pulled him flat, as a searchlight passed over the truck.

They lay exhausted, listening to the deafening roar of the diesel and the tanks lumbering through the back roads of Maryland.

When Bradley noticed her bleeding, he ripped off the tails of his shirt and used them as bandages. Helene gazed at him adoringly, feeling an emotion she had not experienced since childhood: a sense of wholeness and security because of a man. She ran her fingers over his sweating brow.

"We're falling apart, you and I," he said. They lay side by side, staring at the full moon.

"If for some reason we don't . . ."

Bradley placed a finger on her lips.

"But just in case . . ."

"There is no just in case."

"*Merde!*" She pulled back. "*Toujours le dernier mot.*" She lay face downward on the flatbed.

"Wait a minute! If you're going to insult me . . . *s'il vous plaît, en anglais!*" His broad American accent made her smile. His need to control her made her mad.

Bradley raised up on his left arm and stroked her hair with his right hand. "One moment you're a comrade in arms; and the next, you're in a pout . . ." He turned her over so that she was facing him. In the soft light of the moon she looked beautiful.

"You're moody," he told her.

"I resent that."

"Then what would you call someone who is in love one moment and angry the next?"

"Manic-depressive." She laughed. How absurd, here on this rumbling war machine, to have their own *petite guerre.*

"I prefer the term moody," he insisted. She turned to Bradley and studied his face.

"Are you always so steady and sure of yourself?

"Yes, when I first met you."

"You're making fun of me!" she snapped and turned away.

"Are you afraid?" Bradley pulled her around to face him again.

"Yes."

"Of what?"

"Many things."

"Are you afraid of what will happen to us when we get to the river?"

"Partly."

"Are you afraid of us?"

She looked at him, fearful he might not understand. "You are so tender," she sighed.

"Do you mean tender or innocent?"

"As usual, you're right." She turned away.

"No, please don't! Whatever time we have left, let's talk it out. We can solve whatever problems we might have between us."

"Talk it out? You Americans think that talking out feelings will make everything all right."

"What is it? What's bothering you?" She was hiding something from him. He knew it.

A sudden jolt threw them against the side of the truck. The vehicle had stopped moving. The tanks behind them had also stopped, closing the gap between them and the truck to about thirty feet. Four soldiers carrying M16s walked around the truck with flashlights, examining each of its twenty-four wheels. Bradley pulled Helene back into the darkest shadows of the bridge. He slipped his left hand over her mouth as a soldier shone his flashlight onto the truck bed. The beam of light skirted past them. Bradley relaxed his grip only when the truck started to move again. As soon as the truck seemed to be rolling along at a clip, he released her and they resumed their conversation.

"I'm sorry. I had no other choice." He examined her bandages and found them soaked with blood. He tore new strips from his shirt and tied them around her. He pulled her toward him whispering, "I would never want to hurt you."

"I know . . . but you did."

He flinched. She left very little room for empathy. She was as hard on herself as she was on him. He leaned against a steel beam, gazing at her as the truck bumped along.

"There's so much I want to know about you. What about your mother?" It was an odd question to ask her in the midst of all this danger. But he wanted to share a part of her history so that he could understand something about what he sensed was a troubled soul.

"She died in childbirth. My father, his second wife, and a few nannies here and there raised me."

"You had nannies?"

"At certain points in my father's career we were wealthy. At other times we were—shall I say—poorer. It depended strictly on the fortunes of the market. It was a life of continuous boom or bust, giving me a taste for making money—and a great skepticism about man. At an early age I learned some very basic lessons of life. The first is that we can only trust ourselves. The second is that greed and fear are the two basic motivators of man."

"What about love?"

"Love?" She placed her arms around his neck. "What *about* love?"

"I think it's wonderful when you find it and know how to hold onto it."

"But where does it fit into the everyday world? After work? Before work? On long weekends? On short vacations?"

"Is that a recrimination? Even before you and I have started?" he protested.

"No . . . you asked me about my past, so I tell you about my past, in part by telling what I believe in the present—particularly, what I believe about values that concern you and me."

"And your father? What happened to him?"

"He grew to prosper again, making his fortune in the Orient at a time when everyone thought he was crazy."

"Japan?"

"Japan, Hong Kong, Macao. Even some investments in Canton, on mainland China. But the Communists eventually expropriated those holdings."

"And you?"

"I grew to admire him and love him . . . and hate him."

"For what?"

"For having died inconveniently."

"Inconveniently?"

"Yes. For having a stroke at sixty-two and leaving me and my sisters to the wile and deceit of my stepmother, or whatever she was. I learned a stepmother has no more loyalty or affection by instinct than a common household maid. I left home at fifteen to attend parochial school in Lyons, some two to three hundred miles northwest of Toulouse. I stayed with my aunt, my father's sister, a kindly woman who had a deep affection and respect for me—which, I might add, was not shared by my uncle, who on several inebriated occasions tried to seduce me. I resisted, so I was sent away. This time to make my own fortune on *la Bourse.* I went from the stock market to college, graduate school, Japan, and then MTI. *Voilà.*" She sighed as if having released a great burden. "And you, my fine, innocent American?"

"I'm afraid my life isn't very exciting, compared to yours."

"Every life is exciting, depending on how you paint it."

"I grew up in New York. My father, as you already heard, was a POW of the Japanese at Pingfan. He was a WASP; my mother, a hardworking Italian secretary who loved the Greek classics and named me Orestes. She singlehandedly raised Judy and me, saw to it that we had clean clothes for school and food on the table. She adored her son and neglected her daughter. I went through twenty-five-odd years of schooling with one thought in mind—to become a doctor. But not just any doctor, one of those who could, with a single act, help thousands."

"Epidemiology?"

Bradley nodded his head. "I was well rounded, active in extracurricular activities—soccer, track, debate."

"And life?"

"If you mean love . . ."

Helene smiled.

"I have known none," he said. "Perhaps now . . ."

She placed her index finger on his lips. "You've never married?"

"You already know that."

"I simply want to make sure."

"As much as I love my nieces, I never found a woman with whom I wanted to spend the evening just lying on a sofa doing nothing."

"That's a very domesticated picture of life you paint."

"It is. But I am by nature the least domesticated type of animal. Perhaps that's why I never got married."

His profession was all Bradley possessed, Helene realized as she reached over to kiss him. He stopped her with a hand to her chin.

"I think we're slowing down."

The sound of diesel engines had died down. He could hear water rushing in a cascade. Soldiers were jumping down from their vehicles. Men barked orders and blew whistles. The truck stopped. Suddenly, the tank's lights were on them.

"Both of you, raise your arms slowly."

24

Marine and Army soldiers from the Combined Action Platoon, armed with M16 assault rifles, started to build a defense perimeter around the convoy of tanks, jeeps, and trucks. Helicopters hovered overhead, beaming their searchlights across the wooded areas for intruders. At another time, Bradley would have savored the scene like a child playing a game of war with his toy soldiers. Now, he was preoccupied by only one concern—to prevent Webb and the military from disseminating retrovirus II into the water supply, even if it meant destroying the power station.

"Come on down, Russ, Helene!"

Bradley recognized the voice. "Is that you, Kimball?"

"Yeah! You know you shouldn't be here! This is a restricted zone." Drake and Williams flanked Major Kimball, dressed in camouflaged protective gear. He turned to them. "Start assembling the binary bomb for the reservoir. But first make the necessary adjustments on the venturi meter and the flocculation basin."

As they marched away, Kimball shouted after them, "And remember, don't get yourself caught in the goddamn rapid mixer!"

"You're making a big mistake!" Bradley spat at him. "Don't put that retrovirus into the water!"

He skirted behind Helene and tried to unwrap a black adhesive band around some steel cables. If he could only twist one of the cables into a knot, he could knock out the searchlight.

A burst of bullets was fired above their heads from what sounded like a sixty-millimeter machine gun mounted on top of the bridge tank.

"Ezra, tell your gun-happy crew to cool it! They might accidentally kill someone," Bradley said coldly. With one hand he struggled to pry open a metal box marked USMC 1st Engineer Battalion.

"Come on down, then. No one has to get hurt," the ominous voice from the tank continued. "Slowly raise your arms high into the air and walk over to the edge of the truck. All in very slow motion. Do you understand me?"

Bradley tugged at the latch. A little more effort and it would give.

"Move very slowly," Bradley whispered. "Buy me some time."

Helene stood up with difficulty, as if her leg had been severely hurt. She counted ten long seconds before she started moving forward to the edge of the flatbed.

With a sudden jerk, Bradley released the latch and opened the metal box. He picked up a handful of four-inch bolts and threw them at the light. It shattered.

In the darkness he and Helene jumped off the truck and ran toward a thicket in the woods.

"Someone get an auxiliary light source here!" Kimball shouted. He was furious. He should have suspected Bradley would try something like this. "Fan out over the area. Find them before it's time to start." He used his ICPCS radio to communicate with Parker, who was waiting for him at the reservoir, informing him that Helene and Bradley had escaped into the woods.

Bradley and Helene ran through an uncultivated field toward the woods bordering the Patuxent River. Above them three Hueys crisscrossed their searchlights on the ground. It was the sound of the occasional bullets fired overhead that was most frightening. Helene held Bradley tightly as they hid under a clump of bushes.

"Scared?" She could feel his body quiver.

"Only if I breathe, walk, or run."

"At least you've still got your sense of humor."

"I can't be too upset when I finally have an opportunity to get this close to you."

She tightened her grip around him, suddenly exhilarated by this unexpected expression of his desire. And, just as suddenly, a momentary wave of guilt rose within her. She looked at the helicopters flying overhead, and the full protection of the woods only two hundred feet away.

"Russ," she whispered anxiously, "I have to tell you . . ."

A helicopter hovered almost directly overhead.

"It's about Ran . . . and . . ." She hesitated. She wanted to tell everything. But the more she wanted to, the less she was able to. *Sauve qui peut!*

"What about Ran?" Bradley demanded.

The helicopter flew away, only to start another pass toward them. Bradley watched nervously as tiny yellow bolts of light erupted from the machine gun.

"Helene, it will have to wait . . . Let's get out of here."

Bullets hit the ground only a few feet away from them. They ran across the field until they saw soldiers combing the woods. With a helicopter behind and soldiers in front of them, it seemed impossible to get to the river without being caught.

Webb and Ran checked their watches. In fifteen minutes the retrovirus II would be disseminated into the reservoir. They stood nervously next to the flocculation basins and the revolving paddle mixers. Above were two large metal containers and the rapid mixer. Below the containers was a concrete sedimentation basin where dirt-laden floc settled out and clean water was removed from its surface through perforated troughs.

Parker, seated on top of his M-1 Abrams Tank, was dressed in combat fatigues. A dead panatela hung from his mouth in clear defiance of the laws of gravity as he surveyed the field of battle. To the northwest, his First Battalion engineers were setting down metal braces for the TMM bridge-setting trucks. To the right of that, the flatbed truck was backing into the Patuxent River, slowly discharging its contents. On the eastern flank, he watched the M-1 Abrams tanks, fitted with snorkeling tubes, crossing the wide banks of the Patuxent River.

On his western flank, he knew that Squire was supervising a platoon of Marines unloading a truckload of metal boxes marked *Dangerous.* Below this warning, each box was marked with the name of a chemical: lime, ferric chloride, polymer chlorine, carbon, or potassium permanganate. Individually, they were important ingredients required for the purification process of water. Mixed together, they were highly combustible. Anyone with an elementary sense of chemistry could use them to create a Molotov cocktail.

"Sir, we've lost them." Kimball walked briskly up to the tank and saluted Parker.

"How the fuck could you lose a woman running in high-heeled shoes and a flabby-waisted civilian whose greatest exercise in life is to turn his wrist to start his Porsche!"

"I'm sorry, sir." Kimball didn't want to correct Parker. Helene wasn't wearing high-heeled shoes, and both Helene and Bradley were in good physical shape. But this was not the moment to argue. Parker was not only acting as the Army's surgeon general and principal medical officer on the scene, but also as chief of operations. Kimball was well aware of the consequences if he forgot Parker was not only his medical superior, but also his operational superior.

"Sorry? Sorry? My mamma is sorry when she can't have a bowel movement. My girlfriend is sorry when she can't make me come. Two civilians escaping from your alleged custody is a poor excuse for being sorry." The ashes from his cigar fell on the tank. He took out a match to relight.

"Major, would you be so kind as to inform those two gentlemen over near the rapid mixer to come over here. I would like to talk to them."

"Yes, sir!"

Kimball jogged briskly to the mixer and returned with Webb and Ran.

"Doesn't this remind you of the battle for Pingfan?" Parker looked contemptuously at Ran, who appeared distraught. Chasing scientists in the middle of the night was not precisely what Ran had envisioned. Had anyone asked him, he would have preferred to let Helene and Bradley go, and return to his laboratory.

Webb was furious. "This should never have happened, Joe. Never!"

Instead of answering, Parker turned toward Kimball. "Check on your TAG team."

When Kimball was out of earshot, Parker turned back to Webb and hissed, "Where the hell do you get off telling me I screwed up, Captain Webb? This isn't Pingfan. I don't have all these goddamn men here at your disposal. They happen to be serving in the U.S. Army and Marines."

"You've been playing soldier too long, Parker."

Ran smiled. It had been a long time since he had seen these two men argue. It pleased him. He was surprised to see how much each man genuinely disliked the other, despite their forty-year relationship.

"This evening I got a call from you that Helene and Bradley have detailed knowledge about Project Blood Heat." Parker paused, trying to contain himself. "Not only do you and your so-called security men allow them to escape, but you arm them with classified information about the time, place, and reason for the project. Then you have the gall to inform me that we can't postpone Blood Heat for one minute longer. So within an hour's time of your call we are fully mobilized. And now you accuse me of being incompetent because they happened to escape from one of our military vehicles, which they wouldn't have been on had they not escaped from MTI in the first place."

"Sir, we have a slight problem." Kimball raced back toward Parker. "There's a problem with the internal ignition mechanism."

Webb checked his watch as they ran down to the flocculation basins. Only ten minutes left. Had he pushed the system beyond its capabilities by insisting on moving the project up three days?

They watched as Drake and Williams put on their fire-rated protective asbestos coveralls and strapped their auxiliary oxygen tanks to their backs. If the TAG team couldn't make the binary weapon ignite now, then Blood Heat would have to be postponed. The risk that Bradley would then be able to stop the project indefinitely and initiate a full-scale federal investigation was too high—and unacceptable.

"Explain the problem to Mr. Webb and Dr. Ran," Kimball ordered. He glanced nervously at his watch and then at Parker.

Webb inserted himself between Drake and Williams for a better look at the binary weapon. As far as he could determine, it was a simple artillery shell with a small aluminum partition in the middle. Upon ignition by a small fuse cap, it allowed two nontoxic compounds contained in separate plastic containers to join together to produce a toxic compound. The weapon had been tailored to the specific needs of the project by combining binary and delivery systems all in one.

"As you see, Mr. Webb, this is a modified U.S. Army one-hundred-fifty-five-millimeter VX projectile," Williams began as he adjusted the explosive cap. "Major Kimball, is it all right to discuss the intricacies of the dispersal system?"

"I insist on it, young man," Parker responded. "These gentlemen developed the microorganism. Maybe they will know what's wrong with this shell. Continue!"

"Yes, sir! The projectile will be shot out of this modified one-hundred-fifty-millimeter howitzer into the reservoir, where sixty-five percent of its payload up to twenty meters around impact will be dispersed into the air, and then fall into the water. It carries the dried form of your microorganisms that have been preserved using antioxidants."

"Desiccated alpha-tocopherols?" Even Ran had been amazed to discover how an item as common as vitamin E in powdered form could preserve the integrity of a dried mixture of pathogens.

"Mr. Webb, I would caution you not to touch any of the parts inside this shell."

Webb looked sharply at Drake. Had she worked for him, she would have been fired for the way she had said that.

"Please open the two blue plastic containers," Webb ordered. Drake looked toward Kimball for approval. Webb suspected the problem had more to do with the powdered form in which the pathogens were delivered than any particular problem with the mechanics of the shell. His guess was affirmed when Drake unfastened two clips on the side of the box and Webb looked at the inside.

"Just as I suspected. It's clumped together, probably from moisture condensing in the shells."

"We have ten minutes to go, Roy," Parker cut in. "Can we make it work?" Too many things were going wrong, he thought. Bradley, Helene—and now this.

"Ran, I need an anti-agglomerant," Webb ordered hurriedly. He stared at the Japanese doctor; he was concerned about Ran's distracted look.

"Where am I going to get colloidal silica out here at this time of night?" Ran complained. He never trusted U.S. military efficiency; the series of mishaps only reaffirmed how inept Americans really were.

"What if we break some glass and pulverize a very small piece of it?"

"It would contaminate the sterile atmosphere of the retrovirus."

"The area is already contaminated. It will still work." Webb was impatient.

"Gentlemen, may I remind you time is passing. Tell me whether to give the order to abort." Parker chewed nervously on his cigar.

"You can't!" Webb barked.

"Excuse me, Mr. Webb, but would this help you any?" Drake reached into her coverall pockets and pulled out a brown plastic powder compact. Inside was dry, pink face powder—loaded with silicon!

Webb delicately touched the face powder with his index finger and rubbed it over the container. He smiled. "Now it should work!"

"Eight minutes left. Let's go!" Parker motioned Kimball to position his troops accordingly.

One hundred yards away! Bradley and Helene could see the Patuxent River through a small clearing bisecting the woods. As Helene stopped to catch her breath, a helicopter emerged from the darkness of the night with its searchlight glaring like a cyclops. But the helicopter did not pass by them. It hovered in place for thirty seconds until the pulsating beat of its blades lowering to the ground created a gust of wind and dirt that almost knocked them over.

"I can't go on! I'm too exhausted!" Helene's voice was drowned out by the clamor of the landing helicopter.

A glow of bone-white light exploded above their heads, illuminating the turquoise night. For a split second, soldiers in helmets and thick flak jackets were visible, jumping from the helicopter.

Helene tried to move. Toward the clearing! Toward the river! She had willed her mind to forget the moment's fear. But her legs did not respond.

Bradley slapped her across the face.

"Helene! The soldiers are all around us! Helene! We have to run." His voice was strained with fatigue. But the more he screamed, the more remote and glassy-eyed she became. Tracer bullets streaked above their heads. Falling to the ground, Bradley could smell the grass in the wind of the landing chopper. Helene sat transfixed by the sight of the soldiers jumping from the huge machine.

Run! Save yourself! Looking at Helene's face, frozen in a catatonic stare, Bradley felt love and pity.

He glanced toward the helicopter and realized the soldiers were crawling on their bellies, rifles raised slightly above their heads. He still had a few more seconds. Holding the back of Helene's head with his left hand, he made his right hand into a fist and bored his knuckles into the upper part of the orbit of her right eye, where a facial nerve crosses the supraorbital crest. It was an old trick he had used in the emergency room during internship.

"Come on! Helene! Wake up!" Bradley couldn't see the soldiers anymore, except for an occasional glint of light reflecting from the barrel of a rifle. Any time now he would be jumped by one of those charcoal-faced Marines.

"Ahhh! Stop it! You're hurting me!" Helene pulled his hand from her face.

Bradley pulled her suddenly alert body up and, supporting her under her arms, started to run. Her legs were wobbly, her balance was off and she seemed confused. But somehow she trusted Bradley's direction.

"Stop or we'll fire!" Four Marines stood in the grass, their M16s with infrared night vision scopes pointed at Bradley's back.

Bradley and Helene did not stop. Bullets kicked up dirt behind their heels as they ran on to the edge of a steep ravine, covered with bushes and small trees, that led directly to the edge of the Patuxent River. Like children on a playground, they coiled themselves up tightly and rolled down the hill.

"Six minutes to countdown! Assume designated positions!" The authoritative voice came over mobile loudspeakers scattered throughout the area.

The fugitives ignored the bruises on their hands and knees and ran along the banks of the river, staying very close to the treeline. When Bradley could no longer see any soldiers, they slowed down to catch their wind, and hid in the shadow of a tree trunk. About three hundred feet away, they could see tanks, flat trucks, and the outline of the water-purification plant. A group of men huddled near the rapid mixer.

"Ran, Webb, and Parker are over there," Bradley whispered to Helene. "And there's Kimball, the guy who shouted at us to get off that truck. He's head of the bacteriological warfare unit, and the man directly responsible for Blood Heat."

"Five minutes to countdown." The voice on the loudspeaker resonated throughout the wooded area.

They moved quickly toward the water-purification plant.

"See those containers?"

"Four minutes to countdown." The voice on the loudspeaker blared.

"Stay here."

"What am I supposed to do?" asked Helene.

"Pray that I can stop this insanity." He bent to kiss her, then stopped, remembering the time bomb ticking away in his bloodstream. "I was never very good in chemistry. If something should happen to me, I want to be certain that you come out of here alive. I want you to explain to Engel and the press what happened here tonight."

"Someone is over there!"

They watched as the flat truck moved back and forth, discharging its folded bridge into the water. Engineers dressed in combat fatigues directed the unloading. Twenty to thirty feet to the right, the canisters of lime, ferric chloride, polymer chlorine, carbon, and potassium permanganate awaited the proper ignition setting. All Bradley needed was to divert everyone's attention from the canisters of chemicals. He had exactly three minutes to run the fifty-foot distance toward the canisters, ignite the chemicals, and then flee. Just possible!

"Do you have a match?"

Helen took a book of matches from her shirt pocket.

"May I?" Bradley lifted her skirt and tore two strips of cloth from her cotton slip. He took one strip of the slip, lit it, and threw it into a clump of dry bushes.

"Old, but reliable."

He ran along the water's edge to the flat truck as a group of soldiers headed toward the burning foliage. Parker, Kimball, and Ran scurried behind.

"Three minutes to countdown. Prepare for delivery."

Crouching behind the flat truck, Bradley calculated that if he put lime, potassium permanganate, and polymer chlorine in a confined area and ignited them, he would create an incredible explosion. He looked around for a small container to put the chemicals in, but saw nothing acceptable. Not even a discarded bottle.

"Two minutes."

"Shit! This is going to be tougher than I thought," he whispered to himself. He had to ignite those chemicals either with friction . . . heat . . . Suddenly, he ran to the truck, opened the fuel tank, and pushed the second strip of cloth into the gasoline. When it was completely soaked, he removed it.

"One minute to countdown . . ."

Bradley hurried to the container marked Lime and dropped the cloth inside. Then he saturated the cloth with a chlorine compound.

"Fifty seconds."

Carrying the saturated cloth, he rushed back to the gasoline tank and ignited the entire book of matches. The strip of cloth burst into a white-hot flame, the kind of flame he knew could do the trick. He was extremely careful, keeping the cloth at a safe distance from his body.

"Forty seconds."

Bradley threw the burning cloth into the tank.

"Thirty seconds."

"Run, Helene, run! Don't look back!" Bradley shouted to her.

"Twenty seconds."

She ran as fast as her tired legs would take her.

"Ten seconds to countdown."

"Nine seconds."

A ball of light flashed into the night sky. Only the truck's four axles remained intact. A second, even brighter explosion lit up the blackness.

Helene turned and covered her eyes with her hands. Tears were streaming down her cheeks.

25

“Williams, get some water on Drake. Stat! Williams, do you hear me? Isn’t this enough action for you, Williams?” Kimball screamed into his portable R54CA radio pack. He watched nervously as Williams tried to beat out the fire that had spread uncontrollably as Drake inserted the modified VX projectile into the basin. The napalm flames were too fierce. Williams rolled Drake on the ground, trying to rip off her auxiliary oxygen before the flames climbed up her back. Kimball wasn’t prepared to stand by helplessly. Covering his face with a handkerchief doused with canteen water, he rushed from behind the tank through the flames encircling his team.

A voice boomed out over the ICPCS. “Command Center? This is General Parker. We’ve got a fire raging out of control at the reservoir and no available water.”

Absurd! thought Webb. Water not less than fifty feet away, but not a drop for fire control. He looked disdainfully at Parker.

His only thought was to find Bradley and make certain he was dead. "Come with me, Ran! We have some business to finish." Webb picked up the M16 Kimball had discarded.

"I think I will stay with General Parker. I may be of some assistance."

"I'm not asking you, I'm telling you . . ." Webb pointed his rifle threateningly.

"You ain't goin' nowhere, Webb," Parker interrupted. "That's a goddamn inferno out there. You're stickin' right here by my side. This isn't Pingfan. I'm runnin' the show here."

"I see how well you're running the show," Webb sneered. With Ran at his side, he started toward the river.

"Where the hell do you think you're going?"

"We've got some unfinished business." Beyond the burning truck, Webb had seen some movement. If Bradley was still alive . . .

"Jesus Christ!" Parker yelled into the portable phone, "Get me an on-target strike of bromacil!"

Webb motioned forward with the muzzle of his M16. He and Ran covered their faces with water-soaked handkerchiefs and crept down the riverbank. The fire would probably get a lot worse before it got better. An on-target strike meant that the helicopters would soon be dropping a fire retardant, bromacil.

Kimball struggled to undo Drake's belt, avoiding the contorted face peering at him through her fire-resistant plastic visor.

Drake was sweating. Tears welled in her eyes. Her lower lip was bloodied with biting. She was doing everything she could to avoid screaming in agony or passing out.

Kimball was having difficulty with the metal buckle fastening the tank to her clothes. The heat had swollen its release mechanism.

"Please, sir . . ." Drake didn't have to finish the sentence.

"Hush, girl, I'm not getting myself all charcoaled up for a lousy Purple Heart."

Williams was busy smearing moist soil over the tank to cool it down, hoping it would not explode from the intense heat.

Kimball was desperate. There was no way to unfasten the

oxygen tank. The flames were approaching her midriff, and no air was coming into her hood. Under the fiery napalm-like substance she was slowly suffocating. In the distance he saw a Huey helicopter with a copper tank mounted on its side. Bromacil!—standard operating procedure for fires secondary to chemical or biological warfare accidents. But there was a heavy price to pay.

Drake quickly understood Kimball's dilemma. If he and Williams continued to struggle with her oxygen, all three risked being blown up if her tank exploded. If Parker signaled the Huey to drop the bromacil, the fire would be squelched, but they might all die. Within four minutes, bromacil could eradicate fifty percent of the people who inhaled it. And water, although it was only fifteen yards away, would not extinguish the flames. There was only one thing left to do. Summoning all her strength, Drake kicked Kimball away and ran toward the burning truck. Her protective suit was completely ablaze.

"No! Stop!" Kimball and Williams hid behind an M-1 Abrams tank as Drake jumped into the flames and the truck exploded in a blinding flash of light.

The hovering Huey dropped the bromacil on the fire.

Bradley turned his face away and rested his head against the cool, wet sedimentation basin, grateful to be alive. He felt for the piece of paper he had stuffed into his pants pocket, and reread the Japanese and English words.

"Why don't you just hand that thing back to me!" Webb's M16 was aimed at Bradley's chest. Ran stood by his side.

"I won't ask you again."

Bradley continued to clutch the paper and glanced down at it to read one line: Moromi Industries, Noda, Japan.

"Dr. Bradley, please believe me when I say that I am sorry this has come about." Ran's voice sounded genuinely apologetic.

"How am I supposed to interpret that comment, as an Oriental act of contrition?"

"No, simply as my humble desire to assure you that I have had nothing but great personal respect for your professional work . . . and for you."

"Ran, Dr. Bradley is right. Please spare us all this unnecessary sentimentality. And please hand over the paper, Russ. I don't think you'll need it anymore."

"Is Moromi where you manufacture the retrovirus II?"

"What difference does it make to you now?" Webb stretched out his arm to receive the bill of lading.

"I'm extremely curious. That's why I became a clinical epidemiologist."

"Very touching." Webb drew back his hand and cocked his rifle. The bill of lading fell to the ground. A rustling sound made him spin around. "Who's there?" No response. Webb fired off a burst in the direction of the sound. "Move over in front of me, Bradley, away from the basin."

Instead, Bradley rushed Webb. As Webb swung the barrel of the rifle up to defend himself, Ran grabbed the barrel without warning and a burst of gunfire sprayed the trees.

"You stupid son of a bitch!"

Bradley fell on top of Webb, trying to peel his hands off the metal stock of the M16. Bleeding from his left shoulder, Ran clenched Webb's right fist and swung it around, throwing Webb off balance. Bradley grabbed the gun as Webb fled into the darkness of the riverbank, leaving Ran lying wounded on the ground.

"Don't shoot!"

The familiar female voice startled Bradley. As Helene emerged from the woods, he rushed to embrace her. "Are you all right?"

"Except for a lot of fear and worry about you, I'm all right." She examined his face. "Are you all right?"

"Yes. What happened to you?"

"As I ran along the riverbank I saw that horrible explosion and I knew I couldn't leave you. I had to know what happened."

Overhead a Huey began to descend.

"If you flee, they will think you are the culprits," Ran gasped from where he lay on the ground clutching his shoulder. "Don't run. Not before you've explained everything to Parker and Kimball."

"Why? They were Webb's partners in crime."

"Partners—yes! Crime—no!"

Ran's response was drowned by the roar of the helicopter landing in a clearing. Holding Uzi machine guns, Kimball and Parker jumped off the helicopter while it was still several feet above the ground. Five Marines followed them and fanned out across the area.

"Drop that gun, Bradley!" Kimball cocked his Uzi.

"Take it easy! I'm not going anywhere." He dropped the rifle.

"Major, this man is seriously injured," Helene said.

Kimball kicked the M16 aside and motioned for a Marine medic to examine Ran. In less than ninety seconds the private had set up an IV bottle of D5W suspended from a metal pole, with a one-inch butterfly needle inserted into Ran's forearm.

"Please, Major Kimball . . . General Parker. I don't deserve your help. I have made some foolish choices."

"Save your energy, Ran. You'll soon be in a field hospital."

Kimball instructed a Marine to get a stretcher, and told the remaining three, "You keep an eye on this man and woman. Don't let them out of your sight."

Parker turned to Bradley with disgust. "Apparently, the FBI has a search warrant out on you." He felt an urge to pull the trigger of his Uzi.

"Helene and Dr. Bradley must go. They haven't . . ." Ran coughed up specks of blood as he spoke.

"Sir, his BP is falling fast." The medic unwound his sphygmomanometer.

Kimball looked at Ran's pallid face. "What are the vital signs?"

"Eighty over fifty; pulse one hundred ten, irregular."

"You'll bounce back good as new." Kimball lied. "Just let us get you out of here."

A Marine directed Bradley and Helene toward the waiting helicopter.

"Joe, you're in deep shit . . . when the press gets hold of this," Bradley hissed angrily.

"Don't threaten me, Bradley! You're in no position to threaten me or anyone else. Not after you've blown up a major part of the reservoir and killed one soldier!"

"Screw you, Parker!" Bradley went for Parker's throat but was restrained by a Marine. Another secured Helene.

"Joe, you're engaged in the manufacture, production, and testing of biological weapons in total violation of U.S. law." Bradley paused to regain his composure and then continued, "Project Blood Heat was nothing less than the attempted genocide of innocent Americans so you could test a new type of bubonic plague that doesn't require rats or fleas, only a genetically altered retrovirus II, contaminating everything in its path."

"Dr. Bradley, you have only half the story." Ran was having a hard time speaking. His breathing was rapid and shallow.

"Dr. Ran, how am I supposed to believe you? One moment you're with Webb. The next moment you're against him."

Parker was impatient. He walked over to a Marine who had appeared carrying a portable radio on his back. "Tell FBI Agent McDonald we have Dr. Orestes Bradley in our custody." He looked at Bradley with contempt. He certainly wasn't going to let anyone intimidate him, least of all a public health epidemiologist. "Yes . . . tell him . . . we'll keep Bradley until he arrives . . . twenty minutes? . . . Understood."

"Thanks, Joe!" Bradley spat as he tried to pull away from the Marine restraining him.

"Obstructing justice, first-degree murder, destruction of federal property . . . violation of the national security laws—I could have you up before a military court-martial. But quite frankly, it's a lot easier letting the FBI do the dirty work."

"You mean you don't think any of your own dirty linen will be aired in a civil court?"

"That's a reasonable assumption. Although a bit more blunt than I would have stated it."

"Joe, every minute you keep us here means more people will die. We have to stop Webb."

Helene, with her captor in tow, walked over to where Ran

lay. She wiped the perspiration from his brow. "Tell him what you and Webb were doing—"

Bradley interrupted: "while you, Parker, were deploying Project Blood Heat as a means of testing new biological weapons."

Parker spat out the tip of his cigar. "Wait just a minute, son. That's not what Project Blood Heat was or is about!"

Bradley and Helene looked at each other.

"Project Blood Heat was developed as an experimental model for treating and preventing the bubonic plague."

"Treating and preventing the bubonic plague? Come on!"

"Well, Dr. Bradley, I know this may come as quite a shock to you, but the military does not only maim and kill. Project Blood Heat was designed to counteract a plague that had mysteriously infected the civilian population."

"While at Fort Detrick you guys were manufacturing the plague for a new bacteriological weapon."

"I resent that, Bradley!" Kimball interjected angrily. "You saw our laboratory facilities. We don't even have the capability."

"But the greatest concentration of bubonic plague and miscarriages was around the three centers—Detrick, Dugway, and Pine Bluff."

The medic injected ten cc of quinidine sulfate into Ran's IV tube to stop his premature ventricular contractions. "Major, we've got to get him out of here soon. Otherwise . . ." he shook his head.

"What we did was to contract out for its manufacture through Squire and DARPA, to MTI. The protocol was to use the latest and safest techniques to treat a plague-like disease—one that could be used defensively, not offensively." Kimball turned his head toward the distant sound of an incoming helicopter. Behind him, the Marine arrived with a stretcher.

"And you used a retrovirus II rather than the conventional bacteria, *Pasteurella pestis*."

"Correct! No one had ever seen the newly created retrovirus II."

"Then where did the bubonic epidemic begin?"

"I can't answer that because I honestly don't know." Kimball was not defensive. "But once we saw an epidemic coming down the road, we worked on prevention. And discovered that an initial dose of the bubonic plague in the form of retrovirus II could cause the disease in a small percentage of the population at once. If it didn't kill you within forty-eight hours, it could give you immunity for life."

As Kimball talked, Parker bit tightly on his cigar and began searching the awakening skies for the approaching helicopter.

"So if I had been injected with a needle infected with retrovirus II carrying bubonic plague, and didn't die within two days, I could assume I was inoculated for life? Like chickenpox?"

"It depends on the dose and the strength of your immune system. Many people have died because their immune systems weren't strong enough to resist the retrovirus II. But, if you've been able to survive an exposure to the retrovirus II with only minimal symptoms—slight fever, a few aches and pains, and some swollen lymph nodes—then it's a good bet you'll be okay. It's all a matter of degree."

Bradley glanced at Helene reflexively. Instead of sealing his fate, Janet's needle had protected him against future infection.

"Just like the oral Sabin polio vaccine—drink an attenuated polio virus—except on a more massive scale . . ." From the beginning, Parker had been sold on the beautiful efficiency of the project.

"But without anyone's permission or knowledge, Joe . . . don't forget that!" Bradley interjected.

"True. But tell me how we could have explained to the public, given such a short lead time—almost none, as a matter of fact—that we wanted to try an experimental inoculation program that hadn't been tested for the requisite two-year period and did not have FDA approval. We didn't have the luxury of time that you folks do to develop a full-scale program. And at the incredible speed the epidemic was traveling, thousands would die if not given the same disease in a milder, safer form."

"Are you telling me the military had no intention of creating a bubonic plague?"

"Why would we?" Kimball checked Ran's vital signs as he spoke. They were improving: Baseline, normal—90/60. Pulse, regular—100.

"For the same reasons the military conducted experiments in the 1950s and 1960s, disseminating bacteria and viruses through the New York City subway system to determine how easy it would be to poison a city."

Parker exploded: "My God, but you have an overactive imagination, Bradley! We're not talking 1950s—we're talking now. And this operation had nothing to do with creating an epidemic to study its effects on the general population." He paced back and forth, frustrated that McDonald's helicopter was taking so long.

"Believe me, Russ," Kimball came to Parker's defense, "the operation was covert because there was no other way. The first part of the protocol called for developing and storing the bubonic retrovirus as a potential defensive weapon, as well as a vaccine. Within the strictest definition of the law we were running a legal operation as long as we subcontracted to a private concern. The second part involved a slightly illegal procedure, which under more propitious conditions would not have been necessary—covertly disseminating a potentially lethal disease in order to inoculate an entire population of civilians. But I assure you, under no conditions did we intentionally or unintentionally start a bubonic plague. Our intentions here are to protect the American public. We want to get U.S. capabilities on a par with the known CBW capabilities of the Soviets." For the first time, he realized how much he wanted someone with Bradley's integrity to know the true story of Project Blood Heat.

Bradley was hardly satisfied. He wasn't going to let Kimball weasel out of his accountability in running a rogue operation just because he was holding the American flag and waving it. "What about the birth defects? The hemophilia? Where does that fit into your protocol?"

"Perhaps there was an accident in the shipment of our retrovirus."

"What do you mean?"

"I don't know what I mean. We were extremely careful. Checking, double-checking. All the shipments we received were tightly sealed."

"Let's go back to my first question. If you didn't start the epidemic, who did?"

"Webb." Ran's faint voice rose from where he lay. He was trying to pull himself up onto his elbows. "He developed a new bacteriological weapon against which there were no effective defenses, hoping it would enable him to receive an endless number of military contracts. I have been working on such weapons for him for years. Webb created an 'accident' at Fort Detrick, Dugway Proving Ground, and Pine Bluff, and the disease spread. The military believed their negligence was the cause of the spread of the disease. Webb is clever. He knows how to take advantage of the need for a swift cure for the impending disease."

"What do you mean?" Parker nervously lit another cigar.

"Webb needed to raise revenues for MTI. He realized he could use Project Blood Heat, through the retrovirus, to create new and different diseases like the ones you uncovered—hemophilia in girls and methemoglobinemia—for which he is prepared to develop the cure, using genetic engineering. The old diseases have long been cured. How successful can a pharmaceutical company be if there is no need for drugs? But, for some time now, I could no longer support his efforts in disseminating the plague into a population of innocent people—or in creating new diseases. I had serious doubts even while I was operating on Dr. Wilson. But, believe me, Dr. Bradley, even my own inexcusable actions were far more humane than what Webb wanted for him. I performed three operations on Wilson so that I would have a legitimate professional reason to keep him hospitalized at Bethesda as long as possible. Otherwise, Webb would have had him killed sooner. I had no other choice."

"You are telling us that he purposely developed a new disease population to create a need for a new generation of genetically engineered drugs?"

"Correct." Ran lay back, exhausted.

"How could you be a part of it?"

"Webb and I struck a bargain more than forty years ago, at Pingfan. If I worked exclusively for him creating bacteriological weapons, he would not press war crimes charges against me or my colleagues. He promised to destroy all records of Pingfan if we worked together. MTI is the result. He has held us hostage for forty years."

Kimball injected another bolus of quinidine sulfate. Ran's heart was throwing off ten PVCs per minute—dangerously close to total cardiac collapse.

"Thank you, Dr. Kimball," Ran said weakly, "but a dying man should have one last wish . . . and mine is to ask this young man . . . Bradley . . . to forgive."

Tears welled in Bradley's eyes. How could he forgive the man who had killed both his father and his friend?

"So Webb created the epidemic to further his own business interests!" Parker was stunned. He had been played the fool after all.

"Joe, let us go!" Helene pleaded as the Chinook helicopter, a behemoth structure with billowed sides, slowly descended in a deafening roar to the ground.

"I can't! I can't!" Parker shouted through the noise.

"Let us go, or we'll go to the press," she threatened.

"That's blackmail!"

"Joe! There's no time. My silence for our freedom." Everyone watched as the wheels of the helicopter touched ground.

"Joe, you could have stopped Webb. You above everyone else. You knew what he was doing." Helene's threat was not lost on Parker.

"Believe me, I didn't know! I only suspected."

"It was still your job to stop him."

"But the FBI says Bradley is guilty of several major offenses."

"So are you, Joe! So is Kimball. And Squire—and Kuzmack. And it may go right up to the President."

Parker stared at the spinning red light on top of the landing helicopter.

"He's dying. Ran's dying. He wants to say something to you," Kimball shouted to Parker.

Parker rushed to Ran's side and placed his ear near Ran's lips.

"Destroy Moromi. It's the only way . . ."

26

From the window of the Huey, Bradley watched an angry McDonald grow smaller as the ground disappeared quickly beneath them.

"I've telephoned ahead for two business-class tickets; nonstop, Dulles International Airport to Narita, Japan." Parker sat cramped against Bradley. Helene's head rested uncomfortably against Bradley's shoulders. The Huey helicopter had seats for a pilot and copilot located in the front, and two metal bench seats facing each other.

"The ANA flight leaves in exactly twenty minutes." Parker checked his chronometer. "I've arranged for both of you to have a military passport and identification pass. Money will also be provided."

"Sir, I'm afraid we've got a hot pursuit on our tail." The pilot watched the brightly lit blips on the green fluorescent screen.

"It's McDonald's Chinook."

"I'm afraid so, sir!" Helene looked out the window. They were flying into bad weather. She could see the large, cigar-shaped craft silhouetted against the sky.

"About three hundred feet behind us and four hundred feet above us. Traveling at approximately one hundred and twenty knots." The pilot was having a hard time keeping the stick straight, preventing the helicopter from bouncing around.

"What's our speed?" Parker made a few mental calculations.

"We're max at one hundred and forty," the pilot responded, trying to appear calm. "In about one minute he'll be alongside us."

"There's no way we can outfly him, Russ. The Chinook is too fast. The only thing we can do in this bad weather is outmaneuver him. Fly as low as we can over the treetops." Parker pushed away thoughts of his harrowing experiences in Vietnam. "We need maneuverability and stealth."

"You got it!" the pilot called over the scream of the engine. "But I can't afford to take any risks with two extra passengers on board." He banked the helicopter to the extreme right in order to see whether the Chinook would follow. The Chinook mimicked each maneuver he made.

"I can't lose him, sir! He's gaining on us. What should I do?"

The pilot brought the Huey so close to the treetops, Helene felt she could reach out and pull off some of the leaves. Parker watched Bradley, wondering whether all the risks Bradley had taken to stop Project Blood Heat had been worth it.

"How far are we from MTI?" asked Bradley. He had a plan.

"Why?" Parker replied, perplexed. What would Bradley want at MTI?

"I assure you, Webb will not return there," Helene replied.

"How do you know?" Parker had not forgotten her threat to expose him.

"I know Webb," she replied. "He's headed for Noda, Japan. Just where we're supposed to be going. If we don't get to the

Moromi facility before he does, he'll transfer the components that allow him to make the retrovirus II to another site. We'll lose our evidence against him, and he'll continue to spread the plague until *he's* satisfied there is a large enough critical mass of newly diseased people to mandate the manufacture of new drugs."

"Do you think you can get there in time?" Parker asked, perplexed by her eagerness.

"We won't know unless we try."

"Can't our military or diplomatic representatives do something about Moromi now?"

"Sovereignty, Russ," Parker replied. "Governments and their representatives can't do what alleged private citizens could accomplish of their own volition. Remember, you two will be on foreign soil." The 'alleged' was not lost on Bradley. He realized that he, too, was a government official, but in this situation he would be acting as a private citizen.

"She's one hundred feet behind us. In a minute she's going to pull around and force us to land." The pilot pulled up on the stick. The Huey suddenly rose forty feet. Helene grabbed Bradley's hand. She felt sudden nausea. The Huey made a half circle and banked to the right, leaving the Chinook still only one hundred feet away.

"MTI is two minutes from here, due east."

"And from MTI to Dulles?"

"Five minutes." The pilot banked the Huey to the left, the Chinook was still out there, following closely on its tail.

"By car?" Bradley could feel the surge of adrenalin.

"About fifteen by car. But you'd have a good chance of missing the plane."

"Fly us to the MTI parking lot. I think we'll be able to make the plane." Bradley stared self-confidently at Parker.

"All right. Take her due east."

The pilot moved the flight control stick and the Huey banked sharply to the right. Within two minutes, just as the pilot had estimated, they were hovering over the parking lot of MTI, right over Bradley's Porsche.

"If you were to shine your searchlight right at the Chinook, what would happen?"

"You'd blind the pilot for a few seconds. Probably disorient him. At least, for a minute or so."

"Is there any way you can get us down without landing? We need all the time we can get."

Parker stood up and opened the helicopter door. The cold morning wind rushed in. He uncovered a five-foot metal rod on the floor, attached to a winch. At the end of the rod was a steel cable fixed to a leather harness. The pilot turned on the bright searchlight and pointed it toward the Chinook as it flew within fifty feet. Grabbing Helene tightly around the waist, Bradley sat down in the leather harness, she on his lap. He signaled Parker to lower them down the remaining fifteen feet onto the asphalt.

"I've already called ahead. Look for Colonel Squire at the ANA counter. He'll have everything you need."

Parker watched as Bradley and Helene entered the Porsche and sped away down Route 270. In this bad weather, McDonald would have a hard time spotting Bradley from the air. Clever motherfucker, thought Parker, as the Huey banked away from MTI headquarters, heading toward Fort Detrick. Too bad the S.O.B. isn't military.

"Open the glove compartment and take out the Fuzzbuster, please." Too many questions remained about Parker, Moromi, Webb, and Helene. But for the moment, Bradley had to concentrate on reaching Dulles. In precisely fourteen minutes! He pressed down on the accelerator and the speedometer climbed to 90 mph in ten seconds. He began the Bradley One Lap.

"Watch the clock on the dashboard. Give me thirty-second readings, and at the junction of Routes Two Seventy and Four Ninety-five, read off the time to the exact second. Then again at the junction of Four Ninety-five and the Dulles access road. Start now!"

From his previous Lap One practice runs on Route 270, Bradley knew he would have to arrive at his first landmark within

3.5 minutes and the second within 7.5 minutes, averaging 110 miles per hour. Without any anticipated major problems, they would have three minutes to get through passport control and onto the airplane.

"Thirty seconds. Speed of one hundred ten." Helene was too exhausted to be frightened by the onrush of pavement, white lines, street signs, and cars.

Bradley glanced between his side mirror and the road ahead, exhilarated by the run.

"Russ, behind you!"

"The time!"

"The Chinook is behind you."

"The time, Helene—the goddamn time!"

"Take it easy!"

Bradley could see the chopper in his left side mirror, about three hundred yards away and closing in quickly.

"Time!"

"Four Ninety-five—three point nine minutes."

"Shit! We're off by point four seconds."

"So?" She was irritated by his obsession.

"That means I have to average better than one hundred ten miles per hour in early morning traffic to make up the time lost." Turning onto the ramp to 495 West, Bradley saw a state police car lurking on the embankment across the road, clocking the flow of the traffic. In his convex side mirror, Bradley could see the Chinook covering distance quicker than he expected.

He pumped the brakes gently, moved alongside a tractor-trailer in the second lane, and steered into the slowest lane of traffic, invisible to the police car.

"Four point five minutes. Average speed, ninety miles per hour."

Bradley pressed his foot on the accelerator again. He switched quickly from the right-hand lane to the third lane.

"Six minutes. Speed, one hundred fifteen miles." Helene was beginning to enjoy the thrill of the race.

Bradley lost sight of the helicopter. Then, without warning, there was an incredible noise overhead.

"Shit! They're right on top of us."

"Junction Two—eight point five minutes. Ninety-eight miles per hour." He had lost valuable time.

"Bradley, this is FBI Agent Brian McDonald. You're under arrest! Pull over to the side." Blaring through a bullhorn attached to the side of the helicopter, McDonald's voice was intimidating.

"He sounds like a flying Wizard of Oz."

"What can they do to stop you?"

"Shoot at me!"

"In the middle of all these cars?"

Bradley looked around. She was right. As long as he kept the Porsche squeezed between the other cars and trucks, there was little they could do. Once again, he pressed his foot on the accelerator.

"Ninety-seven miles. Nine point nine minutes. At this rate, Russ, we won't make it. We're already two minutes behind."

"There's only one chance left. I have to get McDonald off my ass. He'll blow out my tires if I get clear of these cars."

"Ninety miles. Ten point five minutes. Two point six minutes behind." The roaring noise from the helicopter's engine and the incessant honking of the surrounding vehicles were beginning to give Helene a headache.

"Hold on and pray!"

Bradley jammed the accelerator to the floor and held the steering wheel tightly.

"One hundred sixty-five. One minute behind schedule." The Fuzzbuster started to buzz, and its red light began to flash. "Keep going!"

"Do I have a choice?"

They left the car, motor running, in front of the glass doors of the terminal at Dulles. Squire and Kuzmack stood waiting for them at the escalator.

"Come on! Come on, we don't have all day!" Squire handed

each of them a packet and ran with them down the long corridor toward an empty people-mover.

"We held the plane for you."

Squire signaled the driver to take them to a Boeing 747 sitting on the runway.

"How did you know we'd make it?"

"Overhead surveillance. It's one of the advantages of working for a full-service corporation."

Kuzmack gave them each a carry-on bag filled with clothing. "I'm sorry we don't have anything better to offer you, but I think you'll find them comfortable enough." Reaching into his pocket, Kuzmack pulled out a piece of paper and handed it to Bradley.

Bradley scanned the paper. "This says not to worry about the new federal guidelines for controlling the epidemic because I've been placed on probation by the Public Health Service and dismissed from my job as director of the institute. My pay will be withheld until all investigations are completed. It's signed Dr. Susan Engel, surgeon general. Well, fuck you, Susan Engel."

Squire led them through the open door of the 747SP.

"*Konnichiwa!* We hope you have a pleasant flight!" The stewardess, in a light-blue kimono, bowed gracefully.

27

"*Sugu!*" The taxicab door opened automatically, inviting Bradley and Helene into immaculate doily-covered seats. The driver sped away from the congested Narita Airport into the traffic of Yasukundi-Dori.

"*Tsukiji!*" Helene ordered the taxidriver to proceed directly to the Tsukiji fish market.

"What do you think?"

They sat in silence until they entered the city limits.

"Impressive." Actually, Bradley was shocked. Where was the pearl of the Orient? Pagodas? Small wooden houses framed by Japanese rock gardens? Bonsai trees? All he saw were endless rows of nondescript office buildings with no architectural character. They stood side by side, ten floors high, a myriad of metal-framed windows half-opened, with bundles of electrical wires crisscrossing from buildings to wooden telephone poles. Above the buildings flashed the gaudy red-and-yellow neon signs of familiar brandnames—Honda, Toyota, Sony, Panasonic, Nike. It was 42nd Street on the other side of the planet.

Driving into Tokyo they passed small, two-story wooden houses covered with blue corrugated roofs, planted in the green expanse of irrigated rice paddies. But within the city, the quiet ease of traditional Japan transformed into the smell of diesel exhausts from cloth-covered Isuzu buses and Mitsubishi trucks. Absent were the imagined perfumes of jasmine, chrysanthanum, and cherry blossom. Instead of hand-made silk kimonos, he gazed at a myriad of clotheslines covered with blue jeans, stretched between the windows of apartment buildings. He saw a large metal frame draped with thick rope netting: an ersatz driving range where Japanese businessmen practiced their golf swings during the early morning hours of a weekday. On every other block, rows of men sat mesmerized in front of upright pinball machines, dropping coin after coin to play a game that needed no skill—only a lobotomized attentiveness. The *pachinko* parlors with their eye-catching blue, red, and orange fluorescent signs competed with the morning light in waking the citizenry on its way to work.

He wondered whether he should tell Helene of his profound disappointment. How could someone so cultured and cosmopolitan prefer this unaesthetic pastiche of urban incongruities to the harmonies of Paris or Rome, or even foul-smelling Venice?

After the taxi crossed the Arakawa and Sumida rivers, they rode through an area of impressive rows of cherry blossom trees, manicured gardens, and jogging paths—Hibiya Park, and the Imperial Palace with its impressive wooden Nijubashi Bridge. A right onto Harumi-Dori took the taxi past Shimbashi train station and the surrounding chain of hotels. Bradley wondered whether they would stop at the Shimbashi Da-ichi Hotel.

Helene had been watching Bradley's face during the drive into Tokyo. He looked exhausted. She hoped he would learn, in time, to appreciate the Japan she knew and loved. But she feared it would have to come slowly.

"You're so quiet," Bradley finally said.

She gazed out of the window at the familiar sights. The first time she had arrived in Japan, some eighteen years before, as a "young lady," she was treated accordingly, as a *watakushi.* Her first *Guso* had taught her that the only true value in life was to know oneself. Enlightenment would then ensue. The rest was simply a distraction.

"You're not listening to me." Bradley cupped her face in his hands.

"I'm sorry. You're right!" With his hands pressed on her cheeks she felt comfortable and secure. She pulled his hands away abruptly.

"What is it?" Bradley asked, trying to turn her toward him.

"I love you!" She buried her head on his shoulder.

Bradley felt warm teardrops run down the nape of his neck. All at once, he realized how she must be feeling. She had given up a lot by choosing to stay with him—her career, her patron, her lover. He sensed her anguish and hoped it wouldn't create a distance between them. Could it be that returning to Japan made her feel vulnerable?

"What are you thinking?"

"Over there is the famous Kabukiza Theater where men dress up to play women." Helene straightened up, dabbed her eyes and pointed to a large wooden building with colorful masks affixed over the pagoda-like doorways.

"I'm not interested in drag theater right now. I'm interested in you! We've got to talk about what's been happening. But every time I try, you avoid me. In the plane, you slept all the way—though God knows, you needed it. But for the last half hour you've been gazing out the car window at what I presume are familiar sights, and when I ask what's going on, I get some comment about the kabuki theater."

"*Tsukije!*" The taxi stopped and the driver raised the flag. "Fifteen thousand yen."

"*Domo arigato!*" Helene handed him the money and they exited the cab, carrying their own duffle bags. They walked through clusters of Japanese men dressed in blue denim overalls and knee-length rubber boots. Each wore a blue baseball cap with a number and the name of a fishing company embroidered in bright yellow kanja characters above the visor. Men dressed in aprons and gloves stood on wooden platforms auctioning shipments of iced fish packed in wooden crates to the men below them.

"This is comparable to the trading floor of the New York Stock Exchange. Starting at five each morning, those wholesalers bid on gross quantities of fish. Then they bring them over to their respective stalls to sell them to other buyers or ship them out into the countryside."

As far as Bradley could see, rows of fish were separated by narrow aisles through which men with red kerchiefs rolled around their foreheads pulled packed wooden crates. The five-block-square fish market was filled with more varieties of fish and seafood than Bradley had thought were edible. And what was incredible—the market didn't smell.

"What is it about Japan? Neither the people nor the fish seem to smell."

"The Japanese have an obsession with both personal and public cleanliness," said Helene as she rushed him past a small wooden stall where a fat man sat cutting off the head and the tail of a large red-meat tuna while a woman beside him was collecting the fish's blood in a plastic container.

The entire market was no more than a rusting corrugated metal roof supported by steel bracing from which hung endless rows of naked light bulbs illuminating nothing in particular in the bright morning light. At one end of the market, they stopped in front of a wooden stall three times larger than the others. The purple lettered sign read in English: Daruma Trading Company. Underneath, in small letters: A subsidiary of Trans Nippon Shipping.

Inside, Helene approached a pleasant-looking Oriental man of medium build, sporting a cowboy string tie. They shook hands after her Japanese introduction and pleasantries. "Russ, I want you to meet Mr. Tom Daruma!"

"How do you do, Dr. Bradley? Welcome to Japan. I hope you enjoy your stay here. Please call me Tommy."

With a jolt, Bradley noticed that Daruma's pinky had been amputated. He stared at the hand and felt frustrated. He had a lot of questions to ask.

"You look a little puzzled, Dr. Bradley. Does my hand shock you?" Daruma's open manner at first surprised Bradley. "I could tell you this was a war injury. But, you would soon calculate that I was only eleven years old when World War II started, so that would be a patent lie. Or, more convincingly, I could tell you I acquired this as a result of an accident, cutting a fish with one of my butcher's knives." He went over to the bloodstained wooden chopping block, picked up a black-handled cleaver and slammed it down next to his fingertips. He then burst out in laughter.

"He's a member of an organization called *Yakuza*," Helene stated flatly, not pleased by Daruma's games.

Yakuza—it sounded sinister.

Daruma continued, "*Ya-ku-za* literally means the numbers eight, nine, and three, which add up to a total score of zero in the "flower card" game of *hanafuda*. You see, Dr. Bradley, you are an illustrious professional talking with a mere nobody—a zero."

"Tommy, please!" Helene yelled at Daruma in Japanese. It was also equally clear to Daruma that whatever deference Helene had evidenced in Ran's presence only a few days ago was not to be found today.

"You are quite right, my dear." Daruma's manner sobered.

"I deliberately amputated this pinky as a sign of my unswerving loyalty to the organization of men in Japan who have banded together for what you possibly would consider nefarious deeds."

"What do you mean?"

"I deal in all types of business enterprises that are highly profitable. Yet many, because of their untaxable nature, are considered somewhat wicked."

"Prostitution, drugs, arms?" Bradley was beginning to find Daruma's open manner very appealing.

As Bradley looked more closely at four men who now surrounded the stall, he noticed they also had amputated right pinkies and carried guns in shoulder holsters concealed beneath their gaudy sport jackets. Daruma cut thin slices of *maguro* and handed them to Helene and Bradley.

"You also ship retroviruses into the U.S.?"

"Mr. Raymond was one of our couriers."

"So was my sister, Judy."

"That's right. They worked for Trans Nippon Shipping, but they were never members of *Yakuza*."

"I am a little bewildered by your frankness," Bradley replied. He felt distinctly uncomfortable with the surrealistic nature of the meeting—eating raw tuna and openly discussing criminal activities.

"Open defiance. You see all these *umi-no-sakana?*" Daruma ignored Helene's obvious annoyance with both of them.

"Sea fish," Helene translated, then pointed to her wristwatch.

"This is *anago*." Daruma picked up a long, dark slippery brown-gray eel. "And this *anago* lives next to this *maguro*."

"Tuna." Bradley remembered at least that much from his experience with sushi.

"Very good." Daruma placed the eel on top of a thick slab of fresh tuna. "Catch!"

Bradley reflexively raised his hands and caught a translucent jellyfish.

"*Kurage*. And this octopus is *tako*. So what do we have here? *Tako, kurage, maguro, anago*—all living side by side in peaceful harmony, waiting to be devoured or thrown out. Pretty much like the human condition. *So desho?*"

"*Hai!*"

"Good. You are a fast learner, Dr. Bradley. Well, imagine Webb alongside Helene, alongside . . ." He paused and smiled. "Why not? Alongside you, Dr. Bradley. Or, if you find that offensive, alongside Daruma, alongside *Yakuza*, alongside police . . ."

"I get the point."

"Perhaps, Dr. Bradley . . . Don't be too hasty to jump to conclusions. But our situation is not unlike this fish market: buying and selling different commodities at different prices and at different times. Guided by only one factor—the market. Whether it's guns, drugs—or genetic products that are prohibited from manufacture in the United States."

"Helene, does this mean . . . that you're a *Yakuza?*"

Daruma started to laugh. The four men followed their boss and began laughing as well.

"I warned you, Dr. Bradley, please don't jump to conclusions. Members of the *Yakuza* must amputate their right pinkies to show their unswerving loyalty to the other three hundred thousand or so members." He raised Helene's intact fingers. "Please, Dr. Bradley, I am being frank with you simply because you are a friend of Helene's and we're all here to serve a common purpose."

"What is that?"

"To find and, as you so euphemistically say in the United States, terminate Mr. Roy Webb. A definite *hebi*. Snake!"

"Why are you willing to help us?"

"Why?" He laughed. "Because . . . it suits *my* purposes. Let me just say for now that Helene and I have similar interests."

"Shut up!" Helene was clearly annoyed with Daruma's cavalier manner.

"Why don't we simply go to Noda and apprehend Webb, if he's there?" Bradley said, looking quizzically at Helene.

"First, we received word only this morning from the immigration officials that Webb entered Japan a few hours before you two did. Second, Dr. Bradley, what stops you from taking out the gold in Fort Knox?"

"It can't be *that* difficult!"

"He is very heavily protected. The only way we might be able to get near him is through a regularly scheduled Mori Bus Tour that starts at nine tomorrow morning, or to sneak into his quarters under the cover of night."

"What do you have against Webb?" Bradley wanted to find out what possible interests Daruma could have in common with Helene.

"A need for revenge—not too dissimilar from your own."

"What's that?" Bradley could see that Helene was becoming increasingly impatient with their conversation.

"Your sister. She was, with Mr. Raymond, one of my finest couriers. Webb destroyed an important part of my business when he killed those two." Daruma snapped his fingers and two of the *Yakuza*, each wearing a string tie, left the stall. They returned minutes later in a white convertible Cadillac.

"Don't think too harshly of me, Dr. Bradley. This evening I wish you and Helene to be my guests. First, however, you both must rest. I have already made reservations at a lovely inn. Then you will dine at a restaurant I own in the Ginza." He ushered Helene and Bradley into the car. Waving goodbye, he added, "You may not believe this, but here in Japan most ordinary citizens, and many police and politicians, admire us. They applaud our tradition of samurai courage and our willingness to work outside the mainstream of society."

Headlights blazing, the Cadillac sped off toward the inn near the Shimbashi area, two blocks north of the Imperial Hotel. Helene and Bradley remained silent throughout the drive. By ignoring him, she made it very clear she didn't want to answer any of his questions. She never trusted Japanese chauffeurs. They were by tradition the auxiliary ears of their respective bosses. When the car stopped, the driver rushed to open the rear door and bowed politely. He motioned toward the entrance of a small wooden inn built in the traditional Japanese style with a sloped roof made from brown ceramic tiles.

Before they walked through the oak doors, Helene paused and whispered to Bradley, "I don't trust Daruma, but I need him. Promise me, no questions while we are inside. We will be spied upon."

They entered a small foyer formed of paper-thin sliding walls. A plump woman dressed in a bright-red kimono bowed gracefully and motioned them to proceed to a row of wooden shelves filled with sandals. Bradley imitated Helene as she kicked off her shoes and put on a pair of Japanese wooden shoes and a light cotton kimono. They followed the innkeeper to a room at the end of a corridor walled on both sides by the same paper panels. As she slid open the last *shoji*, she pointed to a sign above the doorway: "*Tori*."

" 'Bird.' Each room has a name. This is called Tori. *Domo arigato!*" Helene bowed to the innkeeper; Bradley nodded his head.

The innkeeper bowed deeply and shuffled back to the entryway as Helene slid the door closed.

As they entered the room, Helene pressed her fingers to Bradley's lips, indicating she didn't want him to say a word. She showed him where to take off his slippers in the *tataki*, the lower entrance of the room. Then he crossed over to her in silence. Helene gently ran her fingers along the deeply etched lines beneath his tired eyes. He had a face she could trust: warm, caring, reassuring. For the first time she would need a man who would be able to accept her with all her faults and vulnerabilities. But how much of herself should she reveal? Slowly, she led him across the room and stepped into a western-style shower located alongside a wooden tub filled with steaming water. Turning on the shower, Helene reached down and began to stroke Bradley's penis with her fingers, softly scratching the underside of his scrotum. She lathered him with soap and water, then ran her slippery hands over his erect member. Bradley closed his eyes, savoring every minute that she was in charge. Then he felt her fingers guide him toward her moist vagina.

"Don't move! Simply hold it in me!" She raised her right foot so he could more easily enter her. Slowly, the head of his penis moved along her outer vulva, guided by her gentle movements.

She teasingly blew in his ear and traced the folds of his earlobe with her tongue. Standing there as one, Bradley lathered her firm breasts and large brown nipples. He ran his tongue over her left nipple and felt her pelvis undulate ever so slowly along his shaft.

"Come into me in the hot tub!" Gently, she raised herself from his erect penis, making certain that all the soapsuds were off both of them, and led him toward the wooden tub. Stepping in first, she sank down slowly and extended her hands in open invitation.

"Oh Christ! It's hot!"

"Dare the heat! See what awaits you." She started to caress her breasts, exciting herself as she watched Bradley enter the tub, once again erect. As he stood straight above her in the tub, she placed his penis into her mouth and ran her fingers firmly up and down the shaft, sending a shudder of pleasure through him. And then, as he lowered himself into the hot tub, she changed positions, placing herself gently on top of him, guiding his penis deep into her. Kissing his lips and watching his glazed eyes begin to close, she raised and lowered herself on him, feeling the soothing warm waves of water lap against her pelvis. The warmth within her began to rise, until she could no longer control her slow, undulating movements. Her thrusts became quicker and harder. She felt the stem of his penis stiffen. If only he could hold on for a few seconds more. His breathing became more rapid. She moved more quickly. He grabbed her with both hands, thrusting in and out while she moved, around and around.

"Aahhh!" She felt herself fuse in the warmth of his explosion. They moved their bodies until they could feel only the pulsating fatigue.

The creaking sound of footsteps brought her out of her reverie. She screamed as the door of the bathroom burst open and three men rushed in.

28

"*Yakuza! Yakuza!*" The innkeeper explained as she applied ice to the swelling on top of Bradley's forehead. She held up five full fingers of her left hand and bent down the top of her pinky, making certain he understood what she was saying.

"*Domo arigato.*" Bradley stepped out of the bathtub and put on the kimono the innkeeper held out to him. On top of that, he placed the thicker *ranzen*. In the mirror Bradley saw a slight bump at his hairline that explained his headache.

"*Kenka! Kenka!*" The innkeeper swung her arms around wildly, indicating that a fight had taken place between the *Yakuza* and Helene. "*Shiro jidosha!*" She placed her hand around an imaginary steering wheel.

"Car?"

The innkeeper shrugged her shoulders. "*Shiro jidosha!*" She pointed to the pearl-white wallpaper lining the bathroom walls. "*Shiro!*"

"*Shiro?*"

"*Shiro!*" She pointed again to the wallpaper and nodded her head.

"White! A white car. The bastards took her away in that white Cadillac!"

The innkeeper smiled, sensing that he had understood her.

Within five minutes Bradley was dressed in his own clothes and standing in the entryway of the inn with a tourist map of Tokyo.

"*Tsukiji?*" He asked the innkeeper. Pleased that he remembered the name of the market, he tried to recall the word Daruma had used for fish.

"*Hai! Tsukiji, sakana.*" The woman covered her mouth, giggling like a girl. She pointed to the street on the map, calling out the names of streets he would cross in order to get to the *Tsukiji* fish market: "Harumi-Dori, Ginza, Sotobori-Dori, Chuo-Dori, Showa-Dori, Shinohashi-Dori."

Bradley resisted giving her a hug and bowed deeply instead. He put on his shoes and walked out into the night. He must have been unconscious for more than a few minutes. It was dark outside, and Bradley felt vaguely disoriented walking through the neon-lit, bustling streets of the infamous Ginza district. People were shopping in the brightly lit Hankyu Department Store. Groups of men dressed in identical black business suits and carrying leather attaché cases staggered over the sidewalks, shouting, singing and, in one case, urinating on the street. Happy drunks, Bradley thought, a marked contrast to his experiences with the offensive drunks of Eastern Europe. He presumed that hours earlier these very same men were the ones he had seen walking with robotic precision into the subway entrances.

It wasn't until he stopped in front of a sidewalk stall to buy a skewer of soy-sauce-dipped chicken teriyaki that he realized an Occidental man in a green U.S. combat jacket was following him. He had thought nothing of it when the man had turned right onto Harumi-Dori, as he had done. He continued at a fast pace through an arcade, distracted by the mélange of sights, smells, and sounds.

The pungent aroma of smoked *anago* mingled with the sweet taffy smell of red soybean paste rolled into little round cookie balls. An omnipresent McDonald's hamburger outlet proudly advertised in both Japanese and English that they were selling more hamburgers in one year than any other store in Japan. Glancing backward, Bradley could see the man with the combat jacket was still in pursuit. Could it be one of the *Yakuza* who had abducted Helene? Bradley walked briskly past small coffee shops with snobbish Anglicized names, like The Scotch, The Checker, The Boxer, then past a row of small fashion boutiques with French names. He stepped into the shadow of a doorway. As his pursuer passed, Bradley grabbed the man by the collar.

"Where the hell is Helene?" he barked in the man's face.

"Hello, Russ!"

"Parker! What the hell are you doing here?" Bradley released his grip.

"I couldn't let you have all the fun, so I hopped on the next plane a few hours after you left and came on over." He took out a cigar and lit it.

"But how did you know where I would be?"

"For the *gaijin*, Tokyo is a small city. Particularly in a season when there are very few tourists."

"Joe, you've got to have a better story than that."

"Okay, okay. I came here as a private citizen to help. But the prefect of police, an old friend of mine, called me a couple of hours ago at my hotel and told me that an American woman had been abducted from an inn in the Shimbashi by a gang of *Yakuza* driving a white Cadillac."

"Daruma!"

"So I went over to the inn and waited for you. When you came out I decided to follow you."

"Why didn't the police come?"

"It's a government-operated inn. And it's in no one's interest to discredit the safety of a state-run business, particularly an inn heavily patronized by *gaijin*."

"That's not an answer. That's an excuse."

"The truth is, the police and the *Yakuza* have many common interests. And as long as it's clear to the police that no major act of violence was committed—namely, the killing of a fellow police officer—they do their best not to destroy their delicate working relationship with the *Yakuza*."

"Who is this Daruma?"

"Hell, I don't know any more than you do. He's a *Yakuza* who has close ties to Webb."

As they approached the dark, empty fish market, Parker took a double-action nine-millimeter Sig-Sauer from his leather shoulder holster. "Stay close to me. These mothers play very rough. I had some of these types in my infantry unit after World War II."

"Over there, at the far end, near the lights. Two of the men I saw earlier are standing near the Daruma and Company sign." Bradley and Parker moved quietly among the stalls.

"What do you mean, you had some *Yakuza* in your unit?" Bradley asked.

The two *Yakuza* turned in the direction of Bradley's voice. Each drew an Astra A-80 from his shoulder holster.

Parker took aim, sighting the shorter of the two. "Watch this, Russ! At two hundred feet, this mother has got the finest combat sights, even in low-light conditions." He pulled back the trigger. The gun fired. The shorter of the two *Yakuza* fell to the ground. Although it was a partially open-air market, the shot made an incredibly loud sound.

The other *Yakuza* spotted Bradley and Parker and raised his gun.

Bradley ducked behind the wooden framing of a stall. Parker kneeled in place and fired three rounds. The second *Yakuza* fell, smashing his face against the concrete floor. Blood splattered over the empty tables and crates.

Bradley watched, paralyzed with horror, as the white Cadillac came barreling toward them out of nowhere, smashing stall after stall as if the car were a reaper, harvesting stalks of wood. Bradley grabbed Parker by the collar and pulled him behind the auctioneer's block. The onrushing car missed them by inches. Parker wheeled around, steadied the gun with both hands, and sighted on the Cadillac as it made a sharp turn. It was once again coming at them. In seconds, the car would be on top of them.

Parker pulled the trigger, first shooting the driver in the head, and then blew out both front tires. The car swerved to the right and crashed against a steel girder.

"Let's get the fuck out of here!" Parker yelled and jerked Bradley up.

"Wait! Helene may be in the car! I've got to see!"

"Look up there at the far end of the fish market—that group of *Yakuza* will be on our ass!" Parker was physically restraining Bradley when the engine of the car exploded, sending up a cloud of smoke.

"But Helene—"

"She's not in there—come on!" Parker pulled Bradley out of the line of fire, and they both ran down Shinohashi-Dori. Parker hailed a cab, pushed Bradley inside, and closed the door behind them.

"*Dozo . . . Moromi . . . Noda!*"

"*Dekiru dake hayaku!*" The driver raised the meter's flag and sped off toward the Edo River, forty miles northeast of Tokyo.

"Christ! I'm too old for this type of shenanigan."

"Why are you so certain that Helene wasn't in that Cadillac?" Through the rear window of the taxicab Bradley saw the *Yakuza* collecting the bodies of their dead. Flames were spreading through the remaining stalls. A blue Brougham Cadillac pulled up alongside the curb.

"You're what—in your early forties?"

"Yeah!" Bradley leaned back against the recently pressed doily. "Going on eighty."

"Well, shit, son . . . I'm in my sixties. Late sixties. As a matter of fact, three years older than when I should have retired."

"Why didn't you retire?"

"Why, I was having too much fun." Parker laughed and slapped Bradley affectionately on the shoulder.

"What the hell is the surgeon general of the Army doing shooting guns and commanding infantry troops?"

"Before I was a medical doctor—an Army M.D.—I was proud to be a Marine grunt—a foot soldier, slugging my way through the malaria-infested jungles of Burma and China. At Harbin I got to know Webb and those samurai assholes shooting at us."

"Helene, what about Helene?"

"You don't give up, do you?"

Bradley shook his head.

"Well . . . I know the way the *Yakuza* think. And Daruma is no different. If they took her as hostage, they wouldn't do anything foolish enough to endanger her life."

"What do you mean 'if'? She was taken by Daruma and his men."

"Probably."

"So why do you say 'if'?"

"I don't treat salmonella poisoning till I see the diarrhea."

"What the hell does that mean?"

"It means . . . stop getting uptight. I'm tired of hearing you ask me the same goddamn question over and over again—I'm not deaf, I heard you the first time. You don't have to trust me, and I don't have to trust you. But we've got to live with each other for a few more hours. I knew I shouldn't have let you anywhere near the reservoir." Parker patted his shoulder holster.

"Are you threatening me?"

"No, I'm simply asking you to let up a little bit."

"Then you wouldn't be having so much fun."

They both laughed until they saw the blue Brougham Cadillac through the back window.

"*Dekiru dake hayaku!*" Parker smashed out the back window with the butt of his gun. Screaming obscenities, the taxidriver pulled over to the side of the highway.

"*Sumima senga* . . ." Parker held the pistol to the driver's head and forced him out of the cab.

"It's not a 928, Russ. But you better drive the hell out of it before those bastards come down on our ass."

Bradley popped the clutch into third and pressed his foot on the accelerator. The Noda exit was twenty-five kilometers away. "Who are the *Yakuza?*" he asked as he swerved, barely missing a motorcyclist. He felt awkward driving on the left side of the road, as if the entire world had suddenly reversed direction.

"They're a group of hoodlums, a confederation of gangs, much like our mafia. But here in Japan the *Yakuza* are highly respected because of the image that they project—a kind of samurai Robin Hood. Historically, their roots are in the unemployed samurai warriors of the medieval era who roamed the countryside robbing the wealthy and, at times, giving to the poor. They were the criminal servants of the shogun."

Aiming carefully at the Brougham with his automatic, Parker pulled the trigger. The bullet hit the radiator grill. The Cadillac swerved, but then resumed its course.

"Shit! Their car is bullet-proof. Let her come alongside, then duck when I tell you."

Bradley downshifted and watched in his rear-view mirror as the Brougham loomed larger.

Parker fired another shot. It bounced off the front window. A white haired *Yakuza* sitting on the passenger side of the Brougham stretched a Ruger semi-automatic rifle through the window.

"Duck! Slow down!"

Bradley sank down into his seat, holding tightly onto the steering wheel. As the Brougham came closer, Parker smashed the right rear window of the taxi with the barrel of his gun and fired three shots at the Cadillac's left front tire.

The Brougham began to swerve uncontrollably.

"Speed up! I think I hit the tire."

Bradley accelerated. Parker took aim again, but held his fire: The Brougham was slowing down.

"The U.S. Army, under General Douglas MacArthur, kept those *Yakuza* fuckers alive—and even nurtured them. They were intended to serve as a political buffer against the rise of left-wing unions and the Communist Party right after the war."

"What the hell are we doing with gangsters?"

"Now, almost nothing. At least, not officially. Webb works with them illegally, importing packages of recombinant DNA retroviruses through couriers like your sister and Raymond."

"You knew about Webb's activities all along?" Bradley asked. The sign in English said Noda was ten kilometers away. He checked the rear-view mirror and saw the Brougham now about a half mile behind.

"Not exactly. Not until you furnished us with your discovery that he was purposely creating new diseases. We suspected something was wrong when our dependents began having a disproportionately high rate of miscarriages with malformed fetuses. But we couldn't prove anything. And we didn't want to stop the recombinant DNA research on the bubonic plague that Webb was already conducting for us covertly."

"So that's where I came in."

"At a most propitious time. Looking back only a few days, I can see that had we implemented Project Blood Heat, we would have helped Webb create a monstrous new set of diseases."

"But why were you willing to take any chance at all, once you suspected Webb?"

"Would you believe bureaucratic momentum? Once the Army sets a thirty-million-dollar project in motion, it's very hard to stop."

"Why didn't you arrest Webb?"

"Where was our evidence? *Your* deductions? Ran's confession? They came a little late. The Army and MTI have been good partners in the past on various covert research projects, some legal, some illegal. So we were hostage to each other. Had he sensed we were suspicious of Project Blood Heat he would have blown the whistle on the Army, the Department of Defense, and the White House."

"Honor among thieves."

"Something like that."

When the exit sign for Noda appeared, Bradley turned off the highway. The two-lane country road meandered through irrigated rice paddies, across a railroad track, and down a narrow main street surrounded by two-story wooden houses capped with blue corrugated roofs. Bradley stopped in front of a large white sign with black lettering in both English and Japanese: Moromi Industries. Beneath the lettering he recognized the logo of the eight-legged beetle—the very sign that had been tattooed onto Raymond's arm. He parked the dented taxi on the side of the road.

In front of them, several dilapidated brown factory buildings were joined by aluminum pipes to large steel vats, eight to ten feet in diameter. In some odd way it reminded Bradley of the facilities at Fort Detrick. Few people were walking about. Those he saw wore white lab coats and white baseball caps with the insignia of the beetle. But the air surrounding Moromi Industries, unlike the atmosphere in Maryland, had a peculiarly pungent odor: fermentation!

"*Ichi . . . ni . . . san . . . shi.*" Parker counted the buildings and pointed to the one with a flagpole in front of it. "That's Building One . . . over there is Building Two." The buildings all looked alike, except for the number of pipes exiting from their sides.

There was no guardhouse to stop them, and they entered Building One. They walked down a long corridor with plate glass windows set into the top half of the walls. The windows looked down into a room with piles of wheat and soybeans. A woman worker, oblivious to their presence, sat behind a large console watching soybeans and wheat sucked into a steel vat in which a rotating blade mixed the two together. A sign in English read: "Welcome to the Moromi Soy Sauce Production Method. Step One: soybeans and wheat are blended together. Aspergillus is introduced into the mixture and allowed to mature for three days."

"Soy sauce!" exclaimed Bradley. Webb was more clever than he had ever suspected.

"So that's how Webb makes his retrovirus," added Parker.

"God, it's so simple, now that we see it. Soy sauce requires fermentation. And fermentation requires active fungi or yeast-like aspergillus. If you substitute for aspergillus an artificially created bacterial retrovirus with a fermenting system, you can produce something that still tastes like soy sauce, but has the bite of the plague." Bradley felt ashamed that he had not thought of the fermentation system as a source of the plague.

The corridor led to Building Two and another corridor that looked down onto seemingly endless steel vats of mash. A sign read: "Step Two: The resulting koji culture of wheat, soybean, and aspergillus is mixed with salt water to produce *moromi*, a mash that brews in fermentation tanks for one year." A woman dressed in a white lab coat and hairnet sat behind a console and controlled the rate at which the matured brown moromi mash poured into burlap-covered frames. Machines stacked one frame on top of another. In the next room, the machines placed the frames on a conveyor belt headed toward a machine that slammed a metal plate down on the burlap, squeezing out a brown liquid. The liquid flowed into plastic pipes that led to large steel vats used to refine and pasteurize the raw soy sauce.

Bradley was enthralled by the brilliance of Webb's scheme. The ramifications were astounding. Any product that required fermentation—beer, cheese, yogurt, bread, in effect, all the staples—could be the source of dissemination. It could happen anywhere in the world. Possibly the process was already underway.

"Do you see," he explained to Parker excitedly, "it's the fermentation process—the amino acids, the media, the nutrients—that would allow the retrovirus to grow."

"Right!" Parker agreed. "But the normal pasteurization procedure would inevitably kill all the bacteria. . . ."

"And the retrovirus! So we have to find a place here where some of the soy sauce is *not* pasteurized, but is sent out without either the bacteria or the retrovirus being killed."

They ran down the corridor, following the pipes with their eyes as they crossed into another room. In this room five women sat at different stations, watching the soy sauce fill two-, four-, and eight-liter plastic bottles. Bradley and Parker walked quietly along a steel catwalk circuiting the room.

"Look over there!" Bradley pulled Parker into the shadow of a steel girder as two security guards walked by.

"So there are guards."

"No—look at that woman with the red cap marking the eight-liter bottles." Parker watched as the woman marked seven bottles with a date-stamping machine. She left the eighth bottle unmarked. A yellow-capped woman controlling the four-liter bottles marked nine bottles and left the tenth unmarked. A woman with a blue cap, controlling the two-liter bottles, marked fifteen bottles out of every sixteen that passed her. The unmarked bottles were placed by another woman on a separate conveyor that immediately exited the building.

Bradley and Parker left through a side door and followed the piping from the conveyor belt into Building Four.

"Welcome, gentlemen. I hope you've enjoyed your tour of the Moromi Soy Sauce Factory."

A shot rang through the air.

29

"Joe, draw that Sig-Sauer out of your shoulder holster—slowly and carefully." Webb stepped forward, brimming with a smile. Next to him stood Daruma armed with an Uzi machine gun and six gray-uniformed guards armed with handguns.

Bradley and Parker had followed the bottles into a packing warehouse. The unmarked bottles were passing beneath a series of automatic needles that pierced the plastic cap tops, squirted a few drops in the bottles, and then dropped them off the conveyor belt into wooden crates marked U.S.A., Canada, France, and West Germany. Obviously, Webb was planning on spreading his new diseases.

"Well, Joe, what do you think? Impressive, isn't it?" Webb pointed with pride around the warehouse as he took Parker's gun.

"Where's Helene?" Bradley demanded.

"Don't worry, Dr. Bradley, your paramour is in good hands." Daruma laughed at the double-entendre.

Bradley lunged at Daruma but was restrained by Parker.

"Please, Dr. Bradley, give me an excuse to fire." Daruma pointed the Uzi two inches from Bradley's head and pretended to pull the trigger.

"I'm very pleased to have you both here to witness the transfer of Moromi Industries to my sole ownership," Webb said with a slight bow.

He led everyone out of the warehouse and into a courtyard enclosing an exquisitely maintained traditional Japanese garden. A small arched wooden bridge, crossing a lily pond, was lit by a row of cleverly hidden floodlights.

"This is where the people at Moromi have made soy sauce for the emperor for over three hundred years." Webb pointed to the small white wooden structure on the other side of the bridge. "A completely separate processing was needed."

The bridge spanned a man-made pond about twenty feet in diameter, stocked with large, whiskered white carp and large, bright-yellow goldfish. The pond itself, Bradley calculated, was no more than four or five feet deep. A table and two chairs were placed beneath a cherry tree. Jagged boulders and rocks of various sizes formed a boundary for the plantings.

"Be careful not to fall against the jagged edges of these rocks near the pond; they are extremely sharp." Daruma gave an ironical smile. "Now that you're our guests, we are concerned above all for your safety." He fired a burst into the pond and watched gleefully as the fish darted about for protection. The guards began to laugh and fire their own guns. Webb, annoyed by the commotion, waved them back into Building Four and bolted the door from outside.

"This is a place of poverty, tranquillity, and symbolic reverence." Webb's arm swept over the courtyard. "Each element of a Japanese garden represents an important part of man's essence. The rocks and stones in the garden represent man's bones. The pond represents man's blood. The small bonsai trees and large cherry tree, all handsculpted daily, represent man's flesh. In this garden, and in many others like it, one can experience the holy trinity of flesh, blood, and bone. Or, depending on one's proclivity, the body and the soul."

As they entered the small wooden building, Webb bade them take off their shoes. The room before them was immaculately clean with a stone mill and four large wooden vats containing *moromi*. Bradley now recognized the pungent odor.

"In this one little factory, twenty feet by twenty feet, the people at Moromi Industries made the soy sauce that went directly to the emperor and his family. One difference between this soy sauce and the one made in the main buildings is that the emperor's *moromi* was allowed to ferment for one year rather than the usual eight months. Most importantly, the *moromi* mash for the emperor was not pasteurized, so it had a more piquant flavor." Webb was clearly proud of the historical pedigree of Moromi Industries. He enjoyed conducting this tour for Bradley and Parker.

"And this is where the unmarked bottles receive their dose of retrovirus. All I really needed in order to create the retrovirus II was the proper growth medium implanted with RNA instructions for additional diseases. Across the way are the laboratory facilities in which we monitor the quality and standards of the different products we make."

Daruma nodded his head with great pride. "We've got all kinds of fancy equipment there. Take a good look." He forced Bradley's forehead against a small glass window.

Suddenly the enormity of what Bradley saw struck him. Before him in neat glass rows was the product of Webb's diabolical scheme: manufacture the lethal retrovirus; ship it in mass distribution to the American public; await the brushfire epidemic; then reap the financial rewards of a stimulated pharmaceutical industry. And the powers that be in Washington had inadvertently helped Webb. The U.S. Army had made a secret pact with Webb's private company, thinking that in doing so they could skirt the international agreements that outlawed the military from producing bacteriological weapons. But Ezra Kimball and his superiors had soon found themselves in deadly collusion with Webb. The Army had been fooled by Webb into thinking that there had been courier accidents at Fort Detrick, Dugway, and Pine Bluff. In the process they had unleashed an epidemic, lost thousands of lives, and put themselves in the brotherhood of the Yakuza.

Bradley pushed Daruma away, who, in turn, grabbed him by both ears and slammed his head against the window. Blood started to drip down Bradley's forehead.

"Enough, Tommy!" exclaimed Webb. He frowned in mock reproof before continuing nonchalantly, "As you can see, only ten feet away in that brightly lit laboratory, we have everything we need to make the retrovirus II. All this, thanks to the genius of Dr. Futaki Ran, who foresaw the advent of recombinant nucleic acid technology forty years ago. Unfortunately, he became a little squeamish when he realized the magnitude of my endeavor. He objected to the fact that millions of people would die within the next five months. To be precise, I calculated about four-point-five million deaths. Ran was a minor league hitter. At Pingfan, he had killed only a few thousand, at most."

"You're crazy, Webb!" exclaimed Bradley as he wiped the blood from his forehead with a handkerchief.

"Of course," Webb pointed to the four wooden vats, "we really don't need much more than these oversized wooden barrels and the proper fermentation of the *moromi* mash. But now that we've terminated the formal part of the ceremony, let us proceed with the main reason for my being here in the first place. Please allow me."

Bradley and Parker followed Webb out of the emperor's factory, down some carved wooden steps, and into the Japanese garden. Daruma followed behind them, the Uzi pointed straight at Bradley's back, his amputated pinky caressing the trigger.

"Here is an official document written in both Japanese and English, giving me one hundred percent ownership of Moromi Industries. It is very unusual, you realize, for a foreigner to gain full ownership of anything in Japan."

A woman dressed in a blue-and-white handmade silk kimono,

with a gossamer drape covering her face and hair, appeared at a side door of the emperor's factory. She walked to the table and picked up a long-nibbed wooden pen, dipped it into a porcelain cup of octopus ink, and scribbled her name. An eighteen-carat gold chain hung from her wrist. As Webb held out his hand to receive the signed document, the woman lifted her veil.

"Helene!" Bradley rushed toward her, but was restrained by Daruma.

Helene neither spoke nor acknowledged Bradley's presence. She turned to Webb. "Well, Roy, you wanted Moromi Industries, and I, as the sole executrix of my father's estate, have just signed over fifty-one percent, the controlling interest in Moromi. I know it would break my father's heart to know that something he helped to develop in his youth, from one small emperor's building to twenty acres of factory, has come to this. I have violated both his trust and my heritage."

"Ah, my dear, you French are always so dramatic. Fifty or so years ago, your father pillaged a poor Japanese family of the only pride they had—their name and their work—by buying them out for less than twenty thousand dollars. Now look what you have—or, more accurately, what *I* now have—a one-point-four-billion-dollar industry, totally independent of MTI. Think of it merely as a simple business transaction. One of many that occur every minute of every day."

"At least you can never buy the name or the nobility."

"Come, come, my dear—you beginning to sound maudlin. You don't want to disabuse your young frightened friend here that you're anything but an impeturbable comtesse de Perignod. Nobility and names are passé, my dear. You know that, so do I. Why make more of it than there is?"

"Because you are, and always will be, a scoundrel."

"And you, my sweet angel? Please, let's stop this game and hand over the document."

"On one condition." Helene handed Webb a sheet of paper. "In return for the controlling shares of Moromi Industries, I want you to sign over to me your twenty-three percent of MTI."

"Of course, I'll sign it!" Webb laughed. "It's worthless without the remaining forty-two percent, and you'll never leave here alive. You know that!"

Bradley turned toward Daruma, who was pointing his Uzi at Helene. He suddenly felt nauseous. Any second, he would see a burst of fire and Helene would fall. He watched Webb sign the piece of paper.

"It's the least I can do to humor you. And, I might add, as a small gesture of my gratitude for the five wonderful years we spent together."

Bradley thought he saw tears well up in Helene's eyes. But they disappeared as she exchanged the sheets of paper.

"I see you've already accumulated twenty-two percent of the outstanding shares," Webb proclaimed with amusement.

"Yes. With Ran's help—and also by selling you short on the open market, then buying you up at a fifty percent discount," Helene replied coldly.

"But you can't get control without Parker's twenty percent," Webb observed comfortably.

Bradley turned to a flushed Parker. Now he understood how Helene had been able to intimidate Parker into letting them get away. She had known all along that Parker was a major holder of MTI shares. If that fact was made public, Parker and the Army would be subject to serious investigation. Looking at each of them in turn—Webb, Helene, and Parker—Bradley was disgusted by the unholy trinity that had evidently existed for years.

Webb nodded his head and Daruma opened fire. But it was Webb who fell to the ground.

His face twisted in horror, Parker ran to the table and grabbed the wooden pen with the long metal nib and clutched Helene by the throat. "Put that fuckin' gun down, Daruma, or this pen goes right into her carotid!"

"Joe, what are you doing? Let her go!" exclaimed Bradley. With one lightning motion, Daruma grabbed Bradley by the throat and pointed the barrel of the Uzi to his head.

"Tit for tat! You get her! I get him! And then I get you. So

I win! Because I get everything. And the one who gets everything—wins! Right, Dr. Bradley?" asked Daruma.

"I don't understand. Why did you kill Webb and not Helene?" Bradley asked.

"You see Doc, all the education in the world doesn't make you too smart," Daruma replied, adding, "It's a question of Japanese *on*—debt."

"Let him go, Daruma!" Helene ordered. She could barely speak. Although she had only met Daruma recently, she had been aware throughout her life of young Tommy's debt to her father, which was to be called in only when she was in serious trouble.

"Why? We've got the ace in the hole now. We got everything and everyone!"

"Without Parker's signature I don't have control of MTI—only a majority share," replied Helene.

"Is this what all of this was about—all the violence and death—for a bunch of lousy shares of stock?" Bradley gasped.

"It's much more than that, Russ. Much more. It's something you wouldn't understand. It's about a family name—de Perignod—and a banking tradition. *Il faut savoir. Il faut faire savoir. Il faut savoir faire.*"

"But you and Daruma! He kidnapped you as we . . ." Bradley exclaimed incredulously.

"An alliance of convenience," Helene replied coolly.

"Oh, Helene . . . no . . . Helene . . ." Bradley shook his head in agonized disbelief.

"Take it easy, lover boy— I'll soon take you out of your misery," Daruma sneered.

"No!" Helene tried to rush forward, but Parker held her back.

Bradley knew he didn't have any time. He swung around with both hands, taking Daruma by surprise and knocking him backward. When his head hit the sharp edge of one of the jagged rocks that lined the pool, the water turned red. Daruma lay perfectly still.

The guards started to bang on the bolted warehouse door.

Bradley grabbed Daruma's Uzi and pointed it at both Helene and Parker.

"Which one, Russ?" Parker asked.

"Remember, I loved you!" Helene exclaimed.

"She used you and me, Russ. She used you to prove that Webb was no longer fit to remain president and chairman of MTI. She needed your detective skills to uncover Project Blood Heat and your integrity to discredit him and me so she and Ran and Daruma could take over MTI and make Moromi Industries one of the truly giant conglomerates in the world. She used Daruma to exterminate Webb, and now she'll convince you to exterminate me."

"I ask you to remember what we went through trying to destroy Project Blood Heat," Helene's voice said evenly. "And, more than anything else, you must believe that I was not part of these horrendous crimes Webb had committed. I had my suspicions, but I could never prove them. Russ, I honestly thought it could work between us. I wasn't wrong. All we need is one more chance."

Before Bradley could make up his mind, the warehouse door burst open. The guards rushed forward, opening fire. Bradley was hit and fell to the ground. Screaming, Helene rushed over and threw herself over his body. Parker picked up the dropped Uzi and began to fire. A burst of rapid gunshots followed.

When the garden was completely silent, the smell of gunfire permeated the air. Blood ran down Bradley's left arm where Helene's head rested against it. Her face had a peaceful expression. Bradley kissed her gently on the forehead and slowly closed her eyelids. He removed the piece of paper from her hands, lit it, and threw it into the emperor's factory. The yellow flames grew rapidly to an all-consuming fire. Slowly, he unfastened the gold bracelet from Helene's wrist and reread the inscription on the back: *Sauve qui peut.*

Parker lay face downward. A bullet had passed through his skull.

With tears in his eyes, Bradley stared at the tree, the rock, and the water. His body and soul ached.

Epilogue

". . . In confidence, Senator Hall, we in the administration feel that the epidemic of bubonic plague has subsided significantly in the past four weeks since it was discovered, thanks to the brilliant efforts of Dr. Orestes Bradley." Kuzmack addressed his extensively rehearsed remarks to the five senators seated in front of him at the highly publicized Senate Health Subcommittee hearing. He sat next to Squire at a table covered with microphones and lit by the klieg lights brought in by the major networks. "Under the inspiring leadership of Brigadier General Robert Squire, the first nonmedically trained surgeon general of the army, and his colleague, Dr. Susan Engel, the new secretary of health and human services, we will begin to implement the Bradley plan."

"Oh, Uncle, that's you!" Sharon's high-pitched voice could be heard throughout the hearing chambers. She jumped out of her seat from excitement.

"Please, sweetheart, you have to sit down."

Dressed in his blue Public Health Service navy uniform, bedecked with a string of new awards and ribbons, Bradley gently pulled Sharon back into her seat.

"See, Unc, I told you . . . You can't take Sharon anywhere with us. She's such a pest. She'll embarrass us in front of everyone."

"Okay, sophisticated lady, we'll just try to calm that pesty little creature down." Bradley wrapped his arms around the two frail bodies, grateful to the Maryland courts for awarding him custody of the children.

"Stephanie, you're going to have to teach your sister by example." Engel tried to hide her smirk behind a serious face.

"Yes, Dr. Engel . . . I'll try." Stephanie was somewhat frightened of Dr. Engel, who nodded her head gravely in reply.

"According to the Bradley plan," continued Kuzmack, "the new antiplague vaccine will be ready for distribution in one week."

Squire leaned over and whispered something in Kuzmack's ear.

"I'm sorry, Senator, I stand corrected. I've just been informed that it will be ready for distribution later today."

The audience broke into loud applause. Senator Hall was thriving with the media attention his hearing was getting. He and Kuzmack had figured that three days of hearings would barely tax the public's tolerance level.

"Dr. Kuzmack, will you tell this committee how the effort will be funded."

"Of course, Senator." Kuzmack always enjoyed testifying before Hall's committee. Everything, including the applause, had been prearranged. There were no surprises. This episode with the plague was certainly a little more sticky than many other health problems that had arisen in the past year—five million people had been infected. But the incidence of new cases had decreased by more than fifty percent; only two million new cases would appear over the next year. That was, in the parlance of the Jesuits, a significant improvement. If the Jesuits had taught Kuzmack nothing else, they had taught him the importance of resolving a problem to everyone's satisfaction. Make certain everyone received a piece of the action and the glory, and most importantly, that there were enough perks to go around.

"The funds for the inoculation program," continued Kuzmack, "will be allocated in part from Senator Hall's Health Subcommittee, and in part from the General Joseph Parker Memorial Fund, established in memory of General Joseph Parker, who died in the service of his country. The Parker Fund is supported by voluntary contributions from private industry."

Bradley looked at Larry Swann, the new chairman of the board of MTI, sitting smugly in the VIP section of the room. Bradley had extracted a written agreement from him, in return for immunity from prosecution, that all secret contracts between MTI and the military or any other agency were to terminate immediately. Molecular Technology Industries had agreed to manufacture all the necessary new antiplague vaccines gratis, while Swann was committed to selling forty percent of the shares of MTI that had been owned by Helene, Webb, Parker, and Ran to provide the necessary funds to care for the victims of the plague.

"Thank you, Dr. Kuzmack. I think the Parker Fund is an excellent illustration of how well the government and the private sector can work together when they commit themselves to a common cause."

"I would just like to add, Senator Hall, before your next witness testifies, that we no longer find it necessary to quarantine the infected population. The incidence of the disease is already diminishing, and the vaccine will be available late today. Both the Military and the Public Health Service will provide free medical services around the country, through designated regional hospitals, to anyone who is, or has been, infected. Thank you for this unusual opportunity to testify before you and your committee." Both Kuzmack and Squire stood up and returned to their seats next to Bradley.

"Thank you. And now for the main testimony of the day . . ."

Bradley stood, hugged both Sharon and Stephanie, then took a seat at the table in front of Senator Hall and his committee.

"My name is Dr. Orestes Bradley . . ." he paused. "As the surgeon general of the United States, I would like to say that we have just averted a major catastrophe. But it could happen again . . ."